AF/THR   BAL   11/2/
                CLAR

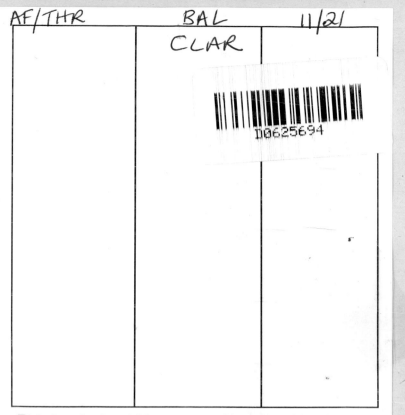

This book should be returned/renewed by the latest date shown above. Overdue items incur charges which prevent self-service renewals. Please contact the library.

Wandsworth Libraries
24 hour Renewal Hotline
01159 293388
www.wandsworth.gov.uk

Wandsworth

SARAH CLARKE is a writer living in South West London with her husband, children and stubbornly cheerful cockapoo. Over fifteen years, Sarah has built a successful career as a marketing copywriter, but her dream has always been to become a published author. When her youngest child started secondary school, she joined the Faber Academy Writing A Novel course to learn the craft of writing psychological thrillers. Sarah graduated in 2019 and *A Mother Never Lies* is her debut novel.

A Mother Never Lies

SARAH CLARKE

ONE PLACE. MANY STORIES

HQ
An imprint of HarperCollins*Publishers* Ltd
1 London Bridge Street
London SE1 9GF

www.harpercollins.co.uk

HarperCollins*Publishers*
1st Floor, Watermarque Building, Ringsend Road
Dublin 4, Ireland

This paperback edition 2021

1
First published in Great Britain by
HQ, an imprint of HarperCollins*Publishers* Ltd 2021

ISBN: 9780008494889

MIX
Paper from
responsible sources
FSC™ C007454

For Michael

Prologue

She pushes hard against the wound. Her hands slip and slide in the blood as it seeps out across his chest. They start to shake uncontrollably. There's too much blood. But she can't let him die. She made a promise; the two of them against the world. She lets the tears flow but won't allow herself any more weakness. The panic needs to be kept at bay.

She has never done a first aid course or paid much attention to those public service adverts on TV. She doesn't really have a clue what to do. But her instinct tells her to stop the blood. To plug the hole. She rips off her jacket – ignoring her own injuries – and screws it into a ball. She pushes deeper into the wound. Does he flinch? She thinks so. That's a good sign, she decides. He's not dead yet.

Today was supposed to be special. How could it have ended up like this, a scene of such horror? But as she pushes and prays and whispers, 'C'mon, c'mon, c'mon,' over and over, the faint sound of an emergency siren reaches her. 'Thank you,' she gasps through the tears. Seconds count with a wound like this; that's something else her instinct tells her.

Dark green uniforms start running in her direction. Relief floods through her. Someone will save him. Not her, but someone. She has to believe it.

Because how could she possibly survive without him?

Chapter 1

NOVEMBER 2019

Phoebe

He's asking if I'm okay. I want to answer him. He's got kind eyes. But I can't speak. I can only breathe. At least, I can only breathe in.

'Do you need a paper bag? Shall I get you a paper bag, love?'

My chest is huge now. It can't expand any more. What happens next? Will my lungs explode? Why the hell can't I just breathe out?

'Here you go. Do you want to take it? Can you do it yourself, love?'

Shit. I've dropped the bag. My hands are shaking. My fingers are numb.

'Ah, she's dropped it. Should I do it for her? Should we get someone? Jen, you do it. She won't want my fat thumbs all over her face.'

I can't breathe in now either. I might faint. I want to faint.

'Give it here then, you big oaf. Her lips are going blue. Hurry up!'

Paper crinkles around my lips. I know how this works. But I need to blow out first. Pollute the air with glorious carbon dioxide.

'Do it, Phoebe, do it!' my brain screams. Suddenly, my breath rushes out into the bag. I suck it back desperately. Again. I'm hooked now. In and out. In and out. My mind clears. I want to cry. God, I am crying.

'There, there. Nothin' to be embarrassed about. No one even noticed 'cept Dave and me. All them young 'uns rushing around, heads stuck in their phones. Would have left you for dead – wouldn't surprise me.'

Left me for dead. I sometimes wish things had turned out that way.

I've been back in London for two weeks now. The city has moved on over the last fourteen years, but I haven't been here to move with it. And now the smallest thing can knock me off track. I used to love the noise, the frenetic energy of too many people vying for the same space, but not anymore. Of course, I know this fear is not really about being away from the city; it's about what happened before I left.

This evening I thought I'd be okay. Completely exhausted after a day on my feet, I was impatient to get home. Eyes down, I ignored the jostling commuters, and the slouchy teenagers, and made it onto the platform without a problem. But then I saw them, huddled together in their dark coats, and they looked so similar that it took me right back to that night. And that's when Jen and Dave found me.

'This is our train now. You going to be all right? You keep the bag, it's fine. Dave has stuffed his sherbet lemons in his pocket now; they'll be gone in a flash anyway.' I nod at Jen, wiping away my tears and smiling widely to show her just how all right I am.

'You take care of yourself,' Dave adds, heaving himself onto the train. He looks a bit embarrassed now. I'm not sure whether that's down to him hesitating with the paper bag or Jen exposing his sugar habit, but I like him more for it either way.

'Thanks,' I say. 'Thanks for saving me.' I know I sound dramatic. But however many panic attacks I've had, they still make me think I might die – like faulty adrenaline levels really can override vital organs.

'It was nothing, love,' Dave mumbles, and then the doors close and his sloped shoulders gradually disappear inside the busy train.

Now I'm worried about Dave and Jen. I don't even know where they're heading, so it's hard to know when I can relax. When I can be certain they've arrived safely. I feel the panic start to bubble again in my stomach; new tears prick at my eyes. I need to stop feeling like this. I need to get off this platform.

I turn back towards the exit and focus on my breathing as the tide of commuter traffic carries me along. Down the stairs, back through the turnstiles – my new Oyster card registering my failed attempt with a disappointed beep – and out onto Old York Road. I half expect to see ambulances, police cars. Flashing lights and paramedics rushing past. But it's just a regular Wednesday evening. City workers filter out along the various residential streets, heads down, collars up against the November wind. A few don't make it further than the Anchor pub where the big screen is on, ready for some football game or other.

The fresh air calms my nerves but I'm tired. I would be home by now, if I could just have made it onto that train. Not really home, of course. But at the moment, it's the best I can do. Instead, I have nearly an hour's walk ahead of me. There was a time when I would have hailed a black cab without even thinking about the cost. Not anymore.

I know the underpass will get me there quicker, but its dark shadows and hidden threats put me off. So instead, I wait impatiently for three different green men to flash me across the multiple lanes of Wandsworth Bridge roundabout and on to York Road. Then I begin the long walk eastwards, the traffic droning past relentlessly. I watch a skinny cyclist with a flashing head-cam hurl abuse at a white van driver, who just gives him the finger and swaps lanes. And at one point I'm forced to step off the pavement by a homeless man curled up against a bus stop, causing some cyclist-type road rage myself. But I suck in the smell of Middle Eastern food drifting out from the grubby cafés and share a half smile with a young mum herding her kids and it feels good to be back. I've missed this.

When I get to the Volkswagen dealership, I can't help pausing, remembering a visit from a lifetime ago. How good it would be to waltz into that showroom now, actually buy a car, instead of yielding to some misplaced loyalty and leaving empty-handed like last time. Although I waddled more than waltzed back then. I need a car now more than ever, but I can't see my Universal Credit stretching that far. As I continue staring, I notice the salesman looking at me suspiciously through the giant glass panes. Clearly I don't look like a prospective customer anymore either. I drop my gaze to the pavement and keep walking.

Eventually I peel off York Road and head south into Battersea. I know plenty of people who don't like this area – its perfect skin of Edwardian townhouses hiding an underbelly of council-flat blocks – but I do. I'm sure it's partly the familiarity of growing up here. But more than that, I like that everyone – the wealthy and the struggling – walks down the same street, grabs last-minute shopping from the same corner shop. I've never managed to work out where I sit in the British class system, so it's a relief to be somewhere where everyone fits in.

It's not even seven o'clock when I arrive at my old childhood home, but the sky is black and I feel ready for bed. I dream of sinking into a hot bath and then crawling underneath my duvet, giving my aching body as much rest as possible before I go out again tomorrow. My father will be in his study by now, pretending to read an old script while chain-smoking his way through a packet of Marlboro Reds. I feel a momentary pang for a nicotine hit of my own, but I know I'd be crazy to start down that road again.

6

I assume my mother will be asleep, or more accurately coma-tose, after gradually working her way through her daily dose of gin. Unfortunately, I'm proved wrong.

'Is that you, darling? Your father's in a foul mood so I'm in search of a drinking partner. Come have a G&T with me?'

I stifle a sigh. 'Actually, I was going to run a bath ...'

'Can't do that, I'm afraid, darling. No hot water. Boiler's on the blink again. Luckily the fridge is in full working order so the tonic's lovely and cold. It's Sicilian lemon, darling. Divine.'

Her shrill voice and heroic attempt at enunciation can't hide the fact that she's probably been drinking these divine gin and tonics since lunchtime. But I can't refuse her. She's given me somewhere to stay after all.

'Sounds great, Flora,' I reply. My parents have never been fond of traditional titles, so it's been Flora and Paul for as long as I can remember. They've never been fond of traditional parenting either. There was a time when I couldn't wait to get away from them; now I'm grateful for their charity.

As I make my way into the front room, I can't help noticing the decay. This was a splendid house once, although it had already started its downward spiral when we moved in forty years ago. There is still evidence of its former glory, the beautiful ceiling roses in both living spaces and the sturdy oak newel post guarding the staircase. But now the neglect is more obvious. What's left of the carpet is stained with red wine spills, and the windows are spotted with fluffy green mould. Everything is covered in a layer of dust and nothing seems to work properly. Except the fridge, of course.

'Any luck, darling? With the job hunting?' Flora asks, while handing me the perfect gin and tonic, weirdly out of place in this shabby setting.

I look closely at her face to see if I can spot any trace of suspi-cion. I've told her that I spend my days looking for work; she wouldn't approve of my real purpose, so I've kept it to myself for now. I'm relying on her not knowing that job hunting is mainly carried out at home in front of a computer screen these days. 'Nothing today. Maybe tomorrow.'

'And ahh, did you cope okay?' At least she has the good grace to appear concerned. I know she doesn't understand really. She's had her fair share of trauma in life too, but she has always found solace in a bottle, letting the numbing effects of alcohol carry her pain away.

'Yes, all good. It was a sunny day so I decided to walk.' I hope she won't grill me further. Even in her drunken state I worry that she can see right through me. For all her hands-off parenting, she always had a way of knowing when I was keeping something from her.

But she just throws me a quizzical look and – miraculously – chooses discretion. 'Well, you don't need to rush things. And walking is wonderful exercise, of course. You'll be fifty before you know it, and you can't take that slim body of yours for granted forever.'

I look at her slight frame and silently question her logic, but I'm glad she's moved on.

'Perhaps you should take the day off from job hunting tomorrow, darling? Give those legs a rest. You've got your dole money after all. We could do something maybe? Just you and me?'

She's looking for forgiveness, I realise. For my childhood, perhaps. For not doing more to save me when she had the chance. I stare at her. She was a young mum, and beautiful too, but time doesn't stand still, and she's looking her sixty-eight years now. Age spots poke through her cheap cover-up and her once signature chestnut mane has reduced to a slender tangle of home-dyed strands. Her wide smile looks almost ghoulish, lips painted with an unsteady hand and teeth discoloured by years of neglect. But her eyes still sparkle, the depth of their blue undiminished.

'Thanks, Flora, but I should probably keep looking. I can't imagine it's going to be easy to find something and I want to pay my way.' I feel guilty about lying, but not enough to stop. I've been so patient, I can't wait any longer.

'Don't be silly, darling, we don't need more money. We're fine!'

I look around me. Everything is falling apart. The boiler needs replacing, and I'm not convinced the creaking central heating system is going to last the winter. Fine is not a word I would use, but for now, there's not much I can do to help.

At least they own the house without any mortgage to worry about. They bought it with the proceeds from Paul's sole film role when I was eight. We all had such high hopes back then. First Hollywood, then the world. But the film got slated by the critics, so it was soon back to scraping a living in regional theatres and the like. I remember it was around that time that Flora went on a health drive – doing Jane Fonda workouts in front of the TV, leaving bowls of cemented All-Bran everywhere – and I sometimes wondered whether she secretly enjoyed his failure, saw it as a chance to rekindle her own acting career after it was brought to a crashing halt by my unwelcome arrival. It didn't last long though – the contentment or the healthy living. And she never made it back onto the stage either.

'Maybe Saturday,' I suggest as a way of bringing the conversation to an end. But I realise I mean it too. Suddenly I feel a surge of love for this old woman with a twinkle in her eye. I need to forgive her. We've all made some bad choices, none more so than me.

And what am I back in London for, if not to find forgiveness?

Chapter 2

There's noise but it's muffled. Sneering. Crying. I'm trapped, weighted down. He walks towards me. He's smiling. He's coming for me. No, he's coming for Charlie ...

I jolt upright in bed, breathing heavily. I'm drenched in sweat and my body immediately starts to shiver. I throw my sodden T-shirt on the floor and reach for my hoodie, still there from the night before, after I finally managed to extract myself from Flora's company. I'll definitely need a shower this morning. I curse the broken boiler and the falling temperatures and my drunken parents, and how the hell I managed to let my lovely three-bed terrace on the other side of the borough slip away.

It's still pitch-black outside but I know I won't get back to sleep now. So I lie back against the lumpy pillow, close my eyes and allow myself to think about him. It's purgatory of course. But addictive purgatory.

Time has taken its toll and I can't remember Charlie as a living, moving human being anymore. I can't remember his smell or the feel of his touch against my skin. But I have preserved images of him, like a pack of camera stills. I see him in his highchair with mashed banana sticking to his rosy cheeks. I see him experimenting with sand and water, all mucky fingers and serious expression. I see him horizontal on the sofa with one thumb in his mouth and the other clutching his chewed cloth rabbit, spellbound by *Teletubbies* or *Peppa Pig*.

But suddenly I see him petrified. And I want to be sick all over again.

I get out of bed and head for the shower. I am almost glad for the freezing cold water now, hitting me like sharp needles. But as my body temperature drops, my mind calms. He's my son, whatever mistakes I've made. My flesh and blood. They say time heals, but not for me.

I start getting dressed, while mentally running through my plans for the day. I'll try Hollybrook Academy, I decide. I know it's not exactly a scientific approach – eyeballing every 17-year-old in the borough – but I have to do something. In a few months' time he'll turn 18, and I hope he will come looking for me. But I refuse to rely on that. I can't just sit by and leave it to fate.

Most importantly, I hope that he's still in Wandsworth. I learned a lot about adoption during those dark days. Not through my own research – I wasn't capable of concentrating on anything much back then – but through the solicitor that the family court assigned me. She was young and earnest and desperate to please. Looking back, I should have been more grateful, but I was too lost in my own grief for that.

However, she did explain – slowly, kindly – that the local authority always tries to help its own list of prospective adoptive parents first, so they would place Charlie locally if they could. Remembering his crinkly nose and solemn, innocent eyes, I can't believe any childless couple could turn down such an adorable 3-year-old, so he must have stayed in Wandsworth.

I have had letters from his adoptive parents, twice a year, ever since it became official – always exactly six months apart, as fixed by the Family Court. Knowing that I would keep that connection with Charlie was the only thing that got me through the adoption process. Of course, I didn't realise then how distancing the letters would be. How unrevealing a page of writing about a boy doing well at school, having friends, enjoying sport could be. All I've really got are the memories.

Discounting the all-girl schools, there are eleven secondary schools in Wandsworth that Charlie could be a student at, and I've been to five so far. He'll be in upper sixth, or Year 13 as they call it nowadays, and I've come to realise what a relief that is. It's almost impossible to distinguish one teenager from another when they're all wearing the same uniform and moving around in packs, but sixth formers wear their own clothes, which makes things easier. There are moments when I question whether I'd recognise him after all this time, but it doesn't take long to silence those doubts.

For the last couple of days I've stood outside Rushton School in Putney with no luck. But today could be different. I have to believe that.

I'm working out which of my jumpers is the thickest – the cold shower has left me desperate for warmth – when I hear a knock on the front door. There's a frustration to their rap, which I realise is probably the result of them trying the broken doorbell first, so I towel-dry my mess of curls into a half-civilised style and race down the stairs. There's no way either of my parents will be raising themselves this early in the morning.

I open the door to a middle-aged woman in ill-fitting jeans and an anorak, standing on my parents' broken paving slabs.

'Can I help you?' I ask.

'Hello, Phoebe.'

Her directness knocks me off guard and I take an involuntary step backwards, which unfortunately she treats as an invite. Before I can do anything to stop her, she pushes open the door and steps inside.

'I wonder if we can have a chat?'

The patronising tone, the tilt of her head; I can almost smell social work on her. I want to refuse, to just slam the door in her face and pretend this never happened. But I know that kind of behaviour will bring its own repercussions, so I surrender to the inevitable and stand aside.

For a woman who wears no make-up and keeps her mousy hair sensibly short, she has a surprising air of authority, and I feel more like the visitor than the host as she walks purposefully down the hallway.

'In here?' she asks, inclining her head towards the living room.

I nod and watch as she scans the room before choosing to perch on the edge of Paul's prized leather Chesterfield, which is cracked and dulled now of course.

'We never met back in 2005,' she starts. 'I know that Taisha was your social worker through it all.'

My heart starts thudding faster as she pauses; I know what she's about to say.

'I'm Clare Morris. I was Charlie's social worker.'

The woman who took my son away. A massive shot of adrenaline surges through me, and I struggle not to act on it. My hands ball into tight fists and my breathing gets shallower. Shit. I can't do this. I think about why I'm back, how I will find him, and it gives me the strength to find my voice. 'What are you doing here?'

'I heard that you were back.'

'From who?'

She ignores my question. 'I thought it would be a good idea to drop by, see how you're settling in, now you're living locally again.'

'From who?' I repeat. My tone is more assertive now and it works because, after a moment of indecision, her shoulders droop a little. She leans forward, resting her elbows on her knees.

'I was chatting to your mum; she mentioned that you'd moved in.'

'Flora?' I ask, surprise knocking me off guard.

'We've kept in touch over the years.' She says it as though it's obvious they would be friends. Perhaps it is. In many ways they were on the same side back then. 'I give her a ring every now and again; she didn't have the professional support that you got, remember.'

I stare at the social worker expectantly; I still don't know why she's come.

'She says you spend every day out of the house.'

'I've been job hunting,' I whisper.

'Yes, she said that too.' Her words hang heavy with disbelief. She's clearly less naive than Flora; less drunk too, of course. 'Look, I just want to make sure ...' she pauses for a moment and I enjoy her discomfort as she struggles for the right words '... that you're not being distracted by the past.'

I shift my weight from one foot to the other. 'So this is a threat, is it?' I ask. 'Forget about Charlie, or else?'

'It's not like that.' She speeds up her words as though suddenly desperate to get it over with. 'Look, I'm not here to run you out of town or dredge up the past. I know that you've suffered. But my responsibility isn't to you.'

'He'll be 18 soon,' I throw back. 'He won't be your responsibility then.' I don't add that I'm counting the days until his birthday, spending every minute wondering if he'll come looking for me. Dreaming about that knock on the door.

'Officially, Charlie hasn't been my responsibility since 2007. His care was signed over when he was adopted. But that doesn't mean I stopped thinking about him. He was a lovely kid, *is* a lovely kid,' she corrects herself. 'And I don't want to see him hurt again.'

'And you think I'll hurt him?' I'm spitting my words out now.

'I know how much you loved him, and I'm sure you still do. But the Charlie you remember doesn't exist anymore. He's got a new name and a new family.' She pauses again, and I realise I'm holding my breath. 'Phoebe, he doesn't know anything about you.'

Her words burn into me, scalding my eyes. They also don't make sense. 'But I wrote to him twice a year,' I remind her. 'Via the council. They *encouraged* it, for his Life Story project.'

'Look, Charlie was very quiet when he was first adopted, withdrawn. He was clearly very traumatised—'

'And?' I interrupt, even though I don't want to hear the rest.

'Normally we suggest adopted children should know about their past, keep that connection to their birth parents, but Charlie's wasn't a normal case. His adoptive parents decided it would be best to make a clean break. Give him a completely fresh start.'

'My letters?' I repeat, like a broken toy. 'And the photos I gave Taisha?' I can sense her trying to make eye contact with me, so I turn to face the window.

Eventually she sighs. 'Phoebe, you know that his parents aren't legally obliged to give Charlie those items until he's 18.'

Perhaps I do know that. It registers somewhere in the back of my mind. But that's not what I've been dreaming about all these years. I've imagined Charlie waiting by the front door, eagerly ripping open the envelope, devouring my words. Not my letters being shoved to the back of some unused drawer by his new parents. Maybe they didn't even keep them. Now I see them ripped in half, thrown into the bin alongside cracked eggshells and soggy teabags. I shake that thought away. It's their legal duty to keep them until he's an adult; I only have another three months to wait.

'Do you have children?' I ask, sensing the answer will be no.

'I work with children every day. And I've been trained to always put their needs first. As a social worker, the paramountcy principle rules everything. But isn't that also the job of parents? To put the needs of their child before their own?'

'To you, needs are surface-deep.' My voice rises in anger. 'A warm bed, clean clothes, GCSEs and family camping trips. But needs run deeper than that. My own mother has let me down countless times – is still letting me down,' I add pointedly. 'But we have a bond. You can't play God just because a parent doesn't fit your idea of what makes the perfect family.'

15

I watch Clare dip her head towards the floor, before raising her eyes up, shining with a new resolve. 'You were angry back then, broken; I know that. You'd lost someone very special. But just think about how much Charlie suffered. Doesn't he deserve some distance from that?'

My eyes smart with tears; acid forms in my mouth. How dare she say these things? I'm his mother. But I can't speak, I can't even move. The silence hangs between us for a moment before she continues.

'Leave him alone, Phoebe. You lost your maternal rights to him a long time ago.' She stands up but doesn't move any further; she's not finished. 'And don't forget, it's against the law to approach him. He may be turning 18 soon, but his right to anonymity from you is permanent.'

I watch her zip up her anorak, hover over me. Hairs prickle on my neck.

'And, Phoebe, you need to prepare yourself for him never coming to look for you.'

I want to shout and scream at her, to slap that patronising expression off her face. 'Why are you so sure?'

'I've spoken to his adoptive parents. Phoebe, he has absolutely no memory of you.' And with that, she disappears into the hallway, and out of my parents' front door with a thud and a clatter.

*

I sit perfectly still and process her parting words. I think about my memories of Charlie. How I've nurtured and preserved them over the years. The effort it has taken to carry him with me. Perhaps it is too much to ask for him to have done the same. He hadn't even turned four when I was forced to give him up.

The Life Story project had been my glimmer of hope. I remember that earnest young woman explaining it to me, how Charlie would be given some mementos – like family photos – to remember Dan and me by. How I could write to him twice a year. I didn't mention Dan's death in my letters, or everything that came after. Those details I wanted to explain softly, gently, in person. But I told him how much better I was feeling, and how much I hoped that we'd see each other again one day. I never thought he might not read them. Or that his adoptive parents would make sure I was wiped from his memory.

Suddenly desperate for fresh air, I grab my jacket off the broken peg in the hallway and head outside, into the park opposite my parents' house. Park is an exaggeration, more a postage stamp of green space plus two swings, a slide and a rusty roundabout. But it has a kind of urban peace about it that I like. I sink onto the metal bench, its unforgiving bars digging into my back.

I replay the social worker's words. *Doesn't he deserve some distance from that?* A speck of doubt starts to worm its way into my thoughts. Could she be right? Is our relationship beyond repair? But I shake the feeling away. No, I've waited so long for this chance; I'm his mother, and I'm not walking away now. And if his adoptive parents have kept me from him, severed our bond, then it's even more important that I find him. I take a deep breath and stand up. I'm fed up of being controlled by other people. It's my turn now.

After nothing but gin, tonic and a grab bag of McCoy's crinkle cut crisps for dinner, I realise I'm starving. I should go back to the house, make myself something nutritious, but I can't face going back inside. My mission feels more urgent now. So instead, I stop at the first café on my route and order a fried egg bap and takeaway tea. At the last minute I ask her to add bacon, and the taste of that sizzling fat is worth every extra penny.

It takes me an hour to reach Hollybrook Academy, a small school on the edge of Wandsworth Common. Everything is quiet when I arrive, so I find a wall to lean against and try to blend into the background. I feel a quiver of excitement in my belly. Like I've found Charlie's school. Like today is going to be when

17

I see my son for the first time in fourteen years. I check myself. This is exactly how I felt yesterday morning and look how that day turned out.

The waiting gives me time to think about what Charlie might look like now. The last time I saw him his hair was a deep brown colour, the same shade as my own before the speckles of grey appeared. He has my eyes too – mid-blue with indigo flecks. But he's Dan from the nose down. Slight hook, with a solid square jawline. Handsome. Height-wise, I imagine him to be about six foot. He was three foot exactly when I measured him at 2 years old, and I remember the old wives' tale about your full height being double that. And with parents the shape of Dan and me, he's unlikely to be picked for the rugby forward pack any time soon.

Suddenly the bell goes and a few seconds later the noise hits me. A few hundred children emerge from a maze of different doorways, chatting and barging their way into the playground, seemingly undaunted by the wall of blazers obstructing their path. It must be break time. Somehow the sea of blue uniform shifts and settles. Some younger students start kicking a football in one corner; others cluster around illicit phones.

That's when I notice a group of taller, lankier boys materialising from a separate building. This is good. They're definitely sixth formers and they're loping so slowly I can easily make out their faces. I look at each boy, searching for some familiar features. Nothing jumps out. Is it the wrong school? The wrong crowd? Or is there a chance I don't recognise him anymore?

'Can I help you?' a voice asks, local accent.

'No thanks,' I respond without turning around. The boys will be back inside soon and I can't miss this opportunity.

'A parent?' it continues, still friendly, but with a slight edge this time. I realise I need to tread carefully.

'Prospective parent.' I turn to face the man in uniform and force a smile.

'That so?' The security guard doesn't believe me. Perhaps I look too old.

'Sixth form,' I respond, in a higher pitch than I planned. 'My son is at Rushton School at the moment. I'm thinking of moving him.'

'Right, well Hollybrook is a great school. Takes security very seriously too,' he adds with meaning. 'See that sign over there?' He points at a large banner attached to the school fence, advertising a sixth form open evening in a couple of weeks' time. 'Why don't you come back then?'

I pause for a moment. I so want to stay, but I know he's moving me on. 'Great. I'll do that,' I answer through gritted teeth and slowly turn away. I can't risk being on some school watchlist, so I know I have to play along. I walk away from the school and deeper into Wandsworth Common, sensing his eyes following me until I reach the cover of the trees.

Chapter 3

MAY 1998

Phoebe

'Everyone's staring at us.'

'Well, that's kind of the point.'

I feel a giggle threatening to escape, so I bury my head into Dan's shoulder. All this pomp and ceremony seems ridiculous to me, but still, there is something intoxicating about being the centre of attention.

'I'm not sure our choice of song is helping,' he continues.

Now laughter does erupt from my belly – which people seem to take as their cue to join us. I relax a little as our first dance gets swallowed up by more enthusiastic guests twirling and whirling around us. 'What's wrong with All Saints?' I ask, feigning ignorance. 'They're a great band.'

'*Never Ever* isn't exactly romantic.'

'They've just won two Brit awards – trust me, everyone loves this song.'

Dan sings along with mock gravity, lines about black holes and feeling low. It fuels my laughter, but secretly I do start to wonder why I chose such ominous lyrics. 'Stop it,' I warn him, between the giggles.

To my relief, he changes tack. 'Okay, make me.' The challenge is set and I happily oblige, leaning in to give his lips something else to focus on. I was planning for it to be a quick kiss to shut him up, but somehow I melt a little and can't help lingering, exploring his mouth. I know every part of him so well, and yet somehow it all feels different today.

'Phoebe darling, sorry to interrupt.' An apologetic voice reaches into my consciousness and I pull away from my new husband. 'I think we're going to slope off now.'

My father's deep burgundy bow tie that had given him a dapper edge earlier in the day is now stuffed into his breast pocket, and there's a couple of red wine splatters on his dress shirt. 'Really?' I say, but I'm not surprised. Traditional weddings aren't my parents' thing. When Paul and Flora got married, they opted for the Old Marylebone Town Hall followed by a booze-up in the Rose Tavern on Marylebone High Street. I find it ironic that it's now one of the smartest streets in London, but my parents are yet to see the funny side.

'It's been a wonderful day. Now it's time for you young things to enjoy yourself. And Flora's ready to go.'

I look over at my mother, perched on one of the chairs that's been pushed to the side of the room to make way for the dance floor. I see her glazed expression, vacant smile firmly set, body swaying not quite in time with the music. But this isn't new. Flora is always drunk on occasions like this, when free booze flows and new drinking buddies spring up from every direction. No, her wanting to leave is about something else – those little wedding conventions that Dan insisted upon, but that make my mother's skin itch.

Dan pulls me closer. 'No problem, Paul. I'll make sure she enjoys herself.'

'Yes, I'm sure you will.' Even being an actor, Paul has never managed to hide his dislike for Dan. Both Flora and Paul were excited when I first told them about my new boyfriend. Dan and I met in a pub when I spilled my drink on his new suede boots. It was more instant attraction than love at first sight, but I didn't leave his place much after that, and when he asked me to move in a week later, I didn't hesitate.

At first my free-spirited parents loved my impulsiveness, my whirlwind romance, but that was before they met him. When they visited his flat, our flat by then, its overt uniformity horrified Flora. Dan's legal magazines, neatly stacked in issue order, clearly offended her too because she managed to spill her entire cup of tea on them. 'You're a fish out of water here,' she'd whispered as I'd seen her out that day. 'He will suffocate you.' It's a shame she never realised how much I was floundering when I lived with them.

'Are you okay?' Dan asks, as we watch Paul navigate Flora towards the exit.

I turn to face my husband. I know looks shouldn't matter, that what's on the inside is more important. But I can't help a surge of pride rushing through me as I stare at him, because he is so very handsome. His strong chiselled jaw, those deep brown eyes and perfect white teeth, always ready with a smile. People keep saying what a beautiful couple we make and today – all pampered and polished – I've been willing to accept the compliment. 'Very okay,' I answer, and rest my head against his chest, my long dark curls blending in with his dinner jacket.

*

'Is it crazy to admit I feel nervous?'

Dan takes hold of my hand without looking at me, his concentration taken up by trying to slot the credit-card-style room key at just the right angle to unlock the hotel room door. 'Yes, it's crazy,' he says softly. The door clicks and Dan raises his eyeline to meet mine. 'But also sexy as hell.'

Butterflies lurch in my tummy and I let him lead me into the unlit room, or honeymoon suite to be more exact. When we first started planning the wedding, we knew there'd be no financial help from either side of the family, so we had to make some sensible decisions along the way. But Dan wouldn't compromise on our wedding night. The element that is purely for us.

We stop in the middle of the room and look at each other. I know there's a bottle of champagne resting in an ice bucket at the bottom of the bed and a bouquet of flowers stood upright on the dressing table, but they seem immaterial now. I don't need any more reminders of how special this day is. Dan places his hands either side of my face and pushes his lips against mine. He's both claiming me and protecting me; telling me I'm his, whilst promising to take care of me. This normally modern man is showing some caveman impulses, and in my virgin-white dress it feels nothing short of perfect.

Except getting the dress off isn't quite so movie-smooth. There are a hundred baby buttons and hidden hooks to work through, and equality reigns again as we both battle to get them open.

'This better be worth it,' Dan threatens, and I pick up on his fictional tale of pre-marital celibacy.

'Oh, my naked body is quite something.'

'I bet it is,' Dan concurs, just as my dress finally slips to the floor. Then the giggling stops once again and he reaches for me. I feel a deep ache of love for this man who swept me off my feet and put me in the centre of his life. Our lips join together and my bony hips slot underneath his more musclebound ones. Our curves rise and dip so neatly against each other that it feels as though we were pre-moulded this way.

'I love you, Dan.' I need to say it, to be clear.

'I love you too.'

'Do you think we'll be this perfect forever?'

'Of course we will. You and me, against the world.'

He picks me up and lowers my naked body onto the four-poster bed. I pull him towards me and very quickly any thoughts of the wider world disappear.

Chapter 4

NOVEMBER 2019

Ben

Fucking unbelievable.

Ben feels the familiar surge of rage flood his body. Adrenaline grabs at his muscles; his pupils dilate, and the red F blurs out of focus.

He shouldn't give a shit really.

But it just doesn't make sense; he'd actually tried in that geography essay.

He hadn't bothered much during his first year of A-levels, so two fails in his summer exams were understandable (while his A in art and design was so expected that it hardly drew comment). His parents' reaction had been predictable of course: a mix of disappointment and sympathy laced up with a thread of *we'll always love you, however much of a failure you turn out to be.*

Ben could have taken them at their word. Left school, holed up in his room with his Xbox. But he hadn't. He'd started Year

13 with something close to a positive attitude – and look where that effort has got him.

Next to the letter F is an illegible paragraph of writing, also in red biro. Teacher's tips for rising up the letter ladder. *Well, fuck you.* Ben drags his fingers along the essay, crinkling the paper into his cupped palm.

'Moreton? Not a good idea,' Mr Saunders calls out evenly. Ben stares at his teacher. He could – should – remove his hand and smile that fake apology he's practised over the years. His teacher would pretend not to recognise his insincerity and the class could move on, giving him the chance to get his shit together. Or he could wrap the essay into a tight ball and throw it at the bastard.

He sucks in air, then expels it slowly. 'Sorry sir, just a bit disappointed, you know.' Beaming smile, gritted teeth. He releases his fingers and rubs his clammy palms along the underside of his desk; no point sweating over a stupid essay.

'No problem, Ben. Come and see me after and we can run through your paper together. Now, you lot, deforestation ...'

With the tension in his muscles starting to ease, Ben switches the class onto mute mode and lets his mind wander. While he is no great fan of school, he does prefer the anonymity of his life during termtime. The half-term holidays had been a different story, trapped with his family in Berlin for ten long days. Ever-perfect Rosie had steered the conversation away from school whenever their parents ventured onto the subject, but that had infuriated him as well, her constant do-gooder-ness. Thank God he'd managed to escape to the city's Kreuzberg district a couple of times and lose himself in its mind-blowing street art scene for a while.

The bell rings, breaking into Ben's daydream. He's got a free period next and had planned to revise for the next day's chemistry test, but he's not in the mood for that anymore. He trudges out of his geography classroom – avoiding eye contact with Mr Saunders in case his teacher plays out his earlier offer of help – and contemplates going to the art studio instead, adding more chaos to the oil painting he's working on for his portfolio. But he doesn't make it further than a few steps down the corridor before he's waylaid.

'Hey, bro, you got a free period next?'

Ben smiles at his friend. Jake only joined the school in Year 12 but has already gained himself quite a reputation for flouting the rules; it didn't take them long to find each other.

'Yep.'

'Got plans?'

'Well, I have a chemistry test tomorrow,' Ben mutters vaguely.

'Fancy a bit of hands-on revision?'

There's a glint in Jake's eye and it doesn't take much for Ben to work out what he's suggesting. He can almost taste that first drag, feel the relief of it filtering through his body. 'Any chance those chemicals involve THC?' he asks in a low voice.

'See? You know it already. You're gonna beast that test.'

Ben smiles again, wider this time because this is exactly what he needs, a chance to dispel the anger still bubbling under the surface. And to do it with someone who feels close to being a kindred spirit. Of course he couldn't expect Jake to have the same life history as him – that would be too fucked up. But having a 28-year-old stepfather who regularly posts topless pictures of himself on Instagram is pretty messy too. And Jake isn't blessed with the same amnesia about his sordid past that Ben is.

Shoulder to shoulder, they wander down the noisy corridor, but instead of turning left into the sixth form centre they carry on out of the main exit.

'Science block?' Jake asks, pausing to check Ben's willing to take the risk. They could disappear off site, but that means a walk across the rugby pitches to get to the back gate, and the sky's already threatening rain. The science block is much closer, but the chance of getting caught is higher too.

'Works for me,' Ben answers without hesitation.

The school grounds are quiet as they stride across the

playground, the rest of the school now sucked into the final period of the day. They arrive at the modern redbrick construction and Ben concentrates on the wall in front of him.

'I'll go first, follow me,' he instructs, with a rare confidence saved for distinct occasions like this. After three miserable years underperforming on a football pitch followed by a season doing the same thing – yet more painfully – on a rugby pitch, Ben's parents finally surrendered to the realisation that their son wasn't into traditional sports like his sister. So at 12 years old Ben had started spending his Saturday mornings climbing. It wasn't always fun. He would get so angry with himself if he couldn't make a particular climb or grabbed onto the wrong colour hold, disqualifying him from whatever level he was trying to conquer. But making it to the top gave him such a rush that the sport proved addictive in the end, although nowadays he tends to use his skills away from the climbing centre.

With Jake falling in step behind him, Ben squeezes his toes into a gap in the brickwork and powers up with his legs, pushing his hips square against the wall. Four grabs are all it takes for him to reach the roof overhang and then he swings his body to get the momentum, before thrusting an arm and leg in one dynamic movement onto the roof. He's made it. He manoeuvres the rest of his body onto the asphalt surface and rolls onto his back, enjoying the sensation of his heart racing.

'Smooth moves,' Jake pants as he appears next to him. 'You're stronger than you look.'

'Can't promise the same precision on the way down.'

Jake responds with a loud laugh and Ben wonders if they're being stupid, smoking their illegal drugs up here. There are four labs underneath him, and all of them will be full of students right now, staring into Bunsen burner flames or throwing acid blanched litmus paper at each other. He imagines getting so stoned that he decides to drop through the skylight like some psychedelic Messiah. The fuss that would cause.

'What you smiling about?' Jake asks, handing Ben a well-packed spliff.

Ben takes a long pull and feels the sweet aroma fill his mouth, and then his lungs. He takes a couple more puffs, then hands the joint back to his friend, his world nicely spinning. 'Getting off my head, I guess,' he finally answers.

'Yeah, life's good when you're fucked.'

Ben considers that. He vaguely knows that Jake is talking rubbish; that there's no meaning behind his words. But what if he's right? Does being fucked give you a unique insight into life? Something regular people will never know or feel? Is being constantly slung with shit actually life-enriching?

'My life must be frickin' rosy then,' he answers, with what he planned on being ironic laughter, before accepting the proffered spliff back and filling his lungs one more time.

*

The bell goes and Ben stuffs his empty chemistry notes into his bag, trying not to make eye contact with anyone in case they notice how bloodshot his are. After smoking and talking shit for half an hour, he and Jake had managed to get off the roof without anyone noticing them, and into the sixth form centre with only a passing look of suspicion from their Head of Year. But now that everyone is heading for the exit, he feels more exposed. He keeps his head down and manages to make it outside without having to engage with anyone.

He's passing the main school building, a looming sixteenth-century mansion, when fingers pinch him at the elbow. With a sharp intake of breath, his arms fly skywards, as if they're programmed to over-react by some outside force.

'Whoa, steady!' Rosie ducks neatly under Ben's arm as it comes back down to earth.

Ben tries to focus on his sister, while slipping his hand back down to his side. If his physical rejection disappoints her, she shows no sign of it.

'Who did you think it was? Is that Arabella girl stalking you again? Don't worry, she freaks me out too. Shouldn't be so damn pretty, should you, little brother?'

Ben vaguely considers pointing out that he actually towers over Rosie now. She's tall, but over the last year, it's like he's been sleeping on some sort of torture rack. Rosie gave him the nickname when he was a mute 5-year-old, during that car ride back from the courthouse. It was her way of reminding him that she was the eldest, if only by five months. And maybe a note on her status. The biological child. In the end, the nickname stuck, and even his new height hasn't persuaded her to change it.

'Nah, Arabella moved on pretty quickly.' Ben chooses not to mention the way he brought that situation to a close, the shock on the girl's face when he couldn't take her constant whining anymore. 'You heading home?'

'Yep. Netball practice was cancelled so I thought I'd make a start on my history essay instead.'

'Do you ever let up being perfect?' Ben asks with more resentment than he'd intended – clearly the numbing effects of the marijuana are wearing off – and her hurt expression rouses a guilt he's never quite managed to shake where Rosie's concerned. 'Sorry, sis. Bad day.'

'Jesus, Ben,' Rosie responds impatiently. 'You've just won that art prize, out of like fifty million kids, and you think *I'm* perfect?'

Ben shakes his head at his sister's wild exaggeration – there were actually about 500 entries in his category of the Wandsworth Young Artist of the Year Award. Secretly he was proud to win the top prize, but he's not admitted that to anyone else. He knows his parents aren't interested in his artistic talent and the thought of their fake congratulations is enough to put him off saying very much.

'All that means is I'm allowed to be *im*perfect,' Ben responds, his mask firmly back in place. 'I'm clearly just too creative for geography, or chemistry, or chores, or being civil—' But he can't finish goading his sister because she starts whacking him with her sports bag.

'You're such a dick,' she giggles, and Ben can hear the affection in her voice. Pride, relief and resentment all flood through him at the same time, one jumbled shot of emotion that could have knocked him off balance if he hadn't learned to cope with his mixed feelings for Rosie many years ago.

Her mood actually proves quite infectious and Ben feels his earlier weed-induced good humour return as they reach their home on Milada Road – a large Victorian terrace, unremarkable from its neighbours with its perfect frontage guarded by iron railings. But as Rosie unlocks the door, his heart sinks. Their mother is back from work.

'Hi, guys,' she calls out, all bright and breezy, like she hasn't been sat in an office for most of the day, appeasing clients with bigger egos than budgets. 'Good day? Any news on that geography essay, Ben?' All casual, unconcerned, like she hasn't got her fingers crossed underneath the work surface.

'Yeah,' he answers, not willing to lie, not caring enough to keep her hopes up. Why the hell is it so important anyway? He hasn't even had a chance to take his shoes off.

'Netball practice was cancelled today, Mum,' Rosie calls out, seemingly desperate to share her own news all of a sudden. 'I reckon Miss Guthrie's pregnant. Either that or hungover. She looked properly green when she told us it was off.'

Ben knows Rosie is trying to divert their mother's attention to give him time to disappear upstairs. He feels that familiar indecision grip at his stomach. Of course he should take this opportunity to avoid an argument, give himself the chance to calm down like he did in his geography class. But the tension isn't letting up this time.

'Well, calling it morning sickness has to be one of life's greatest inaccuracies if my experience was anything to go by,' their mother calls from the kitchen. 'Is she married?' she continues.

Rosie smiles and rolls her eyes at him. The tightness between his shoulders releases a little.

'And sorry, Ben, what grade did you say you got?'

'Don't rise to it,' Rosie whispers urgently. 'She's been brainwashed by all those alpha mums at their annoying little coffee mornings. You've got more talent in your little finger than all of their darling offspring put together. She knows it too, really. She just forgets sometimes.'

As Ben looks at his sister's imploring eyes, his mind flashes back to his first few weeks in this house. Rosie had been so bossy back then – at least she'd seemed that way compared to his nervous ways. She would grab his hand and pull him into the den, talk incessantly and demand he play with her. It could be schools, families, hospitals or zoos. But whatever the game, Rosie would always be in charge. Until the time he refused to play her game. With an anger and force that none of them had expected. She wasn't so bossy after that.

But this time she's right; his brainwashed mother isn't worth it. Ben throws his sister a grateful look, grabs hold of the newel post and hoists himself upstairs. Avoiding confrontation with his parents has been his mantra for years. Why is he forgetting that now?

His bedroom overlooks the garden. It's the smallest room in the house but has always been his favourite. Rosie has the front room with two large windows facing the street, filled with a collection of Annie Sloan painted furniture. Even from the landing Ben can see that most of it is hidden under piles of clothes, messiness being the one chink in his sister's otherwise perfect armour. Where Rosie's bedroom is spacious and exposed, his is compact and private. But that suits Ben fine. He takes off his jacket and tie – compulsory for sixth formers unfortunately – and falls onto his bed. His left hand drops to the side of the oak frame and finds the canvas case that he knows is under there. It would be too risky to open it now, Rosie or even his mother could walk in, but just touching it feels reassuring.

As he closes his eyes, Ben becomes more aware of how fast his heart is racing. He knows he needs to slow it down before he leaves for work, and he doesn't have the option of weed this time – buying it has always been Jake's domain. So he forces himself to remember those breathing exercises he found on the internet. Fuck, that had been a low point. Even in the complete privacy of an empty house he'd felt sick researching the subject, and he'd wiped his browser history as soon as he'd committed the technique to memory. But he knows what happens if he lets the adrenaline take control, has been there too many times. He had to get help from somewhere.

As he focuses on the rise and fall of his chest, Ben feels the thud of his heart slowly recede to normal speed and the muscles in his neck and shoulders start to relax. In these moments of calmness, he feels something akin to love for his parents; he knows how much they've done for him over the last twelve and a half years. It's just a shame that calmness isn't a state he finds himself in very often.

With a small sigh, Ben checks his watch. Time to get ready for work. He sprays some deodorant across his upper body, then changes into jeans and the required plain white T-shirt; he would add the *Bittersweet* apron once he arrived at the café. He pauses at his bedroom door for a moment, then retraces his steps and grabs a small navy rucksack from inside his wardrobe. After his day, he might need it.

Taking care not to alert his mother, who is still busying herself in the kitchen but now with a glass of wine by her side, Ben tiptoes down the stairs and out of the front door, quietly pulling it closed behind him. The temperature has dropped in the last hour and he shivers slightly in the breeze. But he likes the cold air against his skin so decides to make the ten-minute walk across West Hill and onto Old York Road without a coat.

*

'Hey! It's Posh Boy. Grab an apron, Ben, and clear those plates.'

Ben gives Marco a half smile, and wonders, not for the first time, where his bouncy manager gets his energy from.

'The after-school rush was crazy. And Hana's crazy too. I mean, how can you forget how to make an extra hot skinny decaf macchiato?'

'I didn't forget, arsehole!' the diminutive Czech barista retaliates. 'He asked for a flat white. Not my problem the guy's got dementia.'

But the lanky Italian just erupts into laughter while simultaneously pirouetting on his white Converse trainers to face the next customer in the queue. 'Please accept my sincere apologies for my colleague's terrible outburst, madam. Now what can I get you?'

Ben smiles as he walks behind the coffee bar and retreats into the small kitchen at the rear of the café; he likes the easy banter of his work colleagues. He hangs his bag on a peg behind the back of the door – it's more public than he would have liked, but in the year he has worked at Bittersweet, no one has ever thought to look inside it – and pulls off a long grey apron, embroidered with the café's name.

The next couple of hours are busy for the team. The clientele is mainly made up of tired mums choosing the easy option for their children's tea, while sneaking in another latte or even a bottle of the craft beer that they've recently started selling. There's also a steady stream of commuters stopping by for a pick-me-up, or the opportunity to send those awkward emails without the risk of colleagues reading the sordid details over their shoulder.

But by 8 p.m. the crowd is starting to thin out and the students with their laptops and single-shot Americanos don't need much attention.

'Smoke?' Marco proffers a packet of Camels towards Ben.

'Yeah, thanks.' Tobacco doesn't give him the release that weed does, so he's still not sure whether he smokes to relax or to rebel, but the addiction is developing nicely either way.

'Hana, you're in charge. If anyone orders a macchiato, we're just outside.' The two young men disappear out of the back door to the sound of Hana's indignant cries.

'You got any plans for New Year, Posh Boy?' Marco asks, breaking the silence that the task of lighting up against the damp November night has created. 'I've got some friends coming over from Italy; thought we might head up to Edinburgh. You want to come?'

Ben stays quiet for a moment, considering the invite. He likes his manager at Bittersweet, his easy-going manner and hedonistic attitude. And he would love to go to Edinburgh, see Hogmanay in its spiritual home. But the thought of being with a group of strangers exhausts him. And of course he can't be sure that he wouldn't end up doing something that even his streetwise manager couldn't save him from.

'Sorry, man. I have plans.'

Chapter 5

Phoebe

I fumble with my coins. Six pounds fifty for a glass of wine. I only gave her a fiver and suddenly I'm all fingers and thumbs as I try to find the difference. Eventually I find the right change and pick my glass of house red off the bar with an apologetic smile. There are a few spare tables, so I choose one in the corner and sink down onto the accompanying bar stool, its deep red cushion proving a welcome comfort after a day on my feet. I take a large gulp and enjoy the feeling of the wine travelling through my veins. At least that's how it seems as my shoulders relax and my brain buzzes.

And I need it this evening. Being moved on by that security guard this morning unsettled me – if I can't wait outside schools without being noticed, how am I supposed to find Charlie? After retreating from Hollybrook, I'd wandered around Wandsworth Common for a while. The large green space is split in half by a railway line that carries people from the south-west of the country into Waterloo, and the track is set about thirty metres below the Common. The higher vantage point had felt quite empowering, so I'd leaned my forehead against the iron railings for a while, watching the blue and red trains hurtle by.

Beyond the railway, I could see a grand period building surrounded by more modest structures. I recognised it as Wandsworth College, a private secondary school that is on my list, but not one I've prioritised. Even when life was on an upward swing, I could never have imagined living in that world of stiff collars and cricket teas, not with my bohemian upbringing. And though Charlie is part of a different family now, I can't believe he's travelled that far from his roots.

The pub is getting noisier and I watch a group of twenty-somethings slide into a nearby booth, grand goblets of gin and tonic in their hands. They bump shoulders and lean into each other, and their easy movements remind me of when I was that age – before I met Dan and life became a little more grown up. At 18, I'd seen the chance of a steady wage as an escape route from my chaotic home, so had convinced Paul's agent to give me a job. While I could never have followed my parents into an acting career, as much for my lack of talent as anything else, theatre was the only world I knew, so it made sense to stay involved. By my early twenties, I was partying hard and had racked up a string of scandalous stories to entertain my friends with in London boozers like this one.

'Another one?' the bartender asks, hovering over me with a leaning tower of dirty pint glasses in her hand. I shouldn't really have a second drink. The first glass has done its job and relaxation is already turning to exhaustion. But I can't face going back to my parents' house just yet, so I nod, mumble thanks, and hand over another fortune. She then turns to ask the man sitting at the next table, and I notice him for the first time. Headphones cover his ears, and he's staring at his laptop. As she leans down to get his attention, I wonder why he's here, oblivious to the atmosphere that I'm soaking up. But as I scan the room, I realise there are a scattering of other young people sitting alone, having replaced friends or partners with various pieces of tech. This would have been bizarre behaviour when I was their age, but it's normal now. Change can happen like this, a stealthy creep that you never really notice. Or it can hit you like a juggernaut and knock you off course forever.

Two of the twenty-somethings – a boy and a girl – shift out of the booth, both armed with a packet of cigarettes and a coat. I stifle the urge to go with them. I haven't smoked for over a year now, but it was a regular thing for more than a decade, and the craving is never far away. *Smoking kills* it says on the packet now. But for someone who's spent the last fourteen years wondering if they're better off dead, it's not much of a deterrent.

The bartender arrives with the wine, and as we catch eyes, I see the familiar mix of curiosity and apprehension in her expression. My combination of dark brown hair and blue eyes has always sparked a level of interest, but I know she's seeing beyond that. Now my eyes emit a wary glow, and my once open expression has folded inwards. For years my natural urge was to please people – my parents, Dan, Charlie – but then I left them all behind, and it seems their absence has left an indelible mark on my face. I try to soften my features with a smile, and after a moment's pause, she returns it.

As she places a full pint of lager on the table next to me, the man removes his headphones and I hear him say thank you. His voice is light and melodic, and it makes me think of water trickling over pebbles. I suddenly feel bad for my earlier disapproval and smile at him.

'Hey.' He raises both his pint and his eyebrows, his smooth forehead wrinkling for a moment.

I mirror his toast with my wine glass, then turn away. I used to love meeting new people, widening my network of experience or opportunity, but not anymore. However, he doesn't pick up on my cue, and keeps on talking.

'Listen, I'm desperate for a fag. I know it's a disgusting habit.'

He raises his hands in a half shrug, half gesture of surrender. 'But would you mind keeping an eye on my laptop while I nip out?'

I look at the sleek rectangle of grey metal, the slight indent of the Apple logo shining on the top. 'No problem,' I hear myself saying, and then he smiles, and places it in front of me.

'Great, thank you. I'll only be five minutes.'

I watch him pick up his jacket, then head towards the pub door. I look down at the laptop and my fingers itch. It's not like I haven't searched for Charlie online before, typing a concoction of different terms into Google, ghosts hovering over my shoulder all the while. But since I've been back in London, I've felt a fresh urge to try harder. I wasn't surprised to discover neither Flora nor Paul had invested in a computer since I'd been away, and my old Nokia isn't set up for Wi-Fi or internet either. So this is the first chance I've had in a while.

With one eye towards the pub door, I slowly lift the screen lid. Google Chrome is already open and there are three tabs displayed along the top. YouTube. Soundtrap. iTunes. Perhaps he's a singer. With the thud of my heartbeat getting louder, I click open a new tab and consider what to type. From what that social worker told me, there's no point in trying Charlie anymore. With a sigh of imminent failure, I type *17-year-old boy Wandsworth* into Google, but all that comes up is a local knife attack and a disability initiative from Wandsworth Council. I swap to an image search and scroll down the page, but still, I come up blank.

In a fit of frustration, and perhaps indulgence, I type Dan's name into the search engine. Another toxic habit of mine, but one I've not managed to give up. There are the same news articles about him, nothing too in-depth; perhaps he wasn't young or beautiful enough for his death to be headline news. It's a relief really. I can't stand the thought of Charlie searching for information about his real father when he finds out his name and being confronted by the graphic details of his injuries. How he lived is a much better story.

I should close the laptop really. The man could be back from his cigarette break any moment. But I can see Dan's Flickr account listed on the page and I can't bear to miss this chance. I scan the room again, then click the link and fill in his login. I haven't done this for so long but the details are easy to retrieve from my memory, sizzling in the rush of adrenaline that's cascading over me. The page opens and I stare at the most recent photos uploaded. The last time my family was together, happy. Charlie with ice cream smudges, and Dan's bronzed torso, his wedding ring glistening in the sunshine. Chocolate-brown eyes and wide, generous smile.

I reach forward and let my fingertip gently trace the outline of his face on the computer screen. I wish we could go back there, before the violence and loss that erupted so soon after. My eyelids blink back tears.

'So, um, thanks for looking after my laptop.'

I slam the lid down, a gasp escaping before I can stop it. 'Sorry, I was just checking; I hope you don't mind; you see, my phone broke.' Excuses swarm out of my mouth, like bees drunk on pollen.

'Don't worry about it.' He wafts them away. 'My identity's not worth nicking. Not yet anyway.' He grins then and retreats to his seat, lifting his headphones back over his ears. How can people be so easy-going? I think about my brittle exterior, how life has hardened it, and tears threaten again. Charlie is the only person who can soften my shell, and at this rate, I'll never find him.

I drain the rest of my drink and make sure I avoid any more eye contact as I scurry out of the pub. With wine sloshing around in my stomach, I stop at the Sainsbury's Local and buy a couple of discounted sandwiches. I need some solid food to mop it up. Devouring them as I walk the last mile back, I wonder why my parents never feel the urge to eat. How they can just drink all day without craving something more substantial.

It's almost ten o'clock when I get home and everything is quiet. I take off my coat and head into the kitchen, praying there's milk in the fridge for a cup of tea. I'm in luck. I don't check whether it's in date but at least it's neither yellowed nor lumpy. As I stir in two spoonfuls of sugar – a habit I picked up after Dan's death and never managed to give up – I also try to stir up some resolve inside me.

I wish I could tell Flora about my search for Charlie. If I got her excited at the prospect of seeing her grandson again, that would give me the extra push I need to keep going. But after that visit from the social worker, their friendship revealed, I can't risk it. It was the children's guardian from Cafcass that recommended against leaving Charlie with my parents – their dependence on alcohol probably all too plain to see – but Paul and Flora never tried to change the court's opinion. Perhaps they were secretly relieved to have the decision taken out of their hands.

With my tea drunk and mug rinsed, I turn back towards the stairs. Suddenly there's a loud THUD followed by the sound of broken glass, then distant retching. I take the stairs two at a time. My parents' room is at the front of the house and the door is wide open. I see my mother lying on the floor, face down in her own vomit. A shard of glass is sticking delicately into her forearm and there's a thin line of blood trickling towards the carpet. She's laughing, spitting out the remnants of her sick with each giggle.

'For God's sake, Flora! You can't just lie there. Get up, woman!' Paul is barking orders at her, but I know his harsh words stem from worry rather than anger.

'It's all right, Dad, I'll sort it.' I can't help calling him that; he looks so old and vulnerable.

'Phoebe, darling. I didn't want you to see her like this.'

'Trust me, I've seen worse.'

'But she's your mother. She's supposed to look after you. Not the other way around. What must you think of us?'

I stare at the faded pyjamas covering his skinny frame; his small potbelly so out of place against the rest of him that I can't help thinking it's not physically attached – like a prosthetic he's trying on for a new part. His hairline has receded, but what's left is still thick and a lustrous shade of grey.

'We are who we are,' I respond vaguely. I wouldn't tell him what I really thought of them. 'You take my room. I'll stay with Flora tonight.'

After a slight pause, Paul backs out of the room. He's failed too many times to think he can make a difference now. Alone with my mother, I manoeuvre her into a sitting position. I find an old hand towel in a dusty chest and gently wipe the sick off her face. This will have to do. I can't bear the thought of trying to manhandle her into the shower in her current state. I carefully pull the piece of glass out of her arm. The blood oozes for a moment and then settles; no need for a plaster, thank goodness. She murmurs as I pick her up and lower her onto the bed, but within seconds of hitting the mattress, she's fast asleep. I roll her into the recovery position.

I fight the urge to leave the mess until morning. However exhausted I am, that smell is revolting. Instead, I work my way back to the kitchen in search of a dustpan and brush, plus some old newspaper for the glass. Miraculously, I find both. The bristles on the brush are black with dirt and slightly stuck together, but it will do. And there's a collection of *Wandsworth Times* in a box behind the back door.

Almost pure liquid, the sick has seeped into the carpet by the time I get back. I rub at it vigorously with the towel but I'm not sure I achieve much. After brushing the broken glass into the pan, I rip a few pages off the newspaper and scrunch it up to create a makeshift container that I can pour the glass into. As I fold the package away, I look down at the newspaper – now exposed at page seven.

And that's when my chest clamps shut.

Because it's him.

The picture of the boy holding an award.

Absolutely no question, it's him.

Then suddenly my chest releases and my heart starts racing. But it's excitement I feel this time, not fear. Struggling to focus, I desperately try to read the small article accompanying the picture.

Local student Ben Moreton (17) was recently awarded first place in the 15–17-year-old category of the Wandsworth Young Artist of the Year competition – beating five hundred other talented artists to win the top prize. Ben is currently a pupil at Wandsworth College, where he is studying Art, Geography and Chemistry A-levels. Congratulations to Ben from all of us at the Wandsworth Times.

A Wandsworth Young Artist of the Year exhibition will be held at the Battersea Art Centre from 7th to 10th November where all finalist pieces will be on display.

Ben Moreton. I roll the name around my mouth over and over, trying to make it sound familiar. Ben Moreton. Charlie Taylor. So different, but still one and the same. My son. And at Wandsworth College, so close to where I stood today.

After all my earlier doubts, just like that, I've found him.

Chapter 6

JUNE 2000

Phoebe

I try not to catch Richie's eye as I push my chair underneath the desk and reach down for my bag. Saskia Reeves' new contract, confirming her role in the new *Witches of Eastwick* musical at the Theatre Royal, is still strewn across it, my scrawled notes in green biro adding some colour to the otherwise dull legalese. I know I should file it away before leaving for the evening, but I'm in too much of a hurry for that.

'Got plans?' Richie asks with genuine curiosity. It's past the official end of the day, but that doesn't mean much in this office, and I'm usually here until at least seven, unless I'm going to watch a client in a show.

'Emergency love sickness call, I'm afraid.'

'Eurgh, really?' Katie pipes up. 'It's been two years now. Isn't it time you guys gave that love stuff up?'

I could remind her that marriage is actually classed as a

permanent thing, but I know that her husband lasted a lot less than two years after their son Dylan was born, so I move the conversation on instead. 'Apparently he's got news – and needs me and wine in equal measure.'

'I'm not sure that's a compliment.'

We all smile at that and I know I'm forgiven for my early departure. 'See you tomorrow,' I shout as I make my way up the stairs from our basement office and out onto the well-heeled streets of north-west London. I make it to the tube station in under ten minutes and the first train to leave is going in my direction. My luck even extends to a seat being available, so I settle in for the journey south with the review section of *Time Out*. I'm always on the lookout for new talent to add to my list, so I'm still working really; at least that's what I persuade myself.

When I get to Southfields tube station, five minutes' walk from our flat, Dan is waiting at the top of the stairs.

'Hi, babe.' He leans in for a kiss and I'm happy to oblige. I can taste the day of a junior solicitor – multiple cups of coffee, chicken sandwich washed down with Perrier water, a square of chocolate cake in recognition of someone's birthday – and I take it in with the rest of him. 'That was exactly what I needed,' he says as we pull away from each other.

'So I came a notch up from wine in the end?'

'Only just. Let's go.' He grabs my hand and we run across the road, dodging the slow-moving traffic, and into our favourite bar. Set in a typical Victorian terrace, Lexi's is narrow and deep with its bar on the right side, and a slim table ledge with stools running down its left. There are little round tables further towards the back, but we're creatures of habit so I don't say anything before climbing onto one of the nearest bar stools in the line while Dan makes his way to the bar. I watch him chat easily with David, Lexi's manager and other half, as he orders two glasses of Chablis and a dish of green olives.

'Cheers?' I say it as a question because the look on Dan's face is a long way off cheerful, but he clinks my glass anyway and even manages half a smile before taking a large gulp. I join him; the cool citrusy liquid tastes delicious and I pop an olive in my mouth to add a salty twist. I love these simple pleasures. Before I met Dan, my life was littered with big moments – meeting celebrities, going to premieres, celebrating new client wins on glamorous nights out. My friends would listen to my stories with wide, wishful eyes and I'd feel quite smug about the life I'd carved for myself. But looking back, I'm not sure how much I enjoyed all that fun. What I have now – Dan, this bar, our little routines – this is what makes me happy. Except Dan isn't looking exactly joyful now. 'Bad day?' I ask.

'It actually started quite well. Had my review with Henry first thing and he was uncharacteristically positive. He reckons I could make partner in ten years if I put enough hours in.'

'That's amazing, honey.' I'm not sure it is; working night and day for some vague dream of future riches isn't really the life I want, but I sense that now isn't the right time to bring up my opinion on work-life balance. 'So what changed?'

'My dad called.'

'Oh.' That explains Dan's bleak face, and his already empty glass. Dan was 10 when his mum died of an undiagnosed heart condition, running for the bus on her way to pick him up from school. Of course he blamed himself, even though she picked him up practically every day of the school year. But Tony – Dan's dad – had more of a reason to feel guilty. It had been a Thursday, so Dan was finishing late after football club. It was cold and rainy, and Tony had offered to pick his son up on his way home from work. But then a client had dropped by, stayed for longer than anticipated. The whole confusion had knocked Anne off her normal routine, hence running for the bus.

'Actually, let me get another drink first. You want one?'

I look at my half-full glass of wine and hesitate for a moment before answering with a nod. We do things together, and if tonight requires a two-drink preliminary, then so be it. The bar is busier now and I watch Dan waiting patiently to be served. I love his fondness for rules and order, but sometimes I wonder if he'd felt the same way before his mother died.

'I'm going to be a brother.' Dan puts a new glass of wine in front of me.

'What?'

'At the grand old age of 31, I'm getting my first sibling.'

My brain finally clicks into gear. 'Trudy's pregnant?'

'For twenty years my father hasn't shown anyone an ounce of commitment. Then he meets someone half his age and gets all starry-eyed. And now, what? We're meant to believe he's ready to become a father again? I don't buy it.'

'Did he sound happy when you spoke to him?' I first met Trudy last summer, when we took a road trip to Cornwall and stopped en route for a cup of tea. It was a flying visit, but I noticed instantly how smitten Tony was with his new girlfriend. I remember wondering whether he'd finally decided to forgive himself.

'Of course he's happy now, but what about when the baby comes and it's all smelly nappies and sleepless nights?'

'He's done it before.'

'And look how that turned out.'

I pause for a moment, loyalty and reason sparring. 'He never abandoned you,' I finally say. Tony might not have been the perfect father, but I feel an urge to defend him; he brought Dan up on his own after all.

'Not physically maybe, but in every other way. I reminded him of her. It was easiest to pretend I wasn't there. Whatever I did, however much I achieved. He was oblivious.'

'I'm sure he's proud of you.' I instantly regret my words, my empty platitudes. Flora doesn't notice my successes, so why should Tony be any better? It's true that he's never shown an interest in our lives or congratulated Dan on his journey up the career ladder. Perhaps he really is the selfish prick that Dan describes.

'He doesn't give a shit about me – we both know that.'

'Maybe that's why we get on so well. Equally shit parents.'

Dan's face opens up into a wider smile, and I return it quickly. I pick up his hand and kiss each one of his neatly trimmed fingernails. 'Maybe he'll be a better father this time round, without the burden of grief hanging over him.'

'So he gets a second chance at being a good father, but I don't get another childhood. Dan the reject, make way for the new and improved version.'

'Be angry with Tony sure, but don't be jealous of a baby.'

Dan looks up at me, instantly chagrined. 'You're right, I'm being pathetic. I've got you; I don't need anyone else.' He leans in for a kiss and I return it.

The bar is busy now and I can feel a few curious eyes looking over. 'Let's go home, maybe we can practise some baby-making of our own.'

'As long as it's only practising,' he warns with a low chuckle. 'Remember, three's a crowd.'

I smile as we walk out of the bar together, but still, a small sense of unease forms in my belly.

Chapter 7

NOVEMBER 2019

Ben

Ben shivers against the cold wind and swears at his stupid decision not to bring a jacket. The warmth generated by his rucksack is good for his back but does little to improve things for the rest of his body. Bittersweet officially closed at nine o'clock and even the last few stragglers had left by twenty past, but Marco then offered to open a few bottles of craft beer and Ben hadn't been in a hurry to get home. As it turned out, Hana's flatmate had recently moved back to Poland, so she was looking for company too, and the three of them happily worked their way through a crate.

Hana is small and feisty with wild curls and curvy hips. Ben's never properly fancied anyone before, so it's hard to tell what he thinks of her, but he did feel jealous – a more familiar emotion – as he watched Marco flirt so easily. The beer helped Ben behave less awkwardly around her, but he still struggled to think of anything interesting to say. It's all pretty theoretical though; there's no way Hana would be interested in him.

Traffic on East Hill has shrunk to the odd car cruising past, so Ben doesn't change his pace as he walks across the wide road. He'll be home in five minutes and, with any luck, his family will all be tucked up in bed. He can grab a bowl of Rice Krispies, his all-time favourite meal, and head upstairs. It's been a long day and he's exhausted. He prays silently that the late hour and four beers he's drunk will give him the uninterrupted sleep that he craves.

But as he opens the front door, his plans disintegrate. The kitchen light is on and his father is sat behind the island unit, facing Ben. His laptop is open, but he slides it to one side, a silent invitation for Ben to join him.

Fuck. This is the very last thing he needs right now. He decides to try his sister's tactic of dodging an unwanted conversation by unleashing his own torrent of words.

'Hey, Dad, you're up late. I'm done in. Just going to grab some cereal and head upstairs.'

'I waited up for you.' Greg's upbeat tone does little to disguise his own weariness. 'Eat it down here, Ben. It gives us a chance to talk, and your mother doesn't like you having food in your room anyway.'

Ben looks at his father. What is it with people constantly picking at him?

'Look, the truth is, we're worried about you,' his dad continues, filling the silence. 'Hiding in your room all the time. Refusing to engage with the rest of the family. The whiff of tobacco, or that sweeter smell, that follows you around.'

'Dad, I just need to get to bed.'

'Come on, mate, I waited up for you. Can't you give me five minutes?'

He can't stop it now. He's avoided this all day but he's tired and his dad's loaded air of companionship fires up his belly. 'For what?' he hisses.

That patronising sigh again. 'We found your geography essay ... saw the grade.'

'You've been in my room, through my bag?' he asks incredulously.

'We think your job might be impacting your studies, Ben. We want you to consider giving it up.'

The fury spills out. 'So first you want me to get a job – which, by the way, is actually about making you feel better about being so freakin' rich, and jack shit to do with my work ethic. And now you want me to walk away from it? And just so that Mum can finally admit to having two children at those dumb coffee mornings instead of just Perfect Rosie!'

'Don't be ridiculous. Your A-levels are important.'

'Not to me! I don't give a shit about my grades, my qualifications, my fucking future!' Ben likes the sound of his shouting, the release it brings. 'Jesus, just surviving a day in this family is an achievement!' He can't remember feeling this good in ages. But he needs to draw breath.

'Have you finished?' his dad asks, far too calmly for Ben's liking.

No, he hasn't finished. 'I BET YOU REGRET PICKING THE FUCKED-UP KID NOW, DON'T YOU, DAD!' he screams at his father, spittle flying in every direction.

Ben knows he's gone too far when his father propels upwards, the bar stool crashing loudly against the tiled floor. Greg is on him in a second, grabbing Ben around the neck and pushing him against the shiny American fridge. 'Don't you dare say that!'

A primal fear suddenly grabs at Ben's insides and he feels his legs weaken, his bladder loosen.

'You are my son and I love you. But stop pushing me, Ben.'

Ben realises his legs can't hold him up. His knees shake as his Dad's hands unknowingly keep him upright. He freezes in fear. His mind starts shutting down.

Suddenly there's a scream.

'What the hell are you doing?!' His mother's hair is dishevelled, but her eyes are alert as she races into the kitchen. 'Get your hands off him!'

With that command, the pressure against Ben's skin suddenly disappears. He falls to the ground.

'Oh my God, Greg. What were you thinking?' She's whispering now, as though Ben might not be able to hear her from his new position. Or perhaps the neighbours have returned to being her first concern now that imminent danger has been averted.

'I don't know. He just … I just … Oh God, I don't know.' Ben hears his father's voice crack and muffle as his head falls into his hands, but he doesn't care. All Ben feels is relief flooding through him, and a desperate urge to escape.

'Ben, darling, are you okay?' His mum reaches out, but he bats her arm away. He can't bear her touching him.

'I'm fine,' he spits out. 'Just need some air.' He drags himself up, then lurches out of the room and towards the front door. As he opens it, the burst of night air reminds him how cold he felt on his walk home from work, so he grabs the first jacket he finds on the row of pegs. As he runs down Milada Road, the terror gradually leaking out of him with every new step, he realises he's holding his dad's prized Barbour. He removes his rucksack and puts on the jacket. The heavy material makes him feel hemmed in, claustrophobic even; a bit like its owner, he thinks with a scowl.

The adrenaline has worn off now and Ben's body is pleading for rest. But his mind is still racing, and he knows he needs to calm down if he's going to stand any chance of sleeping tonight. When he first felt the urge to pick up his rucksack, before he even left for work, was that a premonition for how things would turn out? He pulls a flattened packet of cigarettes out of his jeans pocket and lights one up with the bright green plastic lighter stuffed inside.

With the anger gone, and the memory of his intense fear shut away, Ben can't stop regret forming. His dad just wanted to talk. That's what dads do. Why does he have to get so angry about it?

His parents have been caring about Ben for over twelve years. They do treat him differently to Rosie. And he hates that. But they do it with the best intentions. He was a broken 5-year-old boy when they picked him up from that foster home, and they offered to fix him. Why can't he be more grateful?

The problem is, Ben can't remember why he became that broken kid in the first place. He knows that his real dad died, and his real mum couldn't look after him anymore. And of course any child would be broken after that. But his first memory is of the intense fear he felt living with a gaggle of rowdy strangers – his foster family – and the confusion of all those women talking over him in concerned whispers. When he met the Moretons all those months later, it was their calmness, the order of their home, that he was drawn to. Ironic really, because it's that same order that suffocates him now.

Of course, in February he'll get the chance to learn more. Once he turns 18, he'll be able to find out his real parents' names, where his mother lives, everything about them. But actually, the thought horrifies him. If he can't make things work with Greg and Lucy, two reasonable people who were prepared to love him when no one else would, how the hell would things go with a grief-stricken fuck-up who clearly has zero maternal instincts?

Ten minutes later, Ben crosses onto a narrower, winding road. If he walks to the end, he will pass Wandsworth Prison, an imposing Victorian period building that appears much more civilised from the outside than it's reputed to be on the inside. But, instead, he stops when he reaches the slightly ramshackle bridge that carries traffic over the railway line. As he stares out over the tracks, adrenaline starts to work its way back into his system.

The walls that stand either side of the bridge are about three metres high and made of London brick. Flanked on both edges by security fencing topped with anti-climb guards, the only way onto the track is directly over the wall. Ben runs his hand along the brickwork. It's damp in the moist air, and moss has grown over the pointing. He hasn't been here since late summer and he knows how much more dangerous it is in these wetter conditions.

He walks to the side of the wall to get a better view through the fencing. The climb up will be easy enough; the rutted brickwork offers a wide choice of holds. But then Ben will need to drop himself over the wall onto a narrow ledge. If he slips off, he'll fall thirty metres onto the railway line.

Ben hesitates for a moment, closing his eyes and listening to the faraway calls of prison inmates. He should just go home. His parents will be in bed by now. Not asleep of course, but they won't risk another row tonight. He pulls the straps of his rucksack tight against his shoulders. Of course he's not going home.

Checking to make sure there are no cars close by, Ben digs his right toe into a shadowy groove and reaches his arms up, burrowing his fingertips in between the bricks. With just the dim glow of streetlamps radiating from Trinity Road, Ben must rely mainly on touch, and his memory.

He hoists himself up, fleetingly remembering his far less dangerous ascent earlier in the day, and manoeuvres himself over to the left where the light shines slightly brighter. One more push up with his legs and he reaches the top of the wall. He lets the right side of his body roll over it, his left side providing the ballast he needs to stay balanced. He lies belly down against the damp bricks.

Ben knows he must keep his body close to the wall, and every muscle taut. He's scared, but he loves the kick that being scared gives him. Slowly, carefully, he lets his right foot scrape down the back side of the wall. As his hips follow, Ben pushes them against the bricks, holding on to the wall with all his strength. His biceps scream in protest, but he ignores the pain. His heart bangs against the surface and his breathing labours. As his left leg follows his right, his feet start searching for the ledge. Ben feels panic form at the edges of his focus. His arms can't hold on for much longer.

Suddenly, it's there. Under his right foot. The relief is enormous, and Ben finds himself grinning as he slowly releases his weight onto the slender ledge. He shuffles along the wall and over to the bank, where he jumps gratefully into knee-high grass. He looks down at the jacket he's borrowed for the night and sees the mixture of dirt and moss stains smeared across the Barbour logo. Something else for his dad to be pissed off about.

But as he tumbles down the bank, his mind clears. He loves being on the railway line at night, with no one but foxes for company. His school is only a few hundred metres away, and his home not much further than that. But being thirty metres down, surrounded by metal tracks and green camouflage, feels like a different world. The wall Ben is looking for is just a short walk up from the bridge. When he arrives, he pauses a moment to check his previous work – Ben is by far his own biggest critic – and then, satisfied, unzips his bag.

Ben is particular about his paints. He travels to the London Graphic Centre in Covent Garden to find the exact brand he likes. And he's choosy about colours too. He likes them fiery and loud. Oranges and deep yellows. Gaslight blue. So alien to him really, but maybe that's the point. His tag is pure black though, the hardest colour to remove.

Ben shakes a can of paint and aims it at the wall. He's already sketched the idea in his black book, which he keeps locked in the case under his bed alongside his uglier, more shameful pictures, so he knows what he needs to do. As the spray floats onto the concrete building, his shoulders start to relax. This is his favourite drug. Better than smoking or craft lager. The sound and the smell of the airborne paint, the mix of destruction and creation, and the covert language only other taggers will understand.

*

Two hours later, the first stage of Ben's design is finished. The writing is there; he'll come back another night to add the symbols

55

that he's planned. He's prouder of his graffiti than he is of the painting that won him his award. Not because it is technically better – he knows the limitations of tagging – but because it's always harder fought. One day he'll get even braver, tag a heaven spot and really ramp his reputation up. It might not be as sensible as an A level, but at least it's something he'll do off his own back, for himself.

Calm, satisfied and dog-tired, Ben decides to take an easier route off the railway line half a kilometre up the track. It's a longer walk home, and he's supposed to be up in four hours' time, but he enjoys the peacefulness of the empty streets. He will apologise to his dad in the morning. They will make up. And an uneasy truce will hold for a while. Hopefully that will give Ben enough time to put out the fire burning behind his eyes.

Chapter 8

Phoebe

Finally darkness has started to lift. Physically I'm exhausted; between Flora's snoring and my own stomach churning, I've hardly slept. But my mind is doing somersaults. At last, after fourteen long years, I'm going to see my son again. Will he recognise me? Should I even give him the opportunity? I don't have a plan beyond standing outside the school gates, but hopefully the rest will come to me once I see him.

As I slip out of bed, trying not to disturb Flora, I catch my reflection in the mirror attached to her dressing table. At 47, I should be pleased that there's no sign of wrinkles, and that my body hasn't sagged or swollen. Especially after what I've lived through. But my lack of ageing hides an uncomfortable truth: that the shell I've built around myself is so brittle that one day it could shatter completely.

I wander over and sink down onto the velvet stool. I have so many memories of Flora sitting here, absorbed in the serious task of make-up application, oblivious to the unkempt urchin staring from the doorway. I feel like an imposter now, sat on her makeshift throne.

To distract myself, I start opening the drawers underneath

the dressing table. The left drawer is full of jewellery. Tarnished chains so knotted together that they look more like a piece of dirty industrial mesh. All manner of pendants are buried inside, as well as an array of brooches, rings and garish costume jewellery. I close the drawer untouched.

The large middle drawer is dedicated to Flora's make-up. As I handle the different bottles, cases, brushes and lipsticks, I realise that I can track Flora's decline through these products. Older Chanel and Dior products sit at the back, foundation that's hardened and cracked, and eye shadow that has turned from powder to a solid block with a film of fingertip grease. The front of the drawer is different; a mixture of Boots No. 7 and Superdrug own-brand products.

I look back at my reflection and wonder. I was never a heavy make-up user but I had my routine, like most other women. A little contour cream to smudge out the imperfections. A mix of light and dark eye shadow, grey pencil and black mascara to give my blue eyes some definition. Except on the few occasions when other people convinced me it would help, I haven't worn make-up since I left home that evening. But today is different; I finally have a reason to look my best again.

Flora groans slightly in the bed behind me as I pick up her primer, squeeze a nugget out onto my index finger and smooth it across my face. My features seem to soften so I keep going, using every product I recognise from Flora's more recent stash, and a few I don't. When I'm finally finished, I sit back and observe my handiwork. It's incredible really. The internal scars I carry have completely disappeared from my face. I can even see remnants of the old me. And if I'm going to meet Charlie today, this is the Phoebe I want him to see.

As I swivel to get off the small cushioned stool, I notice a dog-eared corner of paper sticking out of the right-hand drawer. I turn back and pull it open, releasing a flood of handwritten notes. I recognise them instantly. I don't know where the urge to write to Flora first came from, perhaps the therapy sparked something, but I made it part of my routine, a habit I never gave up in all that time. My parents wrote to me too, but their letters were always signed off with both their names, and as they were written in Paul's looping script, I was never sure how much input Flora had. With a stab of fondness, I look back at her. She's sleeping silently now, looking beautiful if it wasn't for the tell-tale signs of the previous night still speckled through her tangled hair.

As I return the letters, in a neater pile than I found them, I notice a different style of note towards the back of the drawer. With my heart rate increasing, I pull it out and unfold the dried-out paper. There's a short message scribbled on one side.

Charlie drew this in his session today. It's small steps, but he loves art therapy and I remain optimistic, so please don't worry about him. Regards, Clare Morris 16.11.05

With tears welling in my eyes, I turn the paper over, and take in the picture. A boy with brown hair and blue eyes is standing on a yellow beach, with a bright sun shining down on him. But the sea is scrawled in red, and two black dots peer out from the waves. I hold my breath and, with shaking fingers, slam the note back inside the drawer.

The noise filters into Flora's conscious and I turn to watch her wake up, relieved for the distraction.

'Morning, darling,' she starts with surprising vigour. 'You look spectacular. I'm not sure those pyjamas quite do your face justice though. What's the occasion? Job interview?'

I nod awkwardly. At least Clare didn't share her suspicions about my job hunting with Flora. 'Nothing too exciting, office admin, that sort of thing.'

Luckily – predictably – she doesn't ask for more details. 'Well, my mouth tastes like the proverbial vermin's nether regions, darling. Did I embarrass myself again last night?'

I weigh up my response. All I really want is for her to lay off the booze for a while. 'If you're feeling rubbish, why not give the gin a miss today? Give you a clear head for our day together tomorrow?'

'Absolutely, darling. That is exactly what I'm going to do.' We smile at each other, both happy with our own private lies.

I need to get dressed, but after making such an effort with my make-up, I don't want to just throw on my clothes from yesterday. I cross the landing in five steps and knock gently on my bedroom door. While Flora snores in short indignant snorts, Paul's snoring is much more rhythmical. In fact, it's slightly hypnotic and I get lulled into it for a few moments as I listen at the door. But I'm on a schedule; I can't miss the start of the school day. I knock louder.

A slightly flustered voice calls out. 'What time is it?'

'It's still early.' I know that I'm forcing my parents up hours before they normally wake, and hope this doesn't mean they'll pour their first glass earlier too. While Flora's drink problem is more obvious, I know that Paul relies on alcohol too these days. Because he only drinks red wine (full of healthy polyphenols, he tells me) and rarely starts before noon, he doesn't view it as a problem. Just like he thinks forty cigarettes a day are good for his concentration. He hasn't seen a doctor in twenty years though, just in case he's forced to face the truth head on.

'I just need to get dressed,' I call between the cracks in the door panels. 'I have a job interview today.' It's easier now; the first lie is always the hardest.

'Congratulations, darling. Do I know the agent? Can I put in a word?'

I sigh inwardly as I hear him whip back the duvet and thud thud out of bed. 'It's not with an agent. Just an admin job. Just a job, really.' The defeat in my voice is ridiculous. How can I feel embarrassed about a job that doesn't actually exist?

'Ah yes, of course,' he responds, realisation hitting home; the limited job opportunities for damaged goods. 'Well, I'm sure you'll get it, whatever it is.'

The door opens and my father gives me an awkward pat on the shoulder before scuttling off into the bathroom. Paul has never wanted to talk about what happened that night, so little gestures like this mean a lot. A smile forms on my face as I close the door behind me.

When our house in Southfields went up for sale, my parents borrowed a friend's van and drove the four miles across Wandsworth to claim what was mine. I'm pretty sure anything of value has been sold over the years, but the clothes I didn't take with me are still here, in bin bags piled up in the corner of the room. I haven't opened them since I've been back, too scared of what they might trigger, but today, at last, I feel ready.

As I rummage through, I start to connect memories with different items of clothing. The dresses all stand for an occasion – Simon and Amanda's wedding in Derbyshire, the premieres and opening nights that I went to with work – but it's the everyday clothes that threaten to ruin the make-up that I've so painstakingly applied. The H&M skinny jeans with faded knees; my favourite FatFace hoodie, over-washed from too many run-ins with baby food or worse; the Jack Wills gilet that Charlie snuggled inside as a newborn in a baby carrier.

I pull these items out of the bin liner and slowly get dressed. The worn material feels soft against my skin, and it seems to nourish my hard shell. I run trembling fingers up and down each arm of my hoodie and feel wrapped in my memories of him, steadied by touching something tangible from our time together. I'm not sure this well-worn look was quite what I had in mind when I first opened the bag, but I'm not going to give this feeling up.

I check my watch. It's 7.30 a.m. and time for me to go. A tight knot suddenly forms in my stomach. This is it. The day I've been dreaming about for so long. The thought that Charlie could be off sick, or on a school trip, or the dozen other reasons why he might not be at school, is too unbearable to think about. I pop my head around Flora's door to say goodbye and race down the stairs, smiling at the sound of her horrified voice.

'Well, you'll never get the job dressed like that, darling!'

*

I arrive at Wandsworth College in plenty of time to see the start of the school day. Blazer-clad pupils traipse in with varying levels of enthusiasm. The youngest stumble under a haphazard mix of bags and musical instruments. Older girls in long socks and short skirts amble in, checking their phones and occasionally screaming in either delight or horror – it's hard to tell which.

Dotted amongst the navy-blue blazers is the odd polyester business suit, top and tailed with scruffy haircuts and scuffed shoes. They must be sixth formers, I realise, and zone in on them. I have the picture of Charlie from the newspaper with me, but I won't need it; he may have grown cheekbones and stubble, but the essence of him is still imprinted on my brain.

As I watch from the opposite side of the road, I begin to notice that these young men share more than a dress code. I want to call their body language confidence, but I know it's more than that, a sense of entitlement that private education breeds. I think back to when I was their age, how determined I was to escape Paul and Flora's volatile lifestyle. But it was desperation rather than self-importance that led to my bold choices. Is Charlie like these boys? And if he is, what is he going to think of me?

The rush reduces to a slow trickle and then the bell goes, encouraging the last few stragglers to scurry past the security hut and into the main school grounds. With them inside, the entranceway is finally deserted. I stand for a while longer, staring into the quiet. A growing realisation seeps in.

He's not coming.

The disappointment is so intense that I feel it physically. Stupid really. This is just a temporary setback. I have found him; he goes to this school and I can try again tomorrow. But it doesn't work. Everything has been building up to this moment and it's just another huge disappointment. My knees weaken and I allow my body to sink onto the damp pavement. My vision starts to blur. I try to blink the tears away, but they spill out anyway, taking

Flora's cheap mascara with them. I was so excited. Why can't something just go right for a change?

And that's when he appears.

Late for school, running with surprising grace in an ill-fitting navy suit. I only catch a glimpse of him, but it's enough to take my breath away. Because it's my son. Charlie. His blue eyes are still as deep as I remember, and Dan's beautiful bone structure has found a new home. A thousand thoughts rush through my mind as I stare, half in disbelief that this is actually happening. He looks different; tall and lean, and with a stiffness that I don't remember. But he's also completely familiar. All those years apart from him physically seem to just melt away.

Even though I've been dreaming about this moment for so long, now it's here, I suddenly don't want him to recognise me – my tear-stained face and worn-out clothes. Who would want that for a mother? Instinctively I lower my head and it's only when he's safely past me that I allow myself to watch his tall frame disappear into the school.

Once he's gone, a surge of energy races through me and I leap to my feet. It's all so confusing. There's the joy of seeing him of course, but also the realisation of what I am now. No home; no job; no money. And what I did, of course. Could he ever accept me as his mother again? Do I even deserve a second chance? Perhaps I should follow the advice of that social worker and leave him be. But then again, I haven't waited all this time to just walk away now.

I don't know how long I spend staring at his school, frozen in indecision. But eventually the cold wind drags me out of my trance and I head towards the busy crossroads of Northcote Road and St John's Hill.

Chapter 9

JANUARY 2002

Phoebe

A moment of lightness, a tiny squawk, and then he's lain on my chest. My baby son. Tears form in the corner of my eyes and my smile stretches so wide that it aches. 'Hello, baby,' I whisper. His tiny body feels so vulnerable and I lift the soft blanket a little higher up his back. 'Welcome to the world.'

Dan leans in as close as he can get, the narrow hospital bed almost taking his weight as he lowers down beside me. He strokes our baby's fuzzy head and kisses me. 'He's so perfect, just like his mum.'

I look into my husband's adoring eyes and sigh with relief; it's going to be okay after all. I kiss him back, the warmth of our son radiating through both of us.

'Please remember there is major surgery going on down this end.'

The stern voice wafts over the thin blue curtain separating us and I wonder at the craziness of modern childbirth. As Dan and I celebrate being parents for the first time, the consultant surgeon is doing his best to sew up my insides. I'd always thought I'd give birth naturally; I'd practised the breathing, written a birth plan, tried to mentally prepare for the hours of pain. But our son had had other ideas, and adamantly refused to turn from his breech position. So we'd booked in for an elective caesarean section, and I'd tried not to feel too relieved.

Never comfortable either breaking the rules or being chastised, Dan apologises and straightens up. I see how hard it is for him to pull away though, and the fear that's tied me in knots for the last nine months relaxes even more. It was the Christmas before last when I first brought up the subject of children. I knew it wasn't a good time; Eloise was just born, and Dan hadn't really warmed to his baby sister. But her birth had the opposite effect on me, hitting me with this crushing maternal urge. Suddenly I needed to be a mum, a better one than my own. And with Dan, I knew I could be. So I'd suggested it, and then watched him grapple with the idea, his desire for convention pitted against his apparent lack of paternal instinct. By February he was on board, and two months later I was pregnant. We'd celebrated the news together, but that niggle of doubt – that I'd forced his hand – never quite left me.

'He's gorgeous.' The midwife smiles down at me. 'I just need to take him for a moment, weigh him and so on. You'll have him back in two ticks.'

I've only been holding him for a couple of minutes, but I feel his absence and follow the midwife's actions impatiently. But when she finishes her checks, she doesn't give him back to me.

'Would Dad like to hold him?'

Dan nods with only the smallest hint of hesitation. He carefully takes our son from the midwife, positions him in the crook of one arm, while keeping his other hand underneath our baby's head. The look of concentration on his face is absolute as he carries out this manoeuvre. It's not natural, I realise with a pang of disappointment, but he's trying, and that's what really matters.

The surgeon appears around the side of the curtain. 'All done. The team will take you up to the ward now. Oh, and congratulations.'

I start to say thank you, but he's disappeared again, pulling off his surgical gloves with a thwack, thwack. It reminds me that childbirth is both momentous and entirely routine.

'What are you going to call him?' the nurse asks, bouncing along next to my bed in light blue scrubs and trainers as the porter wheels me into the lift. It's a little disconcerting being so public again, my nakedness under the blankets apparent to me, if not to anyone else. For most types of surgery people look away out of a sense of respect. But with a new baby in your arms, people want to stare, to smile their congratulations. I feel like a celebrity caught popping out for a pint of milk in their pyjamas.

'Charles. Charlie,' Dan says with certainty.

I feel of stab of disappointment that Dan didn't look towards me first, check I was still happy with Charles before announcing it out loud, but I have no second thoughts. I like how solid the name sounds, dependable. A normal name. A regular family.

*

'He won't stop crying.'

'Have you tried feeding him?' The heavyset nurse checks my pulse but doesn't look at Charlie.

'I haven't stopped trying to feed him. He's not really interested. But then he screams when I put him back into the cot.'

'Are you swaddling him the way I showed you?'

'Yes, exactly the way you showed me.' I know I sound rude, but it's past 3 a.m. and I'm exhausted; I just want to get some sleep.

She pauses then, but still seems more interested in my health than my newborn's. Perhaps this is the way it works, maybe I am the vulnerable one. 'Why don't I take him to the nurse's station for a while,' she suggests. 'Try him with a bottle and give you a chance for some rest.'

I look at Charlie, writhing and wriggling in the clear plastic cot beside me. Anger etched into his tiny face, all red with the effort of screaming. I imagine that noise gradually dying away as the nurse disappears down the corridor with him, of closing my eyes and letting myself drift off; my son's welfare in the capable hands of someone much more qualified than me.

'No thanks.'

'Are you sure? It's just that ...' She pauses for a moment. 'It's just that the other mums seem to be struggling to sleep too.'

I look around the room for what feels like the first time. My world has shrunk so much today, and I've been oblivious to anyone but Charlie for the last few hours. There are three other beds and cots in here. A curtain screens the bed next to me, but I can see both mums on the opposite side of the room. One is trying to sleep, her baby silent next to her, and I feel a stab of guilt. But the woman directly opposite me is sitting up, her baby snuggled into her arms. 'Don't worry,' she mouths. 'We're fine.' I smile my gratitude and as she smiles back, I feel an unfamiliar sense of sisterhood.

'I'll try feeding him again,' I say, hoping that this will be enough to persuade the nurse to leave us alone. She gives me one final look of concern before shrugging her shoulders and bustling out of the room.

When I'm certain the nurse isn't coming back, I lean over and pick Charlie out of his cot. I undo the cocoon of swaddled blankets, and an arm pushes out, fist curled. This is what he needs, I realise, a bit of freedom. I try feeding him again, but he pulls away after a couple of minutes. I can't blame him; the sticky yellow colostrum milk is hardly appealing. Reluctantly, I start to wrap him in the blanket again, albeit with looser folds. I don't know what else to do.

'Don't put him back in the cot.'

I look up at the woman opposite me, her baby asleep on her chest.

'This one's my fourth. I learned with my second that they don't like being that far away from you.'

'But the nurse said—'

She cuts me off. 'They worry that the baby will fall out of the bed. That you'll go to sleep and loosen your grip.'

'Maybe I would?'

'Look, you can put pillows down the side, just in case. But I promise you won't let him fall. It's instinctive; awake or asleep, a mother will always keep their child safe.'

I look down at Charlie's contented face, so different from the scrunched-up anger I'd seen only a few minutes earlier. It makes sense, of course. He's been feeling the rhythm of my heartbeat for the last nine months; it's not surprising that it comforts him now. But am I putting Charlie at risk if I listen to this stranger instead of the nurse? I know what Dan would want me to do, the man who functions on a clear set of rules. Then I think about Flora; no doubt she would have relinquished me to the nurse's station as soon as the offer was made. But what do I think is right?

I pull one of the pillows from under my head and position it down my right side. I shift down the bed until I'm lying flat, Charlie still resting silently on my chest. Seven pounds exactly, the midwife had called out earlier, clearly enjoying the roundness of the number, and I feel that weight now, anchoring me down. This is so natural, I realise: us nestled together in our den of starched sheets and hospital blankets.

'I'll always keep you safe,' I whisper to my sleeping child. 'You and me, against the world.' Then I close my eyes and let myself drift away.

Chapter 10

Phoebe

Six hours later I'm back at the school gates. It was watching a group of pre-school children singing nursery rhymes in the back section of a café that helped me decide. With continual maracas shaking and the odd episode of outraged bawling, it was hard to tell what tune they were singing a lot of the time. But then the lady with the wide smile and honey-coated voice started, *See the little bunnies sleeping, 'til it's nearly noon,* and suddenly everything went quiet as twelve 2-year-olds lay down and closed their eyes.

I closed my eyes too, but only to stop the tears escaping again. That had been Charlie's favourite song at playgroup when he was their age, and he would respond with the same astounding obedience. Of course it wouldn't last long; we would get to, *Hop little bunnies, hop hop hop,* and Charlie would be jumping up and down with his friends again. But he loved the anticipation

69

of that moment; eyes screwed closed, waiting for the command. And I loved watching him grapple with his constrained energy.

That was the moment when I decided I couldn't walk away. But I need to take things slowly. Suddenly announcing I'm his mother is too risky; what if I'm a disappointment to him? Or even worse, if I cause the wrong memories to flood back? There's the social worker's words to consider too, of course. The laws I'm breaking. So I will find him, discover him, but keep my distance. Not disrupt his life. Who knows what will happen in the future, but as long as the possibility of us reconciling is there, that's enough for now.

The bell goes, signalling the end of school, and I don't have to wait long. In less than a minute, Charlie appears, walking quickly through the crowd of younger children, seemingly desperate to escape. Perhaps school isn't such a wonderful place after all. As he turns left out of the gates, I follow.

Just before he reaches the bus stop, a female voice calls out from behind me. 'Hey, Ben! Wait up a second.'

Charlie pauses for a moment and then turns his head to look. Ben, of course. I keep forgetting that's his name now. As he waits for the girl to catch up, I study his expression; there's fondness there, but also a trace of annoyance. I can't work out whether he's pleased for the interruption or not.

'Hey, Rosie. You heading home?' His monotone response doesn't give anything away. I edge a bit closer.

'Yes. Think so. Mimi's invited me to hers for a movie night sleepover thing but there's talk about nicking a bottle of vodka from her parents' drinks cupboard and I can't be bothered with the fallout.'

Rosie sounds nice. I wonder vaguely if she's Charlie's girlfriend.

'Jesus, Rosie, ever heard the phrase *live a little*?'

Or maybe not.

'Oh, while you're living it up serving skinny lattes to yummy mummies, you mean?'

70

'Trust me, if I had mates offering me free vodka, I wouldn't hesitate.'

Charlie's hard words send a cold shudder through me as I wonder if I've passed on my parents' alcohol addiction. But he's nearly 18. Drinking straight vodka is a rite of passage.

'You do have mates, little brother,' Rosie says in a softer voice, and slips her arm inside Charlie's.

Little brother? The realisation takes my breath away. Of course they're siblings, their conversation was pure brother-sister bickering. But for all the hours I've spent wondering what his new mum and dad were like, I never thought that there might be siblings too. My eyes burn with the effort of forcing back the memory of Charlie's real sibling, but I manage it. This is too important.

I continue to follow but their voices are too low to make out now. Rosie is still hanging on Charlie's arm, while his body language shows that he wishes she wouldn't. Why can't she let him go? Either she's needy or controlling, neither of which are good. She's talking constantly too, not letting him get a word in. No wonder he bites back every now and again.

As the streets become quieter, I hang back a bit. Even after living in the borough for most of my life, I'm not familiar with this part of Wandsworth. But in many ways, it reminds me of my old street, just a grander, more polished version. It has the same tree-lined roads and pretty Victorian houses, except with lots of shiny black four by fours parked in front of them.

After walking for fifteen minutes, the pair of teenagers pause outside a house on Milada Road, still talking in low whispers. If the frontage is anything to go by, Charlie's new parents suffer from a severe case of OCD. Three identical bay trees line up in square pots against gleaming black railings, shimmering with tiny fairy lights. The traditional black and white hexagonal pathway is shiny and smooth, and uplighters give the gunmetal grey front door a regal glow. A bit different from Paul and Flora's ramshackle frontage, with overgrown weeds sprouting through the cracked paving slabs and the collection of rubbish blown in from the street. I'll tidy that up tomorrow.

Eventually the two of them walk inside. Charlie seems a bit reluctant as he follows his sister with his head down. Perhaps things aren't as good as they appear on the outside. The door closes behind them and, absurdly, I feel abandoned. I can't bear to go home now, but equally I can't just stand here staring at a closed door. Rosie had said something about making lattes. Does Charlie work in a café? Is he going to reappear soon, having swapped his suit for a barista's apron? If so, could I risk ordering a coffee from him?

I jump suddenly as the quiet is broken by a high-pitched crash, like glass smashing against tile. I see now that the large front window is open a couple of inches. Raised voices spill outside. It's hard to make out exactly what's being said but it's clearly an argument between him and his adoptive mother. She's screaming at him now. *A ruined jacket. No respect.* Why is she being so harsh on him? Does she not remember what he's been through?

There's plenty more muffled shouting before a young man's voice rings out with much more clarity. *'JUST FUCK OFF!'* it screams, followed by the thudding of footsteps up carpeted stairs. Silence follows, except that I can just make out the heavy breaths of a woman crying.

I'm not sure how long I stand there, rooted to the spot. But it's long enough for the daylight to disappear. As I shiver in the darkness, I hear movement again. More thuds on the stairs. Then the front door flies open and Charlie hurtles out, a look of fury etched on his face. I look away quickly – I don't want to be caught staring – but he doesn't notice me. He storms past, a rucksack held between two white-knuckled fists, and disappears down the dark street.

Without thinking, I follow. His long legs and urgent pace mean I have to jog to keep up, and we're soon beyond the residential streets and heading down the hill towards Wandsworth's central hub. The streets are busy here so I can move much closer to him. The bag is on his shoulders now. Anger still shows on his face, but I can see pain too.

He hesitates for a moment, then takes a packet of cigarettes out of his pocket. I watch him light one up with shaking hands and suck deeply on its filter. I find myself drawing a big breath too, like I'm smoking it with him. The hit has given him something, because he ups his pace again, skirting behind a row of brightly lit shopfronts. This back street is darker and my heart rate quickens. Shadows start dancing around my head, but I bat them away. I need to stay focused on my son.

A sprawling park comes into view, and, as I realise that's where he's heading, my apprehension grows. I remember this park. In the daytime, it's got a lot to offer – playground, football pitches, open parkland – but the place has a more sinister reputation after dark. I brought Charlie here plenty of times when he was little, but I'd never stay beyond the end of the school day. I feel the urge to run now, but I fight it. I can't leave Charlie on his own.

I see a group of teenagers in the far corner of the park. A couple of the younger ones are on BMX bikes, trying, and failing, to get the attention of their older peers with their tricks. It's hard to make out much more than silhouettes in the night sky, but they don't look friendly, so I'm shocked when Charlie walks straight up to them, bold as anything. I move as close as I can without being noticed. They don't seem happy about the intrusion.

'Yeah?' one of the older boys says, not politely.

'Wondered if I could borrow a bike. Take it for a spin.'

What the hell is he doing?

'You fucking high or something, man? Why the fuck would we do that?' The rest of the group sniggers but there's menace in their laughter.

'It's not for me. It's for your mates.' Charlie speaks slowly, as though he thinks they're stupid. *He's the stupid one.*

The kid swaggers over to Charlie, stands so close their noses almost touch. 'Oh yeah? How's that then?'

'I can show them how it's really done, can't I? I reckon they need a few lessons.'

'You fucking bitching me?!' a new voice shouts out, stunned fury adding a new level of danger. The two cyclists throw down their bikes and stride over to where Charlie still stands, seemingly oblivious to the shitstorm he's creating. They're younger than him, shorter too, but God knows what weapons they might be carrying. The weird thing is, he doesn't seem to care; it's almost like he's enjoying it.

The sting of a slap rings out and I gasp in horror. I know this is just the start. I can't stand by and let him take a beating, or worse. But my feet won't move. *Don't let him down*, my head screams, *not again*.

But I'm so scared.

With a silent warrior cry, I force my body into action, lunging forward. And it works. One by one, I take stiff strides towards the group.

'What the hell are you doing?' I shout, trying to drown out the wobble in my voice by turning up the volume.

'Piss off, old lady.'

I need to find the upper hand, and quickly. 'That's *DS* old lady to you,' I counter, emphasising the police title. 'Let him go, or I'm calling it in.' I pray to God that he can't spot my shaking hands, now shoved into my pockets.

The boy pauses for a moment, so I keep staring, desperate to hold my ground. They're just kids. Fifteen at the most. I spot a trace of confusion in his eyes, and I realise with a growing euphoria that he's not going to risk it. I swallow the urge to laugh. He may think he's tough, but he hasn't lost the naivety of childhood yet.

'Fucking pigs,' he mumbles in a bid to save face, and storms off towards the road, his group following obediently.

Slowly I feel my breathing return to some acceptable level. I can't let myself replay what just happened, how differently things could have turned out. That may be for another day, but I have different priorities right now. I look at Charlie, stood less than a metre away from me. This wasn't in the plan. A range of physical reactions threaten to expose me – racing heart, pricking tears, Cheshire Cat smile – but I need to control them all. He hasn't shown any sign of recognition; I can't risk raising suspicion now.

'Are you really police?'

'No,' I manage. At least I'm not worried about him recognising my voice. A decade of smoking has given me a new rasp.

'You look like police.'

'Really?'

'Like you can handle yourself.'

I think of my hardened face and wiry frame, of having to adapt to a life I could never have imagined. 'You just looked like you needed a hand.'

'I didn't.'

His tone is defensive, closed. This isn't how I wanted things to go, but of course he's not going to be grateful; he orchestrated the whole thing after all. 'You just seemed …' But I don't know what to say that won't make him feel embarrassed. As well as being risky, goading gangs of kids is a strange way to behave.

'I've got to go. I'm meant to be at work.' With that, he turns his back on me. I know I should let him go, but now I've got this close, I don't want him to just walk away.

'Where do you work?' I call out after him, sounding more desperate than I planned.

He pauses. Silence hangs in the cold air and I don't think he's going to answer. But finally he does. 'Just a café, not far from here.'

I don't believe in telepathy, but I try it anyway, inwardly begging him to say more. Eventually he sighs and turns towards me. His hostility has faded, and I can see a trace of regret in his eyes, maybe even gratitude. 'I suppose I probably owe you a coffee.'

The sheer joy sparked by those words threatens to overwhelm me, but I can't let it derail this opportunity. 'Why not,' I whisper, trying to match his nonchalance. 'Thank you.'

'It's on Old York Road,' he adds. 'Just five minutes on the bus.'

The significance of that comment starts rapping at my temples. I haven't been on a London bus since I moved back. But I can't walk away from Charlie now, I've spent too long dreaming about this moment to cut it short.

The stop is across the road from the park and I realise, with a mix of dismay and relief, that the bus we need to get is already there. A line of would-be passengers is shuffling towards the front door, while a trickle of people alights from the mid-section. Charlie joins the back of the queue and I focus on the collar of his jacket as I slot in behind him and try to keep my mind clear. I can do this.

Finally Charlie reaches the front of the bus. I watch him climb up without hesitation and hover his phone over the yellow pad. Suddenly all my fears transfer to him and I feel a desperate urge to grab his collar and hoist him back onto the pavement. I want to hold his hand and run away, run backwards fourteen years and start again. How differently I would do things, if I had another chance.

'You coming?' He looks confused, embarrassed even. There are people behind me and I'm blocking their way. I need to do this.

'Coming,' I answer, but my brain and limbs aren't connected. However much I scream at myself, my body isn't moving. The other passengers barge past me, murmuring with impatience, while I stand stock-still. Frozen in fear.

Chapter 11

Ben

What the hell is wrong with this woman? Why can't she just get on the bus? Ben hesitates for a moment, unsure what to do next. His evening would be a lot simpler if she did just stay put and let him get to work saviour-free. And it's not like he really owes her anything after she spoiled his fun. Well, not fun exactly. More like a burst of pure oxygen in his otherwise suffocating existence.

Other people choose self-harm. Pinched skin for the beginner, a razor blade for the more advanced. Ben understands the release, the euphoria, that pain brings. But self-inflicted pain just feels like cheating. He tried it once – running his Swiss Army knife along his abdomen, with just enough force to allow the blood to bubble before thickening into a scab – but it left him feeling even more of a failure. Like a child playing with safety matches. No, goading others, not knowing how things will end up – that's the kind of justice he deserves.

He stares at the woman's wide eyes, both fear and resolve shining through them. Against his better judgement, he feels a pang of sympathy for her. She did put her own safety on the line to stick up for him; she must have seen how the whole episode started, but hasn't pulled him up on what a jerk he is.

Without making a conscious decision to move, Ben finds himself reaching out, taking hold of her arm. He looks straight into her eyes, less vivid now behind the thin film of tears, and whispers, 'It's okay.' Pathetic words really, but miraculously they seem to help. He feels her body relax, just slightly, and he takes the opportunity to steer her inside. The bus driver is either feeling sympathetic or simply in a hurry to leave because he doesn't even ask for payment. Just swings the doors closed and sets off.

But Ben's still holding her arm. He hates this level of intimacy, but it's shaking so much that if he loosens his grip, he can't be sure she won't just drop to the floor in a heap. And that would be even more humiliating. So he just stands there. Holding on. He doesn't want to make eye contact with her again either, so he stares out of the window and wills the bus to reach his stop as quickly as possible.

What feels like hours later, although is about five minutes, the bus draws into the Alma Road stop. He'd been worried that the woman would adopt the same painfully slow pace getting off the bus, but actually, perhaps obviously, she reacts in the opposite way, and within seconds they're standing awkwardly together at the top of East Hill, like the final stage of some embarrassing blind date. He watches as she gulps at the fresh air and he feels the urge to do the same. Eventually he turns down Alma Road and starts walking towards the café, aware that she's fallen in step beside him. With the calming effect of the cold November air, he decides to risk a glance in her direction.

He's always been quite amused by how easy it is to read people. Everyone thinks they're unique, but it's not true. Whether it's builders from Eastern Europe, or city boys from the East End, people find their clan, and can't help following its code. But this woman is harder to pinpoint. She's dressed in that fake scruffy way that loads of new mums love: skinny jeans and trainers, branded hoodie poking out of a navy Puffa jacket. But her face tells a different story. It's hardened, like she's got six kids at home and a husband who doesn't give a shit. Her eyes are a special shade of blue though, and there's something strangely familiar about them.

She turns towards him and Ben realises with horror that he's staring at her. Their eyes catch for a moment, and then he whips his head round, smarting with embarrassment. To distract himself, he reaches into his pocket and pulls out his packet of cigarettes. He extracts one and positions it between his lips. Then he proffers the packet towards her, keeping his eyeline facing downwards, and after a moment of indecision she accepts. Her mumble of thanks breaks the silence and Ben feels a notch more relaxed as they stop for him to light it for her.

'Sorry about all that on the bus.'

There's genuine apology in her voice and Ben feels the tension drop a bit further. He could ask her about it, where it stems from, what she's actually scared of. But he doesn't want to know. He's got enough issues of his own to deal with. 'No problem,' he says, in a tone designed to halt the conversation. A few minutes later they reach the bottom of the hill and he guides her left past a couple of boutiques, a dentist surgery and a yoga studio.

'We're here,' he says when they arrive outside Bittersweet. He pauses, the awkwardness suddenly glaring. How is he going to explain this woman to Marco or Hana? *Oh, hi guys, I was out looking for a kicking, and this badass superhero saved me from myself. And now we're best friends because, as it turns out, she's as much of a freak as I am.* Ben shudders at the thought of how accurate that explanation would be.

'I know you have to work,' she says. It's as though she's read his mind. 'I'll just sit in the corner and you can bring me a coffee when you get a chance.' She pauses then, as though weighing up her next comment before deciding to say it. 'After all, we don't want you getting into trouble, do we?'

It's subtle, but Ben catches it. The tease in her voice. The tiny smirk at the corners of her mouth. She's only known him for half an hour, but already seems to have got the measure of him. The boy who goes looking for trouble. It should infuriate him, her taking the piss like that, but weirdly it has a different effect; almost like he's touched by her attention. He raises one eyebrow in response and pushes open the door.

'Hey, Posh Boy, you made it! I thought maybe you'd had a better offer.'

'Sorry, man,' Ben apologises flippantly, knowing his easy-going manager doesn't care about him being a few minutes late. 'Bus issues.' But Marco has already lost interest in Ben. He's looking at the woman stood next to him, plastering a grown-up smile on his face. Holding out his hand in the formal British way that he thinks people still do in the UK. That some people do still do, Ben has to acknowledge, like his parents.

Parents. It hits him that Marco has never met his mum. That this crazy Italian is holding back his usual chat because he thinks this woman is Ben's mother. He can't help erupting into laughter, while also feeling suddenly anxious to put him straight. While he quite enjoys the thought of how horrified his actual mother would be to get mistaken for this woman, the truth is, he's not particularly keen on the idea of her being his mum either.

'Marco, let me introduce you to—' Jesus, he doesn't even know her name.

'I'm F-F-Fiona,' she pipes up, saving him. He hadn't noticed a stammer before. He's starting to think this woman has even more problems than him.

'Yeah, um, Fiona helped me out earlier. So I said I'd shout her a coffee.' Ben finds that he can't make eye contact with his boss; he knows his explanation doesn't stand up to scrutiny. So he's grateful when Marco chooses not to push it.

'Of course! A coffee on the house, no problem. What can I get you? Latte? Flat white? Or Hana could make you a macchiato. She's in training you see ...'

'*Jdi do prdele, Marco!*' a voice carries from behind the coffee bar. Ben has no idea what his co-barista has said in her native Czech, but guesses it's not a compliment. However, Marco only seems pleased with her fiery reaction, like it's some affirmation of her secret love for him. Ben can't help feeling a stab of jealousy as he watches his boss guide Fiona to the table closest to the window, gesticulating wildly while regaling some anecdote or other. Why the hell can't life be that easy for him?

Chapter 12

Phoebe

I'm trapped, there's no escape. A hand grabs at my arm. A face. It's Dan. Has he come to save me? But no, it's not Dan. It's him. He's pulling me close. He's smiling. It's now, he's going to do it now …

I clamp my hand over my mouth just in time to smother the scream. I couldn't bear Flora coming to check on me; one part concern, four parts confusion on her sagging face. I sit up against the headboard and try to push the images away. It's not hard, I have much better ones to replace them with now. I think about Charlie reaching for my arm last night, reassuring me as my heart thudded along with the chug of the bus's engine. It was as though, in that one moment, he was offering his forgiveness. Stupid really; he doesn't even know who I am.

The cigarette was a mistake though. After the bus ride I felt like I'd earned it, and I didn't want to turn Charlie down, that sense of sharing something with him was so good. But I can already feel the urge for another.

I reach over for my watch to check the time. It's still early. I'd promised Flora that we'd spend today together but she's not going to be up for hours and I need to work off this itch of adrenaline. I met my son last night! And he's handsome and kind and funny. But he's also angry, especially with himself. I need to make some sense of how I'm feeling. I need some fresh air.

A few minutes later I pull the front door closed behind me. The cold air is soothing against my flushed face and I draw in two or three big breaths before heading down the street and turning north towards Battersea Park. The huge green space is so familiar. It was a constant during my childhood; a place to hang out with friends after school, or disappear to on my own when things got too crazy at home. But I have a specific reason to visit there now. I need to tell someone about meeting Charlie, otherwise I'll burst.

My grandma only moved out of London once – she was sent to live with an aunt in Sussex for a year when the Blitz was at its worst – but that time in the countryside turned her into a lifelong nature lover. She began volunteering at Battersea Park as soon as my Aunt Clemmy started school, so I could always find her pruning or potting on a Friday afternoon. She'd been there almost forty years when her breast cancer was first diagnosed, and it was one of the last things she gave up when it spread to her bones. So it was never in doubt that her ashes would be scattered here.

I sit down on the bench opposite a bank of rose bushes, a few still holding on to their autumnal bloom. *In Loving Memory of Violet Simpson*, the bench is inscribed. That's not my grandma, of course; Flora would never have been that organised. But this was her favourite place to sit, and Dan and I brought her here a few times towards the end of her life. He would butt her wheelchair up against the edge of the bench and I'd hold her hand. He'd leave us to it for a while then, offer to get coffees from the little hut by the petting zoo. Whether it was to give me precious moments alone with my grandma, or just a break for him, I never really knew.

As I listen to the morning birdsong, I can see why she liked it here. I relax into the bench a little more. 'I found him, Nana,' I whisper. My grandma died two years before Charlie was born so the only way she could meet him was like this, me bringing him to be inspected by a rose bush, so it doesn't feel strange, talking to her about him now. 'Although he's not Charlie anymore, he's called Ben.'

And I'm Fiona. Where did that come from? I think of Fiona Bruce – glamorous, intelligent, easily holding a rabble of politicians to account on *Question Time* – and the name feels even more out of place. But I couldn't tell him I was called Phoebe, just in case it conjured up some memories. Now I've found him, I can't let the truth derail things.

'And he goes to a private school, like Flora always pretended she'd been to.' My mother was an enigma from the day she was born apparently, this dazzling star in an otherwise ordinary family. My grandparents were in awe of Flora, while they were mainly a disappointment to her. She adopted a posh accent when she was still in primary school, and even the swinging Sixties couldn't persuade her to give it up. With such grand castles in the air, perhaps her life was always predestined to be a disappointment.

'But he's hurting, Nana. Is that my fault? For what I did to him?' I can almost see her weighing up the question, the rose petals wafting side to side in the breeze. She was never very sure of herself and didn't like giving advice, so it would take her ages to say anything. I always appreciated that reflection, but as I listen to her silent response now, I find it deafening.

'But it must be my job to fix him too?' There's an unattractive whine in my voice now. 'They've had him for years, and they've failed. I'm the only chance he has left. I have to make this right, don't I?' I was one of three grandchildren but my cousins grew up in Leeds so I was always her favourite. It also helps that I'm a carbon copy of Flora – but a calmer, less exhausting version. She could never deny me anything for long, and with that final beg I feel her comforting cloak of approval descend onto me.

I stand up with a fresh resolve and pull one of the dying roses off its stem. By the time I get home its petals have disintegrated between my fingers, but at least I managed to stop myself buying a packet of cigarettes at the corner shop.

*

It's lunchtime by the time Flora and I head off. As we totter down the road, I notice that my mother has made an effort for our day out. She looks like a cross between Vivienne Westwood and Joan Collins. If I tried to wear a glittery orange coat and bright pink scarf over a black cocktail dress and leopard print heels, I'd look ridiculous. But somehow Flora manages to pull it off. Just about.

'Battersea Arts Centre?' she exclaims when I tell her where we're going. 'What a lovely idea! I was there last month, actually. Helping a young theatre group with their performance. They call it Scratch – getting feedback from experienced actors to help them develop their ideas. Wonderful initiative. Awful name, of course. Makes me itch every time I think of it.'

I know that Scratch is open to everyone, not just people with acting backgrounds, but I don't take the opportunity to put her straight. 'It's not a performance,' I begin carefully. 'There's an art display in the Grand Hall. Finalists from the Wandsworth Young Artist of the Year competition.'

My explanation hangs in the air for a moment as I try to gauge her reaction. She loves the venue, with its own history of populist campaigning, and art is one of the few things that can drag her attention away from her next drink for a while. But there's always the chance she'll make the connection, so I hold my breath.

Of course I'd love to tell Flora the truth about Charlie; she had a better relationship with him than she ever did with me. Being a grandparent proved perfect for her: dip in and out as you please, have all the fun with none of the responsibility. Maybe she'd be on my side; her respect for the law is flimsy at best. But what if she didn't approve? And decided to tell that social worker? I just can't risk it.

'Does that sound okay?' I ask, and this time she answers immediately.

'Wonderful, darling!'

I sigh with relief and try to ignore the niggling sense of guilt.

'And perhaps we can stop by the Scratch Bar after – my treat?'

*

The exhibition is free to enter and the Grand Hall, with its ornate features and impressive domed ceiling, is full of people wandering from piece to piece, making admiring noises while trying to rein in small children as they slide around the polished floor. I remember the relentless energy that Charlie had at that age, especially when I needed him to behave. Racing around supermarkets, refusing to sit in the trolley. Pouring endless plastic cups of water at the doctors' surgery, obsessed with the glug-glug sound of the water dispenser. How annoyed I would get with him then. What a waste of precious time, I realise now.

'Gosh what a wonderful collection of art, Phoebe darling. Can you believe this artist is only 14!' Flora almost shrieks as she stares at an Andy Warhol-style self-portrait. 'Can you imagine having a talent like that?' It's true that the teenager is a far better artist than me, but her implied insult rankles all the same, so I take the opportunity to wander off. Now that I'm this close, the urge to find Charlie's winning painting is almost painful.

There are three different age categories within the Wandsworth Young Artist of the Year competition, and I know that's Charlie entry will be in the 15 to 17 years group. While the standard of art created by the younger children is impressive, I'm impatient to get to the back of the room where the oldest category is on display.

But as I weave my way through the crowd of visitors, a thought pops into my mind. Charlie could be here. Of course he'd want to see his own work on display, and he wouldn't get chance to visit during the week. I can't risk bumping into him again. I slow my pace and scan the room. Most of the visitors are older than Charlie; proud parents and grandparents, as well as the odd genuine art lover, plus plenty of young families and senior citizens looking for a cheap and warm way to spend their afternoon. It seems that the art students have stayed away, I decide with relief.

Once I'm sure Charlie's not here, I walk towards the final display and his work jumps out instantly, a large oil painting on canvas, its title printed on a small piece of card, Blu-tacked to the wall. *London Streets Through a Child's Eyes*. The angle is captivating. Is that really what children see? Hundreds of human legs, and buildings towering above them like mountains. Almost without realising what I'm doing, I bend down, trying to find the same perspective. I'm fully crouching by the time I reach it. I feel hemmed in and free to roam all at the same time. It's been a long time since I was that size, and the discovery is quite exhilarating.

Until I realise that I'm the height of a 3-year-old. Is that why he painted this picture? Has he held on to that viewpoint ever since I left him? I swallow back the acid forming in my mouth. Carefully I straighten up, reach hold of the table behind me. Flora is here somewhere. At any moment she could pounce on me, drag me to see some other amazing piece of child art or off to the Scratch Bar for a gin and tonic. I try to exhale slowly, but it comes out in heaves. The room starts to spin.

'Worthy winner, I'd say.'

A loud voice cuts through my rising panic and I cling on to it, use it to pull me back. 'The painting?' I manage.

'His use of colour, how the shading graduates. It's very impressive.' The man booms with praise; large, callused hands wave towards the easel with enthusiasm.

Steeling myself, I look back at Charlie's picture. I had been so lost in the perspective that I hadn't noticed how intricately the busy cityscape is painted, or how he's managed to give the tiny commuters a harassed edge. 'It's got a special energy about it,' I say. A sense of awe has crept into my tone and the man turns to look at me, a curious expression on his ruddy face.

'Do you know him, the artist?'

Uniquely, I want to say. But of course, I don't really know him at all. I imagine him getting the envelope through his shiny letterbox, announcing his success, and the family celebration that followed. With a house like that, they're bound to have a spare bottle of champagne in the fridge. The dad would have opened it, poured everyone a glass. The pretty blonde sister would have giggled as she raised hers, made some comment about him having the brain of a toddler too maybe. And the mother. She would have looked on proudly, like it was her doing, his talent, even without the gift of DNA. I look back at the man, his dense grey beard splaying out over the high collar of his navy Rohan fleece, and shake my head.

'Well, I imagine he's a good lad,' he continues. 'It's hard work, painting something like this. The layering, this level of detail. He's clearly got some grit.'

I think back to the night I met Charlie again, his determination to get a beating, the sacrifice he was willing to make to satisfy some compulsion. It's good to see that steeliness translated into something as mesmerising as this picture. But before I respond, a woman's voice drifts over, a lady my age standing just the other side of Charlie's newest fan.

'I never thought of it like that.' It's a simple comment, spoken quietly, but it still makes the hairs on the back of my neck stand up, like I can sense danger in her clipped, upper-class accent. I take a few steps backwards and drop my gaze to the floor.

'Oh certainly. This would have taken ages.' The man's attention is now with the posh woman. I slink a bit further away, then risk looking at her. Her long blonde hair is regulation straight without the slightest wave or tangle. She's wearing a black cashmere jumper underneath a grey herringbone jacket, and her ears sparkle with twin diamonds. I have never seen her before, and yet I know exactly who she is. I watch her drop her head slightly to the right as though she's seeing the picture for the first time.

'Thank you for your insight,' she says finally. 'Hard work is usually his sister's domain.'

And there it is. What my gut knew all along.

'You're his mother?' the man asks. 'Well, I must congratulate you on raising a very talented artist.'

I watch her smile her thanks and I fight the urge to scratch it off her face.

Chapter 13

FEBRUARY 2004

Phoebe

'To a new start.'

We clink glasses and I make a silent wish that he's right. That this perfect little house – albeit with its eye-wateringly large mortgage – will be the catalyst that allows us to reclaim what we have somehow managed to lose. Clanwell Street is only a ten-minute walk from our old flat, but it feels like a world away. This neat grid of small Victorian terrace houses is full of young families, smiling as they pass each other with their matching Bugaboo pushchairs. I have the same model, and I'm torn between happiness at being part of the gang and mourning the Phoebe who preferred to trailblaze.

'I think it's good that you're going back to work too.'

I nod. It's what he wants to see, but that decision wasn't easy either. The first six months with Charlie were hard work: sleepless nights, unexplained temperature spikes, those long hours listening to him cry; but I loved them. Feeling so completely necessary. It was only after that, when he was sleeping through the night and had settled into a comfortable routine, that I started to get bored. And that's when I began wondering if I could be a working mum without damaging him, or weakening our bond. Dan was desperate to move up the property ladder; his promotion to associate partner had fuelled a desire to own a house, so the extra salary would come in handy too. In the end, I'd met with Richie and we'd scrabbled together a plan – three days in the office plus part-time hours from home. I'll keep my demanding clients happy, and be there for Charlie. It's still a leap though; I haven't thought much beyond feeding techniques and infant sleeping patterns for nearly a year.

I look around at the dozens of storage boxes, the neatness of their stacking not hiding the huge task ahead of us. The movers sorted out the big stuff – the sofas and beds, Charlie's cot. But the rest of it is down to us, and Dan has already told me that he can't take any more time off work. I start back with Richie in March, which gives me a month to get this place feeling like a home.

'Life will get busier though,' I warn. 'When I'm back at work.'

'We'll handle it. And it will do you good, being back out there. A reason to do your hair, put some make-up on again.'

His words sting and I find myself struggling not to cry. That's something else new, my much thinner skin. Of course I know he's right; I don't bother with myself like I used to. It's not a conscious decision; there's just never a point in the day when I think about needing lipstick. Parenthood hasn't had the same effect on Dan; his body is still firm from his regular gym visits, and his investment in designer clothes hasn't dropped. I can smell expensive aftershave on him now, while perfume wasn't a factor for me in getting ready to move house this morning. The imbalance makes me feel nervous.

'We should make sure we set aside some time for us too.' I shuffle closer along the sofa. I know it's not just my declining appearance that has caused this rift, that I've made bigger mistakes. Those first two nights in hospital with Charlie were exhausting, but also life-changing. It was just me and him, so pure and perfect, and I didn't want that to change when we got home. It didn't take me long to realise my misstep, that Dan was part of our family too. But the damage was done by then. Perhaps not to their relationship – Dan would still slip into Charlie's bedroom every night after work, gently stroke his sleeping body – but to ours.

'Good idea,' he says, and smiles at me. But I'm not sure it reaches his eyes.

I don't get chance to probe any further though because we're distracted by the buzz of his new Blackberry, a perk of having *partner* in his title now. I watch him pick it up and check the number before answering it, and I wonder who has managed to make his eyes smile.

'I think I should come in,' he says into the slab of black plastic. 'It's fine, we're all unpacked. I can be there in half an hour.' The unnamed colleague isn't even asking him to go in; Dan is practically forcing it on him – or her. I suddenly feel stupid for shuffling up to him on the sofa.

'Sorry, Phoebs,' he says when the phone call ends. 'GFR are threatening to pull the plug on the Bathgate acquisition. I can't let the team handle it on their own.'

'Can't it wait 'til tomorrow?' I hate the whine in my voice, how needy it sounds.

'It doesn't work that way, you know that. If they can't get it signed off tonight, the deal's off.'

I do know that; the arrogance of solicitors and how they think their world is too important for sleep. There have been plenty of nights when Dan hasn't made it home at all, making do with a few naps on his desk in between contract negotiations.

'But it's our first night in our new house. It should be special.'

'Well, let's not forget what's paying for this special new house.'

He kisses me on the forehead and I feel like a house pet, getting a scrap of affection before my master carries on with his life. He disappears out of the living room and I hear him put his trainers on – the smart suit rule not applicable at this time of night – and pick a set of keys off the table in the hallway. The door slams and then it's just me. The setting might have changed but, it seems, not much else.

I carry the half-finished glasses of now-flat champagne into the open-plan kitchen at the back of the house. I'm not used to so much space. The house I grew up in – where my parents still live – has a similar footprint but without the extension; even if they had the money (which they didn't) there's no way Flora and Paul would have had the wherewithal to organise building work on this scale. Flora might have liked the idea of an entertaining space, but it would never have got further than a periodic whim. So it was this room that sold the house to me when we first looked round. The children's drawings Blu-tacked to the wall, magnetic letters spelling out random words on the fridge. Happy families. It was a game I wanted to play too.

The silence is broken by a whimper, followed by a louder cry. When I put Charlie to bed this evening, I'd noticed how red his cheeks were, the tell-tale sign of teething, so I'm not surprised that he's breaking his recently formed habit of sleeping through the night. I take the stairs two at a time.

I peer over the cot and he instantly stops crying. I know this will only last a couple of seconds, that if I fail to lift him out, he'll just start wailing again, but still, this power to comfort him is exhilarating. I reach down and pick him up. He likes to be held against my chest, with his head nestled into my neck. I arrange him into position and stroke his back underneath the quilted sleeping bag. His face is damp with tears against my skin and I gently rock from side to side to try and lull him back to sleep.

'I'm sorry your teeth are hurting you,' I whisper. It doesn't feel right, that babies have to endure this pain; so small and innocent, and yet having to cope with breaking skin and aching jaws. 'Mummy's going to take care of you.'

Eventually he falls silent. He's fast asleep against my swaying chest now, but I don't want to put him back. He feels substantial in my arms, something solid within the fragility of my marriage. I imagine life with just him and I; appealing in some ways, but I understand the loneliness of being an only child in an unconventional family. I'm not going to allow that to happen to Charlie. Finally I kiss his smooth head – the fuzziness he had as a newborn long gone but not replaced by hair yet – and lay him back in the cot. I need to try harder with Dan; I can't let our marriage fail. For Charlie as much as for me. We will be a family, whatever it takes to get there.

Chapter 14

NOVEMBER 2019

Ben

Ben leans his head back against the cool bedroom wall. His T-shirt is damp from sweat and it's not long before he's shivering – no heating on at this time of night. He's sitting on the floor between the bottom of his bed and the wardrobe, so it's not difficult to reach up for his duvet, drag it over him. The warmth is more comforting than he expected, so he makes the extra effort to wrap it all the way around him, and pull it up to his neck.

That nightmare again. He's never told anyone about it, even though it's been part of his life for as long as he can remember. In the early days, he'd wake up crying. His mum would rush in, sit on his bed and pull him in to her. He hated that too, but he taught himself to expect it and then it was manageable. But she never asked what the dream was about, and so he never told her.

Although even now, he's not sure how to explain it. It's as though his eyes are closed in the dream. He can sense it, and hear the screaming. Other than that, all he remembers when he wakes up is a mess of dark shadows, colour seeping out around the edges. And just two piercing black dots, like a pair of eyes staring out at him. He's tried to explain it through art, something else he keeps to himself, but while the process calms him down a bit, the paintings haven't given him any clues as to what his dreams mean.

He reaches his hand under the bed and feels the familiar art case. Foul dreams splattered on pieces of textured paper. It's pathetic really. Being so scared of something he can't see properly; of a dream that he can't even explain. It's not something he likes to repeat when he's awake if he can help it, except that's exactly what he did at school yesterday. Stuck in the main hall, struggling to breathe.

Maybe that's why the dream came tonight, because life has actually been pretty good over the last few days. The weekend could even be described as enjoyable. His mum went to see his painting on Saturday, which was a miracle in itself. And even more surprisingly, she'd come back looking almost proud. The mood was clearly catching, because his dad had then suggested going out for Sunday brunch to Ben's favourite café on Northcote Road. There'd been no arguments over their avocado on toast (or in Ben's case, doorstep bacon sandwich), no innocent questions laced with not-so-hidden meaning. His dad had even apologised for suggesting Ben give up his job. There'd been the odd Rosie worship of course, but he could cope with that.

So Ben had woken up on Monday morning feeling quite good. He'd even suggested to Rosie that they walk to school together, although she'd looked so panicked at the idea – he wasn't exactly known for his timekeeping – that he'd let her off the hook. He'd wandered in by himself, enjoying the half-hearted warmth of winter sunshine on his back, and even considered paying more attention in class.

Which is why he didn't expect to start panicking in the middle of assembly.

Some guy had come to talk to them from the Violent Crime Task Force, one of the London Mayor's pet projects apparently. No one was particularly interested in what he had to say. Serious youth violence up 46 per cent in five years. Stab wounds making up 38 per cent of under-25 hospital admissions. Him trying to shock. No one in the audience that bothered. *Nothing to do with us posh white kids, sir.*

But as he kept reinforcing his message – nearly fifteen thousand knife crimes in London last year, how every young person needs to be vigilant – Ben started thinking about his run-in with those kids. What would he have done if one of them had pulled a knife on him? Stood in that overheated assembly hall, swaying slightly, he'd started to see the glint of a blade. Feel it stab inside him. Imagine himself lying in the muddy park, sticky blood oozing out of him.

His vision had started to blur then. And when he'd tried to draw some deeper breaths, his tie suddenly felt too tight, his throat squeezed. He struggled to hold it together but still, the man went on. Listing the risk factors for violent behaviour. By the time he got to how looked after children make up 50 per cent of young people in custody, Ben had been shaking so much that he could barely stand up.

In the end, he made it through. Managed to block out the images and concentrate on those breathing exercises he secretly relied on. But he didn't dare take his suit jacket off for the rest of the day. The sweat patches were disgusting.

Ben looks over at his clock. It's only 2 a.m. but he knows he won't get back to sleep now. He starts thinking about his project on the railway line and feels that familiar itch. Decision made, he pushes back the duvet and quietly removes his black sweatpants and hoodie from the wardrobe, as well as his rucksack of paints.

He's practised this before, leaving the house in something close to silence. He knows which stairs to avoid and how to unbolt the front door without making a sound, so he's outside his house in minutes without disturbing anyone. The freedom of roaming the empty streets sends a rush of pleasure through his limbs and he starts striding, pumping his arms a little against the night air.

He thought that the dry weather over the last few days would make his descent easier, but as he gets closer to the bridge he realises that the clear skies and cold temperatures have caused a film of frost to develop across the brickwork. Thank God he brought his climbing gloves with him this time. He pulls them on, draws the Velcro strap tight at his wrists, and starts the climb.

*

Ben stares at his writing and lets out a sigh of relief. It was unlikely that the authorities would have removed it this quickly, but there's always the chance that some other tagger could have sabotaged it. There's a code amongst graffiti writers to respect each other's work, but a community built on anarchy isn't always good at following the rules. But thankfully it's there, just as he left it early Friday morning.

Havana. *Have Hana.*

Ben opens his rucksack and pulls out his spray cans. He plans to draw Che Guevara sitting in a bright pink American Cadillac. History, irony and revolution: the true markings of genuine graffiti art. And a red-lipped Czech barista serving Cuban cigars: the sign of a fucked-up graffiti artist.

Ben is so lost in his work that he doesn't notice anything until the three men are less than fifty metres away, running along the tracks screaming in laughter. Instinctively he knows they're taggers too. For people like him, the railway is a second home, not the dangerous environment Network Rail tries to make out. And that's what he can hear in their voices. Excitement. Of course people have died, Ben forces himself to remember, but there are risks everywhere. And right now, Ben's immediate risk is four rail track workers in fluorescent orange jackets chasing after the taggers.

He could run with them, but he's pretty sure their pursuers haven't noticed him yet. His best bet is to lie low and hope he stays hidden. The human hyenas are making so much noise that the workers aren't likely to look in his direction anyway. Ben carefully drops to the ground and buries his face into the long grass; with a slight turn of his head, he can still watch the action.

The hyenas sprint past him, although their laughter is more raspy now as the effort of running catches up with them. The railway workers are showing their fitness levels too as most of them start to flag, one of them stopping completely, hands on his knees, heaving like he's going to be sick. But one of them is fitter than the others, upping his pace if anything.

There's a tangible shift in mood as the kids – not men, Ben can see that now – realise marathon man is gaining on them. Their fight-or-flight hormone kicks in properly and suddenly the only noise Ben can hear is their feet smacking against the metal tracks. They reach his bridge, and he watches as they fling themselves at the brick wall, scaling its many foot holes with a speed that shows they've done it before. The rail track worker apparently doesn't count climbing amongst his hobbies because he just stands at the bottom, shaking his fist and shouting at them; offsetting his failure by hurling abuse at them.

He's still pissed off when his colleagues catch up with him, but some backslapping and gold medal talk seems to lighten his mood, and, as they wander back along the track, it's as though nothing has happened. What do they care really? It'll be the end of their shift soon and someone else's problem.

Finally it's quiet again. Ben sits up and inspects his clothes. His jumper and sweatpants are soaked, and he can feel the dampness seeping through to his T-shirt. He'll be freezing cold in minutes. Checking his watch, he realises the trains will start running in half an hour anyway. It's time to go home.

He collects up his cans and traces the boys' steps back along the railway line. He could take the easier way home, but he wants to play homage to their escape. It's his way of recognising the risk they took, the risk they all take to spread their art. He's almost at the bridge when he notices a dark shadow at the side of the tracks. Getting closer, he realises it's a rucksack similar to his.

Ben picks it up and can hear the tell-tale signs of cans clinking against each other. One of the taggers must have thrown it when their escape was in the balance. He pauses for a moment, unsure what to do. While spray paint is expensive and you can never have too many cans, he doesn't want to steal from one of his own. But on the other hand, rather Ben has it than one of those railway workers. It could even be used as evidence against the taggers if they're ever caught.

Decision made, he hoists the bag onto his shoulders, above his own rucksack, and pulls the straps as tight as they'll go. He'll notice the extra weight when he's climbing up, but he's capable of adjusting for that so it doesn't faze him. With a drop that's only the height of the wall, he doesn't even feel an adrenaline spike as he levers himself over and lowers his feet onto the road. It's an uneventful walk home too, just a nod from a passing milkman, and within twenty minutes of leaving the track Ben is back in his room.

His body is crying out for sleep, so he scrawls a lie on a Post-it note and sticks it outside his bedroom door. *Study period first thing. Don't wake me.* He puts both bags inside the file box in his wardrobe, then strips off his wet clothes – for the second time that night – and finds a dry T-shirt in his drawer. He pulls the duvet back onto his bed and slips underneath. He's so tired that he can almost feel the heavy weight of nothingness descend on him.

Except it doesn't. He can't relax; something is stopping him. Curiosity, he realises. He needs to look inside that bag. With his body still screaming in protest, he pushes back the duvet and retrieves it from the wardrobe. Crawling back under the covers with his new hoard, he slowly unzips it.

There are four cans inside. Green, yellow and two shades of

blue. Taking commuters to some paradise island through graffiti; those guys should get medals, not abuse. There's also a sketchpad; a black book of past designs and future plans. He leaves through it. The colours might be happy, but the messages are angry. The voices of people who want to destroy the status quo, to say *fuck you* to the establishment.

Ben wants to say *fuck you* too, but he's not sure what his anger is aimed at. Not lack of opportunity. Not poverty, or gang violence, or a chaotic family life. He's got no excuses, but still he can't stop the urge. To destroy things. To stick two fingers up. Just like these taggers.

He reaches further into the bag and finds a hard plastic handle. Not a paintbrush, he knows that. His heart rate seems to slow a bit as he realises what he's holding. Self-protection probably. He pulls the duvet a bit further over his head and carefully lifts the knife out of the bag. It looks innocent enough with just its handle on show, but Ben can't help opening it up, releasing the three-inch blade.

Even in the darkness the knife manages to glint a little and Ben fights the urge to run his finger along its edge, feel the sharp sting of splitting skin. He thinks back to that talk at school, the warnings about too many young people carrying knives. In this moment, with the weapon in his hand, he understands what drives them; the feeling of power that a knife brings.

Eventually he folds the blade back inside the contoured handle. The bag can go back in the wardrobe, but the knife needs a better hiding place. He pulls the art case out from under his bed, clicks it open with the four-digit code, and slips the knife inside.

Chapter 15

Phoebe

'It's good to see you again, Phoebe. How've you been?'

I shouldn't feel nervous here. This is only the second time I've met Tom, but I liked him straight away, and talking to him came easily enough in our first session. But now that I have a secret, one that I'm not ready to share, I don't feel so comfortable anymore. 'Yes, fine thanks. Good, I think.' I shuffle in the chair and check my watch.

'Do you have somewhere else to be?'

I look up at him, force myself to make eye contact. Tom has one of those open faces, curious without being nosy. Warm hazel eyes and faint freckles across his cheeks. He doesn't deserve my frostiness. 'Nowhere special,' I say, and force myself to lean back against the soft cushioning of the armchair with a smile. 'I've got plenty of time.'

He smiles back and reaches for his mug of coffee. 'It's good that you're keeping busy.'

I try to resist, but we both know it's a statement loaded with questions. *How are you keeping busy, Phoebe? Are you avoiding those memories, staying on track?* 'Well, I've been job hunting,' I offer, my go-to lie since I've been back in London.

'That's great to hear. Any ideas on what you want to do?'

'Be a theatrical agent,' I murmur, sadness creeping into my voice. I almost didn't go back to work after having Charlie, and perhaps things would have turned out differently if I'd stayed at home, made Charlie and Dan the centre of my world. But I always loved my job, the rollercoaster ride of carving careers for creative people, their crazy dreams and unpredictable responses to every job offer. I can't regret making that decision now.

'Perhaps you could go back?'

I think about how I've changed over the past fourteen years, how scared I now get when I'm in crowds, or alone when it's dark. The panic attacks that come almost without warning. Not like the old Phoebe who paraded around the West End like it was a second home. 'I think it's time for something new.'

He nods. Perhaps he was just being polite all along. 'A new start; put the past behind you. That sounds like a good plan.'

'Exactly,' I say, shuffling again, Charlie's teenage face gate-crashing my mind.

'Perhaps you could look for work closer to home,' he continues carefully. 'Something …' He pauses for a moment. 'Something less demanding.'

'That's a good idea.' I smile again, because I know he's right. The job centre is less than five minutes from here. If I dropped in after our session, I'd probably have a job by the time I left. As a cleaner maybe. Or a care assistant at one the local care homes. But I know I won't go. Not because I think these roles are beneath me; I've done plenty of menial jobs over the last fourteen years and I know they're important. But I have Charlie to think about now, and how would that look to him, his birth mother working as a cleaner?

But I also know that I can't rely on my Universal Credit forever – even living rent-free, seventy-odd pounds a week doesn't last long. And now that I've found Charlie, I don't have to dedicate all my time to searching for him anymore. But the thought of actually looking for roles, writing a CV, figuring out LinkedIn, selling my experience to interviewers half my age. It's just too overwhelming. 'I'm sure I'll find something soon,' I promise.

Tom nods, then his voice softens. 'And, ah, have you thought about Charlie at all? Since you've been back?'

A gasp rises in my chest, but I catch it before it escapes. Of course he was going to ask about Charlie, that's his job. He's read my notes, understands what I've lost. He gets that my welfare is inextricably linked with my son's. But he can't see inside my head. I get to choose how much he knows. 'Not really.' I smile. 'I need to focus on the future now.'

A look of relief spreads across his face, like he doesn't want to have a difficult conversation with me and he's grateful that I'm playing ball. A knot of tension forms in my belly. Why is everyone so sure that Charlie and I should be kept apart? The maternal bond has been around for millions of years, long before adoption processes or court rulings. Why am I the only person who gets that?

I see out the rest of our fifty-minute appointment, make positive noises about settling in with Flora and Paul when Tom asks, but I'm not really engaged anymore; I'm back in Bittersweet, staring at my son.

*

I decide to buy a book. I've never been a big reader, but it feels like the perfect prop for my afternoon plans. So I browse the shelves in Waterstones, dismiss the psychological thrillers, and choose a new romantic comedy by Sophie Kinsella. When the shop assistant asks for seven pounds in exchange, and I scrabble around in my purse, another wave of frustration hits me for my dire financial state. And for the decision my parents took on my

104

behalf. I know they were trying to help me, and that they possibly saved my life. But spending all my money from the house sale on sending me to that clinic feels so wasteful now. And here I am, in my mid-forties, and totally broke. The other half of the proceeds will be waiting for Charlie somewhere. Not a fortune – most of it went on paying the mortgage back – but a nice nest egg all the same. He's richer than me, I realise, even if he doesn't know it yet.

My desire to get a job comes in waves, and I feel another one washing over me now. I've found Charlie, so there's nothing holding me back. It might be too much to ask for him to be proud of me, but if I could find something half decent, perhaps I can avoid him being too disappointed. It won't be easy, persuading an employer to take me on, but it's true that I haven't even tried. I'll go to the library, I resolve, use one of their computers to register with job websites, apply for anything going in Wandsworth.

But not today. Right now, I've got somewhere more important to be.

I wander up Old York Road. It's past 4.30 p.m. and if Charlie is on shift today, he'll be arriving soon. By the time I reach Bittersweet I'm so nervous that my tummy is doing backflips. I stand in the queue and try to distract myself by reading the long list of drinks on offer. It's a whole new language, and not one I understand. I decide on an Americano. It's one of the cheaper options and its heat gives me an excuse to stay longer.

There are at least five people in front of me, and the two baristas are clearly feeling the pressure. I hope this doesn't mean that Charlie's late for work. Or even worse, that he's quit. As I look hopefully towards the café door, it suddenly flies open. But it's a whirlwind of blonde hair and grey pashmina that rushes inside.

'Sorry! Sorry, guys. I got caught up at the wholesaler's. I'm here now. Traffic was a nightmare too. Give me a sec to get an apron.' The volume trails off as she disappears into the back room, but the monologue continues. 'Thanks for covering. Honestly that Jim can talk. I was trying to get away for ages. Now what shall I do?'

'Everything needs restocking, Jo. Can I leave that with you?' The Italian guy. Sounding a lot more professional than he did on Friday.

'No problem, Marco.'

'And maybe another barista, while you're there?'

The sarcasm is sneaking through now, but she isn't offended. 'You're right,' she sighs, pausing at last. 'Ben was supposed to be helping out on our busier days – Thursday, Friday and Saturday – but actually every afternoon is busy now, and those days are even worse. I'll put an advert in the window today.'

I can't help feeling a stab of disappointment that Charlie doesn't work Tuesdays, so I won't see him today, but at least he hasn't quit. I think about her need for staff and my conversation with Tom, how desperate I felt handing over seven pounds for a book. Then I think about spending three days a week in Charlie's company. Could I do this?

No, this is crazy. It's one thing getting to know him from a distance, but working with him would be way too risky. And anyway, I've never worked in a café before. I wouldn't have the first clue how to operate a coffee machine.

But I need a job. And I've been away from him for so long. This is the best chance I'm ever going to get to spend time with him. Am I really going to let this opportunity pass me by?

'Good afternoon, madam. What can I get you?'

I've reached the front of the queue, but before I get chance to order, I see a spark of recognition cross the café manager's face. 'Hi, Marco,' I start cautiously, unsure whether this level of familiarity is appropriate after just one meeting. I doubt he's been replaying the evening in his mind since Friday.

Luckily, his recall is good. 'Ah, of course! It's Ben's friend, Fiona isn't it?'

Fiona. I need to remember that.

'I'm afraid Ben's not working tonight. Or is it a coffee you're after?'

'Yes, a coffee, Americano.' I pause. 'Maybe something else too.'

Mistaking my vagueness for indecision over my order, Marco leans over and whispers, 'The banana and walnut cake's good.'

Instinctively I follow his gaze. It does look good too. My body relaxes a little and with it, my resolve grows. 'I overheard you talking about a job; I'm looking for one you see. I just wondered …' I pause, before spurting it out. 'I wondered if I could apply?'

'Wow, I didn't think it was going to be this easy! Grab a table with your coffee and I'll get Jo. She's the owner – you can have a chat.'

Relieved that he can't hear the drumbeat of my racing heart, I give Marco a grateful smile and carry my mug over to the window. The wonky wooden table in the corner already feels like mine so I'm grateful that it's empty. I sink into one of the chairs and stir a packet of sugar into the steaming liquid. I can't decide whether to feel elated or petrified about the wheels I've just put in motion. Could this work? Will she need all my details for her records? Of course she will, I realise. Marco even thinks I'm called Fiona. This is stupid; I need to get out of here.

But before I get chance to escape, Jo is suddenly there, standing by my table. 'I hear you're looking for a job?' She sits down opposite me. 'And that you're a friend of Ben's? That is so amazing. Fate. No, serendipity. Is that right? I think that's right. Anyway, we'd love to have you. Are you okay with cash in hand for a while? It's my accountant. Adding headcount makes him sweat. If things work out, we can make things more formal in the New Year? What do you think?'

If I believed in God, I'd think it was a miracle. But I gave up faith in almost everything on that terrible night, so actually I don't know what to think. Except that perhaps this is what I'm owed, after fourteen years of purgatory.

And that maybe my sentence is finally coming to an end.

'When can I start?'

Chapter 16

FEBRUARY 2005

Phoebe

I swear under my breath. In the silent house it sounds louder, bouncing off the pale Travertine tiles as I reach over to open the bathroom cupboard. I grab a tampon from the open box, pull at the plastic wrapping with my teeth and try to blink away the tears that are forming across my eyes. I should be relieved really, under the circumstances. But I can't help remembering how differently I felt last month; grieving for my non-child. There was guilt too, for still not being able to give Charlie a sibling or Dan another child. I throw the plastic packet in the pedal bin and slam down the lid with my foot.

I've arranged for Charlie to have a sleepover with his best friend Jude from nursery, and Dan has promised to be home by 8 p.m. The house is spotless and dinner is on a slow cook in the oven. There's a bottle of champagne in the fridge; Dan doesn't approve of real champagne without a tangible reason anymore, but I'm not in the mood for appeasing him tonight. And I've set the kitchen table for two, even lit a couple of candles.

I wash my hands and stare into the mirror. Dan's prediction turned out to be right; going back to work did change my appearance. I put make-up on every day now and wear my hair down when I don't have Charlie's sticky hands to worry about. I even manage to get to the gym a couple of times a week, so my body has returned to its pre-baby shape too. Part of me misses the old Phoebe, the one who didn't care about having tired eyes or a wobbly tummy, but I need to look my most attractive tonight, so loose curls hang over my shoulders and my denim blue eyes sparkle behind Bobbi Brown eye shadow.

I hear Dan's key in the door and look at my watch; he's fifteen minutes ahead of schedule and my stomach lurches in annoyance. He chooses tonight, the one night when I'm dreading seeing him, to break his habit. I think about the nights that he rolls in at 11 p.m., telling me he had to work late but smelling of booze. Or the Saturday mornings when he pops out for a bike ride, then phones me from Brighton because he was feeling too 'in the zone' to stop. Of course, I'll never know whether they were all lies, or just some of them. I close the bathroom door and walk downstairs.

'Wow, you look amazing.'

I'm wearing a plain black dress; it has nothing to offer itself except being short and tight, which seems to do it for Dan. 'It's date night, remember?'

'Yeah, I know.' He looks uncomfortable now and I'm not sure whether I want to cry or slap his chiselled face. 'Just let me go and kiss Charlie goodnight.'

'He's not here.'

'What?' Dan didn't know about this part. He's never liked surprises and I enjoy the power it gives me. 'He's not with your parents, is he?'

That stings more than it should. When Charlie was born, I was surprised at how delighted my parents were to have a grandson;

I've been even more amazed that their initial excitement has grown into something akin to genuine love. I never knew they were capable of it. Flora will spend hours with him, playing hide-and-seek, or Power Rangers if Charlie gets his way. I watch them together, feel the bittersweetness of it, but I never forget what fuels Flora's creativity nowadays. I hardly leave them alone together, and I would never let Charlie stay overnight.

'Of course not. He's at Cara's.' Every working mother needs a wingman, and Cara is mine. I've only known her since we moved to this house, a meeting of prams that became an invite for a cup of tea, a friendship spawned by our parallel lives. But I rely on her more than anyone. Last-minute texts when the District Line is delayed, a beaker of milk when Charlie refuses to go to bed without one and our fridge is empty. It's not all one way – we help each other out – but I suspect the scales are tipped in my direction. Perhaps because her husband is more trustworthy than mine.

'Champagne?' I ask, turning towards the kitchen. I don't want him to see the dread in my eyes, I'm doing this in my own time.

'A little extravagant just for date night, don't you think?'

I hand him a flute, still fizzing with escaping bubbles. 'I want tonight to be special.'

'I assume that means you're ovulating?' He takes a long gulp and I wonder again how we got to this. How wanting another child could feel like such an injustice to him.

'I got my period actually.'

'Oh, okay. I'm sorry.' But there's no regret in his eyes, only relief. Tears threaten again and I realise how wafer-thin my mask is; I can't keep up the pretence much longer.

'Shall we eat?' I use the task of serving up our chicken tagine to turn my back on him. To finish my glass of champagne and pour another. To remember the anger and use it to recharge.

He's sat at the table when I finally turn around; our eyes catch for a moment and then he smiles. It's so rare these days, to connect like this, and I can't help pausing under its warmth. Then the moment is gone. I set the plates down, take a deep breath, and start my confession.

'I know.'

Dan's fork halts mid-air, then slowly works its way back onto his plate. 'Know what?'

'That you're having an affair.' My words dance around the room. The truth that I discovered three nights ago, that I've kept hoping might somehow disappear if I try hard enough; I can't hide from it anymore.

He looks at me but doesn't speak. His eyes widen, then narrow.

'I saw the photo on your phone.' I need to sound calm, to look like I'm in control, even though my heart is punching at my ribcage like a boxer on speed. 'And I read the message that went with it.' After years of unbroken sleep, Charlie has started to wake in the night, his eyes bright and head sweaty. I looked it up on the internet. Night terrors are common at his age apparently, especially for children with a vivid imagination. So when Charlie woke up the other night, I just silently cursed Flora's genes and took him downstairs for a glass of milk. Dan had left his Blackberry on the breakfast bar. It was curiosity rather than mistrust that led me to pick it up, but it didn't take me long to start scrolling through his texts. Opening the one from Jess. Seeing the seductive photo and slutty message. It was revealing enough to remove any opportunity for doubt.

'Don't be stupid.' But he can't summon up a proper denial.

'I am stupid though, aren't I? Believing your shit. You and me, against the world. Remember that, Dan?'

'It wasn't me who broke that promise.'

'Don't you dare blame this on me!'

'So you didn't shut me out when Charlie was born?'

'He needed me.'

'And you didn't make it obvious that I wasn't good enough to parent him, that only you could settle him, or feed him, or understand what the hell his different cries meant?'

'I never treated you like that.' But I can hear the hesitation creeping in my voice. How can he do this? How can he twist things?

'Don't lie! As soon as Charlie arrived, I became surplus to requirements. Until now of course, now that you want another kid. Suddenly it's all champagne and fuck-me dresses again. Well, I can't just perform to order.'

'Why not? You love order!' I'm not letting him win this. 'I bet she's your secretary, isn't she? Or your personal trainer? Predictable Dan – can't even use his imagination when he's finding someone else to fuck. In fact, having an affair isn't even original is it? You're just following in Daddy's footsteps.' The real reason Tony didn't show up at school that day. The dirtier, unspoken truth about Dan's mother's death.

The noise is like a roar, guttural and violent. Then Dan pushes our plates, cutlery, the chicken tagine, onto the floor. It's a symphony of chaos, the high pitch of metal slamming against the floorboards mixing with the ugly crash of smashing china. I fall to the floor myself, but whether it's in fear or anger or just frustration I'm not sure. We were perfect together; I worked so hard to keep us that way. Now I'm cowering on my kitchen floor, waiting to see whether Dan storms out of the room or takes his anger out on me; and I'm not even sure which I'd prefer. But in the end, neither happens. The roar is replaced with a growling sound, like an animal stuck in a hunter's trap, and I can't stand to listen to it. 'Shut up!'

'What happened to us, Phoebe?' He drops onto the floor, sits back on his haunches.

I slide backwards until I reach the island unit; I can't let him reel me in. I stare at the metaphor of broken plates, a meal ruined, and use it to fire me back up. 'You don't get to ask that.'

'Why not? Am I not allowed to care about us?'

'You found someone sexier,' I spit out. 'That's what happened.'

'She's not sexier.' An admission of guilt, finally. Even though

I already knew it, his words manage to make me feel more wretched.

'So it's true then.'

'She's nobody.'

'You were willing to risk your marriage for nobody.'

'I was lonely. She was there, always there. Flirting, pouting. Coming on to me. And you weren't.'

'I was always here! Looking after your son, cooking your meals, washing your fucking pants.'

'But not being my wife, my lover. I don't want a cook, or a cleaner. I deserve more than that! I want what we had.'

'And you think the best way to find it is by going elsewhere?'

He doesn't answer me; I watch him make a steeple with his fingers and rest his forehead onto it. The silence is oppressive, and I don't know whether I've broken him, or fuelled some deeper anger. I start to regret my outburst, of bringing up the details of his mother's death. Of uncovering his most vulnerable spot and prodding it. Finally, he lifts his head and looks into my eyes.

'I'm sorry, Phoebe.'

I don't say anything, or move towards him. I sit completely still.

'It's over, you have to believe me. Jesus, it never really began.'

Does he really think we can come back from this?

'Please don't leave me. You're my wife. I love you.'

My arms tingle. I clench my fists and push them into the tiles.

'I can't live without you, Phoebe. You have to forgive me.'

Chapter 17

NOVEMBER 2019

Phoebe

'Skinny decaf cortado please, extra hot.'

'Drink-in or takeaway?' But I'm not really paying attention to the smartly dressed lady in front of me because I'm too busy repeating her order in my head; worried it's going to drift away from my middle-aged brain. And now I've missed her answer. 'Sorry, what was that?'

'Takeaway.' She checks her watch. Her way of hurrying me along. I take a deep breath and turn to face the espresso machine.

This is only my second full shift but so far, so good. When I was forced to admit that I'd never used an espresso machine before, on that first evening when Jo suggested I stick around until it was quieter to learn the ropes, no one seemed to mind. As the café gradually emptied, Marco took me through it step by step, explaining how to make all the different coffees on their menu, as well as the mysterious intricacies of dry

114

cappuccinos, split-shot Americanos and a multitude of other off-menu orders.

It was quite overwhelming at first, all that new information. But once I started making the different coffees, everything fell into place. It turns out that coffee making is a mixture of art, timing and process, so not that different from being a theatrical agent really.

I scoop some freshly ground coffee into the portafilter and secure it into the group head with a decisive twist. As I run the hot water through, I put a dash of skimmed milk into a jug and lift it onto the steam wand; 160 degrees is the ideal heat, a little hotter for this order, but there's no temperature gauge. You have to feel it, according to Marco. Surprisingly, I do.

By the time I hand the coffee over to the woman, my composure has been restored and I manage to ring up her payment without a hitch. I'm not quite such a natural with the cash register, but I'm learning. As she strides out of the café – perhaps she was in a genuine hurry after all – I can't help looking at my watch too. Charlie will be here soon, and I'm not sure whether it's nervousness or excitement that's playing havoc with my insides.

As if on cue, the door opens and there he is. Loping, handsome. I want to take a moment to bask in the glory of it all, but there's a group of expectant mothers to serve so I turn to them instead. He doesn't notice me, just wanders into the kitchen to drop his bag off. But as I'm adding the Bittersweet motif to my third latte, I sense him joining me behind the counter. Ben, I think firmly. His name is Ben now.

'Fiona?'

Shit, that too. I look up. 'Hi, Ben.' I sound more casual than I'd planned. Anything to hide my thumping heartbeat, but now I sound like I think we're best friends. I build in some distance. 'I hope you don't mind, me taking a job here. I was just passing really, but, well, I guess it was good timing. Me needing a job; Jo having one.' Now I'm rambling. I pray for another customer to walk up to the counter, to stop me talking, but the space is uncharacteristically empty now that the pregnant women have sat down.

'Whatever,' he says. Shrugs. And then slips straight into work mode. 'I'll clear the tables while it's quiet. You okay here?'

I nod, but turn away from him. I can't let him see the beam spreading across my face.

Gradually, I feel more at ease in his company. The exchange of duties helps: passing the milk, saving the burning panini, catching the falling teaspoon. And having the others around helps too. I can see why Jo chose Marco to be her manager; he must be one of only a few people who match her pace. He's a skinny thing and good-looking in an ethereal kind of way, his hair just long enough over his eyes to add a touch of mystery. But then he chats so easily, gesticulating wildly with it. It's a contradiction that works in his favour. Hana is polite and generous, but her intelligent eyes flicker with feminist fire. With cupid lips and wide locks of shiny brown hair, she is also gorgeous, but I get the impression she doesn't care too much about that.

As it turns out, they're the leading actors in this performance; Charlie and I are just supporting roles. Marco teases Hana like a younger sister and she reacts every time. I want to tell her to ignore him, that he'll get bored eventually. But teasing siblings is not something that I have any right to comment on. At first, I assumed he fancied her and that's the reason for all the attention. But it didn't take me long to realise he's not interested in women. I worked in theatre for too many years not to notice that.

'Fiona, take a break.'

It's an order not an offer so I grab a bottle of fizzy water from the fridge – I couldn't stomach a coffee after the number I've served – and walk to my table by the window. It's past eight and the night sky has long since set in. I watch couples walk hand in hand to the bars and restaurants dotted along Old York Road. I came here with Dan once, to a restaurant called Konnigans; we spent a fortune on champagne and fillet steak. It was early in our marriage, before responsibility grew and romance dwindled. Our romance anyway.

'Mind if I sit down?' A voice interrupts my thoughts. His voice.

'Of course.' I try to disguise my awkwardness by gesturing at the chair opposite but my arm flicks at the air with too much force and it looks like I'm shooing him away. I quickly pull it back and sit on my fingers.

After a moment's pause, he lowers into the chair. 'Last hour's always a bit quieter,' he says. 'Gives us a chance to tidy up so that we can finish early.'

I nod at him; I can tell he's got more to say so I stay quiet.

'We usually stay behind on Thursdays, for a couple of beers. It's sort of a tradition.' I can't tell whether he's inviting me or warning me off, but after a moment's pause, he continues. 'You're welcome to join us.'

'Thank you,' I say. But there's still more.

'It's just that, well, I was hoping …'

Realisation hits me. Those boys in the park. His self-destruct mode. He's scared I'm going to bring it up, tell Marco and Hana exactly how we met. I shouldn't enjoy his discomfort, but I can't stop a sense of euphoria spreading through me. We share a secret. And I have the power to protect it, and him.

'If you're worried I might say something about the other night, don't be.' I say it firmly; I want him to trust me. 'We've all got our thing. And we're entitled to keep that thing private. You know mine too, remember? It wasn't exactly the smoothest bus ride.'

He acknowledges that with a tiny nod.

'I won't say a word. Not now, not ever.'

His face forms into a small, relieved smile, and then he's off to clear the last few tables.

*

I didn't stay for a beer in the end. It was hard to drag myself away, but I decided that joining your teenage son for a drinking session with his mates is not cool, under any circumstances. More than that, I had such a perfect image of his grateful face imprinted on my mind that I didn't want to do anything that might dislodge it.

Even though I've been on my feet since lunchtime, the walk home is almost a pleasure. People talk about floating when they're happy. It's not quite that, but I do feel a bit anaesthetised as I make the familiar journey back to Battersea. It's past ten when I get home, so I'm surprised to see the light on in the front room. Even more surprised to see Flora and Paul sitting next to each other on the sofa, watching the *BBC News* as though they have a genuine interest in the state of British manufacturing.

'Darling! How was it?' The TV is promptly switched off. 'We wanted to stay up for you, welcome you home after your first day.'

I think back to yesterday. Letting myself into a dark house, exhausted. Slipping into bed gratefully. They've missed a day, but I'm actually surprised they remember at all – I only told them as an offhand comment on Tuesday evening, my instincts telling me not to say too much. It's touching, this newfound interest in my life. 'Exhausting, but I loved it.'

'Loved it?' Paul asks. 'Serving coffee?'

'It's amazing how satisfying it is, making the perfect cappuccino.' Did I just say that?

'Well, I think it's wonderful! I always wanted to have a little teashop by the sea. Where was it, Paul?'

'St Ives.'

'St Ives! Imagine, Paul. Do you think we still could?'

'Maybe,' Paul responds vaguely – he knows that neutral works best with Flora – then he returns to the subject of my job. 'Nice people?'

'A good team, yes.'

A small smile forms on his face. He's decided it's good news. 'I'm so pleased for you, Phoebe. You deserve to be happy, to start

118

rebuilding your life.' His eyes look different too. Not love exactly, but maybe fondness. He hid so much during those dark days that I never knew what he felt, but I had plenty of time to fear the worst. I feel a rush of elation that I might have got that wrong.

I should tell them. I realise it in a flash but with an intensity that almost knocks me over. They deserve to know. And the truth is I want to celebrate finding him; talking to a rose bush isn't enough, I want to shout it from the rooftops. I think about Flora's continued friendship with that social worker, of Paul not being able to hold my gaze for years; their willingness to go along with the adoption. But that's all in the past now. Even if they only feel a tiny proportion of the excitement that I do, surely it will be enough?

'I do feel like I deserve to be happy again,' I start, gauging their reaction.

'Oh, Phoebe, you absolutely do! All that unpleasant business was years ago now.' Flora flaps it away. 'And you weren't, well, thinking straight back then. Dan's death and everything. That lovely lady at the clinic put you back together, didn't she, darling?'

Now it's Paul's turn. It's amazing how good they still are at this, the double act. 'Phoebe, you've been away from us for a long time, but you're back now. There's nothing we want more than to see you happy again.'

It's not true, of course. The booze and the fags will always come first. But the sentiment sounds genuine, and I'm grateful for it. It spurs me on. After all, he's their relation too, their grandson. They deserve to know.

'I've found him, Dad.' I whisper it, but it sounds louder.

'Found him?'

'Found who? What are you two talking about?' Flora can sense the thickening atmosphere, but her brain hasn't caught up.

Paul chooses to ignore his wife, continues staring at me. 'You mean Charlie, I presume?'

I just nod; I can't speak now.

'What do you mean you've found Charlie?' Flora squeals. She's flustered now. 'Oh, Phoebe, what have you done?'

'He's my son,' I throw back. How can they both be so blind to what really matters?

'But it's not allowed! He's not yours anymore,' she continues.

'He'll always be mine. He's part of me. Surely you of all people can see that?'

'It's been a long time, Phoebe. People change.' Paul's calm voice sounds so convincing. I stifle the urge to stick my fingers in my ears.

'No! He might be called Ben now. And go to a posh school. And live in an expensive house. But he's still my son, my flesh and blood. And no one – not you, not that social worker, not that la-di-da fake mother of his – can ever change that.'

No one speaks for a moment and all I can hear is my heavy breathing stabbing at the silence.

'You know a lot about him,' Paul finally observes. The most level-headed amongst us.

'He's an artist, won an award.' I want them to see the connection, to feel excited by the creativity he inherited from them. But my plan backfires.

'Wait a moment.' Flora sounds more composed now, and there's a new steeliness to her voice. 'Our day out. The art exhibition. Is that why you suggested going?'

'I know you love art.'

'Don't lie! You let me think it was about me, but it was just about you getting your fix of him.'

'He's so beautiful, Mum. He has your spirit.' My face is wet with tears.

'My grandson's art was there, and you didn't say a word.' She drops her face into her hands and lets out a cry of anguish.

'You see what you've started, Phoebe?' Paul's voice is louder now. 'Flora and I said goodbye to Charlie over a decade ago. Do you know how hard that was for us? For him?'

'For me too.'

'But it wasn't our doing, was it, Phoebe?'

His words sting. I can see that he instantly regrets saying them, but it's too late. How dare they tell me what to do? Things may have fallen apart between Charlie and I, but I was a better parent in our short time together than Flora and Paul ever were to me.

'I'm not giving it up. You're not taking this away from me.' I'm shouting now.

'Giving it up?'

'I need this job. Don't you dare ruin it.' Again, I've given away too much; I need to control my temper.

'Charlie works at your café?' This time it's Flora who works it out first.

'He doesn't know who I am.'

'You talk to him?'

'We just work together.' I hear the apology in my voice. The pleading. But it doesn't work.

'So you're lying to him too.'

'It's for the best. For now.'

'For you maybe, but not for Charlie.' Paul sounds so reasonable, I can't stand it. 'For his sake, Phoebe, you need to walk away.'

'I can't, Dad, please,' I whisper.

'You were a good mother, I know that.' His voice is gentle now. 'But when you signed those adoption papers, you knew what that meant. If Charlie wants to find you, he'll have every opportunity when he turns 18.'

The social worker's final comments reverberate around my head. *He has absolutely no memory of you.* 'And what if he doesn't?' I demand.

'Then it's proof that he's not yours after all.' And with that, Paul helps Flora off the sofa, and then the pair of them turn towards the door and shuffle out of the room.

Chapter 18

Ben

'Fam, you've got to see this.'

Ben turns to look at Jake. He was deep into his painting, and the interruption is annoying. 'See what?'

'C'mon, quick. Or we'll miss it.'

'Miss what?' he repeats, irritation starting to surface. It's not often he gets the art studio to himself and he was right in the middle of his latest project, a landscape painting of Barnes Bridge over the Thames. At first it was just another A-level piece, but the more time he's spent on it, the more important the painting has become. The traffic on the bridge, boats on the river, cyclists dodging runners, kids and dogs on the towpath. Gradually he's creating chaos, and he loves it.

'A fight. Year 11, I think. Over some girl. Everyone's down there, but no teachers yet.'

'You came all the way up here to tell me that?'

'Look, I promise this is going to be good. It's that medal kid. You know, the one that wins everything.'

Ben plays dumb but he knows exactly who Jake means. He

shouldn't. The kid is two years younger than him. But some people just stand out. It's one of the many lies that parents tell, that everyone is good at something; that talent is handed out equally. The reality is that some people are brilliant at everything while plenty of others don't shine at all. Chris Thorne plays scrum half for the rugby team, striker for the football team and opening batsman for the cricket team. He's an academic scholar and his band played at the last school disco.

'Against who?' Ben can't help warming to the idea of watching Chris Thorne get a kicking.

'Dunno, but he's a big lad. Come on.'

Fuck it. Ben wipes his paintbrush on the nearest rag and drops it into a beaker of cold water. Now he's made the decision, he's suddenly in a rush to get there, so he throws his apron on the side and the two of them race down the stairs and out onto the playground.

'Where?'

'Behind the sports hall.'

They start to hear the sound of kids jeering when they're halfway across the rugby pitch; a blanket of noise rather than a collection of individual voices, like fans at a football match or animals in a field. As they walk around the back of the building, the volume rises.

Ben stares at the scene. Any urge he had to see Chris Thorne paying for his talent dissolves in an instant. How can so many people be enjoying this? There's close to fifty kids watching and almost all of them have their phones out, recording the event.

The main attraction isn't even much of a fight. The two boys are just shoving each other in the chest rather than throwing any punches. But Ben sees that their faces don't match up. The bigger kid – Ben pulls the name Adam from somewhere – has an expression of pure rage on his, while Chris's face is mainly fear, and maybe some regret. Whoever the girl is, Ben can see she was just a conquest to Chris. While to Adam, she's the one. Another powerful shove and Chris falls backwards onto the ground. The crowd surges forward, phones get angled down.

Acid forms in Ben's mouth. 'Let's go,' he says to Jake. 'It's not even a proper fight.'

'Ah man, it's just getting good.' Jake pulls his face into a comedy grimace. 'Ouch! Did you see that?'

Ben didn't see the boot connect with Chris's ribcage, but he heard it. And again the second time. He doesn't really care whether it hurts – people get too dramatic about pain anyway. But watching it feels wrong. He understands how ridiculous that is, the boy who walks headfirst into trouble not being able to stomach a playground fight. But being on the sidelines gives a different perspective, and not one he likes.

'You need to get out more,' he says casually. He's become pretty good at acting cool while his insides fight some phantom enemy.

'And I will, when you stop working every weekend. But for now, I have the downfall of a perfect specimen to watch.'

Jake's grin leers over him and sweat beads on Ben's forehead. He knows he can't walk away. That would single him out as different and he couldn't stand being the target of that kind of school chat. So he steels himself against the noise and waits for it to be over. Surely the teachers will notice the huddle of goading children soon.

Except it's not a teacher who disrupts the fight. A girl in uniform suddenly rushes up, crying and begging for them to stop, like a scene from some low-budget melodrama. Ben feels a strange mix of disgust and sympathy. Does she not realise how many people are watching, filming? It's horrible to witness, but he can't drag his eyes away from her. However, the girl is clearly too upset to care about her audience because she drops to the ground, to Chris Thorne's side. The timing is unfortunate though. Adam's foot connects hard with her head.

Ben screams. Without warning, without the chance to pull it back inside. Heads turn in his direction, surprised looks from boys who know him, smirks from those who don't. For once, Jake doesn't say anything. Just stares at him.

What has he done? Why did he scream? He doesn't give a shit about that girl, two-timing bitch that she is. He doesn't care about any of them, or Jake for that matter. He turns away from all their mocking looks and starts walking, arms pumping. He wants to leave this place forever. Ben feels the familiar throttling at his throat, the oppressiveness of the buildings around him. He knows he needs to calm down, but he can't. He keeps walking, past the refectory, the Fives courts, the science block, until he reaches the two temporary classrooms on the school perimeter, erected during the recent building work but unused now.

Finally he pauses. Out of sight, he rests his forehead against the pre-fabricated building. Then he pulls it back and drops it once more. Harder this time. The pain feels good so he does it again. And again. His vision swims as the nerve endings in his forehead send danger signals to his brain. Except that's where the real danger lives of course.

He knows he needs to stop thumping his head against the wall. He can't let bruises form on his face, allow the whole world to see his shame. But it's so addictive. Too difficult to stop.

With a half-muted cry of anguish, he turns away from the wall. But the urge to destroy doesn't go. He can feel it surging down his arms like electricity. There's a brick on the ground; the last of the builder's rubbish, hidden rather than cleared. He picks it up and hurls it at the window. The sound of smashing glass is magnificent. Exactly what he needs. The laughter bubbles at first, then spills out in huge roars. He knows he sounds crazy, but he doesn't care. He's alone, no one here to film this madness.

Except he's not quite alone.

'Moreton? What the hell is going on? Why did you just smash that window?'

*

Ben stares at his parents across the kitchen table. His mum looks tired, her eyes still carrying the residue of tears she pretended weren't shed. His dad is angrier, ashamed of having to sit opposite the head teacher yet again and apologise on Ben's behalf. Of having to repeat the adopted child excuse, the tired explanation of Ben's difficult start in life.

Mr Shawbridge had been understanding. Like he always is. Talked about normal circumstances, suspension, about how Ben's situation wasn't normal of course. Abnormal then. At least someone has the balls to admit it. He brought up the subject of therapy, how Ben might benefit. This wasn't new. Every time Ben got into trouble at school, he'd give the same spiel. Greg even suggested he was on the Priory's payroll once, before Lucy's sharp stare had cut that joke dead.

His parents had never liked him having therapy, so those visits had stopped as soon as he became a Moreton. He didn't mind. He couldn't remember much about that place he went once a week when he lived with his foster family, but he knew he never felt comfortable there. The woman was too nice, all sympathy smiles and reassurance. She'd get him to draw or play with toys, pretend it was all about having fun. But then ask him stuff that was none of her business. It was a relief when he didn't have to go anymore.

'Well?'

His dad wants an explanation, but what is he meant to say? Who smashes a window rationally? 'Sorry.'

'Really?'

'Won't happen again.'

'Now where have I heard that before?'

Lucy seems to decide that Greg is too angry for this conversation. She leans forward, rests her hand over his fist, takes the baton. 'Ben. We love you. Nothing will ever change that.'

Ben squirms in his chair.

'But we don't always understand you.' A pause. 'We don't understand why you're so angry.'

Ben's got nothing to say; neither does he.

'You're nearly 18, Ben.' Greg's turn again. 'This is crunch time. We've given you all the tools – home, family, good school, fair boundaries – now you have to decide what kind of adult you're going to be.'

'There's no glory in destruction, Ben.'

'It's childish, just throwing your toys. You need to grow up, take responsibility.'

'You should talk to us, Ben. Hiding in your bedroom isn't healthy.'

'We're not monsters, for Christ's sake.'

Like the stereo from hell, their two voices pound at his head. One whines, the other judges. Why can't they just back off? It was just a window of a disued pre-fab. Shawbridge was willing to let it go. Why can't they?

But he can't lose his temper again, not today; the fallout isn't worth it. He looks square on at his parents sitting across the table and tries really hard to appear genuine. 'I know you're not monsters and I am really sorry. I'm not angry with you, or anybody else. It was just a dare from a mate. A stupid dare that I should have ignored, and next time I will, I promise.'

It's an impressive performance and Ben watches Lucy fall for it. Greg isn't so gullible, but he looks defeated. He knows he's lost this one.

'And you'll talk to us more?'

'I will.' That's when Ben realises his acting is too good. Lucy is moving towards him, arms reaching out. 'But not now,' he adds quickly, trying to hide his rising panic, 'or I'll be late for work.' With that, he attempts a Marco-style pirouette and races out of the room.

*

The quick exit means he's actually early for work, so he takes his time to walk down the hill, sucking deeply on a cigarette and enjoying the sensation of nicotine permeating through his lungs, into his brain. He hopes the extra few minutes will help him shed the day's events from his mind; he needs to lock them away if he wants to function properly tonight. It's Friday, which means the early part of his shift will be busy with stay-at-home mums starting their weekend cooking bans early. Then from about 7 p.m. the place will empty quickly. Plenty more exciting places to be on a Friday night than Bittersweet.

Marco and Hana work full-time Monday to Friday, so Ben tries to let them finish early on their last day if it's quiet enough. It's a bit of a ball-ache clearing up without their help, but the gratitude on Hana's face when he offers to cover her last hour helps with his motivation. Of course, there's that new woman too now – Fiona – so it should be easier tonight.

As predicted, it's busy when he walks inside, so he heads straight through to the kitchen to collect an apron.

'Hey, how are you?' Fiona is standing in the doorway. She's trying to look casual but the fingers playing at her neck give her away.

Ben vaguely wonders what her story is, how she manages to look both badass and terrified at the same time. But whatever secrets she's hiding, what's most important is that she hasn't divulged his. 'Glad it's Friday, I guess.'

'Yeah, I remember school being like that. Especially during A-levels. Way too intense.'

It seems weird to Ben, someone that old having done the same exams as him.

'Bet you can't believe they even had A-levels when I was 18.'

What is she, a mind reader? Ben swallows his embarrassment. 'Did you go to school around here?'

'A grammar school in Battersea. I wasn't exactly an A student though.'

'Me neither. Well, except in Art.' Ben flinches. Why did he say that? It's not something he usually brings up.

'I must remember to check out your coffee motifs then,' she quips with a smile.

Ben smiles back. Whatever her background, Fiona seems pretty relaxed. He realises that he's glad she's joined. It had been starting to feel like a crowd of three.

Together they walk through to the café area. Ben accepts Fiona's offer to clear the tables and wanders behind the counter where Hana is serving one of the regulars. He watches her listen patiently to the old guy's story, then, clocking his shaking hands, offer to carry his pot of tea to the table for him. She winks at Ben as she moves past him and it takes a great deal of self-control not to grin like an idiot.

'Looks like someone's pretty into you.' Fiona is back with a deep tray full of empty cups.

Ben feels his face reddening. 'Not me,' he spurts out.

'Oh? Who then?'

'I think Hana and Marco are pretty tight.' Why is he saying this? Confiding in this stranger?

'I don't think so,' she says quietly. 'I'm pretty sure they're just friends.'

Ben looks across at Marco, flirting with two mums, enchanting their children with some magic trick involving a coin. Perhaps she's right. He thinks about Hana's wink again and feels an unfamiliar surge of optimism. He didn't expect that to happen tonight.

His reverie is broken when the café door flies open, its handle hitting the wall with a thump. He watches an old woman with heavy make-up sashay in, or stagger, it's hard to tell at her age. As she walks towards the counter, she seems to be staring at him. Maybe she's a bit confused, Ben thinks. That might explain her mismatched outfit too.

'Fuck.'

It's no louder than a murmur, but the swear word definitely

just rolled out of Fiona's mouth. Her face looks petrified too, like it did on that bus journey. What is she scared of this time? He turns back to the old woman, who's now arrived at the counter, still gawping at him like he's got two heads.

He's about to ask what she wants when Fiona surges forward, pushing him out of the way.

'Flora?'

Ben can tell she's trying to sound normal, but in reality she only manages a margin off horrified. Ben can't blame her really; he'd be pretty mortified if he knew this woman too.

'Hello, Phoebe darling!'

'Phoebe?' Ben says, confused now. 'I thought your name was Fiona?'

Chapter 19

Phoebe

Shit. What the hell do I say? Things had been going so well and now this. My son thinks I'm either crazy or a liar, and on top of that I have Flora to deal with.

'Fiona is my middle name – I prefer it.' I say it quickly, which makes me sound like a 12-year-old girl making some petulant anti-parent protest. I can tell he can't decide whether to believe me or not, but his expression is definitely confusion rather than shock. Has he really forgotten his own mother's name? The feeling is becoming all too familiar now, relief laced with disappointment.

I force myself to focus on the more urgent issue of getting Flora away from him. Holding her gaze, I will her to keep eye contact with me, and away from her grandson, as I scurry out from behind the counter. I put my arm around her shoulder, and with as much force as possible without looking like I'm manhandling her, guide her to the table by the window. It may be my favourite, but this is all about choosing the one furthest away from danger.

'What the hell are you doing here?'

'What do you think?' The words slur, slipping and sliding into one another.

'You said that I should stay away. Then you turn up yourself!'

'You're still here though, aren't you? You didn't listen to us.'

She thinks she's whispering but it's actually a sharp hiss that carries above the normal hum of conversation; I flinch at the thought of her words reaching Charlie. At least I don't worry that he'll recognise his grandma. She's sunk too low for that.

'And you think it helps? Coming here like this? Telling him my name?'

'I couldn't bear it.'

'If he found out who I was?' I'm struggling to follow her swerving train of thought.

'You seeing him, and me not.' Thank goodness her volume has finally dropped.

'That's why you came? To see him?'

'He was taken from me too. In one day, just gone.'

I hold every muscle inside me taut, push away the image of that kind paramedic, holding my hand and asking if I'm okay. Of Charlie's hand waving, his beloved rabbit creased between his slim fingers. Yes, I agreed to the adoption, but I wasn't thinking straight back then. How long do I have to spend paying for one decision?

'You've seen him now.'

'He's handsome.'

I nod; I don't trust myself to speak.

'He has our eyes,' she continues. The unusual dappled blue that Flora inherited from my grandmother, the thread that links four generations. A swell of pride begins to build in my chest, but I can't let her carry me away. I need to focus.

'He's a mix of all of us.'

'And his new family, we mustn't forget them.' There's a mournful tone to her comment but still, I feel annoyance rising up again. Why does she have to keep reminding me? A wave of anger surges over me. I need to get Flora out of Bittersweet, stop her tarnishing our new start. She may have loved Charlie, but not like I did. Otherwise she wouldn't have walked away that night.

'Um, Fiona?'

Oh God, it's him. And he said the name cautiously, like he thought Flora might correct him. With a stab of panic, I think she might too, so I leap up.

'Yes?' I manoeuvre myself between my mother and son. There's not much space so it's awkward, but I can't risk them starting a conversation. He takes a step backwards.

'Marco and Hana usually finish early on a Friday if it's quiet. I said they could go now that it's thinning out, but they wanted to wait 'til you were finished with your, uh, friend?'

'Mother,' Flora corrects from behind me.

My teeth grind with the effort of smiling. 'She was just leaving.'

'She could stay, have a coffee.'

'Thanks, but she needs to go.' I emphasise the word 'go' too much; it sounds like I'm forcing her out, but I can't rephrase it now. He puts his hands up in some kind of mock surrender and backs away.

'It's time to go home, Flora,' I growl, once I'm sure he's out of hearing range. 'Or I'm calling Paul.'

My threat carries weight. Even the talented Flora can't hide the look of fear that darts across her face. I know she wouldn't have told my father about this visit; we both know his disapproval would extend to her interference too.

She pauses, flicks her hair off her shoulders, and stands up; the actress is back. 'Well, I'm not one to outstay my welcome.' For a moment she teeters, and I pray that she doesn't fall; in here, in front of him. But she rebalances herself and throws me that phony smile that's haunted me since childhood.

I watch her try to sashay out of the café. Does she know how damaged she looks? How people feel sympathy for her, not the envy that she likes to believe. Perhaps I'll turn out the same.

I understand the attraction of alcohol; the comfort blanket of oblivion it brings. I've watched it work its magic on my mother; calm the sting of her disappointments, create a false belief in future promise. It could easily have been a choice I made too.

I look up at my son, lost in his own thoughts as he wipes down the counter. What does his future hold for him? Will he turn out like Flora? Or Dan? He might turn out like me of course, except which version of me, before that night or after? He must sense me staring because he looks up.

'One minute,' I mouth to him, raising my index finger in explanation. I slip into the small toilet and pull the lock closed behind me. I need a moment to collect myself, to rebuild my easy-going Fiona persona. I stare at my reflection in the mirror above the sink. The lighting is soft in here and the flecks in my eyes dance in the shadows. I practise smiling. Could the easy-going Phoebe ever reappear? If I can rebuild things with Charlie, then surely anything is possible. I retie my hair and unlock the door.

'You okay?' It's almost like he cares.

'I'm sorry.'

'Don't worry about it. Family tension is my specialist subject.'

'Really?' There it is again, me enjoying his bad news.

'So that was your mum?'

I nod.

'Are you close?'

I think about how tangled up our lives are, how we hold on to each other, but perhaps only to shift the blame between us. 'Yes and no.'

'Families are complicated, I guess.'

'Are you close to your parents?' My heart thuds hard against my ribcage. He has no idea how much his answer matters to me.

'I owe them a lot.'

'But?' There's a 'but', I know. God, I hope there's a 'but'.

'But it's a pain in the arse. Always trying to repay them. Always remembering to be grateful.'

'You, grateful?' I've spurted it out, can't turn back now. 'Shouldn't they feel grateful to have you?'

'I'm not sure that's how they see it.'

I look at his face. The young are so easy to read. They think the swagger, the attitude, hides what they really feel, but it doesn't. It's not hard to see the loneliness and self-doubt behind it all.

'Maybe it's just not how *you* see it.' I say it gently because I don't want to be categorised as one of them, lecturing him, but it carries no gravity. He wafts it away.

'Luckily, there's Rosie.'

'Your sister?'

'Good guess.'

I fix a smile; will him to move on.

'Rosie's perfect. Sporty, clever, musical. Oh, and really nice. Mustn't forget that.'

'And your parents compare you?'

'Not really. I was just some messed up 5-year-old they took pity on. They don't expect me to achieve anything much; although that doesn't stop them hassling me constantly.'

I pause. It would be suspicious if I didn't ask, but still, I feel like I'm sinking into shark-infested water. 'You're adopted?' I try to keep the tremble out of my voice.

'Yeah. Rosie is theirs naturally. But they couldn't have any more children after that, so they adopted me. They wanted a baby I think, something cute to parade down Northcote Road. But supply is a bit lumpy in the orphan trade.'

'You're an orphan?' The sharks snap at my feet. I struggle to stay upright.

'May as well be.' He looks down at the floor.

Tears well in my eyes. He couldn't be clearer; I'm nothing to him anymore.

And yet, he's not happy.

Perhaps that's the problem. Feeling like an orphan. And if I can become someone to him again, maybe then he will start to feel better.

'And how is it, being adopted?'

He shrugs. 'Rosie and I are only five months apart. Such a small age gap isn't usually recommended, but here I am. My parents swung it somehow. But it means we're in the same year at school.'

'So everyone knows.'

He nods. 'She's the real deal, I'm the fake.'

'That must be tough, being the outsider.'

He looks at me quizzically. 'Most people would say that I'm not fake, that being adopted doesn't make me less of a Moreton.'

My cheeks burn. I'm getting this all wrong.

'You're the first person to see it from my point of view,' he continues. 'To accept what's so fucking obvious to me.'

I look up. Was that a compliment? Our eyes catch for a moment, and then he shakes his head and looks away. 'We'd better clear up,' he murmurs.

And that's it. Conversation over.

*

I slip the key in gently and pray for a silent house; my body is crying out for sleep. I sigh with relief as I enter the darkness – no welcome committee this time. I take off my jacket and try to hang it on the peg, but it just slips off on to the floor and I'm too tired to retrieve it.

It's when I step into the kitchen to get a glass of water that I see her. Sitting in a rotting wooden chair in the tiny garden, staring back at me through the window. The whites of her eyes glisten in the moonlight and her freshly painted lips make her look almost doll-like. For a moment, I wonder if I can leave her there. But it's close to zero degrees tonight and I can't be sure she won't fall asleep, and then into some hypothermic coma. I think of Dan, his motionless body, and realise I can't risk it. I open the back door and step outside.

'Time for bed, Flora. It's freezing out here.'

'How could I possibly sleep, knowing what you're doing?' At least her voice has lost its slur. I sigh and sink down into the chair next to her.

'I'm not hurting anyone.'

'You're stalking him.'

'We just work together.'

'It's against the law.'

I snort. 'Like you ever cared about following the rules.'

I watch her grapple with that. She's always been proud of her rebellious streak. She chooses to change tack. 'And what about Charlie? Do you think it's fair on him?'

'Look, there's stuff you don't know, Flora. He needs a friend.'

'I'm sure he has friends.'

I dig the heel of my hand into the wooden armrest. 'So maybe he needs his mum.'

'He has one of those too.'

'Not a good enough one,' I throw back at her.

'What makes you say that?'

'He seems so lost, intent on self-destruction. What if he did something terrible? I couldn't stand it, and neither could you. I can't just walk away from him.' I reach across for her hand, hanging limply over the chair. 'Please let me help him.'

She takes my hand in hers, and aimlessly strokes my fingers. It's the closest she's come to affection in decades and I'm not sure whether to feel shocked or elated by her touch. We both remain quiet for a while and I listen to the sounds of London at night: the wail of a police siren, the strangled cry of a fox.

Eventually she finds her voice. 'If you can't walk away, then you have to tell him the truth.' She places my hand back against the cold wood.

'I can't. He's not ready; I don't want to hurt him.'

'It's you who's not ready.'

She's right, of course. I've only just found him; I can't risk losing him. 'If I tell Charlie now, he might never forgive me,' I start. 'But the Phoebe who left him wasn't the real me. I need time for him to see that. Don't I deserve a second chance?'

'But, darling, what about him? Surely he doesn't deserve to be lied to?'

'I know!' I scream it, frustration spilling over. 'I will tell him, soon.'

'Tomorrow.'

'I need longer.' I try not to sound pleading – it's not her decision after all – but I can't manage it.

'Parenting is about sacrifice. His needs should come before yours.'

A snort escapes from my nostrils; I'm not letting her claim the moral high ground. 'Really? When did that rule ever apply to you?' My voice is getting louder. 'Not when I was a kid, and you couldn't get me to school on time because you were too hungover. Or when I was older, and you'd disappear for days on end just because you'd get a sniff of an audition. Even once Charlie was born, I couldn't rely on you, could I?'

My words pierce the air with their true meaning. How things might have been different if she'd cared a bit more.

'I did my best.' Her voice is low, strained. 'You can't blame me.'

But the memory has flustered her, and I seize on the opportunity. 'Please, Flora, he's fragile. It's not fair on him to suddenly announce who I am.' I wait, but she doesn't speak, so I keep going. 'I will tell him, but I need time to prepare him.' I stare into her soft features and plead with my eyes, will her to remember that she played a role too.

'How long?' she finally asks.

'A few weeks Flora, just a few weeks.'

She pauses, weighing up my request. Putting someone else first isn't normal behaviour for her and I can almost see the rusty cogs whirring. Finally, she makes her decision. 'One month, Phoebe. Otherwise, I'm telling him.' Then she pushes off from the armrests and stands up. She hesitates for a moment as though she's got something else to say, an apology or explanation maybe, but then just turns towards the house and I listen to the back door slam shut behind me.

It's freezing out here, but I don't want to go inside yet; the stillness of the night sky is too comforting. I sink further into the wooden chair, hoping it will give me some protection against the cold air, but it creaks and groans and I'm not sure it isn't going to disintegrate beneath me. Suddenly a wave of fury grabs hold of me. How did my life turn out like this? Haggling for precious moments with my son. It could all have been so different if I'd been stronger, had more self-respect. I stand up, look down at the rotting chair. Then I pick it up and throw it across the garden. The sound of it smashing against the fence gives me the strength I need to walk inside.

Chapter 20

AUGUST 2005

Phoebe

I lean over the suitcase and push the top down with my elbows. The teeth of the zip move together easily – there's plenty of give in Charlie's soft clothes and toys – and I fasten the case without a struggle. My own case will be harder. I found it difficult to work out what to take, what I would need. It's full to the brim, with another layer of clothes perched on top of that, so I sit on it, and luckily my weight, my increasing weight, is enough to force it shut.

'Mummy, is it tomorrow yet?'

I turn to see Charlie standing in the doorway, mindlessly flicking the floppy ears of his cloth rabbit against his cheek. 'Well, did you go to sleep and wake up?'

'I think so.' But he doesn't sound convinced.

'Did you maybe just close your eyes in front of *Peppa Pig* for a minute?'

'Um, maybe.'

'And do you think you need to sleep in your big boy bed for it to actually be tomorrow?

'I s'pose so,' he relents.

'But do you know what will make tomorrow come faster?'

'Chocolate?'

'No, not chocolate.' I walk over and pick Charlie up, prop him on my left hip. He may be three now and losing his toddler chubbiness, but his legs still fit snugly around my waist and his instinct to nestle into my neck hasn't gone away. 'The sooner you go to bed, the quicker tomorrow will come. And you know what happens when you wake up, don't you?'

Charlie nods solemnly, as though the responsibility for sharing all that good news has suddenly forced him into silence.

'What happens then, Charlie?' Dan walks into the room and gently pulls our son off me. The reproachful look he gives me is fleeting, but I acknowledge it, smile, give him an apologetic one back.

The change of position clearly helps Charlie find his voice. 'We're going on holiday!' he shouts into Dan's ear.

'Easy, mate!' Dan rubs his ear in mock pain, but Charlie doesn't appear perturbed. Just laughs a bit harder and wriggles out of Dan's arms. 'Crete, here we come,' Dan continues quietly, looking across at me. There's so much meaning in his expression that my eyes well up. We came close to losing our marriage, but things are different now. There's still the odd late night at work of course – I can't change everything – but Dan is much more present now.

While I hate admitting it, even to myself, his affair and the argument that followed proved to be a turning point. Against all the screaming voices in my head, I gave him a second chance. And so far, I've had no reason to regret it. Overnight, Dan became much more attentive, and for my part, I threw away the ovulation sticks and let nature take its course, which it did a few months later. Funny how these things work out.

'And you're sure the plane ride will be okay for the baby?'

I swat him with a dress that didn't make it into the suitcase; even at eight weeks my belly is starting to protrude, like it knows the deal this time round and is impatient to get on with the task of growing, so I'm already feeling the need to avoid slim-fitting outfits. 'Of course it's fine, you idiot.' This is also new, his fussing over me, and I can't help basking in the warmth of his attentiveness.

'We should leave at six, definitely no later than quarter past.'

Our flight isn't until eleven; leaving that early will mean hours wandering around the departure lounge at Gatwick Airport, trying to keep Charlie entertained. But I don't question his timings because this is part of the deal too. Accepting his imperfections. 'Well in that case, I think all of us should go to bed early, starting with the littlest in the room. Now let me see …'

Charlie starts giggling and scrambling for the doorway. He looks over his shoulder and I know what he's expecting. I raise my tickling fingers and he screams in delight, slowing down his escape to make double sure that I get to him before he reaches his bed, universally accepted as the safe zone. I catch up with him just inside his room, and we tumble onto his small bed together. Eventually the tickling stops, and we hug for a few minutes before I quietly extract myself. He's already fast asleep.

*

'Just try it.'

'Will I like it?' Charlie doesn't sound convinced as he pulls a piece of fried halloumi cheese apart. His neoprene T-shirt is damp after a morning in the sea and the sand still stuck to it shimmers in the sunshine.

'Well, I like it.' Dan picks another slice off the sharing platter in front of us and drops it into his mouth. The beach bar is no more than a shack really, and the menu is limited to a few Greek staples, but it hasn't stopped us coming here for lunch every day of our holiday so far. 'Mmm, delicious.' He gives me a look of encouragement, but the thought of eating the rich salty cheese makes me want to vomit – again – so I pretend to ignore his signal and pick up a bread roll instead.

'If I don't like it, can I spit it out?' This is when I see Dan in our son. The measured decisions, taking all possibilities into account. These moments always give me a sense of relief, that the impulsiveness of my family has been diluted by Dan's more careful genes.

'How about if you eat it all, I'll get you a Coke?'

'Wow, I can have Coke?'

'As a very special holiday treat. And only if you eat the whole slice.'

I watch my two men take up their adversarial positions. Dan leans back as far as the bar stool allows and crosses his arms. Charlie runs his tongue over both lips and then screws up his face. The challenge is on. He retches slightly after his first bite. I can see that he hates it, but amazingly he doesn't stop. Bit by bit the slice of halloumi disappears until finally Charlie's face erupts with a look of pure triumph.

'I'm finished! Can I have my Coke now?'

Dan laughs with a mixture of admiration and pride. 'I definitely think you earned it, buddy.' He kisses Charlie on the nose and heads towards the bar.

'Can I get one too?' I shout after him, and he gives me a languid thumbs up. We've all relaxed so much on this holiday; it really is the paradise island that the travel agent promised. Charlie has loved sitting at the water's edge, collecting seashells and drawing patterns in the wet sand. And Dan and I have had time to talk, to reminisce, as well as to plan our future. We don't talk about her anymore. It was Dan's idea to give ourselves a week to get all the anger and blame out. Nothing was off limits as long as we both promised never to mention it again once the week was up. So I ranted, goaded him about her, begged for an explanation. He rode it out, answered some of my questions, pleaded ignorance on others. At the end of the week I was so exhausted that it wasn't difficult to close that door and open a happier one. And booking a holiday was the first thing we did.

*

Dan places three Cokes on the table and we all reach for one. The icy cold sweetness tastes delicious and I gulp it down, although not quite as quickly as Charlie.

'Hey, slow down, buddy. You'll be burping all afternoon.'

Charlie responds with a deep belch and immediately bursts into laughter. I can almost see the sugar working its way into his bloodstream and know there's going to be a burst of energy any minute now. The beach bar is hardly a confined space, but I still feel our son needs more freedom to work off his first fizzy drink experience.

'Do you want to head back down to the beach?'

'Yes! Daddy, can we build a castle? A big one for my knights?'

'How big?'

'Bigger than our house. Bigger than the biggest castle.'

Dan laughs at Charlie's enthusiasm and his eyes crinkle with love. As I watch Charlie slip his soft hand inside Dan's much larger one, I let my own drop onto my tummy.

'Are you going to help us build this enormous castle?'

'I think Mummy needs a rest.' Charlie pulls at Dan's hand. He wants his father all to himself for a while and I can't blame him for that. Time with Dan is precious for both of us.

'I might stay here for a bit, in the shade.'

Dan reaches down and kisses my cheek, and it's like we're young again, lost in each other. Then he turns his attention back to Charlie and they're off, striding down towards the sea. I sip the last of my Coke and let my hand explore the new swell above my bikini line. It's warm in the Greek sunshine, and I imagine cells busy multiplying with the easy familiarity that thousands of years of practice bring. I know my baby is just a tiny thing, and that statistically the chance of miscarriage is still real. We haven't told anyone – including Charlie – and our first scan is still a month away. But deep down, I know this baby is a girl and that she will survive. She's strong; she came to save us after all.

Chapter 21

DECEMBER 2019

Ben

Ben looks down at the plate.

'To be honest, Marco, I'm not sure one candle stuck in a stale croissant really says *Happy Birthday*.'

'I think she'll love it! It's ironic, you know? You Brits love your irony, don't you?'

'Yeah, I guess. But Hana's Czech. Not sure they do irony so much over there.'

Marco joins him in staring down the drab offering, the red candle now sloping dangerously to the left. 'Oh, Posh Boy, I guess you're right. But it's also the only edible sweet thing left in the kitchen. The muffins went ages ago and I took the last bit of Jo's mum's banana and walnut cake.

'So on Hana's birthday, you took the last slice of cake?'

'I didn't want to, but it was calling me, you know? The little baby walnuts just squeaking, *eat me, eat me*.'

Ben looks up at his manager's lopsided grin, the sparkle in his eyes only semi-obscured by the strands of black hair falling over them. How did he manage to be so happy all the time?

'It's the thought that counts though,' Marco needles on, still not willing to give up on the idea of birthday croissant instead of cake.

Ben considers his options. He could just go along with it. What does he know about girls anyway? Hana might think it's funny, ironic or whatever. But she might also be disappointed that they hadn't made more effort.

'That's not for Hana, is it?' Fiona asks, looking over his shoulder with the same doubtful expression that his own face had shown moments earlier. Fiona, not Phoebe, as she'd politely confirmed when Marco asked, after he'd made some joke about her being a double agent for Starbucks. She'd blushed at that, then explained that only her parents still called her by her first name. Weirdly, Ben had quite liked Phoebe, thought it suited her better. But then the only Fiona he knows is a stuck-up horsey friend of his mother's who snorts when she laughs, so the name doesn't hold the best association for him.

'It's ironic apparently,' he explains.

'Really? Okay.' She draws the second word out to highlight how unconvinced she is. Ben takes it as a friendly warning.

'I could try Martha's Bakery, see if they've got any cakes left?'

'Okay, Posh Boy, you win. My birthday croissant isn't good enough for your la-di-da tastes. But you better go quick. Martha's closed five minutes ago.'

Ben looks at his watch, swears under his breath, and races out of the café door, the jingle of the bell only partially drowning out the sound of Marco crying, 'Maybe another banana and walnut cake?' Martha's is only five doors up so he's outside the artisan bakery in moments. The sign has already been turned to Closed so he waves at the girl behind the counter. He's not sure if it's the bright smile he forces on to his face, or the Bittersweet apron he's wearing, but she wanders over and unlocks the door.

'You short of something over there?'

'Something like that. I need a cake.'

'Ah, don't we all,' she sighs with more intensity than the comment deserves, until Ben notices the slimming magazine lying open on the counter.

'It's a birthday. My coworker. Have you got anything left?'

'Well, there's that red velvet cake,' she says, dipping her eyes longingly towards the glass cabinet in front of them. 'It's been staring at me for hours now.'

'Did it squeak *eat me, eat me*?' Ben mumbles sarcastically, not expecting an answer.

'Did you hear it too?'

What is it with cake? Ben thinks to himself. He's never really been a fan. There would always be a massive one on his birthday, either following his party theme or favourite hobby of the moment. For a few years he'd assumed Lucy made them, but just before his tenth birthday, he'd opened the door to a dishevelled woman with a cake tin in her arms; and that's when he'd discovered the hard work was someone else's. It didn't really matter though. He would always be loitering around the crisps and mini sausages anyway.

'Red velvet cake sounds perfect, thanks. How much do I owe you?'

'Have it on the house. You're doing me a favour.' Ben watches the woman stare wistfully at the cake before placing it inside a Martha's Bakery branded cake box and tying it closed with a piece of ribbon.

'Uh, that's great. Thanks.' It's awkward. This level of feeling for a slab of sponge. Ben takes the box from her without making eye contact and retreats quickly. It's a relief when the door locks again behind him.

The free cake means he's still got some money in his pocket. He looks at the off-licence across the road. Champagne might be out of his budget but maybe he can stretch to something that passes for it with a tenner. He checks if the fake student ID card that Jake got him is still in his wallet. It's there. The name isn't his of course – Harry Wood – but the photo looks so much like him, it's hard to imagine any shop worker questioning the ID's legitimacy. The thought that there's a double of him walking around, living a completely different life, freaks Ben out at times. Makes him jealous as hell at other times, of course.

As he pushes the door open, his mind wanders to his school friend, although ex-friend is probably a more accurate description now. Not that him and Jake have fallen out; they're just keeping their distance from each other. As it turned out, the fallout from Ben's pathetic scream during that fight was kept to a minimum. The girl who got kicked in the head – Becca apparently, of course everyone knows her name now – was taken off to hospital in an ambulance and diagnosed with concussion. The two boys were balled out in front of everyone and then suspended for a week. So there was plenty to gossip about that didn't involve him.

But it's different with Jake. He got every decibel of Ben's scream full pelt, and would have also seen the terror in his eyes. Ben can't risk the ridicule that Jake would no doubt throw at him if he got the chance, or even worse, the possibility that he might be sympathetic. So over the last few weeks, he's stayed away from the sixth form centre as much as he can, preferring to head to the art studio during study periods. He can't say he hasn't felt lonely at times, but his portfolio has definitely benefited. His painting is finished and he's now researching for his final piece. He may screw up his other A-levels, but at least he should do well in one – the only one that matters to him anyway.

The bald man sat behind the counter of the small off-licence apparently recognises the Bittersweet apron too because he lets Ben exchange his tenner for a bottle of prosecco with a twelve-pound price tag. Although the layer of dust he has to wipe off the bottle as he leaves the shop hints at a different explanation.

Ben doesn't want Hana to see what he's carrying, as much

for keeping his effort hidden as for the surprise element, so he looks through the window to check where she is. Watching his coworkers gives him a rare pleasant sensation. The café is still busy with commuter drop-ins – some people just never seem to get enough coffee – and Hana and Fiona are both behind the counter. Fiona's got her back to him, and he can see her move along the coffee machine. Hana is taking the orders, chatting to the customers, while running the till with subversive efficiency. Neither of them are grumbling about where he is; not bitching about him running out on them. The only time he feels close to happy is in this place. With these people.

Marco walks out of the kitchen and spots Ben straight away. With an exaggerated wink, his manager puts his gangly arm around Hana's shoulder and manoeuvres her into the kitchen. The coast is clear. Ben quickly walks inside, shoves the prosecco into the fridge with the craft beer, and hides the cake box behind the milk steamer.

'Bubbles too, nice work,' Fiona whispers under her breath as Hana ambles back, spots the stale croissant, and with a slight tut, slides it into the bin.

*

The meeting of glasses is more crash than clink as the four of them start the birthday celebrations. With the café empty by 8.30 p.m., they'd been able to clear everything away before it officially closed and as soon as the sign was flipped over and the blinds pulled down, Marco had declared the party started.

'Happy birthday, my little Czech mate! Did you get that, guys? You know, like in chess? Checkmate?'

'Yes, Marco, we get the joke,' Hana groans with a smile.

For all her casualness, Hana had seemed quite touched by their birthday surprise, the three of them lining up, holding out cake and prosecco like it was some kind of tribal offering. Marco had insisted they sing happy birthday to her as well, although it was mainly his voice that rang out across the café.

'So how old are you today, Hana, if you don't mind me asking?' Fiona never wants to talk about herself, so perhaps it's not surprising that she includes a get-out clause in her question to Hana.

'I'm 19. God, that sounds so old!'

'Not to me.'

Hana smiles widely at Fiona's answer; it seems that it's not just him who's warming to their newest member of staff.

'Not to me either! I'm going to be 26 in March, and that's nearly 30. Then it will be hairy ears and a flabby belly and my life will be officially over.' Marco drowns his sorrows with another large gulp of prosecco before filling up everyone's glasses again.

'How old are you, Fiona, if you don't mind me asking?' Hana mirrors Fiona's words but adds a playful smile. Ben's pulse quickens, and he forces himself to look away.

'I'm 47. So I was close to 30 when you were born. Don't remember any hairy ears though.'

'Well, that's a relief.' Marco emphasises his point by fake-wiping his brow.

'Do you remember turning 19?' Ben realises with a start that he's just spoken. Weird. He's not usually the one to initiate conversations, especially not with questions like that.

'I remember it very well.' There's a new edge to Fiona's tone.

Hana picks up on it, leans forward. 'Sounds like a story to me. Come on, lovely lady, spill.'

Ben watches Fiona pause for a moment, but whether that's reluctance to tell them more, or just collecting the pieces of her story together, he's not sure.

'Nothing much to tell, just a fun night out.' The sheepish smile. The slightly reddening cheeks. This is a side of Fiona that none of them have seen before. They wait, expectations rising.

'I got lucky, I guess. My birthday was during London Fashion Week. So my boss got me tickets to Vivienne Westwood's Prêt-à-Porter show. And, ah, the after party.'

'Whoa, what? You got to meet Vivienne Westwood? That is the coolest thing I've ever heard.' As usual, Marco doesn't hold back on expressing his awe, but Ben is quietly impressed too. He's always been drawn to Vivienne Westwood's eclectic outfits and mad range of colours.

'Yeah, it was good. She'd won British Designer of the Year the year before, so her show was really popular. Loads of famous faces there too. I remember drinking too much champagne and babbling to Kate Moss about the acting career I was going to carve out for her.'

'Oh *mio Dio*, you are such a dark horse, Fiona! Any more secrets you want to share with us?' Marco is almost fizzing with excitement.

Ben watches Fiona's face flush instantly; maybe she had a wilder past than any of them had given her credit for.

But Hana takes pity on her obvious embarrassment, steering the conversation in a different direction. 'What did you do to have a boss who could get tickets like that?'

Fiona's eyes dart in Ben's direction before she answers, as though she wants his approval or something. He's not sure why she would, but he throws her a look of encouragement anyway. It seems to work.

'I was a theatrical agent. I started at the bottom, straight out of school.'

'Proper job at 18?' Ben can't help asking. It's like a light has flicked on.

'I was impatient back then. Wanted my independence.'

'And did you like it?'

'The job or my independence? Actually, I liked both. Rented a tiny box room in a house-share in Clapham. It wasn't exactly luxury – slugs in the shower room every morning – but my housemates were fun.' A pause. 'And it was good to be away from my parents.'

Ben's mind wanders to his own mum and dad; their fondness for rules and impressive ability to drain the fucking life out of him. Could he do it? Finish school in the summer and just keep on walking? However annoying he finds his parents, Ben has always believed that he couldn't survive without them. But perhaps that was just the narrative they wanted to push, to keep him reliant on them. Perhaps he has got the guts to do it. If Fiona did, why not him?

Chapter 22

Phoebe

The freezing December night takes my breath away as I step out onto the pavement and turn towards home, but it does little to dampen the warm glow inside me; I imagine my own combustion engine will keep me fired up tonight. Perhaps it was being asked to remember my nineteenth birthday like that, and my tiny room in that easy-going house-share. My life was so full of parties back then: bars, all-night clubbing, days spent exchanging outrageous stories with my housemates. But then I met Dan, and I was so head over heels in love that his request that I tone down my lifestyle was easy to agree to. I wonder how different my life might have been if I'd put up more resistance.

'You heading home, Fiona?'

I turn back towards the café and nod. I'm getting used to my new name now, enjoying it even. It's as though it symbolises the fresh start I've been given.

'Is it far, where you live?'

I pause, a habit I've picked up every time he asks me a question. I can't help wondering, will this answer be one clue too many?

Is this the piece of information that makes the penny drop? And the more time I spend with him, the harder it gets because I start to relax, to forget the huge lie that sits between us.

I'm being stupid of course. No 3-year-old knows their grand-parents' address, let alone one who doesn't even recognise their own mother. 'Battersea. Just off Queenstown Road.'

He pauses now, and I watch him weigh up my response, as though he's calculating the route in his head. I think about the first day I met him, his kamikaze mission in the park, and I wonder if he's ever made his way to my part of Battersea. With the highest crime rate in Wandsworth, it would be a dangerous place to look for trouble.

'I was thinking of stopping at the Anchor. For a beer.'

I look beyond him, but he's on his own. Hana was meeting some girlfriends for a birthday night out and Marco had rushed off too, although he'd been much more tight-lipped about his destination. I'm not sure why he wants to keep his life away from Bittersweet so private, but it would be a bit hypocritical of me to push him on it.

'Only, I spent all my money on that prosecco.'

It takes every ounce of effort to stop myself from grinning. Not only is he suggesting we have a drink together, he's trying to sponge some cash off me. In this moment, I've never felt more like a parent. 'I can buy you a beer,' I say, the grin half seeping out.

As we walk inside the busy pub and Ben gestures towards a small table in the corner, his way of telling me he'll wait there, I realise that I'm about to break the law. Ben isn't 18 yet. Of course I'd had plenty of drinking experience by the time I was his age; progressing from bottles of cider in the park at 14 to JD and Coke once I looked old enough to be served, plus any concoction of booze from Flora's extensive stash at home. But things are stricter now, and I feel a bit uncomfortable as the woman behind the bar asks for my order.

'A pint of lager and a glass of merlot please.' My voice sounds strained, but she doesn't do more than glance at me, never mind check out who I'm with.

'Anything else?'

'Two packets of crisps.' As usual, I've swapped lunch and dinner for grazing through a few leftovers in the café kitchen. Usually it satisfies my hunger, but the bubbles seem to have woken up my appetite this evening. 'Salt and vinegar.'

I pick up the crisps and wine in one hand, and the pint of lager in the other. Ben has chosen a high table away from the wide TV screen and close to the window. The swaying silhouettes of half a dozen smokers on the other side cast an eerie shadow over him.

'Your parents are okay with you going out on a school night?' I can't help asking as I slide onto the bar stool next to him.

'It depends on their mood. Sometimes they're in a "let's wipe our hands of him" mood and me staying out makes them feel smug, like they've made the right decision.'

'And other times?'

'They get all protective; knights in shining armour coming to rescue me for the millionth time. Then they feel like failures when I don't play along, so get pissed off. It's a circular thing, I guess.'

'And how do you see it?'

'See what?'

'Bad boy or victim?'

'Both. Neither. I don't know. I'm a crap son though, I know that.' He picks up a beer mat and starts peeling the top layer off. It's an intricate process, lifting the thin section of paper without ripping it.

'Maybe you should stop being so down on yourself.'

'You don't know me, not really.'

That stings a bit, but I shrug it off. 'I work with you three days a week. I know you some.'

'I'm different at work.' He's lifted the layer of paper halfway across the beer mat. I watch him pause; decide what to do. Take pleasure in his achievement, or continue to peel and risk failure? 'I'm happier there,' he continues.

'And how do you feel at home?' I try to say it casually, but it hits a nerve.

He turns the bar mat over and rips it in half. 'Angry. Trapped. Suffocated. God knows why I'm telling you this.'

'Guilty. Confused. Scared.' I want him to know I understand.

'Yes, that too,' he whispers, the bar mat forgotten.

I look into his eyes, my eyes, and the connection is so powerful that I can't believe he doesn't feel it too. Is this the moment? Is this when I tell him who I really am? Let the whole story roll out: Dan, his baby sister. How sorry I am. But the moment goes when he speaks first.

'Damaged goods. That's me.'

His voice is small, and I imagine him at 5 years old, stood on the doorstep of that immaculate house, three perfect strangers beckoning him inside. 'It must have been hard, the adoption.'

Then he laughs. A horrible, guttural sound that I wish I could un-hear. 'I was damaged a long time before that.'

I take a moment to think about what to say next. I could stop this conversation now; change the subject. We could talk about Hana – I can see how much he likes her – or I could share my suspicions about Marco. But instead, like an addict after another fix, I delve in deeper. 'Why? What happened before you were adopted?'

'I lived with this foster woman. Lizzie. She meant well, I think. Took in anyone the council asked her to. I don't remember much to be honest, except being scared all the time. Too many kids. Too much shouting.'

'That must have been horrible for you.' Guilt stabs at me.

'I was glad to get out.'

'And your real mum? Do you remember her?' We could be anywhere right now. The pub, the smokers outside. None of it exists for me anymore.

157

'Real mum?' he scoffs. 'Do you mean the woman who left me when I was 3 years old? No. Nothing. I used to try, when I was younger and more pathetic. Close my eyes and hope I could remember something. But then fat Lizzie would waddle into view and that would be it, back in that house full of angry teenagers. I'd probably fit right in now,' he adds with a bitter smirk.

'And do you think you would you ever look for her?' My voice falters, but I have to know.

'What would be the point? I have a mother. A perfectly reasonable one who has put up with my shit for over twelve years. And she still annoys the hell out of me. How do you reckon I'd get on with a psycho mum?'

'Psycho?' He means me. That's what he thinks of me.

'She went nuts apparently. My dad died and she went crazy, that's all I know. And do you know what the worst thing is?'

I don't have a voice anymore. I sit and wait.

'I reckon my own fucked-up head is down to her.'

*

I offered to buy another round. What else could I do? I needed some space, but I couldn't just walk out, leave him there with those dark thoughts. There's a queue now and I'm grateful. I replay those words in my mind. He thinks I'm crazy. He thinks I made him crazy. How can I ever tell him who I really am now?

I order Ben another beer but choose Coke for me. My judgement is already being tested; I can't risk alcohol adding an extra layer of confusion. As the barman pours the drinks, I turn to look at my son. He's opened one of the crisp packets and is slowly working his way through it. Chewing methodically, one crisp at a time.

I turn back to the bar and try to concentrate on the positives. *I'm different at work. I'm happier there.* He did say those words. Of course Hana will be the main reason for that; first love is a powerful thing. But perhaps I play a part too. He has chosen to confide in me after all. Why am I so desperate to replace our friendship with a mother-child relationship anyway? It's not like I've got a great record with mine. Flora might want me to tell him the truth, but she's got no right to force me. She stood by and watched while he was taken away; surely she can understand that she owes me her silence now?

I walk to the table and set the glasses down. Maybe I can't retrieve what we had, but I can enjoy what we have now.

'I'm thinking of leaving home, like you did.'

'Sorry?' I'm too lost in my own thoughts to keep up with his.

'After my A-levels. Get a job, my own place.'

I think about the sheltered childhood he's had: the private school, comfortable home, plenty of cash to throw around. I'm not sure he'd find the real world an easy place to survive in, but equally I don't want to patronise him. It was the route I took after all.

'If that's what you want, you should do it.'

'But?' So he's heard the *but* in my voice.

'I think you need to live in the moment more. Stop planning, stop questioning yourself. You say you're crazy, and when I first met you, I might have agreed.' I smile at him, to lessen the impact of my words, and it's a relief when he smiles back. 'But now I know you better, I don't see a crazy person anymore.'

'What do you see?'

My son, I want to say. But I don't of course. 'I see Ben. I don't question you, or rate you, or compare you. It's just you.'

For a tiny moment, I see his eyes glisten with excess moisture. Then they're gone, hidden by the bottom of his pint glass as he throws his head back and takes gulp after gulp. I wait patiently, watching his Adam's apple bob up and down, until the glass is empty and he finally makes eye contact again. Only this time the mask is back.

'Thanks for the beers. I better get back.'

159

'Yes, me too.' I say it for his benefit, but actually I'm relieved. I need some space to think about what I've found out tonight, what he thinks about me. It's awkward between us all of a sudden as we shuffle around collecting our coats and bags. I consider pretending I have a train to catch so that I can rush off, save him the embarrassment of saying goodbye. But I've lied to him enough already. So we walk out together in silence, and then just mumble a quick goodnight before heading towards our very different homes.

Chapter 23

Ben

'Where's the ham?' Ben's head has been pounding all day after last night's mix of beer and cheap prosecco, and he's still got to work a full shift tonight. He needs to find some energy from somewhere, and he reckons a few slices of salty processed meat will do the job.

'Oh, I threw it away. There's plenty of cheese.'

'I don't want cheese.'

Lucy looks up from the drawings currently spread across the kitchen table; a client is hell bent on converting a disused car park into an office block and she's trying to figure out how on earth it's going to work. 'Well tough, because this house is now vegetarian.'

'What?' Ben knows Rosie's been banging on about giving up meat lately; she watched some film on climate change and then declared she could never eat another farting thing. But her pledge has only served to make him a more enthusiastic meat-eater.

'Well, Rosie's taken the leap and we thought it would be nice to join her; show some solidarity.'

'But I like ham. And bacon. And chicken.'

'We all have to make sacrifices, Ben. The planet isn't going to save itself.'

'And how is throwing it in the bin going to help the planet? You're just creating rubbish when I could have eaten it.' Ben watches the reaction on Lucy's face, the realisation slowly creeping in. 'God, you're so stupid.'

'Don't speak to me like that.' Part hurt, part warning. But Ben doesn't care about either of those right now.

'Did you not think about checking with me first? Or am I not important enough for that?'

'Ben, why do you always have to make things a competition?'

'Me making things a competition? Are you fucking serious?'

'Can't we just do something positive without you throwing a tantrum? You're nearly 18, Ben. When are you going to grow up?'

Ben expects these kinds of jibes from his father, but his mum has always been on his side, more or less. It looks like both his parents are running out of patience with him now. Well fine, screw them. 'When I move out of here probably,' he shouts. 'And I get to make my own decisions.'

'Oh, I'll get some bloody ham if it's that important to you.' Lucy returns to her drawings, dismissing him. But that just makes him more furious. Why does she always get to set the agenda?

'Don't turn your back on me!' Ben pulls at her shoulder, not with much force, but enough to twist her around. The sudden movement knocks her off balance and she reaches out with her arms. The back of her hand connects with a glass of pomegranate juice on the table, and it crashes over, releasing a torrent of dark red liquid across the drawings.

'Ben, you idiot!' Lucy yanks her arm free and rushes into the kitchen for a cloth. 'Help me clear it up!'

But Ben can't move. He just stands there, rigid with fear.

'God, you're useless.' Lucy lays sheets of kitchen roll over the drawings. 'Why do you have to cause such a drama over nothing anyway?'

Ben stares at the table, mesmerised; the white paper turning blood-red as the juice seeps through.

'If you're not going to help, just go, Ben, okay?'

He doesn't need to be told twice. He backs out of the room, grabs his jacket and rucksack, and slams the front door behind him. What the fuck was that about? She's right: he is useless. Tears are threatening to fall, and he can't let that happen. He could go to the park, find a way to get it knocked out of him there. But he's been trying to kick that habit since the knife crime lecture at school. Maybe he can walk it off, that's what those do-good websites advise anyway.

He takes a left and starts striding. He's not convinced this is going to work, but what choice does he have? He needs to sort his head out before it's time for work.

'Training for the army, mate?'

Ben hears a snigger and looks up. A kid is stood on the pavement – maybe 11 or 12 – working his way through a bag of Haribo. 'What did you say?' he growls.

'Easy, fam, you just looked a bit weird, you know, marching like that.'

Ben stares at the boy; his smirking face littered with tiny pimples. It's the kind of face that might have been called angelic once, before puberty set in and smeared it with grease and hormones. 'Think you're tough, do you, taking the piss like that?'

'Well, I ain't scared of a skinny fucker like you.'

The resurgence of his earlier anger is so intense that it takes Ben a moment to react physically. But then clarity descends. He lunges forward with his right hand, grabs the kid around the face, and pushes his fingers into the boy's soft jowls. He can feel the undulating ridge of new molars. He squeezes harder. 'Scared now though, aren't you?' he goads, dragging the boy by his face and pushing him back against the nearest wall, enjoying the sound of his spine connecting with the brickwork. The boy tries to say something, but Ben's grip has turned his pleas into incoherent babble.

'Name?' he demands. Nothing. 'Tell me your fucking name!'

'It's Dom,' the boy manages through the tears and spit.

'Well, Dom, I'm going to kill you now, okay?' Ben doesn't recognise his own voice, it's so full of venom. He pulls the boy towards him slightly, then uses all his force to whack the smaller body back against the hard bricks.

'I'm sorry all right? Please. I thought ...'

'You need to learn some respect.'

'I know, I'm sorry. I didn't think you would be like this.'

'What?'

'I thought you looked cool, nice.'

Ben suddenly releases his hand in disgust. Self-disgust. What the hell is he doing? The kid is half his size. What was he thinking? He smooths down the boy's collar, but he can't wipe away the fingerprints on his face, or the bruises that will form underneath. He can't wind the clock back and ignore the taunts. Were they even that? He looks down at the boy. He hardly reaches Ben's chest, for Chrissakes. When the distinctive smell of escaped urine reaches his nostrils, he can't look anymore. He turns around and starts running in the opposite direction.

He runs until his lungs run out of oxygen and his leg muscles start cramping. Then he doubles over and vomits on the pavement. He walks on, away from the stench, his heartbeat still roaring in his ears, and finally his hands stop shaking for long enough to light a cigarette. He draws in the bitter taste, feels the instant nicotine hit, and screws up his face against the tears that want to fall. He's such a fuck-up. The adopted kid with wayward genes.

He thinks about his conversation with Fiona the night before, telling her about his birth mother. His words had clearly shocked her, but why? Could it be that she doesn't think he's as crazy as he feels? She is always so encouraging, certain that he has some baseline integrity; he wonders what she would make of him terrorising a child. But the cigarette does its job, and as he flicks the butt onto the road, he feels calm enough to banish the images and start his journey to work.

*

'You okay, Ben?'

Shit. Marco never calls him Ben, never asks if he's okay. His eyes must still look red, his breath stinking of fags.

'Yeah, you?' He tries to sound casual, but it comes out defensive. Marco hesitates. Ben waits.

'I am more than okay. I opened the twelfth window on my advent calendar this morning and out popped a small but perfectly shaped bottle of Aperol. There's nothing that says Christmas more than an Aperol spritz for breakfast, Posh Boy.'

In spite of his day, Ben can't help smiling, as much for Marco's decision not to push things with him as for the image he's conjured up. 'Where do you want me?'

'Hana and Fiona have called shotgun on creating Christmas, so you and me are running the show tonight. I'll clear the tables; you start behind the counter – once you've dropped your pack off.'

Just the mention of his rucksack sends a rush of adrenaline through Ben; like Marco has gained X-ray vision and can see what's inside. As he nods, he pulls the rucksack tight against his frame. He doesn't want to risk the cans clinking together as he makes his way into the kitchen.

Running the orders by himself keeps Ben busy and he's grateful for it. He enjoys the precision of coffee making. Knowing the exact amount of coffee to use, the appropriate intensity of compression, balancing the milk and froth, perfecting the Bittersweet chocolate motif. And he needs the comfort of that certainty this evening.

However, working alone also means regular bouts of humiliation. For someone who is usually so chilled out, Marco is adamant that Ben doesn't sell alcohol directly. So every time a customer decides to have a beer with their panini or pasta salad, Ben has to ask Marco to come and ring up the sale. It highlights what a kid he still is, which is not what he wants in front of Hana. And tonight, it seems to be happening every five minutes.

Hana and Fiona are in *Blue Peter* mode. Apparently Jo dumped a box of decorations off earlier with instructions to transform the place into some kind of Santa's grotto; there's a competition running along Old York Road and Marco said she was quite upfront about her need to win first prize. The fairy lights are up, flashing around the window frame. And the two of them are now decorating the newly acquired Norwegian pine. A fake tree would never satisfy Jo's standards.

Ben has mixed feelings about Christmas. Mainly, he hates it. Spending long, boring days trying to avoid his family. Particularly his mum when her stress levels skyrocket. And those conflicting emotions on Christmas morning: pleasure at getting a massive pile of gifts, guilt for knowing he doesn't deserve them. And always wrapped up in a fundamental disappointment for life being no different from the day before. But the anticipation of Christmas can still, totally irrationally, excite him a bit.

'I gave you a twenty.'

'Sorry?' Ben looks back towards the customer he's just served: a middle-aged man trying to look cooler than he is in Spoke chinos and bright white Nike trainers. He reminds Ben of his dad.

'You've given me change for ten pounds, I gave you twenty.'

Ben looks down at the guy's cupped hand. A fiver, two pound coins and four twenty-pence pieces: exactly the right change required for his takeaway peppermint tea. Because he definitely paid with a ten-pound note.

'You gave me a tenner.'

'Check the till. It was twenty.'

166

If the guy was angry, shocked even, Ben might not mind so much. But he's calm. Patronising. Not a whiff of self-doubt.

'So you're about 45, yeah?'

'What?' The guy's a bit flustered all of a sudden. Good.

'Did you know that you've been losing about ten thousand brain cells a year for the last twenty-five years?'

'Look, I'm not sure what your point is, but—'

'So by my calculation, you've got about a quarter of a million fewer brain cells than me.'

'What are you saying?' He's angry now, Ben notes with satisfaction. Sweat is starting to bead on his shiny forehead.

'That I'm right, and you're fucking dumb.' Ben stares hard at the customer. What does he want? The guy to walk away, defeated, crowning Ben the victor. Or for him to reach over the counter and grab Ben around the face, dig his nails in. Neither happens though because Fiona walks up.

'I am so sorry, sir.' She pings open the till, whips out a ten-pound note. 'Please accept our apologies. It's been a long, busy day.' She pauses, changes her mind, scoops up a few coins. 'Have your drink on the house too, it's the least we can do.'

Ben watches her drop the money into the man's still-open palm, and smile at him pleadingly. After a moment's hesitation, he throws Ben one last disgusted look, and marches out of the café.

Now that it's just the two of them, Ben steels himself for a telling-off. It will be quietly delivered; this is Fiona after all. But after his day, he doesn't know if he can even handle that. Seconds pass without her saying anything. Jesus, he needs to get this over with. 'So what now?'

'Sorry?'

'Are you going to tell Marco?'

'Of course not.' Her answer is immediate, impulsive, and Ben relaxes slightly. 'For all I know, you gave him the right change and the guy was just pulling a fast one.'

Despite his anger still looking for an outlet, Ben feels a surge of gratitude. Plenty of people forgive him, but rarely do they believe him. 'Thanks,' he whispers.

'Separating right from wrong,' she continues. 'It's not always that easy. I'm not going to start pretending I know best.'

Ben shifts from one foot to the other. Fiona's words seem to have a drug-like effect on him. He's not sure they're good for him, but he wants more. 'I'm going for a fag. Do you want to come?'

He likes the smile that forms on her face; it makes him feel powerful, like he's got a voice worth listening to. Ben suddenly realises that he could tell this woman anything; she won't judge him. And he needs to talk to someone otherwise he'll go insane. He pushes the back door open and they walk outside together.

Chapter 24

Phoebe

It's midday when Flora finds me curled up on the sofa. After breakfast I'd considered cleaning the house, but I just couldn't dredge up any enthusiasm, so I'd found an old script of Paul's in his study and tried to lose myself in Pinter instead. My mind had wandered to Charlie of course, the sins he'd confessed to. It breaks my heart to think he's capable of attacking a young boy. I didn't show it of course. I couldn't risk him putting the barriers back up. I just nodded sympathetically, took a second cigarette and assured him that the boy will be fine. Physically he will be, but I know how long the effects of trauma can last. Ben seemed lighter after his confession, like he'd transferred the burden of his anger to me. I suppose I deserve it.

'Not working today, darling?' Flora hasn't mentioned Charlie since our late-night exchange in the garden. Sometimes I daydream that she's forgotten, that all those gin and tonics have eaten away at her memory sufficiently to let me off the hook. I know that's just wishful thinking though.

'Day off.'

'I suppose that's sensible.'

I look up from the script. There's a gravity to her tone that puts me on my guard. 'Why sensible?'

'Well I imagine he'd appreciate some space today.' She walks over to the fireplace. There's an advent calendar on the mantelpiece and she removes it before sinking into the armchair opposite me. I listen to her count the numbers up, get to thirteen and pause. 'Gosh, Friday the thirteenth,' she murmurs, as though warning herself about impending doom. But she recovers quickly, and I watch her slice open the little window with her electric blue talon. 'Ah it's a little robin, how lovely.' She drops the chocolate into her mouth. 'It's a good job we chose yesterday, isn't it? When you still had luck on your side.'

My heartbeat starts thudding faster. 'Yesterday?'

'To tell Charlie the truth.'

The twelfth of December: is it really a month since our show-down in the garden? For fourteen years, every day felt like it dragged; since I've found Charlie, the opposite seems to be true. I look at the advent calendar still in Flora's hands and curse Christmas. Flora hardly knows what month it is usually, let alone the day. But she's never got over the excitement of chocolate being added to advent calendars and has bought one every year since about 1985. Which means, in December, she knows the date on a daily basis.

With panic silently rising, I consider pretending. Make up a story about him being shocked at first, then softening, listening to my explanation and understanding why I had to leave him. But I know she'd see right through me; then uncover my lie by demanding to be introduced. Her deadline was always going to catch up with me.

'I haven't told him,' I finally admit. 'He's still not ready.'

'But Phoebe, you promised.'

'I'm scared.'

'You're being selfish.'

'I'm scared for him, what he might do if I told him.'

'Maybe Charlie is stronger than you think.' She pauses. 'Stronger than you were.'

'Don't compare this to what I suffered!'

'I gave you a month,' she reminds me, extending each word to drill home her point. 'And you promised me.'

Her seriousness has a dramatic edge, and I wonder for a moment if this is just a performance. Flora's world rarely extends beyond herself; perhaps this isn't about Charlie after all. 'Is this about punishing me?' I ask. 'For being weak?'

'Why does everything have to be about you?'

The irony is palpable. I slam the script down on the sofa, but the tinny thwack doesn't satisfy so I jump to my feet. She stands up too, as though she needs to defend herself from me. In five steps I'm close enough to see the heavy foundation already pooling in her expanded pores, the garish lipstick seeping into the many cracks. I ignore the fear that glistens in her eyes.

'Leave us alone,' I growl.

'I gave you plenty of chances.'

'This isn't a game, Flora!'

'It's not me who's playing make-believe.' She pauses. 'But perhaps it's going to be my job to make him believe.' And with that threat, she darts out of the room.

*

It's a relief to get out of the house. I only go as far as Sainsbury's Local on Battersea Park Road, but the winter air calms my temper. I had planned to buy some fresh ingredients and cook a proper meal, spaghetti bolognaise maybe, or chicken stir-fry. But I'm not in the mood anymore. If Charlie can lose control over a slice of ham, how the hell would he react to finding out I'm his mother? And that I've been lying to him all this time? Why has Flora chosen now to be so proactive in my life? I pick up three microwave meals on special offer and whip them through the self-service till.

I walk to the park after that. I had hoped to sit on the swing for a while, let its gentle motion help me decide what to do, but unfortunately both swings are occupied, and the unwelcome stares I get from a group of mothers stood nearby persuade me to leave them to it. I need to stop Flora telling Charlie the truth, but how? My only hope is that her gin-addled brain won't be able to figure out a plan, that the enormity of telling him the truth, of how he might react, will hold her back. But for how long?

I eat my tagliatelle carbonara straight out of the black plastic container. I left it in the microwave for too long and the first mouthful burns the roof of my mouth, but the creamy sauce and salty ham taste delicious and it isn't long before I'm scraping the last of the sauce out of the corners and wishing I could have another. I make myself a cup of tea instead and return to the living room. The rich food has made me sleepy, so I do my best to plump up the saggy cushions and close my eyes; oblivion is exactly the tonic I need right now.

I clearly do fall asleep because the daylight is low when Paul walks into the living room, waking me up. I rub at my eyes, then push myself to sitting and plaster on a smile. I've hardly seen him since the night he found out about Charlie; his style has always been to avoid confrontation and he's stayed predictably hidden ever since.

'I hear it's your day off,' he says, sitting down next to me.

I nod, smile. I search his eyes for a hint of what Flora might have told him, and it's a relief to see no sign of recrimination. 'I picked up some food for your dinner,' I offer. 'Something easy.'

'Ah, apparently your mother and I are going out.'

'What?' They hardly go out separately anymore. They never go out together.

'Yes, I was rather surprised too. But Flora is keen.'

'You're going out?'

'She's being very mysterious. Won't tell me where.'

My heart starts hammering. This is why he doesn't know yet; I know where she's taking him. So much for alcohol delaying her.

'But I bought food. Maybe you could go another time?' I sound shrill but he doesn't seem to notice.

'That's very thoughtful of you, darling, but Flora is quite set on the idea.'

'Perhaps I could come too then?' I suggest, my panic rising. I can't imagine sitting there with them, but I also can't let them loose on Charlie alone.

'Actually, darling, I was hoping that Paul and I could have some quality time together.' Flora has sashayed into the room and the message in her stare is quite clear: *You're not talking me out of this again.*

'Really?' It's Paul turn to look surprised now.

'You wouldn't deny us that, would you, darling?'

Of course I would deny them whatever it took to protect my son, but I hesitate before answering and then it's too late.

She reaches out to Paul with both hands and flashes him her brightest smile. 'It'll be fun, just you and me, like the old days.'

Even after all these years of selfish acts and drunken embarrassments, he can't resist her. With an almost apologetic glance in my direction he gets up off the sofa and lets her lead him out of the room.

The clang of the front door closing feels like a prison sentence. I shut my eyes and imagine the two of them walking into Bittersweet, taking a table close to the counter; Flora holding one of Paul's hands while pointing at Charlie, confirming who he is. What will happen next? Will Flora just get his attention and then blurt out the truth alongside their panini order? Or will they wait until closing, ask for five minutes when he's mopping the floor?

All scenarios are so awful that I don't want to think about it. I start pacing the room, considering my options. I could chase after them; try to persuade them to keep quiet. But Flora is determined to tell Charlie the truth and I don't want to cause a scene in front of him. I could phone the café, try to get him out of there. But what would I say? He'll just go back to thinking I'm crazy.

I wish I could call Flora, try to reason with her somehow. She's got a mobile phone, but she never carries it with her. It will be shoved in some drawer somewhere gathering dust; the landline sees more movement in this house. I stare down at my own cheap Nokia sitting next to me on the sofa. I'm the opposite; I take it with me everywhere. I'm not sure what I'm expecting. There was a time when Dan would text little messages, *I love you* maybe, or more often: *Can you pick up shirts from dry cleaners?* But that was all a long time ago.

For no reason other than to occupy my hands, I pull a bottle of wine out of Paul's antique French wine rack. The contraption looks like it belongs in a torture chamber rather than a living room, with its iron spokes rising out of a series of metal rings, but Paul loves it. He found it in a flea market in Montpelier one holiday and managed to fit it in the back seat of our Ford Cortina somehow. There was a time when it would be full of interesting bottles from across the globe, but now there are just a few screw-tops from Sainsbury's.

I don't usually drink in this house if I can avoid it; seeing the effects of my parents' dependency is enough to put me off. But tonight is different. There's a bottle opener sitting next to the advent calendar on the mantelpiece and it's not long before I'm holding a large glass of some cheap Portuguese merlot in my hand. I'm greedy for its numbing effect so I don't stop until the glass is empty. I stare at my reflection in the tarnished mirror. Is this it? The day that the future I've been so carefully constructing comes crashing down?

While the wine hasn't slowed my thoughts, it has relaxed me enough to sit back down. I slump on to the sofa; bottle in one hand, glass in the other. Maybe I should just give up on being reunited with my son. Kick back with Flora and Paul and drink myself into oblivion. Right now, that doesn't feel like such a bad idea.

*

I'm on my second bottle when they walk through the door but it hasn't had the effect I was hoping for; I still feel wired. I search their faces for clues, but Flora's glazed mask and Paul's stony expression reveal nothing.

'Well?' I spit it out.

'He looks like you.' Paul says it as an insult. Like I've ruined Charlie by giving him my eyes.

'Did you tell him?'

'He works hard. He's a credit to his family.'

'ANSWER MY QUESTION!' The adrenaline has found an outlet and I can't stop it.

'He remembered Flora. I introduced myself.'

'Oh God! How could you? Don't you care what you've done to him?'

'What we've done to him?'

Paul's voice is mocking. I can't stand the sound of it. Why the hell do I have to shoulder the blame for everything? 'You've done this! THIS is on you.' I jab my finger at him.

'Oh, darling, don't you see?' Flora has chosen a wounded tone; she knows exactly how to rile me. 'This is ALL on you.'

I pick up the wine rack then. It's only in my hands for an instant. Then it's sailing across the room, heading for Flora's accusing face. The few remaining bottles fly out midair. Most thud on the carpet but one smashes against the dusty sideboard. Flora screams as she ducks down, trying to avoid the iron spokes. The sound of metal meeting wall is glorious.

I feel hands grab at me. All the adrenaline has gone now, and I let myself be dragged along like a rag doll. When we get to the kitchen, Paul lets go of my jumper, pushes me away from him.

175

'What the hell is wrong with you?!'

'You told him. You ruined everything.'

'You could have killed her!'

'You have no right.'

'Phoebe, we didn't tell him.'

I look up, try to focus my vision amidst the swirling fog of tears.

'I wanted to, but Flora persuaded me to give you more time.'

'He doesn't know?' The wine, the fear, it's jumbling my thoughts.

'And this is how you repay her.'

Chapter 25

SEPTEMBER 2005

Phoebe

I look in the mirror and try not to be disappointed. Pregnancy doesn't just give you a bump, it changes every part of your body. For nine months, you're a warrior, protecting your baby with every biological weapon available to you. But you do this covertly, under the mask of tired eyes, puffy skin, and an expanding waistline.

'I look fat.'

'You're twelve weeks pregnant – you're allowed to look fat.'

I glance at Dan perched on the side of our bed, his head dipped down, eyes squinting at his Blackberry. It took me a full day of traipsing round different shops to find something appropriate to wear, an outfit that said high-flying theatrical agent rather than new mum-to-be; the least he could do is look up. I change tack, soften my voice. 'Do you think the dress makes me look fat?'

A small sigh escapes from his lips, like I've interrupted something more important, but he lifts his head dutifully. Then I feel his eyes roll over me, appraising my ice-blue Fifties-style swing dress with its low-cut V highlighting my deeper than usual cleavage, and I see his expression change, his interest shift. 'Wow, you look amazing.'

With his words, a worm of excitement squirms in my belly. I still can't quite believe I've made the short list for Theatrical Agent of the Year, my welcome-back news when I returned from Greece, let alone Richie's confidence that I'm a dead cert winner. But this evening, as I twirl in my new dress, the reality of my achievement is coming into focus. Husband, son, new baby, and now my career at an all-time high. It almost feels too good to be true.

Of course, the awards ceremony also means a glamorous evening out with my husband. He'd been unsure about the date at first – apparently some big anniversary for his firm – but when Richie had paid for the tickets and then surprised us with a luxury hotel room to finish off the night in style, he'd promised to sort something out. Cara had agreed to have Charlie, and I'd gone shopping.

'I bought new lingerie too,' I add, finding a sexy tone to match his expression. Over the last week or so, my morning sickness has started to subside, and I've felt more able to deal with the exhausting mix of work, childcare and keeping the house in some sort of order. Second pregnancies are not like your first, when everyone treats you like a princess and demands that you put your feet up, but I don't mind. My hand slips to my belly; we've been toughing this one out together. And now, finally, I have the energy for something more fun.

'It feels a bit weird, having a dirty weekend when you're pregnant.'

'It's a night at the Ritz,' I remind him. 'Not exactly seedy.'

'Maybe my priorities have changed.' He sees the hurt flash across my face and grabs my hand. 'Sorry, that came out wrong. I just mean the baby comes first now, protecting it.'

'Protecting her,' I murmur, almost without realising I've spoken. I'm certain that we're having a girl and calling her *it* feels wrong, offensive even. But he takes my comment as acquiescence.

'Exactly.'

I look into his eyes. 'So where do you get your kicks while you're protecting our daughter?'

He drops my hand, leans back further on the bed. 'Shit, Phoebe. That's not fair.'

He looks hurt and I instantly regret my words. 'I'm sorry.'

'We agreed, that's all behind us now.'

'I know; I shouldn't have said that.'

'You promised you'd moved on. We can't make a success of this marriage if you're still angry with me.'

'I guess I just want tonight to be special, romantic. Free champagne, a room at the Ritz. I want to feel like an irresistible wife, not a sensible mother.'

He reaches for my hand again and pulls me down next to him on the bed. He kisses each of my fingernails, their new French polish shining in the low September sunlight. 'You're right, I'm being stupid. This is your night, and I'll make sure it's perfect.' He leans over and kisses my lips, nibbling and exploring. I close my eyes and feel a shiver of anticipation tingle on my skin. Tonight will be special. I can feel it.

Eventually he draws away. 'I better get in the shower, spruce myself up. What time are we leaving?'

Brought out of my reverie, I look at my watch. 'Cara could be here any minute to pick up Charlie. He's so excited; he's already sat on the stairs with his bag packed. Then we're free to go.'

'Well, it's good that it doesn't take me long to look gorgeous then.'

I roll my eyes, pretend to scoff, but we both know it's true. It's so much easier for men, especially ones gifted with natural good looks like Dan.

'Shall I book a cab?' he asks, his brow furrowing slightly. I know he's weighing up the substantial cost of a taxi into the West End against the free rolling he's going to enjoy for the rest of the evening.

'No don't worry. I was planning on driving.'

'Really?'

'It's not like I can take full advantage of the free champagne.'

'The car's been a bit temperamental lately,' he muses. 'What happens if we break down?'

It's true that our 1997 Jeep Wrangler – a legacy from Dan's bachelor days – has had a few issues. A crack in the manifold that meant a new exhaust. Steering issues when the car picks up speed, known rather ominously in the trade as the death wobble. Dan loves it though, won't hear of replacing his precious Jeep with something more akin to a family car, and secretly I'm quite fond of its iconic status too, if not its reliability. 'It's a six-mile journey,' I say to placate him. 'And if I reach thirty miles per hour in rush hour traffic it'll be a miracle. We'll be fine.'

'Well, if you're sure.' He stands up and releases the buttons on his shirt, exposing his solid torso, still tanned from our trip. 'And I guess it means we won't have to wait for a cab at the end of the night.'

'Quicker to our hotel room.'

'And then we'll see what's more attractive after a night in those heels,' he says, nodding at my new strappy stilettos, 'my body or those plumped-up goose-down pillows swathed in freshly washed Egyptian cotton.' He winks at me, but doesn't wait for a response before heading out of the room.

As I turn back to the mirror to apply the finishing touches to my make-up, my phone buzzes next to me. I read the text from Cara and my heart drops. I tap in her number and she picks up on the first ring.

'Chickenpox?' I ask.

'I know, can't believe the timing. Doctor said I need to keep him at home, definitely no sleepovers. I'm so sorry.'

I close my eyes and try not to let the scream of frustration leak out. Charlie is at nursery with Jude twice a week. Chances are he's caught the illness already. But I can't ignore the instructions given by a GP. 'It's fine.'

'I would come to you, except Tim's away overnight. I know how big this is for you, Phoebs. Could your mum look after Charlie?'

Cara has met Flora a few times, fleeting encounters in the park or local play zone. Not long enough to understand how unreliable she is. 'Perhaps. I'll sort something out,' I promise, before ending the call and throwing my phone onto the bed. What now? Charlie has plenty of other friends at nursery, but none that he would feel comfortable staying the night with, especially at this short notice. Paul is away with a new theatre group he's joined, so Flora is on her own. Could I ask her? In some ways she's a brilliant grandparent, happy to play with Charlie for hours. But how could I trust her not to drink herself into oblivion, to ignore my son's cries if he woke from a bad dream?

Dan walks into the room, towel around his waist. 'What's wrong?'

I sigh and sink down onto the bed. 'Jude's got chickenpox; Cara can't have Charlie.'

'Really?'

'I know, what a nightmare.'

Silence hangs in the air for a while as I rock between two grim options – risking Charlie's safety with Flora or giving up the night I've been so looking forward to. But it's Dan who speaks first.

'I'll stay. It's your night, not mine, and Richie will look after you.'

I look up at him. He was so ready with the suggestion, that I wonder if he would prefer to stay. But I see the regret in his eyes, mixed with concern for our son, and my suspicions subside. 'I want you to be there.'

'Me too, Phoebe, I really want that. But what choice do we have?'

I pause, listen to the thud of my heart. 'We could ask Flora.'

His response is immediate, horrified. 'I'm not leaving Charlie overnight with that lush. Honestly, I think I should stay.'

Whether through frustration or the sting of his words, anger surges inside me. I know I have no right to defend my mother; Dan's description is exactly right. But she had made more effort with her grandson than I would ever have imagined – a lot more than Dan's father – and Charlie loves spending time with her. She also raised me for eighteen years and I managed to survive. Maybe it's time we gave her a chance. 'I'll make sure she doesn't drink.'

'And you think she'll listen to you?'

'It's one night.'

'She hasn't been sober in ten years.'

'She's my mother, Dan. She won't let Charlie come to any harm.'

'Are you sure?'

I stand up, run my hand down Dan's bare arm, still warm from the shower. Am I sure? Can I rely on her, just this once? I think about the alternative, sitting next to an empty chair, slipping into a super-king-sized bed alone. 'I would never put Charlie at risk.'

'But Flora … really, Phoebe?'

'Trust me.'

He stands still for a moment, his mind wavering, but finally he gives me a small nod. His consent. I know he's not convinced, but I can't let him talk me out of this; I want this night together too badly. I pick up my phone and make the call. I'm not going to let our perfect night be ruined.

Chapter 26

DECEMBER 2019

Ben

Ben can hear his family talking in the kitchen before he even opens the front door. He can't make out what they're saying, but he can tell the conversation is achievement-related by the pitch of their voices. He sighs behind the wooden panels. He's already apologised to his mum for Thursday's disaster, and even managed to stay calm when his dad added his two pennies' worth, so he knows there'll be no more fallout from that. But still, he's been on his feet for the last seven hours and isn't in the mood for being congratulatory. He knows he won't get away with going straight upstairs though, so he steels himself for the onslaught of positivity.

'Is that you, Ben?'

No, it's a burglar. On a Saturday afternoon. With a key.

'Yeah.'

'Don't disappear upstairs, Rosie's got some news.'

Of course she has. Rosie attracts good news like bluebottles to a dead rat. He saunters into the kitchen. They're all sat around the island unit, fingers clasped around novelty mugs, the remains of a Waitrose lemon cake sat between them. He looks at the writing on his dad's mug. *Silver Fox*. It was a present from Rosie on Father's Day; Ben remembers him opening it, pretending to be offended while puffing out his chest, probably secretly comparing himself to George Clooney.

Rosie has a healthy glow. Her cheeks suit her name and the remnants of a ponytail are hanging over one shoulder. She's dressed in their school tracksuit and smells of outdoor exercise, reminding Ben where she's been, where they've all been. There was some netball tournament going on and Rosie was captaining the first team. That honour had caused a fair amount of excitement in the house, now it looks as though her team did well. Ben's mood sinks lower.

'Go on then, Rosie, tell him.'

'Mum, the poor guy's just got in.' She turns to face him, dulls her tone a bit. 'We're having a cup of tea, Ben. You want one?' She stands up, walks towards the kettle; looks at him expectantly.

God she's so nice. And he's such an arsehole. 'I'm okay thanks. How did you get on?' It's an effort asking, opening the floodgates to more Rosie worship. But he owes her, he supposes.

'Yeah we won.'

'Out of twelve different teams!' his mum adds. 'And I think Rosie scored the most goals – is that right, sweetie?'

'That's great, well done,' Ben mutters.

'That's not the best part though,' his dad chimes in. 'Winning today means they're through to the national championships. It's the first time Wandsworth College has qualified since 2011.'

'Awesome.' Ben wonders if his response sounds enthusiastic or mocking. It's a fine line.

'When is it, Rosie? January? Will it be a weekday?' His mum is now scrolling through her iPhone X, already trying to work out how she can retain super-mum status while keeping her position as the world's greatest architect. He feels a jab of sympathy for her. It must be hard, having to be brilliant at everything.

'It certainly is awesome,' his dad agrees, not a hint of sarcasm in his voice. 'In fact, I think a bottle of champagne is in order.'

Ben watches his dad leap off his bar stool and duck down behind the island unit. There's always at least one bottle of champagne in his wine fridge, chilled and ready for celebratory moments like this. Rosie knocks them out pretty regularly, so it's good to be prepared.

'How was work?' As always, it's his sister who steers the conversation back to him.

'Busy. But fine.' It had been too. While he never likes the idea of working weekends, of having his free time stripped away from him, the reality is always at least fine, sometimes better than that. On Saturdays he works alongside Jo's friend Sammy, a single mum with a toxic sense of humour. It's always quite amusing listening to what she's got planned for her cheating tight-arse of an ex-husband. Although Fiona had gone all tight-lipped when Sammy started ranting today. It made Ben wonder if there was a husband in her past. In fact, she'd been quite reserved all day. Maybe it was mentioning her parents' visit the night before; they clearly embarrass her because she never talks about them. It's funny; he hardly knows anything about her life, while he can't stop telling her stuff about his own.

'I'd love to work in a café. Babysitting is so dull.'

Ben knows Rosie doesn't mean it. Babysitting pays almost as much as he earns and involves practically no work; playing hide-and-seek for half an hour and then flopping in front of the TV with a packet of chocolate chip cookies. Except Rosie doesn't do that, of course. She drinks tap water and writes essays.

'Here you go, son.' His dad hands him a glass flute with a silver base, Vera Wang inscribed on the bottom. Even the glasses have a designer label in this house.

Ben rolls the word around in his head. Son. His dad says it

so casually, makes it sound almost natural. Does he really see Ben that way? 'Thanks,' he says, takes a sip. Then a gulp. He likes champagne. He hates what the drink represents of course. Arrogant rich men showing the world how successful they are. Only prepared to drink fizzy wine from one tiny region out of the whole fucking world. But there's no denying it tastes good.

'Whoa, slow down, Ben. We haven't made a toast yet.'

'I'll do it,' Ben announces. 'If you fill my glass up.' He's not sure who's most surprised by his offer but it does the trick. His dad tops up his drink.

'Hey! Unfair. My win. I should get more than him.' Rosie always seems to get drunk on half a glass and today is no different. She tips her head back and finishes her drink before holding the glass out for a refill. Ben loves it when any hint of mischief surfaces in his sister, so he winks at her and leans forward to clink glasses. She's obviously used up all of her accuracy on the netball court, because she misjudges the distance and smashes her glass into his so hard that it's a miracle they don't both shatter.

'Oops sorry!' Rosie looks at him and starts giggling. His mum looks a bit irritated and his dad starts inspecting their glasses for cracks. Ben smiles at his sister.

'Better hurry up with that toast or there'll be no champagne left, the speed you two are drinking it,' his dad says, a grumpy edge to his voice now.

Ben stands up. He's feeling a bit better about Rosie's win now. 'It is with great pleasure,' he declares while raising his glass, 'that I congratulate my talented sister, for being brilliant ... at playing with balls.'

Rosie erupts into laughter and even his parents seem to find his joke amusing. His dad puts an arm around his shoulder and draws him in for a much more controlled glass clink. 'Very funny, son,' he says wryly.

*

Going out had been Rosie's idea, concocted when they were sprawled out in the den, binge-watching *Teen Wolf* while Greg prepared his 'special surprise' for dinner (which was chilli con carne, like always). Lucy had looked at them suspiciously when Rosie announced that her teammate was throwing a celebration party, and that Ben was invited too, but Greg hadn't questioned her fictional story, had even given them twenty quid for a cab. The champagne had obviously gone to his head too.

Luckily Rosie isn't one of those girls who spend ages on her make-up or choosing an outfit. She loves jeans and has at least twenty pairs of various cuts and washes, but she usually just wears the pair that's easiest to retrieve off the floor. Tonight she's rocking the Californian look. Light-coloured denim and an oversized pink sweatshirt, the words 'Dream Big' scrawled across it. Chunky white Fila trainers complete the image. Ben looks dull in comparison. Black jeans and a grey T-shirt; the tiny Vans logo on the left side of his chest not exactly eye-catching. But invisible has always been his preferred look.

Rosie suggests Angel's Bar on Battersea Rise as soon as they leave the house. Cocktails and shiny bar staff aren't usually his thing, but the idea of losing himself in loud music is quite appealing, so Ben nods his agreement and falls in step beside her. It takes twenty minutes for them to walk to the bar and they do most of it in amiable silence, but it's a different story when they open the door, and Ben has to lip-read more than listen to what his sister is saying.

'I'm thinking Strawberry Daiquiri. Or Peach Cup. What about you?'

Ben looks at the cocktail menu. It's all a bit too bright and sickly for him. 'Bottle of beer for me. I'll order.' But when he looks up, Rosie has already got the bartender's attention. He watches her lean in to make her order heard above the music, laugh at something he says in response. Why does she make everything look so easy? He scans the room and spots an empty table in the corner, two bar stools either side of it. He tries to get Rosie's attention, but she's still focused on the cute guy behind the bar, so he just retreats to the table and sits down.

'There you are. I couldn't see you at first. Well done on getting a table though. My legs are definitely feeling those eight games of netball.'

Ben's mood sinks a bit. He likes drunk Rosie who almost smashes glasses. He doesn't want perfect Rosie who wins netball tournaments. 'I'm sure they'll be back to their bionic best by tomorrow.' His response is laced with sarcasm and he instantly regrets his comment, but when he starts to apologise, Rosie cuts him off. Finally, she's lost patience with him.

'Ben, I don't care that you're a miserable prick most of the time. But all this self-pity? It's pathetic, and really frustrating.'

He sighs. 'What would you know?'

'I know you're an amazing artist!'

The art thing again.

'But it's so much more than that,' she continues.

'Like what? My brilliance at sport? Oh no, that's you. My big brain? Oops, you again. My massive circle of friends? Now hang on, I see a pattern forming here.'

'Stop it, Ben.'

'Do you know how hard it is being your brother, practically the same age and shit at everything compared to you?' Ben knows that councils don't like placing adoptive children in families with a child in the same school year, but they'd made an exception in his case. Lucky him.

'And I suppose that's my fault, is it? Nothing to do with you smashing windows and staying out all night so you're too tired to study?'

Ben draws a quick breath and tries to hide his discomfort by taking a long swig of his beer. If Rosie knows about his late-night trips, what else could she have found out? The fear must show on his face too because her voice softens a bit.

'I'm good at stuff because I'm too scared not to be. If I'm not successful, then I'm nothing. It's different for you.'

'Because I'm such a proven failure?'

'Because you don't care about failing. You've got the confidence to put yourself out there, stick two fingers up. Question everything; give a shit about nothing. I'd love to be more like you.'

Speech over, Ben watches Rosie suck hard on her paper straw, the pink line of daiquiri descending down the glass. She's never admitted to being scared of failure before; she comes across so amazing at everything that he's never thought to ask. But she has got the same demanding parents as him, goes to the same school; of course she must feel the pressure too.

'Another one?'

'Yeah, why not. If I'm going to feel like shit tomorrow, the hangover may as well be worth it.'

Ben gives her a small salute and walks to the bar. There's something quite exhilarating about the thought of Rosie being jealous of him. But is it true? He does stick two fingers up, and question every rule. Break plenty of them too. He's always assumed it's because he's such a moron. Could it really be something to be proud of?

'Same again, mate?' Ben looks up at the bartender. Not only has he remembered their original order, he hasn't even asked to see Ben's ID. And he served him almost immediately. Ben stands up a bit taller and adds a broad smile to his nod.

*

It's past midnight when they leave the bar. They'd run out of money after their third drink but neither of them had been in a hurry to go, so Rosie had sucked pointlessly on her straw, and Ben had scraped every label off his three bottles, and they'd talked. About Rosie's fear of being trapped in a life she's never had chance to question. About how being a round peg in a round hole sounds good, but actually makes it impossible to climb out of. Ben has never compared them in that way, never seen his awkward angles as a positive.

He hasn't felt this connected to his sister in years and he feels quite content as he watches her hop gracefully from slab to slab.

'So what do you get up to when you sneak out in the middle of the night then?' she asks without looking up at him, although not out of tact; for some reason she's decided that walking on the cracks isn't allowed.

'Not much really. I just like being out when the streets are empty.' He may feel a new closeness, but there's no way he's telling her what he actually gets up to.

'Don't you get scared?'

Ben thinks about the many near misses he's had climbing onto the tracks, the knife that he found. He shrugs. 'I like getting scared.'

'Really?' Rosie looks up. 'Oh shit! I stood on a crack. That's your fault.'

Ben smirks. 'So what? Monsters going to get you now?'

'Maybe.' She laughs back, resuming her strange skip.

An idea starts to form in Ben's mind. 'How about I give you something real to be scared of?'

'Like what?'

'You want to be more like me, right? To put yourself out there?'

'Maybe,' she says again, although with less conviction.

'Come with me.' He grabs her hand. The skin on skin feels alien but not altogether unpleasant.

She starts laughing again, albeit with a nervous edge, as they race hand in hand past their school and into Spencer Park. 'What are we doing here?'

'I want to show you something.' They're almost across the park when Ben finally stops in front of a large oak tree. 'The first time I climbed this, it was for the challenge.'

'And then?'

'It became somewhere to hide, to get away from people like

190

you.' He smiles at her though, to remind her they've moved on.

'I like a challenge,' she says thoughtfully, more to herself than him.

'Watch and learn.' Ben grabs hold of the lowest branch and pulls himself up, then kicks out with his right leg to reach the next level. He's done this climb so many times that it's almost second nature and it only takes him a couple of minutes to reach the bough big enough for two people to sit on, about five metres off the ground. 'Come on,' he coaxes.

He watches Rosie copy his ascent. She's definitely slower and a bit tentative, but otherwise matches him move for move. He feels the familiar stab of annoyance at her ability to do everything so well, but this time it's mixed with a sense of pride. It's his thing, his idea, after all.

Suddenly a scream rings out, splitting the night's silence in half. The thud of a body follows, sealing it back together.

Oh God, what has he done?

Ben scrambles down the tree, his heart racing, his inner voice screaming at himself in fury. What was he thinking? Especially in her drunken state. Why the hell didn't he just take her home? 'Rosie! Are you okay?' He shakes her shoulder, desperate for some sort of reaction. It works. It's only a groan but at least she's conscious.

'My arm,' she croaks. 'It really hurts ...'

Ben looks down at his sister's arm, at the bend in her elbow. Except it's not her elbow. The realisation of what he's done makes him feel sick. And what is still to come. Ambulance. Hospital. His parents' accusing faces. Rosie in a cast for Christmas. And for the netball finals, he realises in horror.

Ben digs his fingernails hard into the back of his neck.

Chapter 27

Phoebe

The siren is getting louder. Closer. The ambulance will be here soon. The sound of it burrows into my ears but I can't see its green and yellow glow. All I can see is Dan. And blood. Too much blood. Still the noise penetrates.

My phone's ringing, I realise with a start. I fumble for it, but in the darkness it crashes to the floor. Who could be calling me in the middle of the night? In truth, who's calling me at all? It falls silent, but only for a moment, and seconds later it's ringing again. I grab it and this time I manage to press the green button.

'Hello?'

'Fiona?' The voice is distant, muffled. It's Charlie. We all have each other's numbers at the café in case of any emergencies – Jo insists on it. 'I've really fucked up this time.'

I feel a range of conflicting emotions. Happiness for him wanting to speak to me, but also a wariness for why he's called. 'What's happened?'

'It's Rosie. She's hurt.'

I shudder. I'm not sure if that's the freezing air or the thought of what he might have done. 'What happened?' I repeat.

'They blame me, just like they always do.'

'For what?' I ask it calmly, but on the inside I'm panicking. I remember what he did to that boy.

'For breaking her arm.' Then the sobbing starts and it's as though a dam has burst. For all the shock of his confession, a tiny voice inside my head says this is good, that he needs to release his pain before he can face up to what he's done. But still, it breaks my heart to hear him cry.

'Where are you?'

'At home. Mum and Dad have taken Rosie to hospital, but they didn't want me there.'

'You're alone?' I'm wide awake now, oxygen rushing to waken my tired muscles. 'You shouldn't be on your own.'

'It's always when things are just starting to go right that I ruin everything.'

'I'm coming over.' I know it's risky, going to his house. His parents could be back any minute, and who knows whether they'd recognise me as Charlie's birth mother. But I can't leave him all alone; I know more than most where extreme trauma can lead.

'To my house?' he asks.

'I'm getting a cab.'

Luckily I remember to ask for his address before finishing the call. After pulling on some clothes, I race out of the house and hurry towards Battersea Park Road to hail a cab. I'm not sure why everything feels so urgent, but I just know I need to get there fast. Perhaps it's the memory of when my life hit rock bottom, and how I reacted. Thankfully I don't have to wait long for a black cab to pull over; no doubt the early hours of Sunday morning are still standard hours in the taxi business. I lean back against the headrest, close my eyes and will the driver to speed up.

*

'We were climbing my tree. Rosie broke her arm.'

So it was just an accident. Not the act of violence I was imagining after all. I release a sigh. 'Well, that's not your fault. These things happen.'

Charlie drops his head into his hands. He's sat at their long kitchen table, an empty Coke can by his side. He smells of cigarettes but there's no evidence of them inside the room. It seems he's still got the wherewithal to smoke outside at least. 'They said I got her drunk. That I should have been more responsible.'

'She's older than you, isn't she? She can make her own decisions.'

'She'll miss the national championships.'

'There'll be others.'

'You always say the right thing, you know that, Fiona?'

I don't know how to respond to that, so I use the moment to take in my surroundings. When I first walked inside, I was struck by its similarity to our old house in Southfields. The large, open-plan kitchen and wide glass doors onto the garden. But now I see the differences, the clever mix of modern and classic kitchen units and the striking signature pieces that we could never have afforded. Ours was the underage version of this, I realise, in size as well as style. Perhaps this is the type of house Dan and I would have grown into, if our marriage hadn't died.

'Thanks for coming.' Charlie's voice brings me back to the present.

'I'm glad you called me.'

'Can I ask you something?'

'Of course.' I couldn't possibly give a different answer, but my back stiffens as I wonder what he's going to say, and whether I'll need to feed him yet another lie.

'Do you believe that some people are born bad?'

I think back to that night. 'Yes,' I say. No lying required after all. 'But I don't believe you were.'

'It was an accident, Rosie falling.'

'Exactly. Not your fault.'

'But I wonder if I wanted it, willed it, you know?' His voice isn't much louder than a whisper, but the sound still resonates in the quiet room.

'You can't will a broken arm.'

'Do you ever get nightmares?' His change of subject takes me off guard. I think about the horrible images I'm subjected to most nights, even after all these years. And the number of times I've woken up shivering because I'm drenched in sweat.

'Yes, sometimes.' I try to sound relaxed, but it comes out guarded.

'Are they different or the same one?'

I pause for a moment. 'Different versions of the same one.'

'My nightmare is always the same. And impossible to under-stand. I hear things.'

'What things?' I ask gently.

'Screaming mostly. But my eyes are closed, in the dream. I can't see what's happening.'

'Nothing's happening; it's just a nightmare.'

'It feels more than that,' he whispers. 'More like a memory. I can't shake the feeling that I did something bad.'

Even though he says it quietly, the shock of his words makes me draw breath. He looks up, his eyes shining with fear. I can't stand to see him like this. Should I tell him the truth? Explain why he might feel that way?

I can't risk it.

'Ben, I'm certain you haven't done anything bad.' I need to sound confident.

'Yeah, I know. I'm just talking shit.' But this new dismissive tone isn't derailing me.

'Listen, nightmares aren't a sign you're bad; they're just an outlet for how you're feeling. You're scared that there's something wrong with you, but there isn't, Ben, I promise you that.'

'How can you be so sure? You hardly know me,' he spits out.

The child again, testing my loyalty by pushing me away. I just have to figure out how to reassure him without revealing too much.

'Something happened one night, a long time ago.' I pause, breathe. 'A terrible, tragic thing. Since then, I've found it very hard to trust people.'

'What happened?'

'But I trust you,' I say, ignoring his question. 'You should be proud of who you are.'

He forces out a disbelieving snort. 'Wish you'd tell my parents that.'

'I'm sure they're proud of you.' My comment jolts me back to a different time, when I gave a similar platitude to Dan about his own father all those years ago. It sounded pathetic then, and it doesn't sound any better now. 'But even if they're not,' I continue, 'it shouldn't stop you being proud of yourself.'

He considers that for a moment, then lifts his head and there's a vague optimism in his eyes. 'Maybe you're right.'

'I am right.'

'I don't need their fake sympathy and patronising advice. Rosie is all they care about anyway; it'll be good for everyone.'

'What will be good?'

'I'm going to move out. Quit school. I'm probably going to fail my A-levels anyway, and who cares about art? I can get a job, my own place. You did it, didn't you?'

'Well, I finished school,' I mumble slowly. My head is racing, and I need to buy myself some time. Charlie hasn't had the upbringing that I had, the early independence that comes with parents who don't parent, or the ambition that financial insecurity creates. I'm not sure he could survive on his own. But on the other hand, the further he draws away from his adoptive family, the closer he might grow to me. They've had more than twelve years to put him back together, and they've failed. Surely it's only right that I get my chance now?

'But then, Chemistry and Biology A-levels weren't exactly

critical to my career,' I counter. He looks up at me and I see pure gratitude in his expression. It spurs me on. 'And of course I'll help you in any way I can.'

'That's settled then. New Year's resolution.' He grins widely and lifts his Coke can in a mock cheer before changing his mind. 'Fuck this, we should celebrate properly. That's one good thing about my dad, always a bottle of champagne going spare.' He leaps up from the kitchen table and squats in front of the island unit. It's the first time I notice the wine fridge discreetly set into its base.

'It's four in the morning, Ben.' I don't want to sound like a killjoy, but the last thing I want right now is alcohol.

'Ah come on, Fiona, there's never a bad time for champagne.'

Alarm bells start ringing inside my head. There's too much alcoholism in my family for me to not worry about comments like that. 'I'd love to celebrate with you, but I'm working the lunchtime shift tomorrow.' I look at my watch. 'Well, today.'

'And you still came out in the middle of the night to check I was okay?'

'That's what friends are for.' I sound shy. Even after everything, I still can't quite believe we're got something real, that our relationship exists outside of my imagination.

'Well, err, thanks.' He can't look me in the eye, but I can tell he's touched by my effort.

My heart leaps, almost taking my breath away. I want to wallow in this moment, but his parents could be home any minute, and I need to get some rest before I start work, so reluctantly I break the silence. 'If you're sure you're okay, I should get going.'

'Yes I'm fine, thanks to you.'

I stand up and reach for my coat.

'But I still want to thank you properly.'

'There's the Bittersweet Christmas party next week,' I remind him, but he bats my suggestion away. I'm almost by the front door when he blurts out, 'What are you doing for Christmas, I mean on the actual day?'

I have a sudden image of being stuck at home, Flora and Paul tucking into a Christmas dinner of gin cocktails and red wine. The three of us sitting in silence, me still not forgiven for Friday night's fight, for the chasm that sits between us. 'I haven't thought about it. I'm not really a fan.'

'Come to ours.'

'Sorry?' I wasn't expecting an invitation.

'There'll only be us, and Dad always cooks for about a hundred. May as well feed one more.'

'I can't. I shouldn't. Thanks for the offer but I don't think it's a good idea.'

'Please, Fiona. They're bound to still hate me over Rosie's arm. You'll be doing me a favour.' Charlie gives me his best smile and imploring eyes. It's amazing how this usually angry teenager can turn on the charm sometimes. Necessity, perhaps.

'Your parents won't want me here. They don't even know me.' Although of course if they genuinely didn't know me, I'd be jumping at the offer.

'They always get what they want, I never do. If you came, well, that would be me getting what I want at last. Does that make sense?'

'Maybe I could come.' The words tumble out before the sensible part of my brain can stop them. Of course it's far too risky; I've no idea how much his parents were told about me, but I have to assume they know everything. I need to pull back.

'That's brilliant. You being here will make all the difference.'

And his face lights up so much that, instead of saying anything, I just nod dumbly and lift my hand in a wave before pulling the front door behind me and walking out into the darkness.

Chapter 28

I look in the mirror and don't recognise myself. Which, under the circumstances, feels like a good thing. As a child, Flora loved me having long hair, couldn't care less about the knots that would form after weeks of neither of us bothering to brush it. And that style just continued, became part of who I was. However many regrets I've carried with me, I haven't wanted to risk breaking my connection with the past, and keeping a familiar look felt part of that. So having a pixie cut stare back at me now is unnerving to say the least.

But hopefully it will work. It has to. I know what a gamble I'm taking in accepting Charlie's invite to spend Christmas Day at his house. While I wasn't allowed to know anything about Charlie's new family when he was adopted, the same privacy wasn't afforded to me, so I have to expect that they've searched for me online. It felt like a close call at Battersea Art Centre, sharing the space in front of Charlie's winning painting with his adopted mother. Yet here I am, soon to sit at her table, share her food. What am I thinking? But I just couldn't turn him down. And I couldn't bear the thought of spending it with my parents either, sitting in silence, the memory of my violent outburst still fresh for us all.

I had the idea to get my hair cut on my walk to work last

Sunday morning, but I haven't had chance until today. The flu that has been doing the rounds at the café has meant I've worked eight days straight to cover missing staff, and longer shifts than usual. I'm exhausted, but it's good to have the extra money. There's only another week or so until the end of the year and then Jo will want to make my employment official. I hope I've done enough to prove I'm worthy of it, but until I have the conversation – that awkward conversation – I can't be sure.

I turn away from the mirror and inspect the floor inside my wardrobe. Buying a new dress hadn't been in the plan, but when I'd seen it in the store window, I couldn't help pausing, drawn to its optimistic colour. Spurred on by my bigger than usual pay packet, I'd stepped inside the shop and ten minutes later emerged with a new outfit for the Bittersweet Christmas party. But my impulsiveness hadn't extended to shoes and now I need to work out what will go with a pale blue belted midi-dress in the middle of winter.

Deciding I can get away with Converse trainers, I pull them on and head downstairs. It's only seven o'clock and the party won't start until at least eight-thirty, but I'm keen to get out of the house. Since our argument Flora has taken up painting. She claims that it provides an outlet for her mixed emotions over me finding Charlie, but I think it's just her way of reminding me of him, and that she won't stay silent forever. Either way, the living room is now a mess of discarded canvases, dirty rags and stained paint pots, and so even more uninhabitable than before.

I pull on my thick Puffa coat, and as soon as I step outside, I'm grateful for its warmth. I wonder if I'll ever feel comfortable taking a bus ride again, to travel alongside strangers without fear overwhelming me. I hope so, because I'm tired of walking. The night is biting, but I've made a deal with myself – walk there, cab back – so I pull the zip up a little higher and start the familiar journey.

I arrive on Old York Road soon after eight. The lights are

still bright at Bittersweet and I can see a few customers finishing their coffee, which means I'm too early for the party. I scan the road and my eyes settle on the Anchor pub where Charlie and I shared a drink after Hana's birthday surprise. The thought of sitting down in a warm, cosy pub for half an hour is tempting; one drink to loosen me up, I tell myself, and make my way inside.

*

When I walk through the café door one hour and two drinks later (the first one went down with surprising speed), Bittersweet has been transformed into a mix between Santa's grotto and *Saturday Night Fever*. Four disco balls have been added to the Christmas fairy lights, and the combination of white sparkle and multi-coloured strobes is quite overpowering. The sound system, usually playing soft background music, is blaring out Christmas classics, and a few people are already drunk enough to be taking 'Rocking Around the Christmas Tree' at its word. The place is packed with bodies – many I don't even recognise – clinking glasses and spreading their own version of Christmas joy. Despite spotting Charlie looking equally bemused, I have a strong urge to leave before anyone notices me.

'Hey, nice hair! Guys, Fiona's gone all Cara Delevingne on us.'

It's too late; Marco has spotted me. I take a deep breath and wander over. I have no idea who Cara Delevingne is, but I sense that asking him might incur horror, so I just turn my head towards Charlie. Now I'm here, I find myself wanting his approval for my new look. But it's Hana who speaks next.

'Wow, Fiona. Looks awesome. It's pretty radical though.' She moves a bit closer. 'Come on, spill. New man? New woman?' She giggles at her suggestion, doesn't realise how accurate it is.

'Just fancied a change,' I manage.

'Well, it will look even better with a glass of prosecco in your hand.' Marco hands me a flute of bubbling liquid and I take a

201

long, grateful gulp. I'm not used to all these compliments. Luckily the sharp clink of cutlery on glass makes us all turn around. Jo has climbed onto a table and is now waving her arms around like an aircraft marshal.

'Hey, everyone! Wow, look at you all. I may be three glasses down, but I am SO proud of my amazing team right now.'

She's swaying slightly and I feel the urge to reach my hands up. Her husband Nate obviously has the same idea because he moves a little closer; raises his arms slightly.

'And I have not one, but two surprises for you. The first surprise is ... drum roll please.'

She looks at Marco and he obliges, beating his hands against the table with impressive speed.

'We won the Christmas competition! We are officially the most Christmassy business on Old York Road.'

Without really understanding why that's a good thing, everyone lets out an involuntary cheer and starts clinking glasses with each other.

'Hey, don't forget I have a second surprise!' Jo flaps her hands, trying to recapture everyone's attention.

'Do you need another drum roll?' Marco asks, not waiting for an answer before he starts whacking the table again.

'You've all got the day off tomorrow!' she spurts out.

That gets our attention. It's Christmas Eve tomorrow and the café is going to be full of local families and last-minute shoppers. I can't imagine any of us were looking forward to working that shift.

'Call it a Christmas bonus. You'll get a full day's pay, and a lie-in. So no excuses for not enjoying the party.' A hiccup escapes and Jo thrusts her hand up to her mouth. From the look on her face, she can't decide whether it's horrifying or hilarious.

'So who's going to cover?' Hana asks, ever the responsible employee.

'Don't worry about that. I've got the whole tribe helping. Nate, the kids, my parents, the in-laws, both my sisters; maybe even my brother, although he probably won't turn up.'

She's gabbling now and I force myself to tune out. The more family members she lists, the lonelier I feel. Someone fills up my now-empty glass and I take a long swig. The liquid feels soothing against my constricted throat.

*

I've no idea what time it is but I'm in that fuzzy bubble where it doesn't matter anymore. I lean further in against Marco. We're sitting on a table pushed up against the counter and staring in the same direction. While his legs are swaying in time with the music, mine are still. They need a rest. I was persuaded to dance when The Pogues' 'Fairytale of New York' came on, but then chose to stay on the makeshift dance floor for the next ten or so songs. I'm feeling the effects of those exertions now. And the alcohol of course.

'Well, it's about time,' Marco says with a fatherly wisdom that he's not really old enough for.

I nod and smile and we both continue watching Charlie and Hana kissing. I'm sure they'd prefer not to have an audience, but I don't care. Mother's prerogative.

'They make a great couple,' I say. 'You know, Marco, there was a time when Char ... Ben, thought you had a thing for Hana.' My heart starts pounding at my slip-up, but Marco hasn't even noticed. I silently thank Bing Crosby for drowning out my voice.

'Me? Hah! That's funny.'

'Because you're gay?' I instantly regret my words because Marco's permanent smile completely disappears.

'How did you know?'

Luckily his voice is stilted rather than angry, and I let out a sigh of relief. 'I'm so sorry for blurting it out like that. I don't have a sixth sense or anything. I'm just old. Call it life experience. I promise I haven't said a word to anyone.'

'And you don't care? Don't see me differently?'

I look into Marco's eyes and am shocked to see such uncertainty there. This energetic, confident man, with a funny comment for every situation, is just as vulnerable as the rest of us when the truth is laid bare.

'Differently from what? There's no normal, you know. You are different, I suppose. But only in your ability to light up a room.'

He smiles then. A big one. And puts his arm around my shoulder. 'You make it sound so simple, Fiona. It's a bit more complicated when you're the middle child of a strict Catholic family. My brother works on building sites with our father, my sister is already working on having a bigger brood of kids than our mother. I'm the odd one, moving to England, caring more about clothes than football.'

'So they don't know?'

'Wow, no. Some friends from back home are coming over for New Year and I'm already exhausted at how much pretending I'm going to have to do. I'm taking them to Edinburgh just so that I can avoid my life here.'

'Living a lie never ends well,' I warn, but the sting of hypocrisy is so strong that I struggle to maintain my composure. It's only by continuing to talk that I manage it. 'Look, I don't know your family, but I do know everyone who works here. And no one would care less about you being gay. So at least don't hide from us.'

I miss his response, but I feel his lips against my cheek and his arms pulling me in for a hug. Then he's off the table, grabbing Sammy's hand and whirling her back on to the dance floor. I feel a warm glow for making him feel better. This is my proper family, I realise. With Charlie at its centre.

'Hello.' Hana has sidled up on my left, and the sad look on her face grips at my stomach. Only a few minutes ago I was smiling at the sight of her and Charlie having finally found each other. What could have changed so suddenly?

'Mind if I sit here?' she asks.

204

'Of course not.' We sit in silence for a while, but eventually I break it. 'I saw you with Ben,' I say the name firmly; I'm not making that mistake again.

'Yeah, that was a bad idea.'

Without warning, anger surges up. How dare she mess with his head like that? I manage to control it, just. 'Really?'

'Not because I don't like him, I really like him actually.'

The anger seeps away.

'But the timing ... I had to tell him I'm leaving.'

'Where are you going?'

'Home. For a while. Not sure when I can come back.'

'Back to the Czech Republic?'

'My babicka has cancer. My grandmother. I want to be with her.'

'I'm so sorry, Hana.' Tonight is full of announcements. 'Are you close?'

She hesitates for a moment, weighing up my question. 'Perhaps,' she says eventually. 'She's not a normal grandma; you know, the type who bakes cakes and gives out wise words about boyfriends and house rules. She calls it her nerves. We joke that she's scared of her own shadow. Either way, she's always been someone who needs taking care of. I guess that makes us close in a way.'

'But she doesn't give much back?'

'She loves me. I know that. But her advice is always to say no, to stay at home, to never try anything. It drives me crazy.'

'Mothers, grandmothers. It's their job to worry, I suppose.'

'Mama says she wasn't always that way. That something happened to her during the Prague Spring.'

'Prague Spring?' I ask, embarrassed by my ignorance of Czech history.

'Sorry. There's no reason you should know. It happened in 1968. We were part of Czechoslovakia then, had been communist for twenty years. But the mood was changing and a new leader was voted in, a more liberal one with big plans. My babicka was a student at Prague University. She was so excited, when Dubcek came to power, was certain things would change for the better.'

'So what happened?'

'The Russians didn't like it; thought they would lose their grip on us. So they sent their soldiers. My babicka said it was horrible, watching the Soviet tanks roll in.'

'And that made her scared?'

'At first it made her angry. She became part of the resistance.'

'And then?'

'She was arrested; spent two days in jail. Nothing terrible happened, but they threatened it, over and over. Then they just let her go. Those forty-eight hours created a fear so deep that it changed her forever. Crazy, hey.'

'Not so crazy.' A shiver crawls up my spine. I think of that night, how profoundly it changed me.

'It was over fifty years ago. And she still begged me not to come to London; was scared I'd get mugged, or caught in the crossfire of some gang fight.'

I can see the man now. The whites of his eyes. The glint of his knife. And then Dan, trapped. My skin feels clammy. My breathing starts to stutter.

'Fiona, are you okay?' Fiona. The name was supposed to symbolise a fresh start. But it's bullshit. Those memories, that night, I'll never escape it.

I focus on Marco, still spinning on the dance floor, and his happy grin draws me back to the party. 'Let's dance,' I shout, with a level of mania I didn't intend. I don't wait for Hana's response before grabbing her hand and pulling her onto the dance floor, close to the speaker. I want to drown out those memories with loud Christmas tunes.

I close my eyes and swirl, arms reaching up, body brushing against other dancers as the alcohol boosts our confidence and frees our movement. I need to forget what happened before, concentrate on the future. The Pogues comes back on and I dance with more enthusiasm. I've built something with Charlie, something I barely allowed myself to wish for. The dance floor is packed now. I spin again.

Then *slam!*

Stars explode in my eyes.

'Oh shit, Fiona! Sorry!'

I stagger backwards. Pain threatens to overwhelm me.

'Jesus, get her some tissues, a napkin.'

My nose is on fire, my whole face feels like it's buzzing with an electric shock. Blood gushes down my chin, drips onto my new dress. How can there be so much blood in my nose? My eyes sting with tears, distorting my vision. I can see Marco, rubbing his elbow, his face tight with remorse. And Hana thrusting Santa napkins into my hand.

And I can see Charlie. His eyes wide, his body frozen in fear.

Chapter 29

SEPTEMBER 2005

Phoebe

'Do you need a top-up, Phoebe darling?'

I rest my hand over the top of my glass and shake my head. I know that Richie will be happy for us when he finds out I'm pregnant; he's not the type to fret about how the clients will react. But our first scan isn't until next week, and I don't want to tempt fate by telling him our news prematurely.

'Probably for the best. You'll need a clear head when you collect your award later.' He winks at me, then reaches across the table, proffering the bottle towards Dan.

'There are five of us nominated,' I remind him. 'And Susie Hall has got two clients into the RSC this year. She has to be favourite.'

'Well, that's not the rumour I'm hearing. Dan, you won't force me to drink alone will you?'

'Of course not.' Dan smiles at Richie and reaches forward with his glass, but I notice it's still over half full. That's not like him, and I wonder why he's holding back. Maybe this is part of his promise to make our night together perfect, his recognition of my not drinking. 'Cheers.' He clinks Richie's glass first and then leans over to meet mine. 'I think you're going to win too.'

'Really?'

'You're definitely the best theatrical agent I know, anyway.'

'Gee, thanks,' I tease back. We both know how exclusive that group is.

'Ah, excuse me!' Richie joins in, puffing out his chest and pretending to be offended. 'I taught her everything she knows.'

Our laughter is interrupted by the buzz of a phone. Dan reaches inside his dinner jacket, looks at the number flashing on his Blackberry and frowns. 'I better take this,' he says, pushing back his chair.

I watch him walk to the back of this proudly ostentatious venue. Café de Paris has long been a favourite with London's rich and famous. A heady escape into luxury and flamboyance, it's a natural habitat for people like Flora, adorned with elaborate chandeliers and dramatic sweeping staircases. With its many pillars holding up a line of ornate balconies, I imagine the illicit conversations that have taken place in the shadows, and wonder who has whisked Dan away from my side.

But when he strides back to the table, with a deeper frown and an air of urgency, any hint of jealousy disappears. 'Are you okay?'

'That was Flora.'

I sit more upright and feel my shoulders tense. 'What did she want? Why didn't she call me?'

'She didn't want to disturb you apparently, in case you were on stage or whatever. Charlie's woken up and he won't settle.'

'Did she sound drunk?'

Dan doesn't respond and the silence says it all.

'I need to go, Phoebe.'

'I know.' My eyes well up and I have to concentrate really hard to stop the tears. I should be worried about Charlie, consoling him, protecting him from my awful, irresponsible mother. But all I can think about is how my night with Dan is over. What kind of mother does that make me? Putting my happiness before my child's?

'I'll get a cab – it shouldn't take too long to flag one down.'

I shake my head. 'No, take the car. It'll be quicker, and Charlie deserves to have you home as soon as possible.'

'I would prefer to drive, but only if you promise to stay at the hotel. I don't want you getting a cab home by yourself late at night.'

I look over at Richie, feel the warmth of his concerned gaze, think about the money he's spent. 'I guess I could still stay.'

'You'll love it, Phoebe. And you deserve it, somewhere plush to recharge.'

I picture the hotel room with its jacuzzi bath, luxury bedding and 24/7 room service. It might not be the fairy-tale ending I was hoping for, but perhaps I can salvage something from this mess. 'Are you sure you don't mind?'

'Absolutely. It will be fun, just me and Charlie for a night.'

'Well if you're sure; I can get the bus home in the morning.'

A smile spreads across his face, the relief that I'm okay shining through his expression. I smile back and enjoy the warmth of his kiss, his whisper of good luck. Then I give him the car keys, and with a small salute, he's gone.

*

'And the winner of Theatrical Agent of the Year 2005 is …'

My heart booms inside my chest; my mouth goes dry. I imagine walking onto the stage, pray that I don't trip up the steps, or stumble over my acceptance speech. I look at the trophy, wonder what shelf I'll put it on.

'Susie Hall!'

Not me after all. Applause erupts around me and I respond to Richie's instructions as if on autopilot. *Smile. Clap. Make eye contact.* I didn't even want the award, dammit, it was more than enough just to be nominated. But Richie had been so sure. And Dan isn't here. And now I feel like crying again.

'Oh, darling, I'm so sorry.'

'I'm fine. It's fine.' I smile at Richie, but it's false. The muscles in my cheeks are stiff with the effort.

'Are you sure? Because I've just spotted Oskar Jansen.'

I follow his eyeline until I see the Dutch supermodel-turned-serious actor holding court in a red velvet armchair at the back of the room. He graduated from RADA in the summer with a distinction, and Richie is one of a number of agents trying to sign him.

'Of course, you go. I might do some networking myself.'

'That's my girl. Tougher than you look.'

I watch him scamper in Oskar's direction, nodding and waving to people as he snakes a route around the many tables. It's a small industry and everyone pretends to be friendly, but we're adversaries first and foremost. There are plenty of people I know here too; I should go and say hello. But they'll offer me sympathy, and I'll tell them how honoured I was just to be nominated, and they won't believe a word of it. I just haven't got the energy.

It's past eleven o'clock and the agent of the year award was the last to be announced, the grand finale. The lady from the Globe theatre who handed out the awards has disappeared, probably heading back to her husband, or wife maybe. The venue staff are clearing the tables and a few guests have decided the stage makes a really good dance floor. Richie seems to have hit it off with Oskar, and I can see Piers – Paul's old agent and my first boss – entertaining a tribe of young assistants with his wild stories from yesteryear.

I feel so lonely.

Of course there's nothing keeping me here. I could just pick up my overnight bag from the cloakroom, head west down Piccadilly. Even in these heels I could be at the hotel in under ten minutes, sinking into a bubble bath five minutes later with a box of Pringles and a large glass of Coke.

Except I'd still be alone.

Not tickling Charlie with my monster fingers, or stroking his forehead to lull him back to sleep. Not climbing into bed next to Dan, listening to him promise that awards mean nothing compared to the new life growing inside me. And how he doesn't need a piece of silverware to know how talented I am.

I dig deep into my clutch bag and find an old biro. I scribble a note on a discarded menu and leave it by Richie's jacket. It's the perfect sweetener, and I'm sure Richie won't waste any time in offering my now redundant hotel room to his latest target. I pick up my denim jacket from the glamorous cloakroom assistant and head out into the night air. It had been a warm day, but the temperature has dropped, and I wish I'd thought to wear a thicker coat. Now that I've made the decision to go home, I feel impatient to get there, and I shrug off Dan's plea that I don't get a cab home alone.

Leicester Square is heaving with people: wide-eyed tourists enjoying the buzz of this cosmopolitan city, plus groups of young workers as they move from pub to club or late-night bar. I usually love the energy of this place, the anomaly of such crowded streets after dark, but hailing a taxi here will be impossible, so instead, I head south down the much quieter Whitcomb Street.

My feet are killing me by the time I reach Nelson's Column and I fight the urge to remove my stilettos. But there are plenty of black cabs trundling around Trafalgar Square, or down the Strand, and many of them with their yellow light shining, showing they're free. As one comes towards me, I lift my arm as a signal, but the driver stops twenty metres away, and I watch a man in a business suit climb into the back. I try again with the next cab I see, but either his light is on by mistake or he doesn't notice me because he sails straight past. I wander a bit further down the road to see if my luck improves, but all the empty cabs seem to have disappeared.

And then it starts to rain.

I swear under my breath and head for the nearest cover, which turns out to be a bus shelter next to Pizza Express on the Strand. I know this place, perhaps better than I should, and I find myself smiling as I sink into the plastic seat. As a teenager, I'd get the bus into town with my friends; the 87 would drop us here and we'd wander up to Covent Garden, stare in shop windows and dare each other to pickpocket the tourists (a dare none of us ever played out). There might be a spliff at some point, or a bottle of cider. Then we'd amble back to this bus stop and giggle until the bus arrived to take us home.

The loud sigh of a bus pulling up brings me back to the present. Amazingly, it's the number 87. This will take me back to Wandsworth, then it will only be a short cab ride to Southfields from there. Should I do it? For old times' sake?

Decision made, I extract my Oyster card from my bag. Buses only started accepting these a few months ago and I still feel slightly relieved when the yellow pad beeps its acceptance of me. It's warmer on the bus and I feel my shoulders relax a little as I head upstairs and slip into a window seat close to the back; the seat we'd always choose if it was free. The top deck is almost empty, and the only sound comes from the patter of rain on the window. A dark-haired girl in a leather jacket is sat at the front, big headphones covering her ears, and an old man is fast asleep a couple of seats behind her. It's almost tranquil.

After a minute, the engine rumbles into life, and I see the flash of an indicator through the window. I settle back against the royal blue seat covering and wait for the bus to leave. But before the driver finds space in the traffic, noise erupts below me and then I hear feet pounding up the staircase. Three boys bundle their way to the back of the bus, eyes wide and breathing shallow. I instinctively know they're running away from something and panic starts to rise in my chest. But am I scared for them, or me?

The last in the trio sits at the midway point, opposite the

213

aisle, and I can tell that he feels exposed. We catch eyes for a moment, and I see both fear and bravado in his. He looks so young, 15 at a push, and I find myself thinking that he shouldn't be out this late on a school night. When did I get so middle-aged? I smile, to reassure him. Whatever danger they've run from, they've made it; they're safe now.

But he doesn't smile back because his attention is pulled away by more noise. Loud scuffling, heavy footsteps banging on the stairs. There are four of them, teenagers still perhaps, but also proper men, with wide chests and Parka hoods shadowing their faces. They fall still when they see the boys and I sense what they're thinking; no need to rush now, their prey have nowhere to run. Then they start to move forward, taking their time, intimidating with their swagger and silence.

I push myself back against the window. I'm not part of this argument and I need to create some distance. But I can't help stealing a glance at the three boys, their eyes darting left and right in a futile search for an escape route. Should I pull the emergency cord? Stop what might happen before any damage is done? But what would I say? These teenagers are scaring me, officer; the way they walk, the threat in their stares. What label would that give me? I look at the girl at the front of the bus, her head moving slightly to some beat that only she can hear. The old man is still fast asleep, arms crossed over the gentle curve of his belly. They don't care what's going on. I hear Dan's soothing voice in my head – *Not your problem, Phoebe* – and realise I don't need to care either.

The bus is moving now so I stare out of the window, try to let the grandeur of Whitehall calm my nerves. We pass the Cenotaph, an imposing stone structure built to honour the bravery of British soldiers, and I silently ask them to get me home safely. No one is saying a word behind me, but the air is heavy with simmering testosterone and it would only take a spark to set it on fire.

The bus lurches suddenly, the driver heavy on the brake, and one of the men loses his balance, falling forwards towards the boy facing the aisle. The boy screams in fear and suddenly he's holding a knife, waving it left and right. 'I'll cut you, man. I'll fucking cut you!'

A gasp escapes from my lips, but the man just laughs, reaches inside his coat and pulls out a length of metal pipe. 'Oh yeah?'

Then it starts.

The four men surge forward. It's a blur of rustling coats and clenched fists. I hear muffled swearing and panting, catch the glint of a knife, rising then disappearing again.

I need to do something. Stop this.

But I can't move.

I'm pushed up against the window. I feel my bladder loosen and I squeeze it shut, but I can't stop my heart from pounding in my ears. Like one terrifying monster, the tussling bodies sway towards me. I can smell their sweat, the stench of cortisol leaking out of their pores. If I stay stock-still, if I pretend I'm not here, they won't hurt me.

They'll just hurt each other.

Like the man on the floor, blood pouring out of his head.

The one I'm not looking at, because it's *not my problem*.

But it's too late anyway. The boy, the one I smiled at, the one with the knife, he's heading for me. He's going to stab me. Why me? I haven't seen anything. I'm not a witness. I just want to get home. To Dan and Charlie.

But he's not heading for me.

He's falling on me.

He's bleeding on me.

Chapter 30

DECEMBER 2019

Ben

The angry fire burning inside him has gone out. Not smouldering, ready to reignite with the smallest spark; but absent. The smell of her skin, the taste of her lips. For the first time in forever, Ben feels totally calm.

As the kiss deepens, Ben feels himself falling. In love, yes. But also, physically falling. Descending into somewhere new. Dopamine floods his body, and he can feel it on his skin. A fizz of excitement. How can this be happening? Even dreaming of this moment had felt wrong, like he was tainting Hana just by imagining being with her. But when, fuelled by all that free alcohol, he'd spurted out his true feelings, she'd actually smiled, then leaned in for a kiss. And it had felt so good.

Too good to be true perhaps.

Ben senses Hana pulling away from him. He opens his eyes and tries to hide his disappointment. 'Everything okay?'

'There's something I need to tell you.'

Ben leans back a bit further but stays focused on Hana's face. The words make his stomach lurch, but he loves the deep brown of her eyes, so much better than the dark blue of his own. 'You're married?' he jokes, anything to delay her confession.

'No, idiot.' She stifles a giggle and pushes his knee with hers. It feels good, making her laugh, but the satisfaction is temporary. 'I'm leaving London.'

'What?' Hairs rise on the back of his neck.

'Going home for a while.'

'When will you come back?' he asks, trying to keep his voice steady. Why does this always happen to him? A taste of something good, then bang, it's gone again.

'I don't know, my grandma is sick.'

'Sorry to hear that,' Ben manages. He thinks about what life could have been like, Hana as his girlfriend, someone this amazing in his corner. What it won't be like now. 'It sounds like you could be gone a long time.'

Hana drops her head, and her face disappears from view, her warm eyes out of sight.

'Are you definitely even coming back?' he asks, a new hardness to his tone.

'Yes of course.' But she doesn't look up.

'I'm going to get a drink,' Ben murmurs. He needs to get away. How could he have been so stupid? He'd allowed himself that moment of happiness, opened himself up to thinking life might actually be getting better, yet again. When will he fucking learn?

He pushes his way through to the counter, doubling up as the bar this evening. He's sick of prosecco, its dancing bubbles taunting him; he needs something stronger. He spots an unopened bottle of vodka, and with a satisfying twist, cracks the seal. He half fills a plastic cup and takes a large gulp. He's not used to spirits and the first mouthful sets off his gag reflex, but he swallows it down and the second one is easier. Fuck Hana. He doesn't need her. Fuck his family, his teachers with their condescending smiles, and Jake with his sympathy stare. Fuck them all.

Ben scans the room, his vision more fluid now. Hana is sat on one of the tables, leaning against Fiona, confiding in her. The older woman is listening attentively, asking the odd question, concentrating on the answer. He feels a stab of jealousy. Fiona is the only person he has left; he can't let her be taken from him too. He watches them both stand up, and Fiona lead Hana onto the dance floor. 'Fairytale of New York' is playing again, and Fiona clearly loves the song because she's spinning around, arms swinging high. Not like her at all, and Ben allows himself a little smile at her antics. Marco is dancing too, like a crazy gazelle, limbs flying in every direction.

So it's not surprising that they collide.

Marco's elbow smashes into Fiona's face. Her head flies back. When it rights itself, blood is gushing out of her nose. Ben watches, transfixed, the vodka adding its own vivid filter. The blood is dripping now, down her chin, onto her dress. The brutality of crimson against the tranquillity of pale blue. It looks familiar somehow.

And terrifying.

'You okay, Ben? You look like you've seen a ghost.'

He can't stop looking at her, the shock on her face, the blood-stained dress. He was watching them dance; he should have warned her.

'Poor Fiona, what a klutz Marco is. Hana's looking after her though; nosebleeds always look worse than they are.'

Ben feels Jo's hand run up and down his arm, as though she's trying to rub some life back into him. This is like her. Disrespectful of boundaries, tactile with everyone. He wants to rip her hand away and scream in her face. 'I'm fine, Jo.'

Why can't he stop staring at Fiona?

He forces his head around, away from the bloody scene. Then he takes a step back, and thankfully Jo's hand slips away. 'I might head off now.'

'Really? I thought you teenagers partied until dawn.'

Ben's urge to escape feels primal, so having to delay it for some modern-day social nicety is excruciating, but isn't that what he's taught himself over the years? Hide the compulsions, pretend to be sane? 'Only if there's class A's on offer.' He grins to soften his response, but it does its job, leaving her speechless for a moment, enough time for him to disappear into the shadows of the party, and then out on to the street.

Ben breathes in the freezing cold air and enjoys the relief at being free of them all. But it's so overwhelming that tears threaten. He can't fucking cry. He screws his eyes closed to stop the flow, but there she is again, behind his eyelids. Fiona. Blood on her dress. Then it's Hana, telling him she's leaving. He whips his eyes open and starts to sprint, under the bridge and over the main road. He runs down Smugglers Way, where the borough's waste disposal centre shares prime riverside frontage with high-rise luxury apartments, and out onto the river path. When he gets to the Thames, he leans against the iron railings and stares into the water. Putney Bridge is to his left, a succession of lights under its arches creating a streak of fire beneath, but the glow doesn't stretch to where Ben is.

In the darkness, with the only noise coming from the water lapping against the river wall, Ben allows himself to replay what just happened. Gripping on to the cold iron bar, he brings back the image of Fiona, blood smeared across her dress. Why did it terrify him so much? And if it was so frightening, why couldn't he stop staring?

And why did it feel like it was all his fault?

He closes his eyes and the image gets stronger. He can't see her face though, just the stain of red, the cut of her dress slicing her chest into a V. He opens his eyes. Fiona's dress had a high neck – that's why the blood dripped onto it so quickly from her nose. Why is he getting that mixed up? But the background is different too. In his mind he sees a small window and a front door, not Christmas decorations and disco lights.

Why is his mind playing tricks on him?

Swearing into the darkness, he pushes off the railing and starts walking along the river path. It's eerie and he half wishes that a gang of kids would show up, push him over the railings. Clear his mind permanently. But the path stays empty and eventually he cuts south, nowhere to go except home.

He doesn't know this side of Wandsworth very well, and when he reaches a gridwork of narrow streets, he realises he's lost. Pastel-coloured terrace houses run in long regimental lines, only broken up by three or four matching streets at right angles. With trees planted at regular intervals, bare branches sparkling with frost, Ben finds the pattern comforting, and he walks the length of one street that follows the tube line from Southfields. But when he reaches Wimbledon Park, he realises how far he's walked in the wrong direction. Instead of just retracing his steps, he chooses another street to make the return journey by. It's almost identical, and yet feels different somehow. Safer. He looks up at the street sign attached to one of the houses that sits at the end of a terrace. Clanwell Street. He says the name out loud.

Jesus, now a street sign sounds familiar. He's really losing it.

He looks back at the sign attached to the cream render, then down at the front door. It should be blue, not grey. He knows that for some reason.

Then he sees a child's cuddly toy. A rabbit. Lying on the pavement. Two black eyes staring up at him. He blinks, looks again. There's nothing there. What the hell is happening to him?

Finally, he gives in to the urge that has followed him through the streets of Wandsworth. Tears flow down his face. Loud sobs rack through his ribcage. He's losing his mind; he feels so alone. He suddenly wishes Fiona was there; she's the only person who comes close to understanding him.

He looks back at the house and imagines her standing there. Her hair looks longer, darker; her face a little fuller.

He wants her to hold him, but he's scared.

Because there's blood on her dress.

And he's angry, guilty too.

He turns away from the house with the sign and the wrong colour door, and runs for his life, for his sanity. And the safety of home.

Chapter 31

SEPTEMBER 2005

Phoebe

There's a boy lying on me, bleeding. The brutal irony of carrying a weapon, then having it wrenched from your grip and thrust into your chest.

But I can't look at the boy. I can only stare into the whites of the man's eyes, the one now pointing the knife at me.

The blade isn't shining anymore, it's dirty, smeared with someone else's blood.

'What did you see, lady?' he growls.

I'm sobbing in fear, but I can't let a sound escape in case it makes him angrier, brings me further out of the shadows, so I swallow each one, my body swelling with the effort. 'Nothing,' I whisper. 'I saw nothing.'

'Right answer.' But he still jabs the knife at me, and I can feel it slicing my skin before it even reaches me. I let out a scream, but he just laughs, stopping the knife just short of my face. Then it disappears inside his jacket and he follows his mates down the stairs, banging and clattering, hoods up against the glare of the CCTV cameras.

They're gone, and I want to cry with relief, but I can't. I'm in a warzone, like a scene from one of Dan's PlayStation games. One of the boys has pushed himself into the back corner of the bus, his knees up against his chest. He's shaking like Nana's old washing machine and I love to see it because it means he's alive. Another is lying face down on the floor, blood seeping from his head. I should go to him, try to help, but how can I when the weight of the third boy, the young one who I reassured with a smile, is leaning on me?

'Jesus, fuck!' The girl leaps up out of her seat, her voice ringing out across the bus, headphones crashing to the floor. The old man is awake now too, gasping in horror.

I pull on the boy's shoulder, turning him round. His white sweatshirt is heavy with blood, the stain spreading at a terrifying speed.

The old man lunges for the emergency alarm. A loud siren-type noise explodes in my ears and seconds later the bus heaves to a stop.

But the blood doesn't stop flowing. I spot the small tear in the fabric, less than an inch in size, but right by his heart. How can I possibly save him? All those missed opportunities to stop this, and now it's too late. He will die here, in front of me.

I suck in some air and try to forget everything except his immediate needs. I bunch up some material and, with the heel of my hand, push it into the wound, like a roadblock diverting traffic back to the safe zone.

Footsteps pound up and down the stairs. Screams and cries and swear words sail around the small space. The dark-haired girl wraps a jumper around the head of the boy on the floor. And finally, I hear the faint sound of an ambulance siren, and I pray that it arrives in time.

*

'He's dead, isn't he?'

The police officer looks down at the pavement, pulls at the bottom of his stab vest. 'I'm sorry, I can't …'

'I watched them. The paramedics. I heard them say it.'

He shrugs and I can't look at him anymore. 'Have you been checked over?' he asks. 'You've had a shock too, remember.'

'I'm fine. I just want to get home.'

'I understand that, but why don't I ask one of the paramedics—'

'I'm fine,' I repeat, interrupting him.

He shrugs again. 'It's your call. But I'm afraid you can't go home just yet. I need you to come to the station, give a statement.'

Panic starts to rise again in my chest. My whole body is exhausted; I can't do this now. 'But I've told your colleague everything I know; that guy in the grey hoodie,' I say, pointing to the detective who calmly took notes as I relived each moment, the violent images threatening to overwhelm me with each new revelation. Flashes of the boy's lifeless expression filter into my mind and my belly aches with the sadness of it.

'Thank you, we appreciate that. But we'll need your clothes too, as evidence,' he says quietly. I look down at my dress. I remember being in the shop, picking it off the rack. I was drawn to its ice-blue colour, it seemed so fresh and pure, a blank slate for a new type of future. Now it's stained red. Ruined.

A noise erupts at the edge of the police cordon, distracting us both. The bus stopped on Millbank, a wide road that runs parallel to the River Thames on the north side, and the police have sectioned off a wide area around the bus. It's a busy road, exposed on all sides, and dozens of onlookers are staring at the scene, curiosity shining on their faces. But the noise is coming from one woman. News is so swift nowadays; I know that she is his mother.

'Wait here,' the officer instructs me. I watch him walk over to her, put his arm around her shoulder, hold her up when her knees buckle. My belly moans again and I cover it with my hands, holding my own child up.

I don't make a decision to leave. I just need to get away from the wailing, so I take a few steps backwards. Then a few more. Everyone is looking at the crying woman, so no one notices me slip under the cordon, or start walking towards Vauxhall Bridge. I'll go to the station first thing in the morning, I promise myself. I will wrap my clothes in clingfilm, protect the evidence. There won't be any anyway – he didn't touch me. Not physically at least.

I just need to be with my family.

On Vauxhall Bridge I stop, retrieve a pair of trainers from my overnight bag, and throw my stilettos into the river. They hardly make a sound as they hit the water, and I watch for a moment as they float towards the North Sea. It's quieter on the south side. A run of alleyways cast dark shadows on the pavement as I walk, and I try not to think who might be hiding there. I think about the whites of his eyes, the tip of the blade, the implied threat if I talked.

And I did talk. I told the police every tiny detail that I could remember.

I owed the boy that at least.

Were they watching me confide in that detective?

I look over both shoulders, then quicken my pace. Are they following me now? It's past midnight and the street is all but empty. They could pull me down any one of these alleyways and no one would notice. I start to run. My belly feels heavy, but it's good to give my adrenaline an outlet. I keep going, past the vast warehouses of New Covent Garden Market, then Battersea Dogs Home, where I dreamed of finding a playmate for most of my childhood. I slow down when I get to Battersea Park. I feel safer here, somewhere familiar, but I'm also exhausted. I can't run anymore.

I just hope that the silhouettes that have followed me here are just my imagination.

Chapter 32

DECEMBER 2019

Ben

Tears prick at Ben's eyes yet again, but this time it's out of relief. The house is in darkness; his family all tucked up in bed. He walks into the kitchen and smells the residue of home-baked mince pies. He runs his hand across the smooth marble of the island unit and enjoys the calm of the clean, white surface. Lucy would never go to bed without making sure the house is spotless. Usually it annoys him. Tonight he's grateful for its certainty.

Something catches his eye in the garden beyond the bifold doors, gleaming in the moonlight. It's a robin, skittering around on its tiny toes. He thinks vaguely about something he read once, that robins symbolise Christmas because they reminded people of postmen delivering Christmas cards back in the Victorian times. Is that why the robin is staring at him now? Is he hopping from foot to foot because he has a Christmas revelation for Ben?

Suddenly he can't sit still anymore. He starts pacing the room, ten steps across, ten steps back. The repetitive marching helps, and he finds his mind clearing, just enough to put his thoughts into order. Fiona's nosebleed scared him because it sparked a memory from his childhood. And it's plausible that he recognised the house on Clanwell Street, even that he lived there. He was born in Wandsworth after all, and he had to live somewhere. But Fiona stood there in a bloodstained dress? And wanting her arms around him? That just doesn't make any sense.

Maybe he's mixing things up. Perhaps it's just the dress that's familiar, and he's joining dots that don't exist. Is he remembering his real mother in a similar dress? Is that why he wanted to be held?

But that's not where the memory ends. He was scared, petrified. Something happened that was much worse than a nosebleed. Something terrifying.

And he can't shake the feeling that the terrifying thing was also his fault.

Ben senses that the answer is locked in the case under his bed, that those drawings will give him the clues he needs to kick-start his memories. Feeling like a lifer heading for the electric chair, he walks out of the kitchen and up the stairs towards his room. He's never really questioned why he doesn't remember anything from before he was fostered; he hasn't wanted to know before. But now it's started, he needs to know it all.

With a shaking hand, he drags the case from under his bed into the centre of the room. He twists the four numbers of the code into place until he hears the click, and then empties the contents onto the floor. He sees the knife first, gleaming up at him. He picks it up, holds the cold blade against his flushed face. The cooling effect feels good against his skin. It would be so simple. Twist the knife, disfigure himself forever. He deserves it – he's sure of that.

But why does he deserve it? He needs to find the truth, to work out what he did. With a renewed sense of purpose, he puts the knife down and fans the collection of drawings out onto the carpet. He stares at them, his portfolio of fear and rage. Some of the pictures are crinkled and ageing, others are smoother, newer. But all of them follow a theme.

He picks up one of his most recent drawings. The dark pinpricks stare at him, but they seem different now. Friendly rather than menacing, like the warmth of Hana's eyes. The rest is mainly just a block of thick red brushstrokes, the anger and fear evident from the splatters of paint reaching into the corners. But there's a darker mass in its centre. Is this just the core of his anger, or does it represent something else?

He picks up another, one of the first pictures he saved. The dark part has more form in this one. He fights the urge to look away, forces himself to think about what it represents. He's never done this before. These pictures have always been his dirty little secret. Painted fast, hated instantly and stored away as some act of penance, a reminder of his rottenness. He only ever looks at them when he wants to hate himself even more.

Now that he looks properly, he can see the dark part is made up of two sections. The longer part uses horizontal brushstrokes, left to right; four, five, six times. At the end of it, the shape changes. The strokes are circular here, the paint so thick that the red beneath it has disappeared entirely. He traces the shape with his finger. Long and straight. Round and round. Long and straight. Round and round. With a gasp, he throws the picture back onto the floor.

He knows what the shape is.

What he's painted.

It's a body. He's painted a body.

He starts pacing again then. A prone body, surrounded by red. It doesn't take a genius to work out what that colour represents. Did he see a dead body? Did he kill someone? He shakes that thought out of his head. He was only three when he was taken away from his family.

But maybe it was his fault? A game that went tragically wrong.

Some toddler tantrum so full of anger that he caused a terrible accident. Or something worse. The images from his dream surface from behind his eyelids. Stairs, he can see stairs. A front door maybe. Chaos. Noise. Fear.

But nothing that makes any sense.

He twists round and punches the wardrobe door. The pain feels good, but the sound of splintering wood just infuriates him more. It's just another mistake, another stick for his parents to beat him with. He disgusts himself. He grabs the knife, lifts up his T-shirt, runs the point along his abdomen. A bit more pressure and this could be over, the images turned to blackness, the memories gone for good.

But no, this can't happen, not now. He needs to find the truth. He pulls his hands away, closes his eyes and concentrates on his breathing. Imagines the air coming in through his nose, flooding his body with oxygen, leaving via his mouth. It's amazing how well it works. How it clears his mind, enables him to think properly about things.

About the fact that his dad died.

When he was three.

That it's his dad lying there.

Surrounded by blood. And chaos. And noise. And fear.

His mum may have had blood on her dress, but it was his dad who was killed.

Violently.

Through the glaze of tears, Ben sees the laptop sat open on his desk, the brightly coloured Google sign glowing in the darkening room. He thinks about what he could search for, the clues he could type in. *2005. Clanwell Street. Man killed at home. Child witness.* The answer will be in there, ready to be released onto his screen. He just needs to unlock the right algorithm.

It's time.

Time to find out what he did.

Chapter 33

SEPTEMBER 2005

Phoebe

I slip the key in the door and let the tears roll down my cheeks. I'm finally home. The hallway is in darkness, but I don't turn the light on, I don't want to risk it seeping upstairs and into Charlie's bedroom via his half-open door.

'Mummy?'

I let out a loud gasp. Charlie is curled up on the stairs, his new favourite place since our experiment with a naughty step spectacularly failed.

'What's wrong, Mummy?'

I flick on the light so I can see him properly, work out why he's not in bed at this hour. But it was a bad decision. His expression changes from sleepy relief to absolute terror. The front of my dress is covered in the boy's blood. I quickly pull my jacket tight around me, but it's too late. He starts crying, but when I go towards him, he backs away, squirming against the stair.

'I'm sorry to scare you; it's not my blood.'

'Did you kill someone?' His small voice trembles and I fight the urge to gather him up.

'Gosh, Charlie, of course I didn't! A boy, on the bus. He hurt himself.'

'Did you save him?'

No, I didn't save him. I let him die. 'The ambulance people took him; they'll look after him,' I lie. 'Charlie, why aren't you in bed?'

'I had a dream.'

'A scary dream?'

He nods his head and his bottom lip drops, wobbles. I take a few steps towards him and he doesn't recoil this time. I take his hand in mine. 'Why didn't you go in to see Daddy?'

'Daddy?'

The tiny hairs on the back of my neck stand up, tingle on my skin. 'Did Daddy come home, or is Grandma still here?' I think of our Jeep, its death wobble, Dan's impatience to get home. Was it parked on the street? I can't remember now.

'They argued. It woke me up.'

My shoulders release. He made it home. And of course they would argue – Dan would be furious that Flora couldn't go one night without getting drunk. But then Charlie's words come into focus. 'You were asleep when Daddy got home?'

He nods. 'Grandma told me the best story; she didn't even have a book to read from. Then she tucked me and Rabbit in, and Rabbit wanted to go to sleep, so we did.'

Why would Flora lie, drag Dan home? Had she got bored of playing the perfect grandparent? Did she have somewhere better to go?

'Grandma was really cross when Daddy got home. She said he should trust her more, that she's a good babysitter.'

'Grandma was angry?' It doesn't make sense.

'Then she said that it wasn't her job to open your eyes and that she was going to wash her hands.'

Did Dan just change his mind about Flora babysitting? But if so, who was it that called him? I need to find out what's going on. 'Shall we go upstairs, go see Daddy?'

'I called him, but he didn't come.'

'When you woke from your dream?'

'That's why I got up.'

'Daddy sleeps like a log, remember? Like the biggest, oldest tree in the forest,' I whisper.

Charlie shakes his head. 'He's not asleep, Mummy. He's not in bed.'

I look at my watch. It's nearly two o'clock, but sometimes Dan likes to stay up, watch some sci-fi movie that wouldn't interest me, or battle with virtual teenagers on his PlayStation. But the house is in darkness. I think of the man on the bus, the point of his blade, and the shadows that followed me home. My breathing shallows. I kiss Charlie's soft curls and release my hand. 'Wait here. I'll be back in two ticks.'

Slowly I walk down the hallway towards our kitchen. 'Dan?' I call out, but softly. I don't want to spook Charlie any more than I already have. I push open the door, with an inexplicable certainty that I will see Dan on the floor, blood gushing out of his heart.

But the floor is empty, the tiles shining in the moonlight flooding through the wide glass panels of our bifold doors.

I take a few more steps and then I see them.

A midnight tryst.

Two bodies lying on our new sun lounger. An empty bottle of champagne fallen prone on the decking. I grab hold of the work surface. He thinks I'm out of the picture, sleeping on goose-down pillows at the Ritz. How could he do this? After everything he's promised? I think of him taking the phone call, how far he walked away from the table. Not Flora at all. Did he plan this? My belly contracts in pain, then stabs at me.

Everything comes out in one long, guttural moan. Even the insulation from the thick glass can't shield them from the noise, and they both turn in horror. That's when my cries turn to laughter, and then I'm cackling like a demented witch. Dan looks so *caught out*. I can see his quick brain furiously flicking through which lie to tell, what angle to try, and coming up blank. They move towards the house together, in unison, and then the large glass door slides open.

'Jesus Phoebe, quit the noise.' He's chosen to go on the offensive, and his arrogance is so breathtaking that it works, stunning me into silence. 'Look, it's not what you think, okay? Jess is just a friend.'

'A friend,' I growl back.

'She's had a tough night. She just wanted someone to talk to.'

The weight of irony threatens to crush me, but I can't let it. He doesn't even ask why I'm covered in blood. He's too wrapped up in his own crisis to notice, or perhaps to care. Another wave of anger surges. 'I know that Jess is the slut you were fucking!'

'I should go.' It's the first time she's spoken, and I fight the urge to slap her. She looks so prim and proper, picking up her bag and smoothing down her skirt. All while she's ripping my family apart.

'Who you're clearly still fucking,' I hiss. My hand drops to my belly, but she pulls away from my touch.

'Phoebe …'

It's so obvious now. The late nights that he promised were work, that he swore on our baby's life were about our family's future. All lies. Just the chance for him to be with her. Our holiday, the plans we talked about. How could he say those things? 'You said it was over, promised on our baby's life.'

'It is over,' he pleads, but he can't look at me.

My voice gets louder, the release is addictive. 'Do you know that I've just pushed a dead boy off me to get to you?'

'What?'

'Stabbed in the heart, murdered in front of me.'

'Phoebe, stop.'

'Another boy, his head battered to a pulp, my shoes sliding in it.'

'Phoebe!'

But I don't heed his warning. 'Blood everywhere. Splattered all over me.'

'Mummy, stop!'

I spin round. Charlie is stood in the doorway, his beautiful features all screwed up, tears and snot dripping down his face.

'Now look what you've done!' Dan's booming voice rears up behind me. I'm torn; devastated that I could have been so stupid, but furious that Dan has twisted this to be my fault. I watch Dan dash towards our son, pick him up and rock his trembling body until the tears die down. I watch Jess take advantage of the distraction, scurrying out of the room, and then out of the house. And all the while, I don't move. I stand frozen to the spot.

Until my belly stabs again, and this time I fold over with the pain. I can't help letting out a cry.

'Can't you see what you're doing to him? Go and sort yourself out, for God's sake.'

Perhaps he's right. I'm hurting all over. Maybe I'm not seeing things straight. Could Jess just be a friend now? Did I give him the chance to explain? I don't remember. I reach out to Charlie, but he pulls away, repelled by my appearance or maybe my desperation. I suddenly realise how filthy I am. I need a shower, a jet of water to cleanse my body and clear my head. My tummy clenches again, harder this time.

I turn away from them both and head down the hall to the stairs. I clasp the banister and use it to drag my exhausted body upwards. The pains are coming more regularly now, and I time each step to fall between them. The bathroom is at the top of the stairs and I crawl inside. Our bathmat is large and fluffy; when Charlie was a baby, I would lie him on it after his bath, all snug in a towel, and tickle his feet until he laughed. I lie on it myself now. I don't want a shower; I just need to sleep. But the pain is too strong.

*

I kneel on the sullied bathmat and keen in agony. This can't be happening. I can't have lost her. My beautiful baby.

This is his fault. He promised the affair was over, on her life. Then he broke it.

How could he do that? How could she mean so little to him? He can't get away with this. Not this time.

I stand up. I don't care what I look like anymore. He needs to know what he's done.

I open the bathroom door.

They're at the bottom of the stairs. Charlie is back on the same bottom step, with Dan crouching over him. I can see Charlie's rabbit gently flapping against the side of his face as he rubs him up and down his cheek.

'What's wrong with Mummy?'

I watch Dan pause, look up and directly into Charlie's eyes.

'I'm sorry that you had to hear that, little man. Mummy said some terrible things.'

I said some terrible things? How dare he!

'She's not thinking straight. But I'll keep you safe.'

But you didn't keep our daughter safe, did you?

You let her die.

No, I'm not the monster here.

That's on you, Dan.

A surge of anger rushes through me. Enough. I half run, half fall, down the stairs. Dan looks at me in confusion as I grab his head. It feels so malleable, so vulnerable, in my hands. Like that boy on the bus. His head caved in.

'You killed my daughter, now you're poisoning Charlie!'

Dan tries to break free but I'm so strong now. Not frozen in fear anymore.

'He deserves so much better than you!'

And then I whack his skull against the radiator. Again and again. 'This is for my baby. And for my son!'

I don't stop, and he can't stop me.

And it feels glorious.

Chapter 34

CHRISTMAS DAY 2019

Phoebe

I can't get the damn earrings in. They were my first Christmas present from Charlie and I need to feel them against my skin today. To remind me that I'm not intruding on their family, it's the other way around. But my hands are shaking too much to hold the delicate post still. I roll the tiny diamond between my thumb and forefinger in an effort to calm my nerves. Charlie wouldn't have chosen them of course; not even a ten-month baby as special as him could do that. These little twinkles of love were Dan's doing. Back when he cared enough to make the effort.

I pull my ear taut, close my eyes and use my fingers to guide the earring in. Finally it works. I add the back and then adopt the same strategy with the second earring. After a couple of misplaced jabs that one goes in too. I stare at myself in the mirror. Pixie hair; full make-up to hide the faint bruising still evident across my nose; sparkly ears. It's a new woman staring back at me.

Fiona. Not the Phoebe who tried so hard to make her marriage work, to keep her family together. Or who walked a tightrope for fourteen years, swaying between a deep urge to end her life and an animal compulsion to survive.

And not the woman who walked out of HMP Bronzefield almost three months ago either. The UK's biggest female prison, with its special area for *restricted access* prisoners: the country's most serious offenders.

The solicitor thought I'd get my sentence reduced to manslaughter, that the events of the day would be enough to convince a jury of the defence of momentary lack of control. But I always knew they'd convict me of murder. The CPS made a big thing about me washing the blood off myself, like that showed I was of sound mind. But it wasn't that detail that persuaded the jury. They convicted me much earlier than that.

I saw the growing disgust on their faces during the opening speech, when that smarmy barrister with his clipped public school accent listed Dan's injuries. The shattered cheekbone and multiple fractures to his skull; the massive bleed on his brain. I watched their appalled stares become even more horrified when the presence of our son was added. His ringside seat. Twelve supposedly impartial men and women couldn't look at me after that. They found me guilty before the trial really began.

It was the judge who took pity on me. Perhaps he understood the ripple effect of gang violence more than most. Murder convictions always carry a life sentence, but the judge gets to decide how much of it is custodial, and he gave me fourteen years. I'd already served one of those on remand after leaving the clinic. So October 2019 became my D-Day. Then it would just be fortnightly meetings with my probation officer. Tom.

My barrister told me that I should be grateful to the judge for such a short sentence. He didn't understand what the true sentence for my crime was, who I'd lost forever. I wanted to hate him for his ignorance. But the truth is, I felt nothing. I just followed that prison officer out of the courtroom. Flora and Paul were in there somewhere, but I didn't even bother to look back. There were times when I wanted to kill myself inside. And there's more opportunity to make it happen than you'd think should be possible in prison. But in the end, he kept me alive. The bland letters sent by Charlie's adoptive parents twice a year told me nothing, except for one important thing. That he was still out there. However miserable my life had become, my son existed in the real world, so I had to continue existing too.

And it was the right choice because here I am, about to share Christmas lunch with him. All these months of breaking down his defences, building up his confidence, keeping Flora at bay, have paid off. We may not be mother and son in the traditional sense, but we have developed something better. A friendship. Mutual understanding. Whether that's through shared experience or DNA doesn't really matter. I pick up my phone to check the time and can't help clicking into his text message again. *Are you sure it's okay for me to come?* I'd asked. His response was short, and to the point. But he's expecting me at 1 p.m.

I pull on a pair of Hobbs high-heel boots. I remember the shop assistant calling them timeless classics when I bought them, which is lucky because it was at least twenty years ago. The leather has lasted well so they were clearly worth the two hundred pounds I paid. As I stand up, I realise that I feel braver wearing these. It's ridiculous really, how a pair of shoes can do that. In prison I wore trainers every day, and that habit just continued when I returned to London. It's weird that uncomfortable footwear can feel so liberating.

Flora is in the front room when I get downstairs. The door is closed but I can hear her singing along to the radio. *Pa rum pum pum pum.* I pause for a moment. 'Little Drummer Boy' has always been her favourite Christmas song. Every year she would sit me next to her and explain its story to me, about how the boy couldn't afford a present for Jesus so used his talent as a gift instead. She would then remind me that creative talent should never be underestimated, and I would feel guilty about my role in curbing her acting career yet again. But still, I always enjoyed that moment with her. And she taught me to love the song almost as much as she does.

I had planned to just slip out of the house to avoid any awkward questions, but that feels selfish now. When it came down to it, Flora kept my secret. I'm not sure how long a lifeline she's thrown me – neither of us has been in the mood for talking much since the wine rack incident – but I should at least wish her a merry Christmas. I push open the door. She's stood at the easel, her new favourite position, paintbrush in one hand, gin and tonic in the other. It could be any day of the year if it wasn't for the flimsy paper hat sat lopsidedly on her head, the entrails of a Christmas cracker discarded on the floor. My heart melts a bit more.

'Merry Christmas, Flora.'

Her head jolts upwards. 'Gosh darling, you startled me. It's the hair, I'm not sure I'll ever get used to it being that short.'

'Sorry. I thought a fresh start would be good.'

'Well yes indeed.' She hesitates. This is the most engaged she's been since I lost my temper with her over Charlie, so I wait for her to say more. Perhaps this is our Christmas Day truce, a chance to find some sort of peace. Eventually she continues. 'In fact, Paul and I were saying something similar only yesterday.'

'Oh?'

'Well, you have a job now. Money in your pocket, friends of your own.' She looks me straight in the eye and I realise what's coming. 'And of course there's your duplicity to consider.'

'You want me to move out?'

She nods. 'We do. It's for the best.'

'Because of Charlie?'

'You killed his father, Phoebe.'

Pa rum pum pum pum.

'There were reasons – you said you understood.'

'Charlie was sat so close that there were blood spatters on his

240

clothes. But still, you expect us to feel most sorry for you. Poor Phoebe, her life ruined, her child taken away. What about him though?'

I played my best for Him, pa rum pum pum pum.

'I wasn't thinking straight. The baby ...' My throat closes up. I can't say any more.

'And what about your father and me? Our only grandchild, taken away. But still, you put your own grief before everyone else's.'

'I took my punishment,' I just about manage through the tears. 'I did my time in prison.' How dare she lecture me? She could have stayed that night, demanded a better explanation from Dan. There's blood on her hands too.

'All those years in prison, and you didn't learn a thing.' She puts her paintbrush down, turns to face me. 'Not remorse for Dan's death. Not gratitude that Charlie gets to live a better life. You just licked your wounds and waited it out. And now you think you have the right to see him again. To lie to him; play with him like a toy.'

'I'm protecting him, not me.' Why the hell can't she see that? Shock has given way to anger. I can feel it pulsing through me.

'You can try all you like to convince yourself, but it won't work. We all know what you're capable of.'

I see flashes of Dan's head whacking against the radiator, of Charlie's frozen frame as I tried to hold him. Adrenaline surges through me and I fight the urge to push her stupid easel over, let paint splatter over the threadbare carpet. She walked out that night, told Charlie that she'd washed her hands of me. If she'd fought harder, questioned Dan more, refused to go, then maybe things would have turned out differently.

I reach up to my earlobe and rub the hard diamond between my fingers. She has no idea what kind of mother I was, how good I was. She could never understand the strength of my bond with Charlie, and how much damage it can sustain without breaking. It's not something our own relationship has ever known.

Chapter 35

SEPTEMBER 2005

Phoebe

'How are you feeling today Phoebe?'

I still can't relax in this room. I'm sure the bright seascape on the wall and the fresh flowers on the side table are designed for that purpose, but it's too empty for me. My chair on one side, hers on the other. A chasm between us, both of us knowing what that represents.

'I'm fine.'

She gives me a sympathetic smile. Half of me wants to fall at her feet in gratitude, while the other half wants to scratch it off her face with my fingernails.

'It was a tough session yesterday. I hear you had a difficult night.'

That dream. His dark hood and the white of his eyes. Except in the dream Charlie is with me. And I daren't look down in case the dead weight on top of me is actually my son. Even thinking

242

about it now takes my breath away. I shake the image out of my head and pull my knees up into my chest. My shoes leave dust prints on the dark velvet armchair, but I don't care, and she doesn't seem to either.

'I feel better now,' I lie.

'That's good.' The smile deepens. 'Are you ready to talk about Charlie?'

Her words take me straight to that staircase. My beautiful son, his face crumpled up with fear. I blink furiously. I can't let her break me down again. 'No, I don't want to.'

'I understand how painful it is, Phoebe. But it's only by talking that you can begin to heal.' She falls silent, waits. She's better at this than me, but I have so much more to lose. Seconds pass, perhaps minutes. Eventually she continues. 'And remember that I also have a responsibility to the courts.'

While she says it softly, the meaning is clear. My bail is conditional on staying at this residential clinic, and the magistrate explained that cooperating with my therapist was part of the deal. If I don't keep talking, I'll be transferred to Bronzefield women's prison until my trial. Well, fine. Let's play the game. But don't expect me to be honest.

'Yes, I remember.' I force a smile. 'We can talk about Charlie.'

'He was there – he saw it all,' she coaxes me.

I take a deep breath, wrap my heart in lead, and pick up the story. 'He'd pushed himself back against the wall, covered his face with his rabbit.' I think about his catatonic state, his wide, petrified stare. 'Not his eyes though,' I add.

'And did you go to him?'

'How could I?' I snap back. I need to be careful though; I'm losing my cool already. I pause for a moment to let my pulse rate settle. 'My hands were covered in blood, his father's blood. I couldn't touch him like that.'

'Yes of course, I see.' But she can't see. She could never imagine the horrific scene that I created in our hallway that night.

'I went into the kitchen to wash my hands. The solicitor said that was a mistake, that it weakens the loss of control defence or something. But I couldn't stay like that, could I? It wasn't fair on Charlie.'

My words hang in the air. How ridiculous they sound now, floating around my head. Was it fair that I took his dad away from him, or that I forced him to witness the killing? Was it fair that I left him alone with Dan's corpse so that I could clean myself up? Of course not. Right up to the end, I was putting my needs before his. My chest tightens, so I dig my fingernails into my palms, soak up the pain, and it releases a little.

'And after? Did Charlie allow you to get close then?'

I can't think about that moment; when I reached out, and he squirmed backwards; when I pulled him into my arms and pretended not to understand why his body shook so hard. I was taking comfort, not giving it. Bile forms in my mouth and I wonder if I'm going to be sick.

'Take a moment, Phoebe.'

'I told him how sorry I was. And that I loved him.' I blow my nose and take a few gulps from the glass of water next to me. 'And then I phoned 999.'

'That was brave.'

I look up. Was I brave? I never considered absconding; I always knew that I had to pay for what I'd done. 'Charlie needed help.'

'After everything you'd been through, you put him first.'

'I killed his dad! How is that putting him first?'

'Phoebe, you suffered a terrible trauma, then many more traumas piled on top of the first. Anyone might have been driven to do what you did in the same circumstances.'

'Do you think so?' I whisper. The smallest hint of kindness, and I can't help pushing it, trying to secure some kind of redemption. 'Maybe this is his fault, the boy on the bus, his casual brutality.'

'Go on,' she encourages.

'That night, it was like violence and death had become normal.

There was this ball of tension inside me and releasing it on Dan, well, that felt normal too.'

'And does it still feel that way?'

Seeing his skin split open and not caring. Feeling his skull crack and enjoying it. 'No of course not. Murdering my husband was not normal.'

'Murder? That's for the courts to decide.'

'I know what I've done.' Of course there's no chance of redemption for me. 'I knew it as soon as Dan's broken head slipped out of my hands – that's why I phoned the police.'

'Did Charlie speak at all, before they arrived?'

'He said sorry.'

'Sorry?'

'For wetting his pyjamas.'

Silence hangs between us, both of us mourning a childhood lost. How could I have done that to him? Every choice I ever made was for him. Taking Dan back after his affair, trying so hard to get pregnant, to give Charlie a sibling. All I wanted was to be a better mother than my own. How could I have got it so wrong?

'Did the police take Charlie?' she asks.

I shake my head. 'There were only two of them, both younger than me. I'm not sure they'd really believed my phone call.'

'Who then?'

'Two paramedics. They knelt down and talked to him, told him he would be safe with them. He didn't speak, but he took their hand.'

'Did you get to say goodbye?'

I nod. My whispered words. His little hand, raised in a tentative wave. 'I think they called a social worker after that, but I was upstairs by then.'

'They let you go upstairs?' she asks, surprise in her voice. For some reason it rattles me.

'Don't be stupid. I'm a killer, remember? I was with another paramedic; she'd arrived a few minutes after they took Charlie and noticed that I was bleeding.'

'Your miscarriage.'

'She was the first person to see a mother before a murderer.'

'And she looked after you?'

I can still see her face and the thousand messages it carried: I don't care what you've done; I can see you're in pain. I know what you've lost; I'm here for you. It was the greatest kindness I'd received since my world had shifted hours earlier on that bus. My knees had buckled under the weight of her compassion, but she'd held me up.

'She did everything that she could.'

Chapter 36

CHRISTMAS DAY 2019

Phoebe

The doorknocker makes a louder bang than I was expecting, and I skitter backwards. When Rosie opens the door, I'm trying to regain my balance and cursing the heels that had felt so empowering only an hour before.

'Hello?'

'Hi, I'm Fiona, Ben's friend from work.' It comes out more defensive than I'd planned, and she looks at me suspiciously before opening the door wider.

'Would you like to come in?'

I take a deep breath. 'Yes please. And merry Christmas.' Like a peace offering, I hold out a plastic Sainsbury's bag. It's full of presents, carefully chosen, painstakingly wrapped. But they feel cheap now against the backdrop of this perfect house.

She takes it with her free hand, the one not constrained by plaster cast, but doesn't look inside. 'Thank you. You shouldn't have though.' The honesty in her voice is unsettling. 'Anyway, come in.' She leads me through the mosaic-tiled hallway, but instead of going into the now-familiar kitchen area, she ushers me into a formal living room. The fire is crackling in the hearth and tiny fairy lights twinkle melodically in the Christmas tree. Other than the deep blue fireplace and oak wood flooring, everything in here is a delicate shade of grey. Even the Christmas cards seem to blend in.

'Dad's just opened some champagne so that's good timing.'

My stomach lurches at the thought of more champagne. I definitely drank too much of it at the Bittersweet Christmas party, and spent most of Christmas Eve feeling sorry for myself, necking paracetamol and munching crisp sandwiches while trying not to remember how the night ended. I still can't believe how much blood there was; Hana fussing with tissues, Marco distraught. And Charlie in the distance, looking so upset. Even as my nose throbbed, I'd felt a happy glow when I'd noticed how concerned he was.

'It's a little early for me,' I say, lowering myself onto the velvet sofa so that we don't have to make eye contact.

'Sparkling water then?'

I nod and watch her unscrew the cap of a San Pellegrino bottle using one hand. I want to offer my help but her determined expression holds me back, and it doesn't surprise me when she manages the task without spilling a drop.

'Here you go,' she says, passing me a glass. 'I'm sure Ben will be through in a minute.'

I hope so. Charlie has told me so much about Rosie, but in my nervousness, I'm struggling to filter out the private confessions from the public persona. I take a gulp and wonder whether I should have chosen champagne after all. It's then that I hear the voices.

'Just back off, okay!' Charlie's anger floats through the wall. I shuffle awkwardly on the sofa, smile at Rosie as though I haven't heard a word.

'Don't you dare tell me to back off! You've been holed up in your room since yesterday, haven't lifted a finger to help.'

Rosie returns my smile, but then picks up her phone and starts manically swiping and tapping. Within seconds the room erupts with classical music and I spot the four small speakers nestled into each corner. It does a good job of drowning out the argument, until it reaches a crescendo.

'YOU'RE NOT EVEN MY PROPER DAD!'

I hear a door slam and then feet pound up the stairs. Where did that come from? Charlie has never talked about his real father to me. I think of Dan, what might have been if I'd gone to the hotel, or taken a cab rather than the bus, or even gone to the police station like they'd asked. But none of those things happened. And now Charlie is calling for the father I denied him. Imagining him alone upstairs makes me fidget in my chair; I desperately want to go to him, but of course I can't.

The living room door bursts open and Greg steps inside. He's exactly as Charlie described him: broad chest, wide smile, salesman eyes. The classic rugby player turned advertising executive.

'You must be Fiona.'

I stand up, take his proffered hand, force myself to look into his eyes. There's not a hint of recognition there. Thank God. He must have seen photos of me back then – enough newspapers ran the story. It seems fourteen years in prison and a radical haircut have done their job.

'I must admit, it was rather a surprise,' he continues with contrived geniality, 'Ben announcing that he'd invited a colleague from work.'

'It's kind of you to have me,' I manage, before adding, 'Ben says you make the best Christmas lunch.'

The compliment appears to do its job, as Greg's eyes turn from accusatory to welcoming. He drops into the sofa opposite and accepts a glass of fizz from Rosie with a wink.

'Sorry about the noise,' he continues. 'Ben can be a grumpy sod at times.' That smile, smoothing over the cracks.

'Perhaps I should go. Let you sort things out.'

'Not at all. We can't turf you out on Christmas Day, can we?' There's an undercurrent to his tone. Greg is clearly someone who's used to getting his own way; no wonder Charlie struggles with him. 'Lucy will sort him out. When he's like this, she's the only one who can get through to him.'

I try to match his smile, but I can't stop a snake of envy slithering through me. We spend the next few minutes in polite conversation. Greg is good at this, but I quickly realise that I can't let him ask the questions; there's too much I need to hide. So after a few splutters and false starts I introduce the subject of Rosie and that works a treat. He's mid-flow about her university offer from Durham when I hear new, more gentle, footsteps on the stairs. The door opens slowly.

'Sorry, everyone, Ben will be down in a minute.' I look up at Lucy. Every strand of her sleek blonde hair is perfectly in place; the cobalt blue silk dress looks like it was tailored just for her. She turns her head towards me, and our eyes lock together.

My heart stops.

'Oh God, not you.'

*

'Lucy? What's wrong?' Greg's voice; concerned for his wife.

I can't move. The world is crashing down around me, but I can only sit here. Watch it happen.

'Not who? What do you mean, darling?'

What was I thinking, coming here? Of course she would recognise me. I know she was given my name, details about my life. I can only guess at the number of nights she's spent scrutinising my face on her computer screen, unable to sleep, too worried about her son's murderous birth mother coming to claim him.

250

I imagine her slipping out of bed, making a chamomile tea to calm her nerves, opening up her laptop. Dan's death might not have made the headlines, but it still featured in the inside pages. And the trial was covered more widely. Middle-class family, the link with gang violence, my celebrity clients; it was a scandal worthy of more than a few paragraphs. The accompanying photos were too grainy to give much away, but she could have looked at my Friends Reunited page. Stared at it, committed the contours of my face, the unusual blue of my eyes, to memory.

'Sorry, nothing. Ignore me. Did someone say champagne?'

I don't understand what's happening. Why is she not screaming at me? Kicking me out of her perfect house? The British stiff upper lip is not something I'll ever recognise. Is this what's happening here?

'I'll pour it for you,' a sullen voice rings out from the doorway. It's Charlie. He looks terrible. Those beautiful blue eyes are blood-shot and framed with dark circles and his skin looks even paler than usual. Is this Hana's doing? Kissing him then just upping and leaving? Messing with his head? A jolt of annoyance shoots through me; she might be my friend, but she shouldn't have played with him like that.

'Thanks, darling,' Lucy whispers to Charlie with an intimacy that ratchets my annoyance up further.

I watch her touch his arm protectively as he shuffles past her. I hope to see him flinch, but he doesn't react at all. Then he slouches on the sofa and stares first at her, then at me, like he's at a slow-motion tennis match. I want to connect with him, through our shared eyes, but his are glazed over. Then she turns to me. The look of horror has disappeared but there's a new tautness to her face. I feel like a trapped animal, my fate in someone else's hands.

'So you're the mysterious Fiona. Ben hasn't told us a thing about you. I'll warn you I'm a very nosy person – I want to know everything.' She's challenging me to a fight, but I'm no match for her. I just smile weakly in response.

'Well, while you ladies get to know each other, we'll put the finishing touches to the dinner. I hope you're hungry, Fiona; I might have overdone it on the roasties a little.'

'And the turkey, the stuffing, the pigs in blankets …' Rosie adds, counting them off on her fingers with a giggle. 'We're having a break from vegetarianism today,' she adds with an embarrassed grin.

I watch them look at each other, the mutual adoration clear to see. Even as an outsider it makes me feel uncomfortable; I can't imagine how isolating it must be for Charlie.

'Guilty as charged,' Greg says, lifting his hands up in mock surrender. I look down at mine, can't risk making eye contact with Lucy. 'Now come on, kids, kitchen. And that includes you Ben.'

I watch Greg march, Rosie skip and Charlie saunter reluctantly out of the room. I try to catch his eye again, but he's looking down at his feet now. So that leaves just us. The mothers. I push my palms against the sofa and steel myself for the onslaught. I don't have to wait long.

'What the hell are you doing in my house?' she hisses. That stiff upper lip has curled into a sneer. The social worker, Flora, now Lucy. Why does everyone think they have the right to keep me from my own son? He's half me. No one else can claim that. But I have to play this right, for his sake.

'He doesn't know. I haven't told him.'

'And you think that makes it better?' The incredulity in her voice is brutal.

'I just wanted to see him.'

'Seeing him is buying a coffee from Bittersweet, not getting a job there. Seeing him isn't taking advantage of his vulnerability, wheedling your way into his home, lying to him with your false name and fake sympathy.'

She's twisting things, but I can't let her ruin what I've worked so hard to build. 'You can't tell him; he's too fragile.'

'Don't you dare tell me how to bring up my son!' Then she

stands up, walks over to the window. She's not looking at me when she continues. 'But I don't want him to know about you either, so I won't tell him, as long as you do exactly what I say.'

'What do you mean?'

'We will all sit down for Christmas lunch.' It's like she's relaying instructions to her subordinates; the lack of emotion is chilling. 'You'll laugh at Greg's jokes and listen politely to Rosie's concerns on climate change. You'll ask me about my job and compliment the meal. Then before the brandy sauce is cold, you'll wish us all a merry Christmas and walk out of my house. And keep walking. Away from the café, from the area, and most importantly, away from Ben.'

'And what if I don't?' I want to fight her now. 'What if I take the risk that he'll forgive me?'

She laughs then, a small smug titter that sets my teeth on edge.

'It's not Ben that I'll tell, Phoebe.' I shudder as she drags out my name. 'It's the courts.'

*

I'm still reeling from Lucy's words when Rosie's head appears around the door to tell us lunch is served. My nemesis is all smiles again, and I try to follow suit, but I can't stop my hands from shaking as I reach across the table to share a cracker with her. She claims victory of course and I'm left with just a scrunched-up piece of glittery paper and the smell of smouldering chemicals in the air.

'Here, have this one. I won both of mine.' Of course you did, Rosie; a broken arm wasn't going to affect your performance. I take the body of the identical silver cracker, while remembering the garish red and green one that Flora dropped on the floor this morning. Bright colours must be banned in this house.

'Go on then, Ben, you always have the best joke.'

I can't tell whether Greg is encouraging Charlie or challenging him, but I'm glad to see it causes a reaction. He's been almost motionless since we sat down, just staring at Lucy's face, like he's waiting for something to happen. Has he sensed her unease? Worked out that her hospitality is just a performance? Perhaps he's expecting her snobbery to leak out, I hope it's nothing more than that. I watch him unravel the small piece of paper, read the joke to himself, then look up. I smile at him, try to convey my support. He doesn't react at first, but then suddenly his expression changes and his whole face lights up. And for a tiny moment, the shitstorm around me just disappears.

'Here goes then,' he says. 'Who hides in a bakery at Christmas?'

'Interesting theme.' Lucy looks at me pointedly, but luckily no one seems to notice.

'Oh, that's so easy,' Rosie says, rolling her eyes. 'A mince spy.'

'Nope.'

'Course it is, everyone knows that, Ben.' Greg's irritation bubbles up to the surface. 'You're just being difficult.'

Why is he so impatient with Charlie? I feel another wave of sympathy for my son and try to regain his attention, but his focus is elsewhere now. I watch him weigh up his options.

'A sensible turkey actually,' he says bitterly and throws the piece of paper down on the table. He picks up his knife and fork, starts pushing the food around his plate.

'I think you owe Ben an apology, Greg.' She says it quietly but there's steeliness in Lucy's voice. I have no doubt she would have the courts remove me from Charlie's life without a second thought.

'Yeah sorry, mate. Joke must have had a refresh this year.'

'Whatever.' Charlie shrugs his shoulders, continues toying with his food.

I can hardly swallow myself but I'm mindful of Lucy's demands, and I need to buy myself some time, so I force down a few mouthfuls and try to pretend nothing's wrong. 'Delicious food, Greg. Are you a keen cook?' I add a fake smile that Flora would be proud of.

'I am now, I guess. I learned the hard way though.'

'Oh?' I'm not really interested, but it's a relief to have the spotlight taken away from me.

'Lucy used to do it all. But Rosie's birth was, ah, complicated. She was in hospital for quite a while, so it was a case of learn quick or starve.'

'That must have been traumatic.' I'm on autopilot, saying the right thing; Charlie has already told me the details of Rosie's birth, how Lucy lost so much blood that the only way to save her life was to remove her womb.

'Fiona has had her fair share of trauma too, haven't you?' Ben suddenly announces, turning to face me.

'Sorry?'

'You told me, remember? How something terrible happened. And now you can't trust people. That must have been traumatic.'

My heartbeat slows and my skin feels clammy. Why is he saying this now?

'And it made me think about how you walk everywhere, how much you hate taking the bus.'

Oh God. I've told him too much. He's figuring out my story, and just at the wrong time. I need to stop him saying something that might alert Greg to who I am, connect the dots for him, but I can't speak; my mouth is too dry. I take a swig of wine.

'And I wondered if something had happened to you on a bus, something terrible.'

'Oh my goodness, were you attacked?' Rosie asks, with the ease of someone certain that such dangers will never befall them.

'No, not attacked,' I mumble, pushing the painful memories away, the losses that came after. I can't let myself be dragged down now, there's too much at stake. I watch Greg's eyes dart from me to Charlie and back again, and I feel the pierce of Lucy's stare on him, ordering her husband to keep quiet. Has he worked out who I am? Does it even matter now his cold-hearted wife has recognised me?

The room starts to spin. I can't keep this up; the deception, the fear of losing everything I've fought so hard to get back. I hold my breath. Oh God, I can't exhale; my fingers splay out, then lock. Oh please, not here. Not now. My chest keeps expanding. My breathing is only going one way. I need to get out of here.

'Excuse me,' I inhale, and rush out of the room.

Luckily I find the downstairs toilet in seconds. I lock the door and let my body take over. My arms climb the walls in some futile hunt for more oxygen. The tears fall as I suck more air into my already expanded lungs. Finally, I find the strength to cup my hands in front of my face, to trick my body into accepting carbon dioxide instead of the oxygen it craves.

Gradually my breathing settles but, as always, the tears take longer. And putting myself back together in this cold, unwelcoming house takes longer still. By the time I finally unlock the door, the table has been cleared away and only Lucy is left sitting at the table.

'Where's Ben?' I ask. I hate that he's seen me like that. I don't want him blaming himself because he brought up the subject of my trauma.

'He's tired. I sent him for a lie-down. Greg and Rosie have gone for a walk.'

'I'm sorry. For the panic attack.'

'Perhaps it's a sign,' she says. 'That you shouldn't be here.'

'He's my son. Like Rosie is your daughter.' This woman nearly lost her child too; if I can make her understand perhaps there's a chance for Charlie and me.

'NO!' She pauses, checks herself. 'No,' she repeats in a more measured tone. 'Ben is my son. Legally, functionally and emotionally. You broke him, and I fixed him.'

'That's not true.'

'You beat his father to death in front of him. You think that didn't break him?'

'You haven't fixed him.'

'I've done everything possible.' She believes it too, despite all the evidence.

The urge to make her see the truth is suddenly more important than protecting Charlie's privacy. 'Did you know that he hates himself so much that he goes to parks looking for a beating?

'That's ridiculous,' she says.

But I can hear a flicker of doubt in her voice, so I keep going. 'Has he ever seen a therapist? Had professional help?'

'He saw someone,' she says, flicking the comment away with her rose-painted fingertips, 'in the early days.'

'But not once he came to live with you.' It's not a question. Charlie told me how unwilling his parents were to send him to a therapist.

'It upset him; she upset him. It was better to move on.' It's her turn to go on the defensive now.

'Change his name? Pretend it didn't happen?'

'What good would remembering it do? Replaying Mummy Murders Daddy? Not exactly a happy memory.'

I flinch, but I can't let her words knock me off track. 'Have you researched PTSD?' I ask.

'A little. Enough.'

'So you know that the most successful form of treatment is trauma-focused. That it's only by facing the trauma that sufferers can start to move on.' I don't tell her that these words aren't mine; that they've come from the series of therapists who have treated me over the years. I also don't tell her that I've faced my trauma on countless occasions without any sign of success; that the nightmares still come, and panic attacks are part of my life.

'You have no idea how damaged he was, how much you damaged him. He hardly spoke a word when he came to live with us. Just screamed at night and spent all day in front of that red plastic easel we bought him as a welcome present. Terrible, chaotic pictures that he'd paint and then rip to shreds. When I held him, it was like cuddling a robot. The first time he spoke to me – properly, more than a yes or no – was when I suggested we see the therapist again. He used his newfound voice to beg me not to send him there, promised he'd do anything if I told him he didn't need to go. It was the first conversation we'd had in six weeks. How could I refuse him?'

I stare at her. I remember his beautiful face. His innocent eyes and sweet singsong voice. I can imagine how hard it would have been. But that doesn't excuse her.

'Because you were the adult. And he was five.'

She's silent then and I almost feel sorry for her. Regret is etched across her face, along with a realisation of what she's done.

And how it's not just me who's failed him.

Chapter 37

SEPTEMBER 2005

Charlie

'Hello, Charlie.'

Charlie digs his fingers into the rug. Its bright dots make him feel a bit dizzy, but he likes delving his fingers into it. They're really deep now. He can't even see his nails anymore.

'I'm Celina.'

Charlie knows he should look at the lady, but he doesn't want to. He doesn't want to look at the rug anymore either, so he looks at the table in front of him instead. It's the colour of wood like his table at home. Home. He turns his face towards the window.

'Would you like me to open it? It is a bit stuffy in here.'

As the lady starts pushing at the window, Charlie decides to look at the wall instead. There's a picture in the middle of it. It has lots of blue sky and birds flying around. Charlie has always wondered what it would be like to fly. Always thought he might enjoy it. He especially thinks that now.

'Do you like colouring, Charlie?'

He's surprised by such an easy question. The big woman who lives in the house he's staying at had said 'Good luck' when she left him in the room. He hadn't been sure why she said it but it had worried him a bit. It's what Mummy said to him when she left him with that muscly lady at the swimming pool. Except she didn't really leave him because she sat outside the big window and blew him kisses when he got in the water. Charlie's bottom lip starts to tremble so he bites it.

'Well, your grandma told me that you like colouring, so I thought I'd bring some crayons and some paper. Maybe we can draw together?'

Charlie looks back at the table. There are loads of crayons. Some are in a pot but they look dirty, all different sizes too and the paper around them is ripped. But there are also four new packs with crayons all neatly lined up inside. They look perfect. Charlie picks one of the packs up. The lady asks whether he needs help opening it, but he doesn't answer because he's nearly three and a half so of course he doesn't.

The lady slides a piece of white paper across the table until it's sitting in front of him. Out of the corner of his eye he watches her pick a crayon out of the pot. A grey one. It's a bit dirty, but not too bad. Then she starts drawing on her own piece of paper. The lady is concentrating really hard, so Charlie risks turning his head towards her. She's got light hair like Jude's mum and is wearing a white T-shirt and a really long skirt that hides her legs. Her necklace is pretty. It reminds Charlie of the sea in Greece. Shiny blue balls on a metal chain, bobbing against the bony bit underneath her chin.

He looks back towards the table. His grandma is right: he does like drawing. He picks a crayon out of his pack and carefully folds the flap back inside. The other crayons will be safe now.

What should he draw? He usually draws his family but he doesn't think he wants to today. They've disappeared and left him all by himself so why should he? And he doesn't want to draw the fat lady. He's not sure whether it's her fault, him living in her house now, but he doesn't think he likes her. Just because she gives him ice cream and lets him watch Ben and Holly on TV doesn't mean she's nice.

Without thinking, he draws Rabbit, starting with his beady eyes. He misses Rabbit. When the man in the green uniform took him outside he dropped him on the pavement and he hasn't been back to his house since. A lady got him another rabbit. Not the fat lady or the drawing lady but another one with big brown eyes. She was really nice but he didn't like the rabbit.

He keeps drawing. It's easy once you start. It feels good to draw big lines; zigzag them across the page. He takes another crayon. And another. Now he thinks about it, there are lots of things he wants to draw. He forgets the wooden table and the bobbing necklace and the street noise and concentrates on his picture.

'I've finished mine, Charlie. Would you like to see?'

He doesn't really care about her picture anymore but he looks anyway. It's quite funny actually. She's drawn an elephant from behind with a gigantic bottom and a tiny tail. And a monkey sat on the elephant's head with a silly smile and a banana in his hand.

'Have you finished yours?'

Charlie looks down at his picture. He's not sure he wants her to see it after all. It was supposed to be a drawing of Rabbit but he can't work out where he is now. He's made too much of a mess. How stupid he is; just scrawling all over the paper like that.

The crayons! He realises in a panic that he forgot to put them back. The pack is empty and the flap is undone and the crayons are just strewn about all over the table. He picks up the red one and realises it's snapped. Broken. The black one too. He wanted to look after them and look what's he done.

'Perhaps I could see your picture, Charlie?'

No. Charlie quickly picks up his picture. She mustn't see it. He backs away from the table. One step. Two steps. Finally his back touches a wall. It's the one with the picture of flying birds, only he can't see it now. He sinks down onto the floor.

He wishes he had Rabbit. Even the other rabbit might be okay. But he only has his picture so he holds that to his chest and wonders if the fat lady is coming back.

Chapter 38

CHRISTMAS DAY 2019

Phoebe

'Fiona, can we talk?'

I take a sharp intake of breath and the cold air hits my lungs. 'Wow, you scared me. What are you doing out here?'

'Waiting for you.' Charlie takes a step forward, and the street-lamp shines on his face, lighting up his anguish.

'Lucy said you were tired, that you'd gone for a lie-down?'

'She sent me upstairs when you left the table. But I didn't want you to go without checking that you were okay. I thought it would be easier to wait outside, figured you'd want to leave pretty quickly. After everything.'

'After making a fool of myself, you mean?'

He kicks at the gatepost, won't look me in the eye. This is because I've let him down; I'm supposed to be the stable one, supporting him, not the one who falls apart.

'I shouldn't have asked you to come here.'

The regret in his voice makes me want to cry. I was so looking forward to today, and now I've messed everything up. 'I'm sorry about my panic attack.'

'My family can have that effect on people.'

'You just took me off guard, talking about trauma like that.'

He looks up, stops the monotonous kicking. In the shadowy light his expression casts a menacing glow. I search his face for understanding, or pity, but it's just blank.

'You don't like talking about yourself, do you?'

'I guess I'm quite a private person,' I mumble. *And I have so much to hide.*

'Even from me? You said you trusted me, remember?'

I nod. 'I do trust you.' I know he's challenging me, testing my loyalty. But I don't want to say too much. I took a risk by coming here today, and I'm still trying to process how much damage that has caused.

'Will you tell me what happened to you?'

Should I tell him? He's confided in me so much, perhaps I owe him this, a small piece of the jigsaw. And it's not like this revelation will give away my identity; he's got no idea what I went through before I walked through our front door that night. It some ways, I wish he did.

'Fourteen years ago, I witnessed a fatal stabbing.' I watch him catch his breath, push his hands deeper into his pockets. 'The victim was just a teenager. I did what I could, but he died.'

'That must have been terrible,' he says, his voice low and quiet. 'But fourteen years is a long time. Why does it still affect you so much?'

It's a fair question; it was a lifetime ago. But I can't tell him the real reason I still carry it with me. 'Maybe I never faced up to it properly, the fear.'

'What about guilt?' he asks, his voice suddenly harder.

'Sorry?'

'Survivor's guilt. That's a thing isn't it?'

My heart settles down again. 'Yes, that's a thing. Seeing someone so young die, while I got to live.'

'Do you ever wish you didn't?'

I don't want to talk about this now. I'm exhausted. Lucy's threats are still ringing in my ears, and now Charlie is trying to peel back my layers. I need some time by myself, to decide what to do next. 'It's getting late, I should be going.'

'I'd understand, you know. If you'd preferred to have died instead of that boy.'

'I'm walking home, so I'd better go,' I mumble, trying to block out his words. The truth is, I would never have swapped places with him, not with Charlie at home, and my daughter growing inside me. Although, in the end, I lost them too.

My head feels full of cotton wool. One good night's sleep and then I'll know what to do. I give him an awkward flick of a wave and turn to go.

'Fiona, stop.'

His voice is plaintive rather than demanding, but I pivot back to face him.

'Don't go yet; I want to show you something. Will you come with me?'

'Tonight?' I ask, stalling for time. I want to go home, but he's been in a strange mood all day; perhaps I should try to lift him out of it. And of course the thought of spending time together, just me and him, is always tempting.

'It's important.'

I sigh. 'Of course I will.'

'Thank you.' He reaches his arm out towards me, and I brace myself for his touch. I can't help imagining him drawing me into his arms, feeling my son's heartbeat thud in time with mine. It's been too long. But he changes his mind, drops his arm back down by his side again. He looks at a Ford Fiesta parked on the street. 'Quicker if we drive there.'

'Is that your car?' He's never mentioned being a driver before, but he nods.

'It's mine and Rosie's. It was a joint present for our seventeenths, even though Rosie's birthday is five months before mine. And she passed her test before I'd had a chance to work out the gears.'

'Do you have your licence now?'

'I can drive,' he says, trying to dodge the question.

'I'm not sure that it's a good idea.' I try to sound placatory, but I'm on probation, so any brush with the law could put me back inside. 'If it's far, maybe we should do it another time instead?'

'No.' The forcefulness of his answer shocks me, and I can tell it's taken him by surprise too because he immediately softens his tone. 'I mean, I'd prefer us to go tonight. Since Rosie broke her arm, I've been thinking about stuff. About how angry I get with myself. Yesterday I walked for ages, like you do, and I found somewhere special. A place that makes me feel happier in my own skin. I want to show you.'

I look at his hopeful expression and my heart swells. Even without knowing my true identity, he wants to tell me his secrets, share his more vulnerable side. I wonder where he means, a tranquil spot by the river maybe, or a highpoint with views over London.

'And you could drive,' he continues. 'It's insured for any driver.'

I look at the small car, how the different panels fit securely together. I haven't driven for over fourteen years, but I feel an urge to climb inside now, to let the door clunk closed and drive away, with Charlie. 'If it means that much to you, then let's go tonight,' I say, smiling up at him.

'And you promise not to change your mind once we set off?'

A sense of foreboding tingles on my skin. Why would I do that? Is his special place somewhere illegal? Will I be risking my freedom anyway? I look at his beautiful face, the shared blue of our eyes. 'I promise,' I say, and try to hide the unease growing inside me.

Charlie grins then and it reminds me of the child he used to be, getting an extra ten minutes before bedtime or winning a race in the park. He rummages in his pocket and pulls out a single key, the Ford halo glinting in the dark.

And it leaves me wondering whether he'd planned it all along.

*

As it's Christmas night, the roads are quiet, and we don't pass another car on the spiderweb of streets that take us out of Charlie's neighbourhood. Lots of people have forgotten to close their curtains though and I feel like I'm intruding as I stare at families playing charades or delving into tins of Quality Street in front of the TV. On Charlie's instruction, I turn onto Garratt Lane, the main thoroughfare in the borough that links Wandsworth town with the sprawling treasures of multicultural Tooting. I have walked these streets so much over the last few months that it feels strange, rushing past them at thirty miles per hour. But then he directs me down Kimber Road, a line of tarmac that cuts King George's Park in half, and their familiarity starts to change, become more distant.

'Where are we going?'

'A surprise.'

I pause. The shortness of his answer reminds me of the boy I first encountered all those weeks ago. This isn't the Charlie I've become used to, the one who bares his soul to me with an ease that still fills me with joy. 'I'm not a big fan of surprises,' I say carefully.

'I thought you trusted me?'

The car heater is on full blast, but this new hardness in his tone sends a chill down my spine. I take my eyes off the road for a moment and glance at his face in profile. He's just staring at the road, his hand fiddling mindlessly with something in his pocket. He has been sensitive all day. Is this about Hana? Dare I ask him? The low light and lack of eye contact spur me on.

'I'm sorry about Hana. She told me about her grandmother.'

Charlie doesn't respond, just continues staring out of the window. The silence is too oppressive.

'I'm sure she'll be back as soon as she can. You two are so right for each other.'

'Not right.'

He's so quiet that I can hardly make out what he's saying. 'Of course you are. Don't let her leaving London put you off.'

'NO RIGHT!' His roar makes me jump so much that I nearly swerve into a bollard. Then he drops it to an acidic murmur, which scares me almost as much. 'You have no right to comment on Hana and me. Okay?'

'Okay,' I whisper back. But I can't hide the tremble in my voice.

Especially when I reach the traffic lights and he tells me to go left, then right. We're getting too close to a place I promised I would never set foot in again. The scene of my crime, but also so many others. The loss of my daughter, my husband and finally my son. Losing my liberty meant nothing after that. I want to spin the steering wheel and put my foot down, get the hell away. But instead, I keep driving, following his instructions with my lips sealed and my heart imploding.

Could it just be some terrible coincidence?

Or am I heading for a cliff edge?

But whatever the outcome, after everything I've done, I can't deny him this.

We pass Southfields station and the images come tumbling forward. Dan and I running from our little flat to catch a tube, after I'd convinced him to stay in bed an extra five minutes. Meeting at the exit after work, then going to Lexi's for a glass of Chablis. And later, negotiating Charlie's buggy down those concrete stairs as I attempted a trip to meet Dippy the dinosaur at the Natural History Museum or to explore the real-life magic in the basement of the Science Museum.

So many happy memories. How did it all go so wrong?

Then he gives the direction I've been dreading. And I slowly pull into Clanwell Street.

Even in my petrified state, the memories keep coming. The boozy street party we held in that long summer of 2003, evening strolls with Cara as we tried to get our teething sons to drift off to sleep. But all too soon, Charlie gives his final instruction, and I stop the car outside our old home.

My whole body is shaking, I can't bear to look at the house that once symbolised all my dreams for the future. And I'm not ready for this conversation with my son. I wish I could run home and pretend it isn't happening. But I know there's no chance of that now. Whatever reason Charlie has for bringing me here, to this place where we both lost so much, I need to let him play it out. That's what unconditional love means.

I wonder who told him. Did Flora sneak out when I was at work one day, choose not to warn me? Or did Lucy change her mind, do the big reveal, while I climbed the walls in her downstairs toilet? And how much does he know? Flora might tell him about me, but I can't believe she'd relay Dan's story, label me a murderer without giving me the chance to explain. Lucy might hate me enough, but would she really do that to Charlie on Christmas Day?

'Let's go,' he says, but it's an order not a request. Any friendship we've built up has disappeared now.

I open the car door and the cold air rushes in. I shudder at the thought of leaving the warmth of the little Ford Fiesta. In contrast, he seems oblivious to the freezing temperatures; just launches himself out of the car and starts pacing up and down the pavement.

'Come on,' he shouts impatiently.

I close the car door and dredge up the courage to look at my old house. The front door is a different colour, but otherwise it's the same. To a house built in the 1800s, fourteen years means nothing. I wish it were the same for Charlie.

'Where are we going?' I ask.

He throws me a look of disgust, like I'm even more of a coward than he thought. Still not owning up to what I've done. 'Into that garden,' he replies, playing along. He points to the wall that runs down the side of our old garden. Once it was a symbol of pride, signifying our rare end-of-terrace house. But now it just feels like the end of our journey.

'How will we get in?'

'We can climb over.'

I look at the six-foot wall. Even if I wanted to, there's no way I could climb over that. I don't speak, but the scepticism must show on my face.

'I can get you over.'

'No really, I can't do it Char ... Ben.' Oh God, I'm so tired.

'What did you call me?'

'Ben, I called you Ben.'

He smirks then, and for a moment, he looks evil. 'Come here,' he demands, and I find myself obeying him. He cradles his fingers and instructs me to step up and push off. I'm shaking so much that it's hard to find my balance, but I do as he says, and then I'm reaching for the top and he's pushing me over. I wonder if the police will come, or the owners will rush out of the front door, hurling abuse at us. But the house is in darkness and the streets are still, and a moment later I'm tumbling over the wall.

I stifle a yelp as I lose my balance on landing and fall hard onto my side. My ankle screams and I close my eyes as I try to ride the shot of pain radiating through my leg. I take a deep breath and roll onto my knees. The pain isn't subsiding. I realise I can't put any weight onto my left leg, and it makes me feel even more vulnerable. From my crouched position I watch Charlie appear at the top of the wall, transfer all his weight to his arms and then twist over like a gymnast. His lean frame hides how strong he is.

I gingerly pull myself to standing and look around me. Like most London houses, it's a small garden, patio next to the house, and just enough lawn for a trampoline and a shed. On sunny days, I'd push open the wide bifold doors in the morning and Charlie would potter in and out all day. But the sky is black tonight, and all I can see is Dan and that woman, lying together.

'Is it all coming back then? The memories?'

It comes out as a snarl and I take an unsteady step backwards. I can't bear the acid in his voice, the pain on his face. Not my beautiful Charlie.

'Because it's amazing how much you seem to have forgotten, isn't it, Phoebe?'

And there it is. The truth laid bare.

Tears roll down my face. It wasn't supposed to be this way. I remember the moment I saw his face in that newspaper, the elation I felt on finding him. I remember the first time I saw him, racing through the school gates. And then later, the horror of witnessing his self-destruct mode when he confronted that gang of kids. There have been so many good moments too, shared confidences. Charlie and me against the world.

But now all I see is pure hatred.

He knows it all.

It doesn't matter how anymore.

I can't believe it's come to this.

I need to put this right.

Chapter 39

OCTOBER 2006

Charlie

'Hello, Charlie. It's good to see you again. Do you remember me? I'm Celina.'

Charlie looks around the room. The wood-coloured table is in the same place, although it looks smaller now. And the desk. And the window. He suddenly remembers the sky picture and whips his head round to the wall. It's still there. The birds flying. He can't remember how many times Aunty Lizzie brought him here when he first went to live with her. Quite a lot though. The lady called Celina always asked if he wanted to talk about his mummy and daddy. He never did so he'd shake his head. At first she seemed okay with that but one time she started talking about them anyway. He got really angry with her then. He might have hit her. Maybe that's why Aunty Lizzie stopped bringing him.

'I'm afraid I don't have any crayons today. But I've got some toys. Would you like to play with them?'

Charlie follows her gaze to the corner of the room. He's not sure he wants to play with her toys but there are some knights on horses. He wants to be a knight one day so this might be good practice.

'Okay.'

She walks around the desk towards him. He worries that she might try to hold his hand, but she doesn't; she just bends her knees so that they're the same height and smiles at him. Her face is covered in tiny freckles and her eyes are the colour of water, which isn't really a colour at all. She looks like an angel, Charlie decides. And that makes him feel even worse about hitting her.

'Shall we sit in the corner? There's loads of cushions; it's really cosy.'

Charlie walks to the corner of the room. It's a bit like book corner in his classroom, which is his favourite place to sit. He reaches for the knights on horses. They're really heavy. That's probably because they have big muscles.

'So I hear you've started school now, Charlie?'

The blue knight must protect the king. He's very brave and strong.

'And your teacher says you're brilliant at art.'

Uh-oh. The black knight has arrived. He wants the castle for himself. He's going to kill the king!

'And that you like books, that you love the book corner.'

He attacks the blue knight! Bang bang bang. The horse rears up! But the blue knight is strong. He gets back up, settles his horse. But can he save the king?

'But also that sometimes you're a bit quiet.'

He must kill the black knight. He attacks! Again, again. The black knight is injured. But he must be sure. He keeps hitting him.

'And your foster mum, Aunty Lizzie, said the nightmares have started again.'

Charlie looks up. So that's why he's here. It's a punishment for wetting the bed again. He hates Aunty Lizzie anyway.

'My daddy is dead.'

'Do you miss him?'

The black knight isn't dead after all. He's crawling towards the blue knight. He must be killed. Die, black knight!

'Maybe you could tell me something about your daddy?'

Charlie stops banging. The black knight is dead now. But the blue knight isn't moving. He might be dead too.

'I already told you something.'

'Sorry, Charlie, you did – that's right. What I meant to say was—'

'Someone killed him.'

Charlie feels powerful saying that, like the knight. Her water-coloured eyes look even more watery now.

'I know Charlie. And that must make you feel sad.'

She looks sad, Charlie thinks. Perhaps she loved his daddy too. Like the lady he saw through the banisters that night.

'I was scared at first.'

'Of course you were.'

'But I'm not now.'

'That's good, Charlie. Do you feel safe with Aunty Lizzie?'

'Yes. Because he's gone now.'

'Sorry Charlie, who's gone?'

'The big boy. The one that killed my daddy.'

Charlie can tell that the lady doesn't know about the big boy because she looks really surprised. Well, how could she know about him? She's never been to Aunty Lizzie's house so she won't have seen him. She won't have heard him shouting horrible words or slamming the kitchen door so hard that it cracked the glass either.

'Why do you think the big boy killed your daddy?'

'He's bad.'

The big boy has scary eyes and sometimes he would stare at Charlie and laugh at the same time. One time the big boy laughed so much that Aunty Lizzie shouted back at him. But that was when the scary laughing had made Charlie wet his pants, so she was probably just mad with him.

'I'm sorry that the boy scared you, and I'm glad that he's not living with you and Aunty Lizzie anymore. But it's important for you to know, Charlie, that the boy didn't kill your daddy.'

Stupid lady. Of course he killed Daddy. Charlie saw him do it. At least, he thinks he did. He can't actually remember for sure. But he remembers feeling angry and sad and scared all at the same time. And that's how the big boy made him feel. So it makes sense really.

But he only knew for sure that the big boy killed his daddy when the two policemen came to Aunty Lizzie's house. They all went into the kitchen together and shut the door, made Charlie go into the front room. He watched a whole DVD of Peppa Pig before they came out again. Then one of the policemen winked at Charlie, which must mean they'd caught his daddy's killer. And the big boy never came back after that.

'Yes he did. And one day I'm going to kill him back.'

Chapter 40

CHRISTMAS DAY 2019

Ben

Ben stares at her snivelling face and he wants to punch it. Still acting the victim when she's actually a fucking killer. It hadn't taken him long to work that out. All those news websites flashing up once he'd started the online search. *Man bludgeoned to death. Theatrical agent convicted of husband's murder.* The grainy pictures that proved he wasn't going crazy. He'd been certain it was his fault; he'd almost told her as much. And she'd just let him believe it, hadn't said a word. Fucking bitch.

He can't let himself think about how much he's confided in her, what he's told her about his life. To the woman who murdered his dad, ruined his life. Acid rears up in his chest, but he swallows it down. He won't give her the satisfaction of showing how much this hurts.

'I'm so sorry, Ben, for keeping this from you. I should never have let it come to this. Please, let me explain.'

She's rambling some pathetic apology now. Does she really think that will work? That she can talk herself out of this? *Oh yes, I killed your dad, left you with social services, then when you least expected it, I tricked you into telling me all your secrets. Oops sorry!*

'Please, Ben, say something.'

She's begging now, her voice cracked and desperate. Ben feels a tiny worm of sympathy work its way into his consciousness. But no; he can't allow it. He slaps it away, and the sting of his palm against his face feels good, invigorating. 'How could you do it?' he asks, pleased that his voice is firmer than hers. He watches her hesitate, weigh up how to answer him. Realisation hits and he feels a sudden urge to laugh. She doesn't know what he means, which terrible act he's referring to. How could you murder my dad? How could you leave me? How could you lie to me about who you are? *So many fuck-ups, Mummy dear. Eeny, meeny, miney, moe …*

'I've made a lot of mistakes.'

'Understatement of the fucking year.'

'But I never stopped loving you – you have to believe that.'

'Like you loved my dad, do you mean?'

'I did love him.'

'So what; you're going to kill me too?'

He listens to her sharp intake of breath, then her voice crack. 'No, of course I'm not!'

She can't speak for a while after that. She's crying too hard. Ben watches her fold into herself, collapse onto the patio. He hadn't stuck around for long on the night of the Christmas party, but he'd taken more time on his second visit last night. He'd needed to check that the place was empty, but it was more than that: a craving to reconnect with his roots, to try and make sense of what he read on those websites. He'd climbed over the wall easily enough, then prowled around the garden looking for traces of his past. But it was only when he sat where Phoebe is now, staring through those wide panes of glass at the kitchen beyond, that the memories had started to surface.

Memories of his dad, his hero.

'You chose to kill my dad though, didn't you?'

'It didn't feel like a choice.'

'What? Even now, you won't take responsibility!'

'I was broken. He broke me.'

'HE WAS MY DAD!' The flowerbed by Ben's feet is edged with rocks. He picks one up, then throws it. He's not sure whether he meant to hit her, but it connects with her shoulder and he feels better for it. Calmer.

'I know, I'm sorry. He loved you.' She brushes at her shoulder vaguely, like she didn't notice what just happened, doesn't understand why it's hurting.

Ben stares at the back of the garden. There's a hint of a mound in the turf next to the fence, and it sparks a new memory, the three of them stood solemnly, holding hands and saying goodbye. 'Do you remember Lola?'

'Sorry?'

'We had a hamster. I called her Lola, after the *Charlie and Lola* books.'

'Yes, Lola,' she says in a faraway voice. 'She wasn't with us for long.'

'Seems to be a theme in our family,' Ben growls. But Phoebe doesn't react, it's as though she's become immune to his anger. A coldblooded monster. Ben picks up another rock, but throws it against the back fence this time, enjoys the sound of the wood splintering. 'Do you remember burying her? I do. You finding a little box, me drawing her a picture. Dad digging a hole. All of us stood over it, sending Lola on her way.'

'You were upset. It made you feel better, saying a proper goodbye.'

'Oh yeah? Do you know how many times I've visited my father's grave? Laid flowers for him, honoured his important dates? Jesus, I don't even know if he has a grave!'

'It wasn't my choice,' she whispers. 'To keep the truth from you.'

'So now it's my parents' fault is it? You're developing quite a pattern here, Phoebe. Yeah, they should have fucking told me. Like they should have thrown you out of our house today. I watched; I waited. But you're all the same. Hiding your dirty secrets, thinking you've got the right to keep my truth from me. But whatever they've done, don't you dare use them as your excuse.'

'I wrote to you. Twice a year. They kept those letters from you.'

'And did you explain my dad's death? Own up to what you'd done?' Her silence says it all and any wisp of hope Ben might have felt dies before it was ever really formed.

'I only remembered him yesterday,' he continues. 'I was his little hero; I remember him calling me that now. And yet, for all these years, he's been alone. You killed him, and I forgot him.' The strength in Ben's legs seems to disappear and he fights the urge to collapse down next to her. Instead, he walks across the patio and leans on the arm of a rattan sofa, its cushions elsewhere, packed away for winter.

'Don't think like that. He wasn't so perfect.'

'I remember him pushing me on the swings, daring me to close my eyes.' In honour of the memory, Ben closes his eyes now, imagines swaying from side to side. It isn't difficult; he's hardly slept for the last two days.

'He was never there; I raised you, not him.'

Ben watches Phoebe push herself to standing. Her face contorts in pain and she drops her weight onto her right side. She must have hurt herself on the climb over. It's nowhere near punishment enough.

'He worked hard, nothing wrong with that,' he spits back. The urge to defend his father is intense.

'He always put himself first.'

She's taking uneven steps towards him now. Ben's breathing quickens; pinpricks of adrenaline tap-tap-tap at his arms. 'It's you that I remember shouting, not him,' he throws back. 'He tried to calm you down.'

279

'He pushed me to it. I need you to understand that, Ben.'

She's hovering so close. He can't look at her. How dare she blame his dad, taint Ben's memories. After everything she's done. 'I've only just got him back. And you want to ruin it, even now?'

'He cheated on me; didn't even care enough to hide it from you.'

A stranger with red lips arriving in the darkness, her hand reaching behind Daddy's neck. Ben forces the memory out of his head. 'He didn't deserve to die.'

'I was pregnant. I was sure I was going to give you a sister. But my baby died inside me. That's on him.'

She's lying. A wave of revulsion sweeps over Ben, so powerful that he thinks it might drown him. But instead, it recharges his exhausted body. He lunges forward, grabs her by the neck; pushes against her. He doesn't remember making the decision, but the knife appears in his hand.

Did he plan this? Had he chosen to bring her here because it's where she murdered his dad? A private garden where he could be certain of no witnesses? And he's brought the weapon. He opened his art case, cradled the knife in his hands, zipped it carefully into his jacket pocket. As he stares at the broken little bird in his grip, he knows he didn't need it for self-defence.

It doesn't matter now though. Pre-meditated or impulsive; it's happening either way. Perhaps this is why his parents chose not to love him, not properly like they do Rosie. It's shame that's fuelled their silence. And why he's never made anything of himself at school, or found friends who actually care about him. Maybe this is why Hana left as soon as he admitted how much he liked her. Because they all knew before he did. That his life as a Moreton, a rich kid with a future, was only ever a temporary thing.

He looks at his mother. The murderer. Her blood running through his veins.

This is his destiny.

And his duty. He made a promise to avenge his father's murder. He's remembered that too. He got the wrong person then, but he knows the truth now. She should have been stabbed on the bus with that kid. Then his dad would be alive, and they would be celebrating this Christmas Day together. But she didn't. She survived and got the chance to ruin two lives. Well not anymore. It might be fourteen years too late, but it's still going to be worth it.

He pushes the blade up against her throat. He can feel her shaking beneath his grip.

'Please, Charlie, don't do this.'

She warbles like a bird too. And pecks at him. She needs to shut up. 'Don't ask anything of me,' he growls. 'I owe you nothing.' He pushes harder, can sense the splitting of her skin, the thin dribble of blood trickling down her neck. He listens to her breathing get faster, shallower, her voice starting to panic.

'I'm not asking for me. This is about you. Don't ruin your life like this. I'm not worth it.'

'Don't put this on me!' he howls. 'It was you who ruined my life. The moment you smashed my dad's face in; sprayed his blood all over me. The moment you walked away. Turned me into an orphan. That's when this started.'

'I know what I am, what I've done. Don't you think I haven't longed for this? To have all the guilt and the pain snuffed out by a blade or a packet of pills?'

'Then why didn't you?'

'For you, Charlie. For you.'

He starts to correct her again. His name is Ben. But it isn't anymore, he realises. He's given that life up now. He needs to accept who he really is.

'For those precious three years when you were my world.'

He wishes she'd just shut up. He needs to get on with this.

'It was all so ordinary at the time. Trips to the park, cuddles on the sofa, races down the street. Do you remember that tipi that Grandma got you? You'd sit for ages in there, with your colouring books.'

Ben shakes his head violently. He does remember but he needs to knock the images out of his head. They're confusing him. He pushes her roughly onto the bare sofa, pulls his arm away from her. He can't slice at her neck. But he can stab her. Like that boy she didn't save.

'But then it stopped, and it wasn't ordinary anymore. It was a collection of the most wonderful memories, special moments that no one could take away from me.'

He can see her now. Chasing him with her tickling fingers. Tucking him into bed. Kissing him and his rabbit goodnight. His mum. Her face. Those eyes.

'It wasn't much, Charlie. But it was enough to keep me alive.'

Ben can't bear it anymore. He raises his arm, releases an animal call of pure rage and stabs the knife in, feeling the splitting of flesh, the gush of blood. The release it brings is incredible. A sense of euphoria sweeps over him.

It's done now. There's no turning back.

And it feels so right.

Chapter 41

Phoebe

No, no, no. This can't be happening. Not again. Not here.

'Charlie! What have you done? Please, Charlie, talk to me.'

But he's just looking at me weirdly, like he's high or wasted. For a second I see Flora, her knees buckling, her falling to the ground. But it's not Flora with a knife jutting out of her midriff. It's my beautiful boy.

I don't know what to do. The street is so dark, no one else around; this is on me. But I can't think straight. It easier to just freeze. Sit and watch. Pretend it's not real; just a cheap Netflix movie that I can turn off at any point. I want to turn it off now, but I don't have the control. I can't stop this.

I need to do something.

I lurch forward, almost falling on top of him in my sudden attempt to help. His eyes are open, that's a good sign, but his face is deathly pale and there's a film of sweat forming across his forehead. His breathing is shallow and rapid like an excited puppy. Except it's fear and panic that I see in his eyes now.

'It's okay,' I say. 'It's going to be okay.' Neither of us believes it but it still feels worth saying, if only to mask the horrific sound of him searching for air.

Tentatively I reach my hand towards the knife. It's just under his ribcage on the right side. Not his heart, thank God, but my fingers still squelch in the sea of blood flooding out from the wound. I scream. Then my mouth starts to claw at the air, searching for oxygen.

And with my growing panic, the images come.

The blood seeping out of that tiny hole in the boy's chest, flooding my vision.

The blood in my bathroom; nothing I could do.

And Dan's blood. My doing.

I can't let history repeat itself.

The panic attack is all in your head, I scream at myself. It's enough to halt my constant inhaling; miraculously, it's also enough to force out a long angry blow of carbon dioxide. I reach into Charlie's pocket for his phone. With shaking fingers, I press 999 and prod at the speakerphone button. But it's too passive; I need to do more than that. I rip off my jacket; ignore the cold air that grabs me. With nothing but instinct to guide me, I push it down onto Charlie's body, either side of the knife, and sink my hands into the wound. I couldn't stem the blood of that boy, or stop him dying, but I can't let history repeat itself. Not Charlie.

'Which emergency service do you need?'

'Ambulance.' It's just a whisper though. Too quiet. 'Ambulance!' I repeat.

'Putting you through now.'

'London Ambulance Service. What is your location?'

I want to scream it all out, tell her everything. So that she'll understand how important it is, how they need to save him. But I have to stay calm, do something right for once. The stakes are too high.

'It's 55 Clanwell Street. In the garden. There's a back gate, off

Brookfell Road. I think there's a padlock and chain; you'll need bolt cutters.'

'Thank you. That's very useful. What's your name?'

'Phoebe.' Comply with the rules, don't let your impatience show.

'Are you hurt, Phoebe?'

Yes, I'm hurt. Everywhere hurts. But this isn't about me. This has never been about me, but I've been too blind to see that.

'It's not me. It's my ...' And that must start with me acknowledging who he is. And who he isn't anymore. 'It's a friend of mine. Ben Moreton.'

'What's happened to Ben?' Her voice is so professional. I need to match it.

'He has a stab wound. Self-inflicted. Right side under the ribcage.'

'Is he conscious? Can I talk to him?'

I've been concentrating on his wound. The task of trying to stop the never-ending stream of blood has given me something to focus on, distracted me from the enormity of what's happening. I look back towards his face and see that his eyes have closed. Maybe he's just resting.

'Ben! Wake up.' There's no response so I gently push him with my knee. 'Ben!' I've forgotten the ambulance call handler is on speaker phone so I jump at the sound of her voice.

'It sounds like your friend is unconscious, Phoebe. Is there a lot of blood on his clothes?'

'There's so much blood! It's everywhere!' I know this isn't helping. I need to be more accurate. 'His T-shirt is covered, not his trousers though.' I imagine a carton of milk; it feels about right. 'I think he's lost about a litre.'

'That's so helpful, Phoebe, thank you. I'll let the crew know. Police and first responder will be there in six minutes. Ambulance in seven. But for now, I have a very important job for you.'

'Okay,' I answer meekly. She's become my master; I'll do anything she asks.

'Is the knife still in situ?'

'Yes.'

'Good. You mustn't remove it.'

'I haven't touched it.' It comes out triumphantly, like I deserve a gold star.

'Brilliant. Now I want you to place your hands either side of the knife and push down, apply pressure to the wound. Can you do that for me?'

'I'm doing it! I'm already pushing!' I can't believe it. I'm doing something right for once.

'And is the wound still bleeding?'

I look down at the wound. My hands seem to glow white in the darkness. The blood isn't gushing like before, but I can't stop my scrunched-up jacket turning a darker shade of red.

'Yes. It's still bleeding.' Doing everything right and still getting it wrong. I cry then. Racking sobs that push down between my shoulder blades; test my resolve. But for the next six minutes my hands stay white. I don't stop pushing down on the wound for a moment. Or pleading, 'C'mon, c'mon, c'mon.'

It's all I can do.

*

I hear sirens first, then the snap of a chain breaking, and a gate smacking against the fence. Three paramedics rush towards me, one first responder and an ambulance crew, just like the woman on the phone said. As I turn my head towards them, I also see a blue light still flashing beyond the open gate. The police. They would have been responsible for cutting through the padlock, gaining access for the medical staff, but their presence is also a reminder that there'll be questions to answer. Not now though.

The elation I feel when the paramedics reach me is incredible, but when a gloved set of hands offers to take over my job, I find I can't let go. What if the wound starts gushing blood again while we make the switch? What if that extra blood loss proves too much for his hungry heart? I can almost see it pumping madly in its desperate search for oxygen, totally confused why the usually reliable transport system is failing it so badly.

'Phoebe, you've done an amazing job, but I've got this now.' Her singsong Welsh accent makes the instruction sound casual, but her hands show the level of her determination. They expertly slide mine away and take over applying pressure. It's seamless. I rock back onto my heels to create some distance, pull my knees into my chest, and listen to my teeth chattering inside my head.

'Signs of haemorrhagic shock. I need two IV cannulae please.'

Her instructions are calm and clear, but I can hear the tension in her voice. From my crouched position, I watch the older paramedic put an oxygen mask over Charlie's head and pull two cannula sets out his bag.

'We need to get him to the major trauma centre at St George's ASAP,' the Gaelic lilt continues.

Major trauma. My teeth go into overdrive and they remind me of a comedy toy I once bought for Charlie in a joke shop. I start to laugh at the ridiculousness of it all. A shiny metallic blanket gets wrapped around my shoulders. Fourteen years too late maybe. If I'd asked for help then, let the paramedics look after me and my baby, if I'd understood what really mattered, then perhaps I wouldn't have caused all this devastation. But no one knows for sure of course, because that version of our lives was never written.

'You have a nasty cut there. Want me to take a look?' The third paramedic, the one responsible for the blanket, crouches down next to me. He looks about twenty-five and shines with the energy of youth.

'No,' I say firmly. Still not accepting help after all. 'Will he live?' I'm petrified what he might say, but I have to ask. He pauses for a moment, too long, I think.

'It looks like a laceration to the liver. It's a nasty wound, but you did absolutely everything right. If he survives, it's down to you.'

If. My vision shudders and the small garden around me moves with it. I struggle to ride the wave of nausea that it causes. 'And if he dies?'

'Listen carefully, Phoebe. It's not your fault.' He draws the words out to emphasise his point. 'I don't know the ins and outs of what happened tonight,' he continues, like he's read my mind. 'But from a clinical point of view, he was lucky to have you here.'

Is that true? Could he ever be lucky to have me? Right now, all I can think about is the pain I've caused him, but I need to believe that our first three years together still means something. It has kept me alive for so long, I can't let it go now.

'BP is stabilising. Let's get him in the ambulance.' It's the first time the older paramedic has spoken, and his voice is the sharpest. Perhaps he's become anaesthetised to it all; too many years playing witness to young lives being cut short by knife wounds like this. Or maybe he's just good at hiding his true feelings.

'Will you come in the ambulance, Phoebe?' The Welsh girl thinks she's asking a rhetorical question. She saw the desperation in my eyes when she took over applying pressure, and I can see the gravity in hers. In her mind, there's no way I wouldn't see this through.

Except I can't go with him.

I can't be there when Lucy and Greg arrive. I won't be responsible for the distraction that will cause. 'No,' I whisper robotically, not daring to make eye contact. 'His parents are called Greg and Lucy Moreton. They live at 16 Milada Road, Wandsworth. Their number will be in Ben's phone.' I dip my head towards the patio where the phone is still lying, redundant now.

'Are you sure?' There's both surprise and concern in her voice.

'Yes, I'm sure.' I try to sound genuine. She doesn't need to know that I'll go to the hospital anyway, find somewhere in the shadows to wait; that I won't rest until I know whether he lives or dies. She shrugs and turns to go. There's no time for discussion anyway. I watch the three of them carefully lift the stretcher and transfer it to the wheeled trolley. Charlie is covered in blankets and I watch her secure his motionless body with thick black straps.

He might not survive the night, I realise suddenly. I need to say goodbye, to see his face one more time. I scramble to my feet, ignore the pain in my ankle, and run the few steps it takes to reach his side. His eyes are closed; he looks calm, at peace. I wish I could see the anger again, the rage that shows me he's still alive. Even the look of hatred, that felt so painful only an hour or so ago, would be welcome now.

I stroke his hair, gently guide it away from his face, and kiss him on the forehead. It's the most intimate moment we've shared since he was 3 years old, and it took a loss of consciousness, the threat of death, to get here. Over the last two months I've tried so hard to make amends, listened to the tirades against his parents, his school, his sister. Forgiving him for the anger and violence. Did he sense it, my unconditional love? Did he crave it?

I will never get the chance to find out because now I'm just the mother who left him, the liar who tricked him, the woman who murdered his father. I close my eyes and pray for Charlie to survive. There's so much more I want to pray for, but it feels selfish, dangerous, to ask for too much, so I force those pleading voices away.

Then I kiss him one last time, take a step back, and watch the paramedics wheel him away.

Chapter 42

Lucy

Lucy dabs at a stray tear escaping from the corner of her eye. She can't cry now. Not yet. She picks up the waterproof mascara, blue-black, and starts curling it through her eyelashes. She doesn't want to cry later either, not in front of everyone. But deep down, she knows the tears will come.

Sitting back against the soft velvet cushioning of the Regency dressing table chair, she stares at herself in the mirror. Better. But even good make-up can't hide the fact that she looks older. Tired. It's funny, she's spent years rushing around, trying to do everything. Be brilliant at everything. But it's now, when life has become so much stiller, that she feels truly tired.

She turns to look at the dress hanging on her wardrobe door. It's still got the tags on. Of course she already has plenty of dresses inside her wardrobe that would have worked perfectly well today, but she wanted to buy something new. Something special. She owes him that. With shaking hands, she unclasps the tiny safety pin holding the tags in place and drops them into the bin. Lifting her arms into the air, she lets the simple black dress glide down her body, the silk cooling her burning skin as it falls.

A gentle thud-thud on the stairs signals that it must be time to go. Lucy's heart starts racing at the prospect and she dabs frantically at her eyes again. Keeping her emotions at bay is not going to be easy today.

Greg appears at the door, a long raincoat covering his dark suit. He won't let the weather define how smart he looks today. 'Are you ready, darling?' he asks.

Ready? Not really. For so long, her life had been what she made it. Its success based on her working hard, finding solutions, believing that anything was possible. Even the trauma of Rosie's birth had been fixable. She'd fixed it. On the day Greg agreed to try adoption, and then again when their darling Ben walked into their lives. A child who had suffered such trauma, who she was going to save. At least, she thought so at the time.

Things are different now. Out of her control. But she knows that she has to learn to live with this new normal. 'Yes, I'm ready,' she answers.

Greg reaches for her hand and they walk slowly down the stairs. Rosie is waiting for them by the front door and they confront the miserable day together.

*

The journey doesn't take too long and they do it in almost silence, each of them with their own thoughts on what today means, and what might have been. At one time, Lucy would have disapproved of Rosie's chosen outfit, the preference for comfort over etiquette. But she's learned a lot about priorities lately and now she's just glad that Rosie is here. She leans over, squeezes her daughter's hand. Then she risks looking into her eyes. In them she sees the reminder *we're here to celebrate Ben* and she smiles in response. It feels good.

At least the rain has stopped when they arrive. They walk up the steps and into a group of people. The oldest amongst them are quiet, more respectful of the occasion perhaps, while the young people chatter and giggle. Maybe it's their way of dealing with the day's magnitude. Either way, the unexpected crowd makes Lucy feel claustrophobic and she slips her arm inside Greg's for support. She looks around her until she sees a familiar face.

'Hi, Mum.'

Lucy turns to face her son and straight away the waterproof mascara is put to the test. Ben even manages to make his academic robe look scruffy, and there's no hiding the blue streak in his hair, but there's an energy behind his eyes that overwhelms her. Because she still remembers seeing those eyes almost lifeless. Christmas Day 2019. Four and a half years ago. But etched in her memory like it was yesterday. She still can't quite believe they've come this far, that they're about to watch him graduate from the Slade School of Fine Art, one the best art schools in the world. On that dark night when her phone rang, and the world came crashing down, all she cared about was having him back.

'Good to see you, fella.' Lucy watches her husband and son embrace. A proper hug, held for many moments. Greg blamed himself, of course. For trying to stem Ben's anger rather than letting him release it. For thinking he knew best. But the reality is they were all guilty of keeping the truth from him, not letting him mourn the family he'd lost. Even on that Christmas Day. Still trying to brush Ben's past under the carpet, forcing him to deal with what he'd discovered all by himself.

The relief of Ben surviving spurred them into action. Making good on all those deals they made with God during those long hours outside the operating theatre. *If you give him back to us, I promise to work less, get him help, listen to him more.* But it was the therapy that gave them the framework to move forward. For all those years, she'd thought she was doing the right thing. Putting his trauma behind them. Helping him avoid those terrible memories. But in reality, she just let them live inside Ben, eat away at him. He never confided in her about the nightmares he had, or about how he was feeling, but of course there were clues. If she'd looked hard enough.

'Shall we go inside? The ceremony will be starting soon.' For all her more relaxed approach to life, Lucy still can't bear being late. Old habits die hard.

'We just need to wait for Hana. She'll be here any minute.'

Lucy looks into the crowd again and sees Ben's girlfriend walking towards them, her curly hair bouncing as she hurries along. She probably shouldn't approve of the relationship of course. He was too young, too troubled, too vulnerable, when they met. But the truth is, Hana is impossible to disapprove of. The way she accepted Ben's mental illness without question or judgement, invited him out to the Czech Republic to help him heal; those are the things that endeared her to Lucy forever. And rightly or wrongly, the partnership is still going strong. Who knows what the future will hold, but that's another thing Lucy's trying not to worry about so much these days.

'Hi, everyone, sorry I'm late.'

'Probably stuck in the Ferrari showroom organising my graduation gift.' Ben leans down and kisses his girlfriend on the cheek. This is new too; his easiness with affection, and Lucy hasn't managed to take it in her stride yet. Her heart still does a mini jig every time she witnesses it.

'Ah Ferrari! I should have thought of that,' Hana responds, clicking her fingers in mock frustration. 'I went with the stale croissant in the end.'

'Sentimental value?' they both say in unison and start laughing.

This is going to be a good day.

The Slade is part of University College London, but they hold their graduation ceremonies at the Royal Festival Hall on the Southbank, a modernist building more loved for its soul than its looks. They walk inside the huge auditorium and Ben lopes off to his designated seat, self-conscious all of a sudden as he joins his peers. Big crowds will never be his thing. As they take their seats, Lucy can't help being awed by the ambition of the building. It was constructed soon after the Second World War when confidence could have been low, but instead they created this monumental space. Optimism. It's still a daily battle for her, but she's getting there.

'God, I hope he doesn't talk as much as my provost,' Rosie whispers behind her hand as a small man in a gown and spectacles bounds onto the stage. 'I honestly thought we were all going to die of heatstroke before he finished raving on about our future potential.'

'Well I'm not sure it was his fault that temperatures topped thirty degrees that day.' Lucy feels the need to defend the man; she was actually rather inspired by his talk at Rosie's graduation. 'Although it is hard to believe it was only a week ago,' she continues, making an involuntary shudder and pulling her grey silk shawl further round her shoulders. She didn't plan her outfit for drizzly rain and gusty winds. Not what you'd usually expect in July.

Rosie didn't go to Durham University in the end. She told most people that she'd changed her mind about the course, but it wasn't just that. Durham is at the other end of the country and Rosie decided that she didn't want to be that far away from home. From Ben. King's College London had happily offered her a place and she now holds both a first-class law degree and a wonderful relationship with her brother. She still hasn't worked out how to remove her clothes from the bedroom floor unfortunately.

'Ladies and gentlemen, friends and family. Today you can be justly proud ...'

Lucy relaxes back against the foam cushioning of her seat, focuses in on her son as he plays idly with his new hairstyle, and lets the provost's words roll over her. Ben is alive, and from her perspective, she doesn't need a better future than that.

Chapter 43

Phoebe

'Look at me. You're going to be okay.'

'No, can't breathe.' A tiny whisper, hardly a sound at all.

'I'm here now. I'm going to help you.'

My fingers point and flex with the effort.

'I'm going to put this paper bag around your lips and I want you to breath into it. That's brilliant. Now let go of that breath, force it out. That's it. You're doing it, see? You're breathing.'

I smile at the woman kneeling in front of me, get drawn into her shining brown eyes.

'Thank you,' she whispers, louder this time. 'Thanks for saving me.'

Her words jolt me back to a different time; to the memory of Dave and Jen helping me on that busy platform nearly five years ago. How life has changed since then. I tilt back on my sturdy black boots, enjoy the sound of my stiff jacket rustling as I move. 'You were having a panic attack,' I explain gently. 'I used to get them too, so I know how scary they can be. But you would have beaten it without my help, I promise. We're stronger than we think.' Not my words originally, but I've adopted them. I believe them now.

'Survival instinct,' she replies and there's a real gravity to her voice. It makes me wonder what her story is, what she might have been through; her heavy accent suggests that London is new to her. But I haven't got time to delve any deeper. Friday evenings in South London are too busy for that.

'Everything all right here? Only we've had another call come in.'

I look up at my crew mate, Mo. Then back down at my patient.

'I'm fine now,' she assures me, pushing against the kerb and up onto her feet. She starts brushing the dust off her jeans, the act slightly out of kilter against the worn-out denim. 'Could you just tell me where Geneva Drive is? I'm a little lost.'

She makes it sound like an offhand comment, but instinctively I know this is what caused her panic attack. The loss of direction, fear of the unknown. I pause for a moment, think of the questions I'd like to ask. But I'm a paramedic, not a counsellor. She's physically okay now, so my job is done. 'First right, then first left,' I say, pointing at Somerleyton Road, just a hundred metres up from where we're standing.

She smiles her gratitude as my brief directions connect the dots for her. She turns to go, and I watch to make sure she takes the right corner before climbing into the truck next to Mo. He's the senior medic between us but has elected to drive tonight, which means I'm front of house. 'Where to next?'

'Frequent flyer, I'm afraid.' He checks his wing mirror and swings out onto the road. 'Nice guy though, just wants to see a friendly face probably.'

'Tea and biscuits?'

'Always.'

I settle back against the firm headrest and let my eyes close for a minute. We've been on shift since eight this morning and it's been non-stop ever since. No knife injuries today though, thank goodness. I still remember the first time, back when I was studying, on placement with the ambulance team working out of St George's Hospital. I pretended to observe the paramedics working on that poor boy. I even managed to grab the right kit out of the wagon when they asked. But I wasn't really with them, I was back in my old garden with Ben. Luckily, as a student, I wasn't expected to do much other than observe. Since I qualified a year ago, I've dealt with seventeen knife attacks, and each time the memory of my son clinging on to life fades a little. I'm still not sure whether that's a good thing or bad.

Mo pulls up outside a large Victorian house, which would be a lot more impressive if it weren't for the overflowing wheelie bins lined up against the grubby brick wall, and the long-abandoned grass in the tiny front garden reaching halfway up the windows. 'Geoff's got a little flat on the ground floor,' he explains. 'His daughter owns the whole building and she used to live upstairs with her family, but she got a job in the Middle East somewhere, so they've moved over there and let their part out. Not sure the tenants are quite so house proud.'

'Bit of a change for Geoff then.' I have to shout my response because Mo is already out of the ambulance. I grab my bag and join him on the pavement.

'Yeah, we all moan about family until they're not around anymore.' Mo's easy grin reminds me how close he is to his own family; his mum holds legendary status at the ambulance station for the various baked goods she sends him in with. Flora has never reached that pinnacle, but we have built something. She never once said *I told you so* about Ben's suicide attempt, and I stopped blaming her for my mistakes. It took time, but now I look forward to our monthly theatre trips more than I'm willing to admit.

The bell doesn't work, so I rap hard on the front door. After a moment, I hear the sound of shuffling feet, getting louder as they work their way towards me. When Geoff opens the door, the look of pleasure on his face goes some way to both reveal the true motive for his call and melt my heart. I give him a big smile and then Mo and I walk into the musty flat. A quick cup of tea won't hurt.

*

It's nearly ten o'clock by the time I get home. Finishing a shift on time is always a luxury so I'm neither surprised nor bothered that Friday night has all but disappeared without me. Especially knowing that I have the next week off, holiday signed off six months ago by a manager grateful that I'll be back before the school summer holidays kick in.

I find a half full bottle of wine in the fridge and pour myself a glass. There's a hint of vinegar about it but I swallow it anyway; one of the downsides of never allowing myself more than one glass, but a discomfort I deserve. Four and a half years ago I sat outside the A&E block at St George's Hospital in my bloodstained jacket, praying to every God I'd ever heard of to let Charlie live. And finally Meghan – my friend now, but just the kind Welsh paramedic to me then – gave me the best news I could possibly hope for. And I celebrated by buying a quarter litre of vodka and drinking the whole lot on my unsteady walk back to Battersea. And I didn't stop there. Joined by Flora, and unopposed by Paul, I spent the rest of the festive season with a drink in my hand, the safe cocoon of alcoholic indifference proving too powerful to resist.

Incredibly, it was Lucy who dragged me back. Prickly, perfect Lucy. Only she didn't look so perfect when she turned up on my doorstep that cold January morning. She looked raw, dried out, like the oily layers of wealth and privilege had been stripped away from her. She looked more like me. Except that Lucy's eyes were clear while mine were dazed and bloodshot. Even in my hungover state I knew that I didn't want her to see how we lived, the empty gin bottles and layer of dust, so I guided her into the park across the road. It was my idea to sit on the swings – I wanted to avoid her eyes that were still sharp enough to judge me – but those swings seemed to release something in her. Before long she was flying up and back, rolling her body through the motions. Finally she stopped, and that's when she said it.

Thank you.

The doctors had told her that I saved Charlie's life. That he would have died from blood loss if I hadn't acted so quickly, so correctly. It's amazing how powerful those two words can be in the right context. I cried, then she cried. The two toddlers playing on the slide eyed us suspiciously and that made us laugh. We didn't hug, or even dare touch each other, but something happened between us. Her look of respect for me was only fleeting, but I caught it. Returned it. And then I walked back into my parents' house and started clearing up.

It was Tom who suggested I train as a paramedic, at one of our meetings after I finally came clean about Ben; I don't think of him as Charlie anymore. He said it might be a way of turning my experience into something positive. At first the idea seemed ridiculous – I'd had my chance at a proper life and thrown it away. But then I remembered the way Meghan treated Ben that night, how she mixed efficiency with compassion so perfectly. And I thought about the paramedic who looked after me all those years before, the only person in the house to see a mother before a murderer. So I applied. Even with my two science A-levels, I knew I wasn't a standard applicant, so I put everything into my personal statement. Sometimes I'm still amazed that it actually worked.

With only the smallest hint of some not quite dormant craving, I pour the rest of the wine down the sink and drop the bottle into the recycling bag. There's no way the wine will be drinkable when I get back anyway. I walk the four steps to my bedroom door and pull the small suitcase from inside the wardrobe, bought last weekend specially for this occasion. Tiredness is starting to weigh me down now, which is a good thing because it stops me worrying too much about what to pack; or dwelling on what will happen when I get there. I throw in some T-shirts and shorts, a couple of long skirts and a cardigan. After a moment's hesitation, a swimming costume too. When I'm done, I take a quick shower to wash off the South London grime, set my alarm for 5 a.m., and crawl under my duvet.

*

The blast of warm air feels alien but not unpleasant as I step off the aeroplane and into the midday Mediterranean heat. I take a deep breath and let the scent of Greece permeate through my pores. It feels good to be back here, in Crete, where I can still remember Charlie looking in wonder at the blueness of the sea, and where those few precious weeks of new life grew inside me. I know my emotions will run high on this holiday, but I feel strong enough to cope with them now. To enjoy the memories rather than dwell on what I lost. But perhaps I'm not as ready as I think because as I turn towards the stairs, I stumble slightly. An arm reaches out to steady me.

'You okay?'

I look down at my son's hand, now holding on to my arm, and it takes me back to that bus journey, on the day that I found him. I was so elated to see him back then that I chose not to notice his disgust at the thought of touching me. His desperation to create some distance between us. It's taken some time, but things are very different now, and I have Lucy to thank for that. She made me a promise on that cold day in the park to give Charlie the letters I had written throughout my time in prison, and the rest would be up to him. All I could do was hope that those messages of love, of hope for some kind of future together, would be enough.

It wasn't until April that I heard from him, and that was just a text asking if we could meet. I suggested Battersea Park and we sat together on my nana's favourite bench staring at the roses, watching new life form. We weren't there for long, but some silent agreement passed between us: we were going to try. Over time short coffees became longer lunches, and awkward small talk turned into proper conversations. And before we knew it, we had built something. A relationship strong enough to take a trip together, to create new memories on the foundations of old.

'I'm fine thanks,' I answer as we walk down the metal steps together, the gentle breeze having a cooling effect on my mind as well as my body. I steal a look at his languid frame, the relaxed expression on his face and the optimism in his eyes. And with a heady surge of joy, I realise something wonderful.

At last, he's fine too.

Acknowledgements

When I started my research for *A Mother Never Lies*, I was amazed and humbled by the willingness of people to give their time and expertise to a debut author. Thank you Hugh Constant and Susan Ellery for explaining adoption processes, and to Richard for sharing your unique insight. Thank you Malcolm Partridge, for your advice on criminal law – the glaring error of a fourteen-year minimum custodial sentence for murder rather than the correct fifteen years is all mine. Thank you Dr Harriet Tucker for your medical expertise, and Dr Julia Yates for your help with my psychotherapy chapters – as well as your unwavering friendship and support. Thank you also to the team at HQ Digital and especially my editor, Dushiyanthi Horti, for your thoughtful comments – the book is much improved for your input.

Writing a debut novel is a challenging journey. Thank you Faber Academy, and especially my tutor Julia Crouch, for making me a better writer. Thank you Sophie Hannah, your Dream Author programme is inspiring. Thank you Katie Lowe for making me believe it possible, Kitty Walker for your editing skills, and Jane Casey for your invaluable advice and generosity with your time. I have so many friends who supported me, but thank you particularly Bex, Mirella, Jo, Selina, Judy and Hannah for your kind words and constant encouragement. And to my chuffing bats crew, I salute you.

And finally a huge thank you to my family. To my dad who read every draft and my mum who made the whole venture possible. To Scarlett, who is wise and thoughtful beyond her years, and Finn for his contagious good humour. And finally to Chris, who travelled every step by my side.

Dear Reader,

Thank you for putting aside a few hours of your time to read my book. I hope you enjoyed discovering the truth behind Phoebe's actions and why she was compelled to give Charlie away.

I have found that Phoebe divides opinion, and I would love to know what you think of her. Is she deserving of our sympathy after the terrible trauma – and subsequent loss – that she suffered? Or is she selfish, violent and unwilling to put the welfare of her child first? Is there a way that she can be all of these things?

You can reach me by email at sarah@sarahclarkeauthor.com or via social media. I am on Twitter as @SCWwriter, and on Facebook and Instagram as @sarahclarkewriter.

This book began as a private affair between my characters and me, and now I am asking the whole world to read the story. A scary prospect in many ways! If you enjoyed *A Mother Never Lies* I would be hugely grateful if you could spare a few moments to review it.

You can also follow my publisher @HQstories for lots of book news and great giveaways.

Happy reading,
Sarah

Dear Reader,

We hope you enjoyed reading this book. If you did, we'd be so appreciative if you left a review. It really helps us and the author to bring more books like this to you.

Here at HQ Digital we are dedicated to publishing fiction that will keep you turning the pages into the early hours. Don't want to miss a thing? To find out more about our books, promotions, discover exclusive content and enter competitions you can keep in touch in the following ways:

JOIN OUR COMMUNITY:

Sign up to our new email newsletter:
http://smarturl.it/SignUpHQ

Read our new blog www.hqstories.co.uk

🐦 https://twitter.com/HQStories

f www.facebook.com/HQStories

BUDDING WRITER?

We're also looking for authors to join the HQ Digital family!
Find out more here:

https://www.hqstories.co.uk/want-to-write-for-us/

Thanks for reading, from the HQ Digital team

If you enjoyed *A Mother Never Lies*, then why not try
another gripping thriller from HQ Digital?